PETRIFIED

Recent Titles by Graham Masterton available from Severn House

The Jim Rook Series

ROOK
THE TERROR
TOOTH AND CLAW
SNOWMAN
SWIMMER
DARKROOM
DEMON'S DOOR

The Sissy Sawyer Series

TOUCHY AND FEELY
THE PAINTED MAN

Anthologies

FACES OF FEAR
FEELINGS OF FEAR
FORTNIGHT OF FEAR
FLIGHTS OF FEAR

Novels

BASILISK
BLIND PANIC
CHAOS THEORY
DESCENDANT
DOORKEEPERS
EDGEWISE
FIRE SPIRIT
GENIUS
GHOST MUSIC
HIDDEN WORLD
HOLY TERROR
HOUSE OF BONES
MANITOU BLOOD
THE NINTH NIGHTMARE
UNSPEAKABLE

PETRIFIED

Graham Masterton

This first world edition published 2011
in Great Britain and in the USA by
SEVERN HOUSE PUBLISHERS LTD of
9–15 High Street, Sutton, Surrey, England, SM1 1DF.
Trade paperback edition first published
in Great Britain and the USA 2012 by
SEVERN HOUSE PUBLISHERS LTD

British Library Cataloguing in Publication Data

Masterton, Graham.
  Petrified.
  1. Parental kidnapping–Fiction. 2. Traffic accident
  victims–Fiction. 3. Burns and scalds in children–
  Fiction. 4. Stem cells–Research–Fiction. 5. Crush
  syndrome–Fiction. 6. Gargoyles–Fiction. 7. Horror
  tales.
  I. Title
  823.9'2-dc22

ISBN-13: 978-0-7278-8072-7 (cased)
ISBN-13: 978-1-84751-373-1 (trade paper)

All Severn House titles are printed on acid-free paper.

Severn House Publishers support The Forest Stewardship Council [FSC],
the leading international forest certification organisation. All our titles that
are printed on Greenpeace-approved FSC-certified paper carry the FSC logo.

Typeset by Palimpsest Book Production Ltd.,
Falkirk, Stirlingshire, Scotland.
Printed and bound in Great Britain by
MPG Books Ltd., Bodmin, Cornwall.

ONE
Monday, 5:27 p.m.

By the time he reached the intersection with the Vine Street Expressway, Braydon Harris was convinced that God had it in for him.

An electric storm like Judgment Day was flashing and thundering over the center of Philadelphia, and rain was hammering down so hard that it was almost impossible for him to see the highway ahead of him through the spray.

On the back seat of his seven-year-old Dodge Caliber, Sukie was lying fast asleep, snuggled up under a red plaid blanket, clutching that moon-faced doll of hers. Sukie had been overjoyed that Braydon had kidnapped her from Melinda's parents, but this evening it seemed as if the Lord was on the side of Melinda and the Maryland Family Courts, and that He wasn't going to allow Braydon to make an easy getaway.

As he drove north on the Schuylkill Expressway, past the Philadelphia Zoo, there was a bellow of thunder directly overhead, so loud that Braydon was almost deafened. Sukie woke up and screamed in fright, dropping her doll on the floor.

'Daddy! I'm scared! What is it? I dropped Binkie! I dropped Binkie!'

'It's OK, sweetheart! Everything's OK! It's only thunder! It can't hurt you!'

'I'm scared, Daddy! I dropped Binkie! I can't find her!'

There was another devastating cannonade of thunder, and this time Sukie let out a high-pitched shriek, the kind of shriek that only terrified little girls can produce, almost beyond the range of human hearing. The rain began to drum down even harder on the Caliber's roof, as if God were doing His level best to flatten it.

'I can't find Binkie! I've lost her! I can't find Binkie!'

'Don't worry, sweetheart, it's a rainstorm, that's all! There's nothing to be scared of!'

'But Binkie's scared!'

Braydon twisted himself around in the driver's seat and reached behind him with his right hand, trying to locate Sukie's doll on the floor. At first he couldn't feel it at all, but then he arched his back and lifted himself up in his seat a little more, and his fingertips touched the doll's frizzy nylon hair.

'It's OK,' he told Sukie. 'I got her!'

He managed to pinch Binkie's hair between his index finger and his middle finger, and he was just about to pick her up when his windshield was flooded with blinding white light. Through his furiously-flapping windshield wipers he saw a huge truck sliding sideways across the expressway in front of him, and the single word DIAMOND.

Even with both hands on the wheel, he probably couldn't have steered the Caliber out of the path of the jackknifing semi. As it was, his right arm was pinioned between the two front seats, and he had to spin the wheel with his left hand only.

He heard nothing. He didn't even hear Sukie shrieking. The Caliber skidded through one hundred eighty degrees and slid backward underneath the semi's trailer, so that its rear end was instantly crushed to half its height. Braydon was slammed face first into his inflated air-bag, smashing his nose. The side of the trailer hit the back of his seat, forcing him forward and pinning him against the steering wheel.

He sat stunned for almost half a minute, with a beard of blood. Gradually, his hearing returned, and he heard rain pattering against the windshield and people shouting. He tried to turn around to see if Sukie was all right, but his right arm was jammed tight between his seat and the center console.

'Sukie?' he coughed. 'Sukie, are you OK, sweetheart? Please tell Daddy you're OK.'

There was no reply. Only the sound of rain and rumbling thunder and people shouting, and the *scribble-scribble-scribble* of a distant siren.

'Sukie! Can you hear me? Please tell Daddy you haven't been hurt!'

Through his rain-ribbed windshield he saw flashlights coming toward him, and dark silhouettes. Somebody was tugging at his door handle, and then knocking at his window.

'Are you OK in there, buddy? Hold on – we're going to get you out of there ASAP!'

'My daughter,' he said.

'Hold on, buddy! We're going to try to force the door open!'

'*My daughter!*' he repeated, although his ribs were pressed hard against the center of the steering wheel, and he couldn't force enough air out of his lungs to manage anything louder than a croak. 'My daughter's in the back seat! She's not answering me! I think she might be hurt!'

More flashlights criss-crossed in front of his windshield, and then he heard a bang and a creak as somebody forced a tire iron into the side of his door.

'Sukie?' he called her. 'Sukie, please answer me, sweetheart!'

There was another creak, and he felt the Caliber rock from side to side as his rescuers tried to jimmy his door open. He twisted his head around as far as he could, but the vehicle had been crushed so low beneath the trailer that all he could see was the vinyl roof-lining. He prayed that Sukie had still been lying flat on her seat at the moment of impact.

'Dear God I'm so sorry I took her,' Braydon gabbled to himself. 'They told me I wasn't fit to be her father, and look at me, I'm not. Dear God please tell me that I haven't killed her.'

He heard more sirens, wailing and screaming. He inhaled deeply so that he could shout to his would-be rescuers to hurry it up, but when he did so he breathed in the eye-watering pungency of gasoline fumes. The Caliber's fuel tank must have been split open by the collision, and it had been almost full.

'*Hurry!*' he wheezed. '*Hurry! The gas tank's leaking!*'

'Don't panic, buddy!' called back one of his rescuers. 'We almost got the door open.'

Almost as soon as he had spoken, however, Braydon heard a soft explosive *whumph*, and then another, followed by a crackling sound.

'*Hurry!*' he shouted. '*We're on fire in here! For Christ's sake, hurry! We're on fire!*'

Hot air began to swarm through the gap between the front seats, and Braydon smelled shriveling vinyl and scorching wool. A spattering of molten plastic burned the back of his hand, and he tried even more desperately to wrench his arm free, but the force of the collision had trapped it too tightly. He could feel a thick crunching sensation inside his wrist, and for the first time since the crash, his arm began to throb with unbearable pain.

'We're burning up! Get us out of here! We're burning up!'

The interior of the Caliber was rapidly filling up with choking fumes. Braydon coughed and coughed, and then he burst into tears. He didn't want to die like this. He didn't want Sukie to die like this. She was five years old. She had all of her life ahead of her, but he had killed her.

'God almighty we're burning up in here!'

TWO

Monday, 5:34 p.m.

The driver's door burst open and was wrenched right back against its hinges. A big shaven-headed man reached inside with tattooed forearms and released Braydon's seat belt. He grabbed hold of him and tried to drag him out but Braydon's arm was still trapped.

'My little girl – she's in the back seat!' Braydon told him. 'Please get her out of there! Please!'

'OK, buddy, just hold on! Somebody pass me that tire iron! Quick! *Somebody pass me that goddamned tire iron!*'

'I called out to her—' Braydon coughed. 'I called out to her – but she didn't answer! Maybe she's unconscious. She's only – she's only five years old. Please, you have to get her out of there!'

The big shaven-headed man forced the tire iron into the space between the driver's seat and the center console. 'When I say yank your arm out, you yank your arm out, OK?'

Braydon nodded. The big shaven-headed man grunted, and leaned against the tire iron as hard as he could. There was a loud crack of breaking plastic, and then the man said, 'Yank your arm out! Yank it out *now!*'

Braydon twisted his arm forward, even though the pain from his shattered wrist almost made him pass out. As soon as he was free, the man heaved him bodily out of the driver's seat as if he were a child and lifted him clear. Two other men took hold of his legs, and between them they hurried him over to the opposite side of the highway and laid him down on somebody's raincoat. An ambulance had just arrived, its lights flashing red in the rain, and paramedics were opening up its rear doors.

There was another ear-splitting rumble of thunder. Braydon felt rain splattering against his face and he could smell gasoline smoke on the wind.

'My daughter!' he said, hoarsely, trying to sit up. 'My daughter's still in there! I have to get her out of there!'

A fire truck arrived with its klaxons blaring, followed almost nose-to-tail by a heavy rescue vehicle, and then a fire marshal's van. Orange flames were crawling like the tentacles of a fiery octopus from underneath the trailer and people were shouting to each other to stay well back.

'*You have to let me go!*' Braydon demanded. But two paramedics helped Braydon's rescuers to haul him up on to his feet, and between them they practically frogmarched him up to the back of the ambulance and hoisted him up the steps. They tried to make him lie flat on the gurney but he insisted on sitting up so that he could see what was happening.

'Sir – please try to stay calm,' said a black woman paramedic. 'The firefighters are going to do everything they can to get your daughter out of there.'

Braydon was coughing so hard that he couldn't answer her. He tried to swing his legs off the gurney but the paramedic pushed him back. She was chunkily built, and unexpectedly strong.

'Please, sir. Please stay here. There's nothing you can do.'

'My daughter's dying in there!' Braydon told her. 'My daughter could be dead already!'

'I know that, sir. But all we can do right now is pray for her.'

The firefighters were spraying the wreck with compressed-air foam, and clouds of it were dancing across the highway and flying up into the air. The orange flames reluctantly retreated and shrank back under the trailer, and then they died out altogether. Six or seven firefighters approached the burned-out shell of Braydon's Caliber and Braydon could hear them shouting out for hydraulic lifting equipment and cutters.

'You have to let me out of here!' said Braydon. 'That's my Sukie in there! That's my little girl!'

'Sir – please,' said the paramedic. And at that moment, two officers from the Philadelphia Highway Patrol appeared at the back of the ambulance, in their distinctive crushed caps and black leather coats and riding boots. One of them was tall and thin and sandy-haired, and the other was stocky, with a walrus moustache.

'Sir, you really need to stay here. There's absolutely nothing you can do.'

'Oh God,' Braydon wept. He pressed his left hand over his mouth. 'Oh God, it was all my fault.'

'I don't think you should blame yourself, sir,' said the sandy-haired patrolman. 'That semi had a multiple blow-out and skidded clear across to the northbound side of the highway and there wasn't nothing you could have humanly done to avoid it. Wasn't nothing that *nobody* could have done.'

'Here,' said the paramedic. She pulled up his sleeve and gave him a shot of oxycodone for the pain. Then she strapped an FLA splint to his fractured wrist, while the patrolmen asked him his name, and his address, and Sukie's name.

'Susan Amelia Harris,' said Braydon. 'Born April seventeenth, two thousand seven.' He didn't tell them that he had long ago lost custody of her, and that he had been kidnapping her, and taking her back to his home in Connecticut. What would have been the point of it? He felt guilty enough already.

When the patrolmen had finished questioning him, he sat in the ambulance watching the firefighters at work with their cutters and their spreaders. Now that the oxycodone was beginning to take effect, he was beginning to feel strangely detached, as if that burned-out wreck on the other side of the highway wasn't really his car at all. The paramedic gently lifted his elbow into a sling, and all the time she kept on asking him 'Is that OK, sir? Is that comfortable? Does that hurt?' but he didn't answer her, or even glance at her. If he had answered her, that would have confirmed that he was really here, and that his daughter Sukie was really trapped inside his car, and that she had probably been killed.

'How are you feeling, sir?' the paramedic asked him. 'You're not feeling faint at all, are you?' But he still refused to respond. *I'm not feeling anything. This is not me.*

It seemed to take hours for the firefighters to attach a steel hawser to the front of a fire truck and drag the Caliber out from underneath the trailer, so that they could begin to open up its crushed rear section. With a last few spiteful flickers and a last few sulky rumbles, the thunder and lightning were gradually moving off toward the north-east, but the rain continued steadily to dredge across the surface of the highway.

Braydon saw showers of sparks as the vehicle's roof pillars were cut apart, and then four firefighters lifted the roof clear off and laid it down on the road.

Three paramedics reached inside the rear seat. Braydon began to shiver uncontrollably. *Oh God almighty she's dead and I've killed her. Oh God have mercy on me. Oh God, my poor little Sukie.*

The woman paramedic unhooked an oxygen mask and pressed it over his face. 'Just breathe normally, sir. We don't want you going into shock.'

Braydon rolled his eyes and stared up at her. He took four deep breaths and then he lifted the mask away. 'She was so darn *unhappy*. That was the trouble. She kept on begging me to take her away with me. But now look what I've done.'

'Sir, this was an accident. You heard what the officers told you. This was not your fault. But now I think we need to take you to the ER. There's nothing more that you can do here.'

'Please – I have to see her. I have to know for sure.'

Just then, another ambulance backed up to the wreck of Braydon's Caliber, and its rear doors opened. Less than a minute later, it sped away, with its siren screaming.

'What was that? Was that Sukie? Where are they taking her?'

A gray-haired paramedic walked across to the back of the ambulance and climbed up the steps. For some odd reason, he reminded Braydon of the actor Lloyd Bridges. 'We got your daughter out, sir. She's alive.'

Braydon coughed, and coughed again. He could hardly breathe. 'How badly is she hurt?'

The paramedic looked serious. 'I can't yet tell you the full extent of her injuries, sir, not until the doctors have examined her. But I have to warn you that she's suffered some very serious burns.'

'Oh, God. Oh, God, no.'

'We've sent her directly to the burns center at Temple University Hospital. It's the finest burns unit in the country, bar none, and it's only a few minutes from here. We'll take you there right now, so that you can be with her.'

He climbed down and closed the ambulance doors behind him. The woman paramedic said, 'Why don't you lie down, sir, so's I can strap you in? You'll be safer.'

Braydon shook his head. 'Who cares if I'm safe? What difference does it make?'

'It makes *all* the difference, sir. From now on, your Sukie's going to need you more than ever.'

Braydon lay back on the gurney and the woman paramedic buckled him in. He closed his eyes as the ambulance swerved and bumped its way to North Broad Street. He didn't pray any more. All he wanted to do was to fall asleep. If he could fall asleep, maybe he could wake up and find that it was still seven a.m. this morning, and that he hadn't yet set out for Baltimore to kidnap Sukie from Melinda's parents.

He would rather that he had never seen Sukie again than have her burned alive.

He would rather that she had never been born at all.

THREE
Monday, 6:17 p.m.

Nathan tore the wrapper off his Baby Ruth bar and bit off almost half of it at once. 'Well, *compadres*,' he said, with his mouth full of chocolate and peanuts. 'We're about as ready as we're ever going to be. In about ten minutes' time we're going to make scientific history. Either that, or we're going to end up as a laughing stock.'

'We've done everything according to the book, haven't we?' Kavita insisted.

'Oh, sure. But what a book! *Kitab Al-Ajahr, The Book of Stones*. An eighth-century treatise on alchemy. It's not exactly *Kleinman's Mesenchymal Stem Cell Regeneration, Volume Three*, is it?'

'You should have more faith in yourself, Professor,' said Aarif. 'And faith in the wisdom of Abu Musa Jābir ibn Hayyān.'

'Abu Musa Jābir ibn Hayyān died over thirteen centuries ago.'

'What does that matter? It is one of the greatest scientific collaborations of all time, you and he. It is like Francis Crick working with Copernicus.'

'I hope this isn't a prelude to your asking for a pay rise,' said Nathan.

'I admit that I would not refuse one, if it were offered,' Aarif replied. 'However, I am simply speaking the truth. Look what you have done here. You have given life to a creature which has not been seen on this earth since the days of Rameses the Fourth.'

'Well, yes,' said Nathan. 'But like I've said so many times, a worm is one thing and a bird is quite another.'

'We shall just have to see if you and Jābir can prove between you that this is not so, and that a worm can also be a bird, and a bird can also be a worm.'

The early-evening skies were beginning to clear, and in downtown Philadelphia an orange sun was making a brief guest appearance behind the trees around the Schiller Medical Research building, so that Nathan's fourth-floor laboratory was filled up with honey-colored light.

The light lent an almost holy radiance to the huge vivarium made of Pyrex glass that stood in the center of the workspace, reaching nearly to the ceiling. Roughly heaped on the floor of the vivarium was a tangled nest of twigs and leaves and dry vegetation; and resting on top of this nest was a fat pale-gray worm that was nearly twenty-two centimeters in length and eighteen centimeters in circumference. Its skin was thick and wrinkled and covered all over with coarse knobbly spots. Kavita had already dubbed it 'Grubby'.

Nathan was exhausted. His short blond hair was scruffed up and his eyes were puffy. He had been preparing for this final experiment for over a week, and for the last four nights he had slept on an air bed in his office, so that he could carry out two-hourly checks on the worm's development.

For the past forty-eight hours the worm had shown no increase whatsoever in size or weight, and its movements had slowed down to a barely-perceptible ripple, so Nathan guessed that it must have reached maturity. It had to be a guess, because this was the first worm of its kind that had been conceived since 1150 BC.

If the eighth-century alchemist Jābir was right, the worm was ready to enter the most dramatic stage in its life cycle, just as a chrysalis bursts open and a butterfly emerges. As the critical moment came nearer, however, Nathan was beginning to harbor a nagging suspicion that in *The Book of Stones,* Jābir might have simply been retelling a well-known Egyptian myth, rather than describing successful experiments that he had actually carried out in his own laboratory.

He held up the most recent CGI scan. 'This is what concerns me. There's still no suggestion of any incipient bone structure inside the nematode, only these random clumps of fibrous tissue.'

'But Jābir says that once the fire has reached a sufficiently high temperature, the bird's skeleton is created by fusion,' said Aarif.

'Well, that's your interpretation. What he actually says is "at their hottest pitch, the flames of the inferno take on the shape of wings". That's if my ancient Persian serves me right.'

Aarif shook his head. 'You should not be so pessimistic, Professor. After all, this entire project came from your inspiration. We are standing on the brink of a defining moment in modern science.'

'I don't know,' said Nathan. He rubbed his face with both hands. 'I've been here too many times before, standing on the brink of a defining moment in modern science. And what happened? Last time I ended up with a rotten gryphon's egg with a stink that hung around for a week.'

'This will be different, Professor. I am convinced of it.'

'Me, too,' said Kavita. 'It's going to be fame at last! We'll all be on the cover of next month's *Time* magazine. Or *American Biology Today,* anyhow.'

Nathan managed to smile. 'You're right. I guess I'm bushed, is all. Listen – I just want to call Grace and tell her I'm going to be late. Aarif – can you make sure that all of the video and infrared cameras are up and running? And run another soundcheck, too?'

'Of course, Professor,' said Aarif, with a courteous nod of his head.

Aarif was in his late twenties, a tall Egyptian, thin as a rail, with a vertical shock of wiry black hair and near-together eyes and a hawk-like nose. He was a graduate in developmental biology from the University of Cairo. He was polite and good-humored, but almost terrifyingly academic. Nathan had first met him when he flew over to Egypt last summer to collect DNA samples of dragon-worms from the Nile basin at Ain Shams.

Aarif had helped him to collect his samples, and had then volunteered to return with him to Philadelphia so that he could assist with this experiment. After seven months, and more than three hundred tests, they had at last succeeded in fusing the DNA from a dragon-worm with the DNA from an Egyptian scavenger hawk, and the result had been this fat gray phoenix-worm. Half worm, half bird. Theoretically, anyhow.

'How about you, Kavita?' Nathan asked her, laying his hand on her shoulder. 'Are you all set?'

'All set, Professor. I sorted out that glitch with the multi-gas monitor, and all of the other instruments are reading well within tolerance.'

Kavita was a young biochemist whom Nathan had wooed away from SupremeTaste Pet Foods in Pittsburgh. Now that he was privately funded by Schiller, he had been able to tempt her with nearly double the salary that she had been making at SupremeTaste. But it wasn't only the money that had attracted her; the cutting-edge stem cell research that Nathan was working on was infinitely more glamorous than dog-food development.

Kavita's mother was a full-blooded Mohawk, and Kavita had inherited her glossy black hair, her sharp, distinctive cheekbones, and her full, pouting lips. She also had a figure that had led Nathan's son Denver to ask if he could help out in the laboratory after school, even if it meant sweeping up.

It was Kavita's job to filter and analyze the airborne chemical residue that resulted from this experiment. Then she had to produce a computer model of exactly what had happened during combustion – even if it turned out to be a disaster.

'OK, Kavita, that's great,' Nathan told her. 'Just give me a moment and then we'll be good to go.'

He went through to his office, picked up his phone, and punched out his home number. As he waited for Grace to answer, he could see his reflection in the office window, in his white lab coat. Forty-five years old, but very young-looking for his age. Nobody ever believed that he and Grace had a son of nineteen.

Grace sounded out of breath when she answered him.

'Sorry,' she panted. 'The rain eased off so I went out for my run.'

'I've decided to start the test right now,' Nathan told her. 'I guess I could have waited until tomorrow morning but I'm worried that the nematode might have grown too mature to metamorphose by then. So – listen, I don't know what time I'm going to get home, if I get home at all.'

'I'm beginning to suspect that you've got yourself another woman, not a worm. I miss you.'

'I miss you, too, sweetheart. But tonight's the night. Wish me luck, won't you?'

'You don't need *luck*, Nathan. You're the best there ever was. Oh, before I forget – you had three phone calls today. A young man, by the sound of it. He was *very* persistent. I think he must have been German, by his accent. Or maybe Russian, or Polish. Something like that.'

'Did he leave his name?'

'No, but he said he'd be sure to call back tomorrow.'

'What did he want?'

'He said he had something very important to discuss with you. He kept saying, "*I vont to leave no stone unturned, tell Professor Underhill that.*"'

'Hey. Very convincing accent.'

'Well, it wasn't quite as thick as that. But he must have repeated it five times at least. "*I vont to leave no stone unturned. He vill understand.*"'

'Sounds like a nut job to me. Just hang up on him if he calls again. Listen – I have to go. It's T minus two minutes.'

'I love you, Nathan.'

'I love you, too.'

He hesitated for a moment. He felt like saying something more, like telling Grace that she was more important to him than all of the scientific breakthroughs he had ever made, or ever would. But he knew she understood that, and he hung up.

When he came out of his office, Aarif said, 'Everything is ready, Professor! We are all prepared! Video running, infrared running, ultraviolet running, audio on!'

Nathan took one last look at the phoenix-worm lying at the bottom of its glass case. Aarif had constructed its nest exactly in accordance with Jābir's description in *The Book of Stones* – out of oak branches, cinnamon sticks, frankincense, spikenard and twigs of Yemeni myrrh. The myrrh twigs were clustered with thorns, but they didn't seem to cause the phoenix-worm any discomfort. Its skin-surface was gently rippling, and the two glistening sensors just above its mouth were repeatedly rolling and unrolling like a snail's eyes.

'Look at you, Grubby,' said Nathan. 'Only a mother could love an ugly bastard like you. That's if you had a mother, which you don't. If anybody's your mother, it's *me*.'

He paused, and then he turned to Aarif and Kavita and said, 'Hard to believe that Grubby cost upward of eight and a half million dollars, isn't it? Let's hope we're not about to watch all of that investment going up in smoke.'

Aarif swung open a glass panel on the left-hand side of the case and reached inside. He arranged the twigs so that the phoenix-worm was completely covered over. Then he attached a strong magnifying glass to an adjustable chrome stilt, and set up a halogen lamp to direct an intense spot of light into the branches. Even before he had lowered the panel and closed up the case, the dry oak twigs had started to smolder, and a thin wisp of smoke was curling up into the air.

It would have been more practical to light the fire with a match, but in *The Book of Stones*, Jābir was adamant that the nest had to be ignited 'as if by the rays of the sun, shining through a jewel'.

'It is burning, Professor!' said Aarif, clenching his fists in excitement. Already the first thin tongues of flame were flickering up from the nest, and the Pyrex cabinet was filling up with clouds of blue smoke.

Nathan wished that he could have attached electrodes to the worm's outer skin, to monitor its nervous responses, but he had been anxious to follow Jābir's instructions to the letter, and Jābir had insisted that 'the phoenix-worm be not bound nor tied nor trammeled in any way, nor marked with dyes or henna, nor tattooed'.

In countless previous experiments, Nathan had already seen the consequences of trying to recreate mythical creatures without adhering strictly to the ancient formulae. It didn't work and it could be highly dangerous. If this experiment failed, he knew that he would risk losing his sponsors' money. More than that, though, he didn't want anybody to get themselves injured, or even killed. As he had warned Aarif and Kavita over and over, 'We're not dealing with pets here, or even zoo animals. We're dealing with primeval birds and beasts and reptiles, and sometimes a mixture of all three, with powers that we can't even begin to understand. What's more, they've never encountered humans before – unlike wolves and bears and coyotes and alligators – so they have absolutely no fear of us whatsoever.'

FOUR
Monday, 6:22 p.m.

Inside the vivarium, the flames crackled even more briskly. The oak branches began to char, and the spikenard curled up, and the thorny cuttings of *commiphora myrrha* were all reduced to fragile black prickles. There was a strong, aromatic smell of burning spices.

As the nest was reduced to ashes, the phoenix-worm itself gradually reappeared, and Nathan could see that its pale gray skin was starting to shrivel and flake off in the heat. Underneath its skin, however, its flesh was glowing dull red, like a hot coal; and as Nathan watched it, it began to glow brighter and brighter. Within a few seconds, it was incandescent, not like a hot coal any longer, but more like a white gas mantle. It was so bright that Nathan could hardly look at it.

'Can you see if it is metamorphosing, Professor?' asked Aarif, shielding his eyes with his hand. 'There is so much shining! So much smoke!'

Nathan said, 'I don't know yet. To tell you the truth I can't see a goddamned thing.'

Now the phoenix-worm burned more intensely than ever. Even through the thick fire-resistant glass, Nathan could hear a low flaring sound as it burned. The flames leaped up fiercer and higher until they filled the whole vivarium, and as minutes went past they showed no signs of dying down. Nathan began to feel the heat on his face, and he stepped back two or three paces, as did Kavita.

'It is *incredible*,' said Aarif. 'How long can such a small creature burn? And all of the oxygen inside the vivarium, that must be used up. This is against all of the laws of physics!'

At that moment there was an explosive crack, and the front glass panel of the vivarium broke in half diagonally and dropped out on to the floor. Flames rolled out with a hungry roar and enveloped Aarif's video cameras, almost as if the blazing worm was angry at being filmed. Aarif dodged forward to rescue them, but the flames came rolling out again, and he had to back away, both arms crossed in front of him to protect his face.

The heat that came blasting out of the shattered vivarium was overwhelming. Papers strewn on top of the laboratory workbenches caught fire and whirled up into the air. Bottles of chemicals exploded, one after the other. Even the varnish on the floor burst into flames. There was a sharp click, and fire-suppressant F-200 gas began to hiss out of the pipes in the laboratory's ceiling, but to begin with, even that seemed to have no effect.

'*My cameras*!' screamed Aarif.

But Nathan shouted, 'Forget them! Just get the hell out of here!'

They hurried to the door. Nathan opened it and pushed Aarif and Kavita outside, but then he unhooked the fire extinguisher that was hanging beside it and turned back toward the blazing vivarium.

'*Professor*!' said Aarif.

'Call nine-one-one!' Nathan told him. He hit the button on top of the fire extinguisher and slowly started to walk back toward the vivarium, spraying foam from side to side. But the flames continued to blaze with undiminished ferocity. In fact they almost seemed to *eat* the foam that he was spraying at them. The heat was searing. Nathan could feel his forehead and his cheeks scorching, and one by one, the three remaining glass panels in the vivarium cracked and fell out.

'Professor!' called Aarif. 'The fire department will be here in just a few minutes!'

Nathan gave the wreckage of the vivarium a last spray of foam before his extinguisher ran out. He dropped it on to the floor with a clang and retreated toward the door.

He was only halfway there when there was a devastating bang, and for a split second the whole laboratory was filled floor-to-ceiling with fire. Nathan was thrown against the wall so hard that he was stunned and dropped to his knees. Aarif rushed to help him and started hitting him repeatedly on the back of the head.

'What the hell are you doing?' Nathan protested.

'Your hair is alight, Professor. I am putting you out.'

'Is it? Are you? OK, thanks.'

Aarif helped Nathan to his feet. Nathan turned around and saw that the fire had extinguished itself. Nothing was left of the vivarium but its twisted metal frame and its ventilator hood, and two workbenches were scorched and littered with broken glass. Apart from that, however, the damage was superficial. The fire may have burned at an unfeasibly high temperature, but it had burned for only two or three minutes.

Nathan walked across to the remains of the vivarium, his shoes scrunching on shattered glass. He sniffed. The laboratory reeked of smoke, but something else, too, like joss sticks from his student days.

Aarif said, 'Maybe I had better call the fire department and tell them that we have no need of them after all.'

'No . . . they'll want to come and take a look. In any case, the company will have to have the fire marshal's report before they can claim on their insurance. We don't want them accusing us of negligence, do we?'

'It was not our fault. How could we have foreseen this fire would be so intense? It defies all scientific principles.'

'Trying to recreate mythical creatures, Aarif – *that* defies all scientific logic, too.'

Nathan picked up a long steel rule. He bent over the remains of the vivarium and started to poke through the heaps of hot ashes.

Jādir had written that each phoenix was supposed to live for five hundred years. When its time came, it flew to the ancient city of Heliopolis, city of the sun, which used to be located five miles to the east of modern-day Cairo. There, it built a nest out of branches and spices, and crept inside, and died, and became a phoenix-worm. Then the rays of the sun set the nest alight, and out of the flames a new phoenix appeared.

'*Zip*,' said Nathan. 'It didn't work, did it? I'm beginning to think that Jādir never *did* create a phoenix, not for real. Maybe everything he wrote about it was a legend. You know – like something out of *The Arabian Nights*. Like genies, and dragons, and flying carpets.'

He scraped aside the last of the ashes with the edge of the steel rule, and then stood up straight. 'I don't know how the hell I'm going to explain this to Ron Kasabian. He's going to cut off our funding for sure. And he's certainly not going to give us any more money to create a wyvern.'

Aarif was trying to salvage his camera equipment, but the heat had shattered all of the lenses and the legs of his tripods had collapsed.

'I believed so much that this would work,' said Aarif, shaking his head. 'I believed it with all of my heart.'

'Well, I'm sorry,' said Nathan. 'It's always the same with science. You work your butt off for year after year, and in the end you come up with squat. It's not surprising that you get so many mad scientists.'

'*Professor*,' said Kavita.

There was an odd inflection in her voice, which made Nathan turn around and say, 'What is it, Kavita? What's wrong?'

Kavita was staring up at a ventilator hood on top of the burned-out vivarium. Nathan frowned at her and then he looked up to see what she was staring at. On top of the ventilator hood he could just make out a silhouette that looked like a bird's head with a hooked beak.

At first he thought it might be an optical illusion, an angular arrangement of shadows on the ceiling. But then the head jerked sideways, opened its beak, and let out a high, harsh cry.

'Aarif!' said Nathan. 'Aarif – up there, on top of the vent!'

Aarif looked up, too, and then he turned to Nathan with a widening smile on his face. 'You did it, Professor! You did it! I was sure that you could do it!'

'You mean *we* did it, Aarif. Me and you and Kavita. *We* did it. And I think I need to apologize to Jādir, for doubting him.'

'I will bring the stepladder,' said Aarif, and hurried off to the storeroom to fetch it. Nathan crossed over to the far side of the laboratory, where a large parakeet cage was standing ready on a workbench. When he had ordered this cage, he had believed that he was tempting fate, and that he would never be able to create a living phoenix to put inside it. But at last he had done it. He had brought to life a living creature that for centuries had been known only as a myth.

Aarif came back with the stepladder and set it up beside the remains of the vivarium. Nathan made sure it was firm, and then climbed up it very slowly, so that he wouldn't startle the phoenix with any sudden moves.

Little by little, the phoenix came into view. It cocked its head sideways and stared at Nathan with one glistening eye, and then it let out another harsh *crarrrrkk*.

'Come on, baby,' Nathan coaxed it. 'Come to poppa. You're beautiful, aren't you? You're really, really beautiful!'

The phoenix was about the size of a small scavenger hawk. The French author Voltaire had described this mythical bird as having a rose-red beak and feathers covering its head and its neck that were all the colors of the rainbow 'but more brilliant and lively, with a thousand shades of gold glistening on its body and its tail'. But then Voltaire had never seen one, not for real. This real phoenix had brown, lusterless plumage, almost shabby, with darker brown tinges to the tips of its wings.

As Nathan rose higher on the stepladder, it spread its wings a little and backed away, its claws scratching noisily on top of the ventilator hood.

'Come on, baby,' said Nathan. 'Come to poppa.'

The phoenix gave a nervous little skitter and backed even further away. Nathan froze, and then stayed completely motionless, both hands raised, scarcely even breathing, for over half a minute.

Aarif said, 'Do you want me to try, Professor? When I was a boy, I used to catch my uncle's chickens for him.'

Nathan didn't answer, and still didn't move. The phoenix let out yet another *crrarrrk* of alarm, but after a while its curiosity was beginning to get the better of it, and it came a few steps nearer, repeatedly twitching its head from side to side.

Nathan waited until the phoenix had almost reached the near edge of the ventilator hood. It stared at him, making a thin warbling noise in its throat, and ruffling its feathers. Even when it was close enough for him to try snatching it, Nathan held off. He wanted to make sure that he got a good firm grip on it, first time. He didn't know for sure if it was developed enough to fly yet, and he didn't want it to fall off the top of the ventilator hood on to the floor and injure itself. It was only a fledgling, after all.

'Aarif,' he said, 'take off your lab coat and hold it out, just in case it loses its footing.'

Aarif did as he was asked, and he and Kavita stood underneath the phoenix with his lab coat stretched out between them as a safety net.

The phoenix came even closer. Nathan took a deep breath, and then lunged forward and caught hold of both of its scaly legs.

Immediately, with a screech of rage and indignation, the phoenix attacked him. It jabbed at his face with its beak, narrowly missing his left eye, and its claws scrabbled at his wrists. It screeched again and again, its beak hacking at his forehead and his cheeks and splitting his lower lip, and its wings beat so frantically that it almost lifted him off the stepladder.

He tried to take a step down, but the phoenix went for his face yet again, and when he instinctively jerked away from it, he lost his balance. He clattered backward down the stepladder, still holding the phoenix's legs in both hands. Aarif managed to snatch the tail of his lab coat and partially break his fall, but he landed heavily on his right shoulder on the floor. Even as he lay there, winded, the phoenix kept up its furious attack, tearing at his left earlobe with its beak and clawing at his neck.

'*For Christ's sake get this damned thing off me!*' Nathan shouted.

Aarif tried to pin the bird's wings against its body, the way he would have caught a frightened chicken, but the phoenix was like a blizzard of feathers and claws, and it was impossible for him to get his hands around it. He tried instead to seize its neck, but it screeched and twisted its head around and viciously pecked at his hand.

It was Kavita who finally managed to subdue it. She threw Aarif's discarded lab coat right over it, twisting one of the sleeves around its legs and tying it roughly into a knot. The phoenix screeched again and again, and fought with such determination to escape from its makeshift straitjacket that they could barely hold it. Eventually, Aarif managed to keep the struggling creature pressed against his chest long enough for Nathan to be able to climb to his feet. Between the two of them they carried it across to the parakeet cage, opened the door and forced it inside.

Aarif untied the sleeve of his lab coat and dragged it out of the cage, while Nathan quickly fastened the catch. Instantly, the phoenix exploded with fury. It thrashed its wings and hurled itself from one side of the birdcage to the other, crashing against the bars so violently that some of its feathers burst out and floated in the air all around it.

'Aggressive little critter, isn't it?' said Nathan, dabbing the blood from his face with a paper napkin. 'You remember what I told you about mythical creatures not being afraid of humans? I should have remembered it myself.'

'It won't hurt itself, will it?' asked Kavita.

'Maybe we should give it a tranquilizer,' Aarif suggested. 'A small dose of metoserpate hydrochloride, like they give to chickens whenever they get stressed.'

'No,' said Nathan. 'At least, not yet. Let's just give it time to relax. I don't want to risk giving it an overdose.'

Outside in the street, they heard the wailing and honking of sirens. At the same time, the building's super appeared in the doorway, a tall rangy black man called Henry. He wore a flappy gray uniform with the Schiller insignia on the pocket, and a peaked cap.

'Holy Moses, Professor!' he said. 'What happened in here? I heard a bang, but I thought it was just more thunder.'

'Slight accident,' said Nathan.

'You ain't kidding me. Look at this place!'

'Don't worry. We called the fire department, as you can hear.'

'But your *face,* Professor! You're all cut up!'

'It's nothing, Henry. Only a few scratches. Why don't you go back down to the lobby and show the firefighters where we are? And you can tell them that the fire's out now, so they won't be needing their hoses.'

Henry loped around the workbenches in his thick-soled shoes, sniffing and shaking his head. The way he walked always reminded Nathan of Jar Jar Binks. 'You know they had this entire laboratory refurberated just last fall, only a couple of weeks before you moved in. Man, oh man! Mr Kasabian, he's going to go apeshit.'

He passed close to the phoenix cage, and as he did so, the phoenix screeched and scrabbled at the bars. Henry jumped back, and said, '*Shee*-it! That's some seriously cranky bird you got there, Professor!'

He bent down and peered at it more closely. '*Homely*, too. Never saw a bird like that before.'

Nathan was dabbing more blood from his ear, but he couldn't stop himself from smiling. 'No, Henry, you never did. *Nobody* ever did. Nobody in this day and age, anyhow.'

FIVE

Tuesday, 7:43 a.m.

'**M**ore coffee, honey?' asked Trixie.

Detective Jenna Pullet shook her head emphatically from side to side. 'No, thanks, Trixie. I don't want to spend the rest of the morning shaking like a fricking epileptic.'

'You didn't touch your bacon,' said Trixie, frowning at her plate. 'You hardly touched your eggs, neither.'

'That's because the bacon is watery and the eggs are rubbery. And is this a buckwheat pancake or a mouse mat?'

'I don't never know why you come in here,' said Trixie. 'You order breakfast, you always hate it.'

'I come in here to lose weight. It's a whole lot nearer than my gym.'

For Jenna, her weight was a never-ending struggle. She was blonde, with big hair and a wide, generous face, and a wide, generous figure to go with it. In her closet at home she had seven suits of three different sizes – the suits she could comfortably get into, the suits she could get into if she wore her Bali firm-control briefs and held her breath from morning till night, and the suits she could only aspire to get into.

It was the irregular mealtimes that did it. The jelly donuts when they were out on early-morning stake-outs, the hurried Reuben sandwiches before they had to give evidence in court, and then the cheesesteak and beer orgies after they had made a successful arrest. She could never keep track of the calories, and she always imagined that her digestive tract was like the CSX marshaling yard, with food being shunted down her like coupled-up railroad cars.

'So, you doing anything exciting today?' Trixie asked her, taking away her plates.

'Sitting in front of a computer screen, most likely. Things have been real flat for the past couple of weeks. Even the South Philly mob are sitting at home and doing all their racketeering online. These days, I think "Mousie" Massimino employs more hackers than hit men.'

Joe McVitie came out of the kitchen holding up Jenna's plate. 'What the hell's the matter, Jenna, this is best farm bacon, fresh eggs!'

'I know, Joe. It takes real talent to mess them up as bad as that.'

'So why do you keep on coming in here if you think I cook so shit?'

'That's what Trixie asked me. I really don't know, Joe. Maybe it's a Catholic thing. Mortification of the palate – you know, like the nuns force themselves to eat gristle.'

'Well my advice to you is to go eat breakfast someplace else.'

'No, Joe. It's not in my nature. I'm waiting for a miracle. I'm waiting for the morning when I walk in here and the bacon is crispy and the eggs are over easy and the pancakes are light and golden. An angelic choir will start singing and the whole diner will be filled with dazzling sunshine and I will know that my faith in you has at last paid off. And do you know when that will be?'

Joe shook his head, partly because he really couldn't guess and partly because he thought Jenna was nuts.

'Sometime around the year twenty-thirty, if I'm lucky,' Jenna told him.

She climbed down off her red leather stool and lifted her coat off the back. As she did so, her cellphone played 'Blanket on the Ground'. She slid it open and demanded, '*What*?'

It was her partner, Dan Rubik. It sounded as if he were out on the street someplace, because she could hear traffic and sirens and people shouting in the background.

'Jenna – I'm here at the intersection of Green Street and North Twenty-second. Just outside the Convent of Divine Love. We got ourselves a very weird DB here.'

'Weird? What do you mean by *weird*?'

'Looks like the guy got hit by a half a ton of rock, right out in front of the convent. Killed him instantly.'

'What? Did it fall off the roof or something?'

'Couldn't have done. He's nowhere near the roof.'

'OK – I'll get right down there. Do you have backup?'

'There were half a dozen uniforms here by the time I got here, and the medical examiner's on his way.'

'OK. Give me ten minutes.'

Jenna took out her billfold to pay for her breakfast, but Joe McVitie said, 'Forget it. It's on the house. Go be a nun. Eat gristle.'

Officers Steinbeck and Cremer gave Jenna a ride to North Twenty-Second Street. Officer Cremer had a head cold and kept noisily blowing his nose, and the interior of the squad car reeked of menthol.

When they arrived, Jenna saw that the wide paved area in front of the Convent of Divine Love had already been cordoned off with POLICE DO NOT CROSS tape and that the side street was crowded with spectators. A black van from the medical examiner's office was parked nose-to-tail with a van from the crime scene unit and another van from 6 ABC Action News.

Dan Rubik came across the paved area and lifted up the tape for her. He was a young, intense detective with a bright ginger buzz-cut and pale green eyes and freckles. He always wore green coats because he thought that they complemented his gingery complexion.

'OK – we have at least five eyewitnesses already. They all say that the vic was crossing this forecourt, minding his own business, when *crash*! This massive block of stone dropped on top of him, right out of the blue. No warning. Just *crash*!'

Jenna elbowed her way into the knot of officers and CSIs and medical examiners who were gathered around the victim. When they saw who it was, they all stepped aside and let her through. Several of them gave her a wary nod of acknowledgement. One or two of them put on sour expressions and backed away.

The body was that of a man about forty-five years old, wearing a dark blue linen coat and light khaki pants. He was lying with his face pressed flat against the paving slab, still wearing his horn-rimmed Clark Kent spectacles, as if he had made no attempt at all to break his fall. The back of his head was crushed in – a glistening mixture of brains and skull fragments that looked as if somebody had broken a white china pudding basin filled with boysenberry jelly.

Lumps of shattered stone were scattered everywhere. Several of them were still resting on the victim's back, but most of them had exploded in all directions, and now littered an area spanning the street. One chunk was over a foot wide, but few of them were bigger than tennis balls, and most of them were much smaller.

Jenna looked up. The convent's facade was a gray Gothic chapel with a circular stained-glass window like the spokes of a huge cartwheel. Dan was right. The vic was lying at least sixty feet too far away to have been struck by a piece of stonework falling from the roof of the chapel – not that she could see any sign of missing crosses or spires or statues or gaps in the parapet.

Ed Freiburg, one of the crime scene specialists, came up to her. He was short and chunky, with pitted cheeks and steel wool for hair, and he looked more like a boxing coach than a forensic scientist. 'We're guessing there's nearly a thousand pounds of stone here. We can't know for sure until we collect it all up and weigh it, but that's our estimate.'

'So how the hell did nearly half a ton of stone drop out of a clear blue sky?' Jenna asked him. 'Did any of the witnesses hear a helicopter?'

Dan said, 'None of them.'

'All the same, run a check on all helicopter flights in the vicinity. See if some construction company was maybe trying to fly a block of rock across the city for some restoration job.'

She turned back to Ed Freiburg, 'Do you know what kind of stone this is?'

'Limestone,' Ed Freiburg told her. 'And it's some of the best quality limestone I ever saw. Usually used for building and sculpture, that kind of thing. So if it *was* dropped from a helicopter, this is the kind of stone it would most likely be, if that makes sense.'

Jenna looked around. She hated cases like this. More often than not, they turned out to be negligent homicide, and cases of negligent homicide invariably involved weeks or even months of tedious paperwork and hours of Byzantine interviews with evasive executives and slippery corporate lawyers. Eventually, somebody would pay off somebody else and the whole process would be dropped for the lack of anybody willing to point a finger at whoever had added the lethal chemical to the cleaning fluid, or whoever had left off the safety switch, or whoever had allowed the pipes to rust through, or, in this case, whoever had failed to secure half a ton of limestone to whatever it was supposed to have been secured to.

'I presume the vic was carrying some kind of ID,' she said.

Dan passed her a black leather wallet. She opened it up and saw a photograph of two curly-headed girls about eight or nine years old, one with her two front teeth missing. The victim's driving license showed a serious, slightly overweight man with the glassy-eyed look of a contact-lens wearer. His name was Steven Caponigro, and he lived at 4414 Buttonwood Avenue, Maple Shade Township, across the river in New Jersey.

'No relation to Tony "Bananas" Caponigro, I suppose?' asked Jenna, but then she answered her own question. 'Highly unlikely, if he was living in Maple Shade Township.'

She took a business card out of his wallet. It told her that Steven Caponigro was senior manager of Maple Shade Realtors.

'Can't see anybody deliberately wanting to flatten this poor guy. Not unless he'd sold them some overpriced dump that turned out to be riddled with dry rot.'

'You want to talk to any of the witnesses?' Dan asked her. 'I've asked them to wait, in case you did.'

Jenna shook her head. 'You can let them go. It's pretty obvious what happened here, even if it isn't explicable.'

As she circled slowly around the body, she noticed the heavy side door of the convent open up. There was a pause, and then one of the Holy Spirit Adoration Sisters stepped out, dressed in the distinctive rose-colored habit that had earned them the nickname of the Pink Sisters.

The nun hesitated for a moment, and then half-lifted her right hand, as if she were trying to attract Jenna's attention without appearing too obvious.

Jenna said, 'OK, Dan, want to follow up that helicopter thing? Try talking to Stuart What's-his-face at Columbia Heavy Lift Helicopters.'

'Stuart What's-his-face?'

'Just ask to speak to the skinny guy who laughs like Pee-Wee Herman. They'll know who you mean.'

She maneuvered her way through the assembled police officers and CSIs and walked across the paved area until she reached the convent door. The nun waited for her. As she approached, she lowered her hand and said, 'Are you a detective?'

Jenna tugged out her badge. 'Detective Jenna Pullet, Sister. Did you have something you wanted to tell me?'

The Pink Sister nodded. She was in her late thirties, maybe thirty-seven or thirty-eight, with a face so pale that it was almost ivory. She wore rimless spectacles and her eyebrows were dark and unplucked – yet in a strange, asexual way, she was beautiful, like a medieval painting of a saint, either male or female.

'I felt something,' she said, with the slightest of lisps.

'You felt something? What do you mean? You felt it when that rock hit the sidewalk? I'm not surprised. It weighed close to a thousand pounds.'

'No. I felt something before it fell.'

'*Before* it fell?'

'It was during our Eucharistic celebration. We have one every morning at seven. While we were praying in the chapel I felt something pass overhead.'

'I get it. Like a helicopter, or an airplane, something like that?'

The nun shook her head. 'It made no sound. It passed overhead like a shadow passing over the sun, that's the only way that I can describe it.'

'Did you actually see it?'

'No. It was a feeling, that's all. Dark, and cold, and very evil-hearted.'

'What's your name, Sister?' Jenna asked her.

'Sister Mary Emmanuelle.'

'How long have you been a Pink Sister, Mary?'

'Seventeen years this September tenth.'

'So for seventeen long years you've been shut up in this convent, praying? I mean, like, this is a very closed community, so far as I understand it? You don't get out much.'

'We do live a cloistered life, yes. We devote our days and our nights to listening to the Word of God and to keeping a prayerful vigil on behalf of the entire world. But I hope you're not trying to suggest that my years of seclusion have made me susceptible to delusions.'

'No, no. I'm not suggesting that for a second. Or, I don't know. Maybe I am. It's pretty hard for me to understand how you can spend all day every day praying. I'm a Catholic, too, Sister, but I have to confess that there's a limit to how much praying I can do before I start to feel seriously prayed out. My knees won't take it, either, not these days.'

She paused, and then she asked, 'Did any of your fellow sisters experience this same feeling? This cloud passing over the sun?'

Sister Mary Emmanuelle shook her head again. 'If they did, none of them spoke of it.'

'OK . . . so what do *you* think it was? Do you have any kind of explanation for it? Maybe it was intuition? Or maybe a cloud really *did* pass over the sun and the chapel physically went colder and darker and for some reason it gave you the heebie-jeebies?'

'I have no explanation for it,' Sister Mary Emmanuelle admitted. 'I felt it, and I felt that it was cold and ugly and ill-intentioned. But only seconds later it fell out of the sky and killed that poor man, and that's why I thought it important for me to tell you what I felt.'

'Excuse me?' said Jenna. 'You said "cold and ugly and ill-intentioned". It was a half-ton lump of rock, that's all. How could a half-ton lump of rock be ill-intentioned?'

Sister Mary Emmanuelle frowned over Jenna's shoulder toward the fragments of limestone scattered across the pavement.

'It was a living thing, Detective. A creature.'

'A creature? What kind of a creature, exactly?'

'I'm sorry. Please – forget it. I shouldn't have bothered you.'

'No, Mary. I don't think that at all. Tell me what kind of a creature. Please.'

Sister Mary Emmanuelle's eyes darted from side to side behind her rimless spectacles as if they were trapped. 'I can't,' she said. 'I should never have mentioned it. To believe in evil is to give it life.'

'Mary – evil is alive and well whether we believe in it or not. I come across evil every day of my life and some of it is totally unbelievable. But it still exists, and all I can do is try to stamp it out.'

Sister Mary Emmanuelle covered her face with both hands.

When she spoke, she spoke so quietly that Jenna had to tilt her head toward her to hear what she was saying.

'It had a face like a demon, ugly beyond all description, with bulging eyes and horns. It had a hunched back and leathery wings. Instead of feet it had claws.'

She hesitated for a moment, and then she lowered her hands.

Jenna said, 'You told me you didn't see it.'

'I didn't see it. That was what I felt.'

'You felt bulging eyes and horns? You felt claws instead of feet? I don't understand what you're saying. How do you *feel* claws instead of feet?'

'You think I'm hysterical. You think I've been shut up in this convent for too long. You think I've been looking at too many illustrations of hell.'

Jenna didn't know how to answer that. She patted Sister Mary Emmanuelle on the shoulder and said, 'OK, Mary . . . thanks for talking to me. I know where to find you if I need to ask you any more questions, don't I?'

'You don't believe me,' said Sister Mary Emmanuelle.

'Of course I believe you. Jesus, you're a nun.'

'I felt it pass overhead. I felt its coldness. I felt its malevolence. I saw it clearly in my mind's eye. I promise you in the name of Our Lord that I am telling you the truth.'

'And like I said, Mary, I believe you.'

Jenna left Sister Mary Emmanuelle at the convent door and walked back to the victim. The crime scene investigators were taking photographs now, and with each flash of their cameras his body seemed to twitch, as if he wasn't quite dead yet.

'Anything?' asked Ed Freiburg, nodding his head toward Sister Mary Emmanuelle.

'Are you kidding me? I think too much adoration has gone to her head.'

'Well, we'll catalog all of the pieces and that should give us some idea of how high this rock was dropped from. Maybe that should give us some idea of *what* it was dropped from, and how.'

'OK. I'm going to drive over to Maple Shade and talk to this unlucky bastard's nearest and dearest. After that I'll be back at the district.'

One of the CSIs called out, 'Ed! Take a look at this!' She

was holding up a piece of limestone and turning it this way and that.

Ed went over to see what she wanted, and Jenna followed him. Although one side of the stone was broken and rough, the other side was evenly rippled and smooth, as if it had been fashioned to look like a fold of material.

Jenna took it and examined it. 'This has definitely been carved,' she said. 'Look, you can see that it's been chiseled, and then filed.'

'So our vic could have been flattened by a statue?'

'I don't know. Let's see if we can find some more sculpted bits.'

Ed called out, 'Can you all take a closer look at these rocks, people, and check if any of them have evidence of carving on them – like this one I'm showing you here!'

Within a few seconds, one of the police officers held up a triangular fragment of stone and said, 'Here! This piece has some kind of a wing tip carved on it, by the looks of it.'

'And there's a kneecap here! Or maybe it's an elbow.'

'I found a couple of fingers!'

Over the next ten minutes, the officers brought over more and more pieces of stone that bore unmistakable signs of having been carved. Most of the fragments had been smashed so small that at first sight it was impossible to identify what part of a statue they could be, but Jenna knew that once Ed and his team got them back to their laboratory, they would be able to reassemble them and find out what the figure originally looked like. Two years ago they had reconstructed an antique glass vase that had been shattered into more than three thousand pieces.

'Right,' said Jenna, checking her watch. 'I'll leave you to it. Let me know as soon as you've got this baby stuck together again.'

'Oh, for sure. So long as you give us about three months, minimum.'

She was returning to the squad car when one of the CSIs shouted out, 'Detective! Detective Pullet!'

She turned around. The investigator was standing in the raised flower-bed at the side of the convent, more than forty feet away from the point of impact. He was holding up a large gray piece of limestone that looked like a mask that had been broken in half, diagonally. Jenna walked back so that she could look at it more closely.

'Scary-looking sucker, don't you think?' said the CSI.

The piece of limestone must have weighed at least fifteen pounds. It was half of a head, with tangled hair and a single curved horn. Its face had one protuberant eye and a snarling mouth. *It had a face like a demon, ugly beyond all description.*

Jenna looked across to the convent's side door, but Sister Mary Emmanuelle had disappeared now, and the door was closed.

'Shit,' she said. The very last thing she had wanted to find out was that Sister Mary Emmanuelle might have been telling her the truth.

SIX

Tuesday, 2:46 p.m.

B raydon was dreaming that he was trying to find his way through a cemetery, just as the sun was beginning to go down. A bell was tolling to warn visitors that the cemetery gates would soon be closing for the night, but he knew that he couldn't leave yet because he hadn't yet done what he had come here to do.

The trouble was, he had completely forgotten what it was. Was it to visit somebody's grave, or was it to meet somebody? Was it to find out if somebody he knew was dead?

The setting sun made it look as if the trees surrounding the cemetery were on fire, and he had to walk with his hand held up in front of his eyes to stop himself from being dazzled. The gravestones cast extravagantly long shadows across the grass, and his own shadow looked like a circus performer on stilts.

He reached the intersection of two lines of gravestones and stopped. The cemetery was on a hillside and there was a hot wind blowing. In the distance he could see a dark gray lake, with dark gray clouds gathering over it, and lightning flickering. He could hear thunder, too, and he knew that God was angry with him. At least God didn't know where he was – not yet, anyhow.

He hurried on. He could hear crackling and smell smoke. The trees not only *looked* as if they were on fire, they *were* on fire. Flames were leaping up and down like hysterical dancers, and the bushes began to sparkle and shrivel up. The wind rose and blew even more strongly, and Braydon suddenly realized that if he didn't move faster the fire was soon going to encircle him, and he wouldn't be able to escape. *Burned to death in a boneyard,* that would be ironic.

He jogged faster and faster, panting. He jogged past marble cenotaphs and polished granite slabs and statues of weeping angels. The trees were burning more and more fiercely, and now the grass itself was on fire, and the flames were rushing after him as if a fiery rip-tide were coming in.

As he neared the cemetery gates, he saw that they were closed and locked, and that there was no way out. Black smoke was rolling across the cemetery in dense, choking clouds, and everything was blazing, even the statues of weeping angels, as if they were made of white wax instead of stone.

Braydon turned around and around, frantically trying to work out how he was going to escape.

It was then that he heard Sukie's voice. '*Daddy?*' she was calling. '*Daddy, where are you?*'

'I'm here, sweetheart!' Braydon called out. 'Daddy's right here!'

'*I need you, Daddy! Please, Daddy, come save me! Please!*'

'I'm coming, darling! Don't be frightened! Daddy's right here!'

Braydon flailed his way through the thickening smoke, coughing and wheezing. He tripped over the low cast-iron fencing around somebody's granite sepulcher, and stumbled through the flower vases in front of somebody else's headstone. But then the smoke cleared a little and he saw Sukie standing on a white marble plinth, holding Binkie tightly in her arms.

'I'm here, sweetheart! I'm right here! Let's get you out of this horrible place!'

Sukie was wearing the same red sweater and the same OshKosh dungarees that she had been wearing when he had kidnapped her from Miranda's parents' house. Her dark hair was parted in the middle and braided into pigtails, with red ribbons tied in a bow. To Braydon's bewilderment, though, her eyes were closed.

'*Daddy! I need you, Daddy! Please come save me!*'

'I'm here! Open your eyes, sweetheart! I'm right here in front of you!'

'*Save me, Daddy! Save me!*'

As he came nearer, Sukie opened her eyes. Braydon said, 'Oh my God! Oh, sweet Jesus!' Both of her eyes were completely blood red, and translucent, as if she were a vampire.

Braydon had been ready to reach out and scoop her up, but now he hesitated. 'What's happened, Sukie? What's happened to your eyes?'

'*Save me, Daddy! Don't let me burn!*'

'I won't, sweetheart. I promise.' He coughed, and he coughed, and for a while he couldn't stop himself from coughing, and he ended up by retching. 'Here – let's get the hell out of here, before it's too late!'

But it was already too late. Sukie's cherubic, heart-shaped face was beginning to melt – as if she, too, were molded out of wax. Her cheeks slid slowly downward and her lips curled, and then her eyelids drooped like a very old woman.

'*It hurts, Daddy! It hurts so much!*' she repeated, but her throat was constricted and her words were thick and sticky and Braydon could barely understand her. He stayed where he was, unable to move. His brain simply couldn't work out what messages to send to his legs and his arms to make them work, and go to her, and pick her up.

Sukie's forehead collapsed, and then her doll Binkie caught fire, and started to blaze fiercely in her arms. The flames from Binkie's nylon hair licked at Sukie's face, and she started to burn, too. Her skin, her flesh, her pigtails. She burned so fiercely that Braydon could feel the heat on his outstretched hands.

He didn't know how long she burned. Eventually, however, her head collapsed into her neck, and then her chest collapsed, and then she was nothing but two burning legs supporting a burning pelvis, like some kind of sacrificial bowl.

Braydon managed to take one step back, and then another. His eyes were crowded with tears and his throat was raw. His lungs were so filled with smoke that he couldn't even cough.

Sukie. I killed you. Sukie, I burned you alive. How can you ever forgive me?

A woman's voice very close to his left ear said, 'Mr Harris? Are you awake?'

Braydon opened his eyes. He was lying on one of two beds in a small recovery room. A black nurse in a pale blue uniform was leaning over him with her hand on his shoulder.

'How do you feel?' the nurse asked him. 'Do you feel any pain?'

He lifted his head, and saw that his right arm was supported by a gray vinyl sling, and that his right wrist was encased in a hard white plaster cast. He could feel a dull, underlying throbbing, but no real pain.

'I'm OK. I think I'm OK. Where am I?'

'You're in the specialist burns unit at Temple University Hospital. You've been sleeping for over an hour now.'

'Temple University Hospital?'

'Philadelphia, Mr Harris.'

He looked up at her. 'Oh, Jesus,' he said. 'Sukie.'

'I'm sorry,' said the nurse. 'But Doctor Berman has made your daughter comfortable, and she's not in any pain. You can come and see her now. Let me help you put on your shoes.'

Braydon rolled himself sideways on the bed and managed to sit up. When he tried to stand up, however, his knees gave way and he promptly sat back down again. The nurse took hold of his elbow and helped him to his feet. 'How bad is she?' he croaked.

'Well, you can see for yourself. She has deep facial burns, but Doctor Berman is brilliant when it comes to treating children with injuries like hers.'

'I thought – I dreamed she was dead.'

'She's a very sick little girl, Mr Harris. She has damage to her mouth and throat and lungs, and her digestive tract, too. But, like I say, Doctor Berman is one of the world's leading specialists when it comes to pediatric burns.'

Braydon nodded. 'OK. Can I see her now?'

'Of course. But I think there's one more thing I should tell you. Your ex-wife is here, too.'

Miranda was sitting next to Sukie's bed. She didn't turn around when Braydon was ushered into the room. She was wearing a dark green silk scarf tied around her head and from the back she looked bonier than ever – with visible vertebrae and angular shoulders. In the middle of one of their more spectacular rows,

Braydon had told her that she had all the physical charm of a praying mantis.

Doctor Berman was standing on the other side of the bed. He was big and heavily built and bespectacled, with two double chins that were covered with a graying beard. He held out his hand when Braydon came in, and in a booming voice said, 'Mr Harris? How are you? Terrible thing to happen. Just awful. I want you to know that you have all of our sympathy.'

Braydon heard Miranda say, '*Huh!*' but he ignored her and approached the bed. Sukie's face was charred scarlet and black so that it looked like an aerial view of some volcanic island. Her nose and her lips were hideously puffed up and most of her hair had been burned off, so that her scalp was covered with nothing but blackened stubble.

'How is she?' he asked.

'Oh, she's just dandy,' said Miranda, still without looking around. 'You can see for yourself, can't you?'

'In herself, she's doing not too bad,' said Doctor Berman. 'We have her on a drip to replace her fluids and her vital signs are holding up.'

Braydon said, 'She has bandages on her arms but no bandages on her face.'

'That's right. But if you look at her face you'll see that it appears to be shiny. That's because we've covered it with a transparent film medication called Jaloskin. It's a totally new class of biomaterial, a membrane produced by the esterification of hyaluronic acid, which is a naturally-occurring extracellular matrix molecule.'

'Excuse me?'

Doctor Berman smiled. 'I'm sorry. I didn't mean to get too technical. When you're dealing with deep dermal burns like Sukie's, it's important to remove the burned flesh as soon as possible, because that reduces inflammation and scarring.

'Once you've done that, you need to apply a dressing to prevent infection, and that's where Jaloskin comes in. It covers the burns and creates the ideal conditions for very rapid healing. It allows excess fluid to drain away, but at the same time it keeps the wound moist. Using Jaloskin, I've been able to allow young patients with second-degree burns to leave hospital and go home after only twelve days' treatment.'

'How long do you think it's going to take Sukie to get better?'

Doctor Berman shrugged. 'Right now, it's a little early to predict. Her burns are very deep and very serious, and we want to make sure that she suffers minimal aesthetic impact.'

Miranda twisted around in her chair. Her pale blue eyes were narrowed with fury, and she looked as if her mouth was crammed with broken glass.

'You know what that means, Braydon – "minimal aesthetic impact"? That means that the good doctor here is going to do everything he can to stop your daughter looking like too much of a freak!'

'Now, come on, Mrs Harris,' said Doctor Berman. 'If everything goes according to plan, Sukie should eventually be left with only the faintest of scars.'

'She wouldn't have any scars at all if my deadbeat ex-husband hadn't tried to kidnap her! I can tell you where I'm going as soon as I leave here, Braydon. I'm going to contact the FBI, and I'm going to have you arrested for violating a court order and for taking my daughter over a state line and for wrecking her life! You stupid, selfish, irresponsible, careless, pig-headed piece of worthless shit!'

Braydon looked down at Sukie, lying on the bed with her scorched face shining under its protective membrane.

'You can do what you like, Miranda,' he said, his voice still hoarse from the smoke. 'I think I've been punished quite enough already.'

SEVEN

Tuesday, 7:17 p.m.

Nathan arrived home that evening to find a strange car blocking his driveway, nose-to-bumper behind Grace's Explorer, so that he had to park his own car halfway up the curb. The offending vehicle was a purple Chevrolet Impala, and when he squeezed past it he saw that it had an Avis rental sticker in the window, from Philadelphia International Airport.

He opened the front door and immediately heard voices in the living room. When he walked through, still carrying his briefcase, he found Grace sitting on the couch, talking to a young man in a light-gray three-piece suit. The young man had prickly black hair, almost military cut, and eyeglasses with black rectangular frames, as if he were looking through the slots in a mailbox. He turned around when Nathan came in, and as he did so, Nathan could see that he had a white zigzag scar that ran all the way from his right cheekbone to his chin.

'Hi, honey,' he said. 'Didn't know that we were expecting a visitor.'

He was feeling sweaty and ratty. In spite of his success in creating the phoenix, he had been looking forward all afternoon to coming home, taking a shower, and then collapsing into his armchair with a very cold can of Dale's Pale Ale.

The young man stood up, tugged down his vest, and held out his hand.

'I called yesterday, sir,' he said, in a strong German accent. 'Unfortunately I could not contact you so I decided to take a chance and call in person. I am Theodor Zauber.'

Nathan put down his briefcase, but he didn't shake the young man's hand.

'Theodor *Zauber*? Any relation to the late Doctor Christian Zauber?'

'He was my father, sir.'

'I see. So what brings you here to see me? I would have thought that I was the last person on earth you would have wanted to make contact with.'

'My father and you, sir, you were two sides of the same coin, so to speak.'

Nathan said, 'I don't know if you should have come here, really. What happened between me and your father – well, I think it's best forgotten.'

'It was a tragedy, Professor Underhill. But it would be even more of a tragedy if all of his life's work were to be wasted.'

Grace said, 'Would you like a beer, darling?'

'In a minute. After Mr Zauber has left.' He turned back to Theodor Zauber and said, 'To be straight with you, Mr Zauber, I don't think we have anything to talk about. Your father managed to bring a basilisk to life, which would have been an incredible achievement if he hadn't sacrificed the lives of dozens of elderly people in order to do so. He almost killed my wife, too. He put her into a coma from which she was very lucky ever to recover.'

Theodor Zauber nodded. 'Yes, Professor. I know about all of this. I can only tell you that I am profoundly regretful for all of those deaths, and for what my father did to Mrs Underhill. Of course his actions were criminal. But I think it would be even more criminal if all of the advances he made in the field of cryptozoology were to be ignored.'

'I'm sorry, Mr Zauber. Your father was a genius, no doubt about it. Anybody who could take a spell devised by an eighth-century sorcerer and make it work in a modern laboratory was inspired. But that still doesn't excuse what he did. The whole purpose of recreating mythical beasts is to *save* lives.'

'In all medical research there is some risk,' Theodor Zauber replied. 'However – *ja* – I have to accept what you say about my father.'

'Then, goodnight,' said Nathan. 'I hope you understand that it's nothing personal.'

Theodor Zauber said, 'Of course. The only reason I wanted to talk to you was because you have already made such impressive strides in recreating gryphons and basilisks and wyverns. I gather from the scientific media that you have also been trying to recreate a phoenix.'

'That's right, Mr Zauber, I have. But I've had a very long day and I really have nothing more to say to you.'

'Please, Professor. I do not know how far you have advanced with this phoenix project, or any of your other enterprises. But if you were to have unlimited access to all of my father's papers – there is no question that you could save yourself years of laborious research and millions of dollars.'

Nathan shook his head. He wasn't going to tell Theodor Zauber that he had successfully managed to breed a phoenix already. He hadn't even told Ron Kasabian yet, the CEO of Schiller Medical Research Division, who was funding him. Neither had he told Grace, although when she had called him at his laboratory today and asked him how his experiment had worked out, he had told her 'pretty darn good, on the whole. I think we're making some serious headway.' Obviously she hadn't heard the phoenix in the background calling out '*skrrrarrrkkk*!'

Theodor Zauber said, 'It is not just in recreating mythical creatures from scratch that my father's research could help you.'

'What do you mean?'

'I read in *Modern Zoology* that you were trying to create your phoenix by combining the DNA from a dragon-worm with the DNA from a scavenger-hawk. This is correct, yes? But there are other mythical creatures which have survived from previous centuries in their fully-developed form, except that they remain in what you might call suspended animation.'

'I'm sorry. I don't understand what you're talking about.'

'Let me put it this way, Professor – they are not unlike a mammoth that is found frozen in a glacier after forty thousand years. Fully formed, fully developed, not at all decayed – but, of course, inanimate. All it requires is for somebody with the right scientific know-how to bring them back to life. Somebody who has both belief in thaumaturgy and expertise in science.'

Nathan stared at him in bewilderment. 'Are you trying to tell me that your father found one of these creatures, whatever they are?'

'Oh no, Professor. He found many of them. In fact he found *thousands*. It was one of the last great discoveries of his career.'

'How could there possibly be thousands of them? Somebody would have dug up at least some of them by now.'

'No, Professor. You would never have found any of these creatures by digging.'

'Then where the hell are they?'

Theodor Zauber raised both of his hands in surrender. 'Forgive me, please. I think I have said too much already. It is obvious that you do not wish to take advantage of my late father's research, and I cannot say that I blame you. He was quite ruthless. He thought nothing of taking an innocent human life if it would further his experiments and eventually make him rich. I apologize for troubling you.'

'So you're not going to tell me where these creatures are? Or even *what* they are?'

'Unless you are interested in carrying on my father's work, it is better that I do not. As I say, I apologize if I intruded on your evening. I realize that you must be very tired. Goodnight.

He bowed to Grace and said, 'Thank you for your hospitality, Mrs Underhill. You were most *gastfreundlich*.'

'Wait up,' said Nathan. 'You're serious about this, aren't you?'

'Of course. Why do you think I went to such trouble to find out where you lived?'

'Sit down,' Nathan told him. 'If you really do know the where-abouts of fully-developed cryptozoological creatures, then *I* want to know, too.'

'Very well. But you have to understand that they may not have the same medical application as the creatures that you have been trying to develop yourself.'

'I can't be any judge of that, can I, unless you tell me what they are, and what kind of condition they're in.'

Theodor Zauber hesitated for a long time, with his hand over his mouth. Nathan waited, without saying anything. Grace said, 'I'll get you a beer, OK?' and Nathan nodded.

Eventually, Theodor Zauber walked back to the couch and sat down. 'I suppose I have to tell you,' he said. 'After all, you are probably the only person in the world who can help me. Who else has come so close to bringing mythical creatures back to life? My father was full of admiration for your work, and for your persistence in the face of so much skepticism from the scientific community. He always said "whatever has existed once can exist again".'

Nathan sat down opposite him. Grace brought him a can of beer and he popped it open and took a long, cold swallow. Theodor Zauber couldn't help saying, '*Prost!*' although he didn't smile when he said it.

'So,' said Nathan. 'What exactly *was* your father's last great discovery?'

'Petrification, Professor. The turning of living beings into stone.'

Nathan had been about to take another mouthful of beer but he slowly lowered his can. 'Is this a joke?'

'Absolutely not. What would be the point?'

'I really don't know. Maybe you want to make a fool out of me because of what happened between me and your father.'

'Please, Professor. I am one hundred percent seriously talking about creatures whose flesh has been deposed into solid stone.'

'I see. Your father didn't find Medusa's head, by any chance?'

'Of course not. But he did discover a formula that was used by thirteenth-century alchemists to convert a vertebrate being into what is essentially a statue. It is a process first mentioned by Ibn ar-Tafiz, sometimes known as Artephius.'

'OK, Artephius, I've heard of him. He wrote *The Secret Book of Artephius*, didn't he? Not that I've ever read it.'

'You should, Professor, although it is not an easy book to understand, even for an eminent scientist such as yourself. Artephius devised a way of converting solids into gases without first becoming liquids, and many other important chemical reactions. He lived on his family's cattle farm near Cordoba, and he discovered many new methods for making cheese and yogurt.

'His most important discovery, though, was what he calls "secret fire". This fire is actually a volatile liquid that can permeate a living body within a matter of hours and transform flesh into stone. It is exactly the same process by which mineral-rich spring water can gradually petrify anything that is immersed in it for long enough. Because of the active chemicals that Artephius added to his water, however, it all happens considerably quicker.'

'And so what are you telling me? That at some time in the past, thousands of mythical creatures were turned to stone, and that your father found out where they are?'

'Yes, Professor. Precisely that. But he found out much more than that. He found out how to turn them back into living flesh.'

EIGHT
Tuesday, 8:34 p.m.

Jenna switched off the lamp on her desk and shrugged on her quilted brown parka. 'That's me for tonight,' she told Detective Brubaker, who was still hunched over a pile of paperwork. He was appearing in Municipal Court tomorrow, giving evidence in a case of two young girls who had died after taking contaminated ecstasy tablets.

'See you, sweet cheeks. Have a brewski for me, will you? I won't be through till way past midnight.'

Jenna paused beside Detective Brubaker's desk. '*Gerry*?' she said.

Detective Brubaker caught the seriousness in her voice. He took off his reading glasses and looked up at her.

'What is it? Not that daughter of yours giving you trouble again?'

'No. Nothing like that. I was just wondering if you think that I'm likeable.'

'*Likeable*? What kind of a question is that?'

'I don't know. Sometimes I get the feeling that I put people's backs up. You know, losing my temper too quick, opening my yap and putting my size six sneaker in it. That kind of thing.'

Detective Brubaker made a *moue*. 'Nah. I don't think anybody gets too aerated when you say what you think. Now and then it might be better if you kept your opinions to yourself. Like Sergeant Mulvaney's hairpiece. The poor guy's real sensitive about it.'

'I know he is. But, my God. He could have warned us he was going to walk into the squad room with Punxsutawney Phil on his head.'

Detective Brubaker couldn't help smirking. 'Let me tell you this, Jenna. Most of the guys don't believe that women should be detectives at all. They think women should be home doing the laundry and baking brownies and changing the kids' shitty diapers, and that every night they should welcome their husbands back to the bosom of the family with a cold beer and a warm blow-job. They certainly don't believe that women should be detectives who say it the way they find it.'

He replaced his spectacles and went back to his paperwork, but Jenna stayed where she was.

'But, what?' she asked him.

Detective Brubaker looked up again. 'Did I say "but"?'

'I'm a trained interrogator, Gerry. I know when somebody has a "but" on the tip of their tongue.'

'OK. You asked me if you were likeable, and you are. I like you. You're sassy and you're funny and you're tough and you're good at what you do. Underneath, I think all of the guys like you, too. It's just that they're scared of you. In fact I think that they're scared of most women, especially women who talk back to them and won't take any bullshit.'

'Hm. I think you're just trying to get into my thong.'

'I didn't know you wore a thong.'

'And you never will, Gerry. Not for sure, anyhow. I'll see you tomorrow, OK? And – you know – thanks for the heads up. I'll try not to be so goddamned outspoken in future, especially when it comes to toupees. I'd hate it if everybody in the district thought that I was some kind of harridan.'

She was making her way to the squad room door when her telephone rang. It had a particularly loud, unpleasant jangle that always left a salty taste in her mouth.

Detective Brubaker waved his hand dismissively. 'I'd leave it, if I were you. Go home.'

Jenna hesitated. She was very tired, and she was anxious to get back in time to make sure that Ellie had eaten a proper supper. Ellie was neurotic about her weight at the moment, almost to the point of anorexia, and Jenna was growing increasingly worried about it. She knew what it was like to look in the mirror every morning and see a big-breasted, big-bellied, big-hipped lard-butt staring back at you, even if you didn't really look like that at all.

The phone kept on jangling and she knew that she would have to answer it. She went back to her desk, put down her pocketbook and picked up the receiver. '*What*?'

'Jenna, it's Dan. I'm at the Nectarine Tower Apartments on North Nineteenth. Up on the roof. We have two DBs up here.'

'For Christ's sake, Dan. I thought you were supposed to be home.'

'Well, yes, I was on my way. I'd even bought myself a pizza at Dolce Carini. But I saw two squad cars and a bus pulling up outside and I couldn't very well drive past without checking what was going down here.'

'You're not on duty, Dan. *I'm* not on duty. Our shift is over, and I'm frazzled. Why didn't dispatch put it through to Smith and Collard?'

'Because I told them not to. I told them that you and me would handle it.'

'And why the hell would you want to do that?'

'Because three eyewitnesses say they saw something drop out of the sky. Something dropped out of the sky and they heard screaming up on the roof and when they went up to see what it was all about, they found these two DBs. They've been ripped right open, Jenna. I mean they have literally been torn to shreds. I never saw anything like it.'

'Something dropped out of the sky?'

'That's right. All three witnesses saw it. Or at least they caught a glimpse of it.'

'Do they have any idea what it was?'

'They're not sure. One of them only saw its shadow, but they all agreed it was like some kind of a bird, even though it wasn't a bird. Like, it had wings. But two of them agreed that it had horns, and one of them said it had bulging eyes like Don Rickles.'

'Don Rickles? I don't believe this. Two people were ripped to pieces by something with wings that looked like Don Rickles?'

'I guess it was the eyes, that's all.'

'Jesus. And you thought you and me needed to take this case up for why? Because of that statue that fell out of the sky?'

'Well, yes. You have to admit they could be connected. The horns. The bulging eyes. The feet that looked like claws. It all seems like kind of a coincidence.'

Jenna took a deep breath.

'You still there?' Dan asked her.

'Yes, I'm still here, for my sins. Give me ten minutes. I have to call home first.'

'The crime scene team have just arrived. My God. One of them barfed. One of them actually barfed.'

Jenna hung up. Detective Brubaker looked across at her and said, 'No peace for the wicked, hunh?'

'Two DBs on top of the Nectarine Tower Apartments. According to Dan they were both torn to pieces.'

She punched out her home number and waited for Ellie to pick up. Detective Brubaker stretched and said, 'It totally beats me, you know. Homo sapiens has been living on this planet for five hundred thousand years and we're still tearing lumps out of each other. Homo sapiens? More like homo asinus.'

Ellie answered, '*Mom*?' She sounded tired, or dreamy, as if she had just woken up. Jenna hoped she wasn't high. Some of her school friends had been caught last week taking mephedrone, and she knew for sure that several of them regularly smoked weed, particularly that Ricky Martinez.

'Hi, baby. Listen, I'm going to be later than I thought. I'm sorry. Something real important came up and I have to go deal with it.'

'A murder?'

'Yes, well, something like that. You don't want to hear all the grisly details. Did you eat the lasagne I left you? I made sure I left you only a small piece.'

'I ate some of it.'

'You ate *some* of it? Ellie, it was only a mouthful to begin with.'

'I had lunch. I wasn't hungry.'

'So what did you have for lunch? Come on, tell me the truth.'

There was a pause, and then Ellie said, 'A Kellogg's cereal bar and half an apple. And a diet Dr Pepper.'

'OK, fine,' Jenna told her. Maybe a Kellogg's cereal bar and half an apple wasn't a banquet but at least she had eaten something, and she didn't want to make Ellie feel any more stressed about it than she did already. 'I'll see you when I see you, OK? And don't stay up too late.'

'Kids today,' said Detective Brubaker, as Jenna hung up. 'When we were young, my mom put us on the Earring Diet.'

'Oh yeah? What was that?'

'You sat down at the table, you said grace, and you ate what was put in front of you. If you didn't, you got a smack round the head, which made your ear ring.'

'Yeah, those were the days,' said Jenna. 'If I did that today, I'd have to arrest myself for assault.'

She parked around the corner on Brandywine Street and crossed over North Nineteenth Street to the Nectarine Tower Apartment building. The entire street was already jam-packed with squad cars, ambulances, a van from the medical examiner's office and press trucks. She pushed her way through the crowds and up the steps to the building's main entrance, showing her badge to the two young officers standing in front of the revolving door, although she knew that they knew perfectly well who she was.

Dan was waiting for her in the lobby, talking to the doorman. When it was first opened in 1968, the Nectarine Tower had been the second most fashionable address in Philadelphia, after the Metropolitan, but these days it had a dated, worn-out look about it. The lighting in the marble-floored lobby was dim, and the brown leather couches were sagging, and the bronze finish on the elevator doors was badly discolored. Even the gold braid on the doorman's maroon uniform had started to fray, and he could have used a shave.

'I've managed to ID them,' said Dan, as Jenna came click-clacking across the lobby. He flipped open his notebook and said, 'They were two friends from different apartments who used to go up on the roof to smoke, because their wives wouldn't let them do it indoors. Chet Huntley, thirty-nine, and William Barrow, fifty-two. Huntley was an insurance assessor and Barrow was an electrical contractor. As far as I can tell they had nothing in common except that they both enjoyed a cigar and they both supported the Phillies.'

'Are the witnesses still here?' asked Jenna. 'This time I need to talk to them.'

'One of them lives in twenty-one-oh-nine. She's the one who saw the bird-thing the clearest.'

'The one who thought it looked like Don Rickles?'

'That's right. Her name's Mary Lugano. The other two live in nineteen-twelve and seventeen-twenty-three respectively. Christine Takenaka and Kenneth Keiller.'

'Which of them found the bodies?'

'Mary Lugano and Kenneth Keiller and another resident from twenty-oh-six.'

'They're OK? They're not in shock or anything?'

'Lucky for them they didn't really see too much. It was pretty dark, up on the roof, and all they could make out was one of the vic's heads, and a leg, and the floor all covered with blood. They came straight back down and called nine-one-one.'

'OK,' said Jenna. 'Let's take a look.'

They went up in the elevator to the twenty-second floor. At the back of the elevator car there was a brown-mottled mirror, and Jenna thought what a mess her hair was, and how tired she looked. These days she found herself wondering more and more frequently why she had chosen to join the police department. Even after all these years, her job frequently gave her horrific nightmares. It had broken up her relationship with Ellie's father Jim, and with several of her closest friends, and she always looked as if she had been dragged backward through a briar patch.

If she quit, though, she knew that she would miss it from the very first day. It was a curse, but it was a calling. It was like being a doctor, or a nun. She had told Sister Mary Emmanuelle that she couldn't understand how she could spend her entire life in prayer, but in reality she *did* understand, only too well. Just like Sister Mary Emmanuelle, she had no choice.

When they reached the twenty-second floor they stepped out of the elevator, crossed the corridor to the stairwell, and climbed up the last flight of stairs. Outside, the roof was brightly lit with portable halogen lamps, and cameras were flashing like summer lightning. Ed Freiburg and two other forensic investigators were waddling around in their noisy blue Tyvek suits, taking photographs and measuring the blood spatter and collecting samples of tissue and skin. Off to the left, two police officers were leaning on the low railing that surrounded the roof, talking to one of the medical examiners and deliberately keeping their backs to the horrors behind them.

The lights of the city twinkled all around them, and a soft damp breeze was blowing. Jenna stepped forward two or three paces, but no further, because of the dark shiny blood that was splashed across the concrete, as if somebody had thrown it from a bucket.

Dan had been right. The two victims had been torn to pieces, but much more explosively than Jenna could have imagined. They reminded her of a young woman who had been hit two years ago by an Acela express locomotive out at Norwood, and whose head had been found seventy-five feet further up the track than her feet, with every other part of her body littered in between. Both Chet Huntley and William Barrow had been ripped apart in a similar way, which indicated that they had been struck by something traveling at an extremely high velocity, and of considerable mass. And at a low angle, too.

Ed Freiburg stood up. His Tyvek suit was smeared with crisscross patterns of blood, like an action painting. He lifted his glove in greeting when he saw Jenna and he called out, 'Come around the edge of the roof – that's it, over to your right. There's not too much residue there.' By 'residue' he meant blood and skin and smashed-apart flesh.

Jenna circled around the roof to the north-east corner, balancing on her toes as delicately as a tightrope walker. Ed Freiburg came over to join her, wiping his nose on the back of his sleeve. Resting in the right angle between the two low retaining walls was a man's torn-off head. Jenna guessed from his age and appearance that it was William Barrow. He was balding, with gray curly hair, and a bulbous nose. His pale blue eyes were wide open and he was staring upward with a concentrated look on his face as if he were trying to identify the stars.

His torso had been hit so hard that it had burst into pieces, and his skeleton and all of his internal organs had been scattered from one side of the roof to the other, a distance of more than a hundred feet. His feet were lying in the south-west corner, still wearing a pair of brown sneakers, with his shin bones protruding from them like turkey drumsticks.

Chet Huntley's body was spread out diagonally across William Barrow's, from the north-west corner to the south-east, so that between them they formed a grisly X. Where the remains of their two bodies intersected, there was a bloody confusion of ribs and livers and sloppy heaps of intestine. Ed Freiburg's assistants were painstakingly trying to separate them, by hand, and heap them into evidence bags.

'No sign of the unfortunate Mr Huntley's head,' said Ed Freiburg. 'Guess it must have bounced clear off of the roof when he was hit. I sent one of my people down to street level to see if they can locate it.'

'Ever see anything like this before?' Jenna asked him. Unexpectedly, a sharp surge of bile rose up in her throat and she had to cover her mouth with her hand. In spite of the breeze, there was a strong smell of human insides up here on the roof.

'I once saw a guy who was tied to two automobiles, which then drove off in opposite directions. That was in the days when "Little Nicky" Scarfo was in charge. But I never saw anything like this. These two guys are standing here, having a quiet smoke, when something that must have weighed the best part of seven hundred pounds hits them by surprise at – what? – a hundred and twenty-five miles an hour, at least. Probably a whole lot faster. And simultaneously tears them open, too, with a jagged instrument of some sort, like three baling-hooks.'

'According to Dan, at least one of the eyewitnesses thinks that it was some kind of massive bird.'

'Yeah, he told me. But, come on. What kind of bird do we know of that could do this? The giant roc, from *Sinbad the Sailor*? That's the only one I can think of. The roc was supposed to be able to pick up elephants and fly away with them. But here? Tonight? A roc? In Philly? I don't think so.'

'Two of the witnesses said it had horns and one of them said it had bulging eyes.'

'Yeah – like that statue we picked up this morning. Dan told me about that, too. He seems to be convinced that there's a link between them. But you don't seriously think so, do you? Whatever that was a statue of, it was carved out of solid limestone. Whatever killed these guys, it was living and breathing and it was plenty mean.'

It was cold and ugly and ill-intentioned. That was what Sister Mary Emmanuelle had told her. *I felt its malevolence.*

NINE

Tuesday, 8:57 p.m.

Theodor Zauber leaned forward and spoke in a low, confidential voice. 'You know from your own research about the *Wasserspeier.*'

'The water-spitters?' Nathan replied. 'Yes, of course I do. That's the German word for gargoyles.'

'But how much do you *really* know about them? The gargoyles?'

'Not a whole lot, I guess. I know that there was a whole plague of them in Europe in the early part of the fourteenth century. They slaughtered sheep and cattle mainly, but they also killed quite a few people, didn't they? Especially little children.'

'Aha! They killed more than "quite a few", Professor. It was many hundreds of people, probably thousands, maybe even *tens* of thousands, all across the Netherlands and Germany and Poland and as far east as Russia.'

'I didn't know that. I've never seen anything about it in any of my textbooks.'

'That is because nobody would openly say the name of the *Wasserspeier* out loud, for fear that the gargoyles would hear them, and come after them seeking retribution. Gargoyles were said to have unnaturally sensitive hearing. Nobody would even dare to write the name down for fear that they would pick up the scratching of the word *Wasserspeier* with a pen – not that many people could write in those days, only monks. It took my father many years to find out how many thousands of people they massacred, the *Wasserspeier*. But – as you probably *do* know – they disappeared from the face of the earth quite suddenly. In less than a year, almost all of the gargoyles were gone.'

Nathan finished his beer and slowly crushed the can in his fist. 'That was round about thirteen fifty-something, wasn't it, from what I read? Nobody knows why they disappeared – not for sure, anyhow.'

'There are many conflicting explanations,' Theodor Zauber agreed. 'But most religious historians agree that they were finally purged by a select band of priests known as the *Bruderschaft der Reinheit* – the Brotherhood of Purity.'

'Really? Who were they?'

'They were all experienced exorcists, of different nationalities, twenty-one of them in all. They were dispatched by the Vatican to travel from country to country, hunting down the *Wasserspeier* one by one and sending the demons who possessed them back to hell.'

'Great idea, a posse of exorcists,' said Nathan. 'Personally I prefer Doctor Jacob Lenz's theory. He thinks the *Wasserspeier* died out because they contracted a highly-infectious strain of diphtheria which was not particularly harmful to humans but which was fatal to gargoyles. Pretty much like the Martians in *The War of the Worlds.*'

'Yes, I am aware of Doctor Lenz's theory.'

Nathan was getting up from his chair to fetch himself another can of pale ale. 'You don't sound very convinced.'

'Doctor Lenz is highly regarded and his theory is very plausible. In fact it is much more plausible than what really happened. But what *really* happened was an extraordinary combination of science and religion and some thaumaturgy, too – what your man in the street would call black magic.'

'Go on.'

'I don't know if I should. And if you knew what this was leading to, maybe you shouldn't ask me to.'

Grace came in from the kitchen. 'Everything OK, darling? Would you like another beer?'

'I was just about to get myself one.'

'That's OK, I'll do it. Mr Zauber? Would you care for a drink? How about something to eat? I could make you a sandwich. I have cheese, or baloney.'

'I think a glass of water please. But, no, no sandwich, *danke sehr*. I have to observe strictly my special diet.'

Theodor Zauber waited until Grace had left the room and then he said, 'My father discovered that the Brotherhood of Purity included more than exorcists. It was led by Bishop Bodzanta from Kraków, who was a fierce opponent of all kinds of corruption and debauchery, especially in the royal courts.

'Also with them was our friend Ibn ar-Tafiz, Artephius, and a Dominican friar called Tomaso Campanella, who had taught himself to become proficient in astrological magic, so that he could defend innocent people against demons. In his later years he was said to have saved Pope Urban the Eighth from a life-threatening attack by evil spirits.'

'Quite a gang, then,' said Nathan.

'As you correctly say, quite a gang. They traveled from one city to another, and as they did so, Tomaso Campanella located each gargoyle in its hiding place by means of a witch-compass. Once the creature was cornered, the priests gathered around to exorcize it and render it powerless. As soon as they had done that, Artephius applied his "secret fire" and the gargoyle would be turned to stone, so that it could not by repossessed by evil spirits. In total, the Brotherhood of Purity hunted down and petrified over a thousand of them. Sometimes they petrified as many as thirty in a single day.'

'OK . . . once they'd done that – turned them to stone – then what?'

'The gargoyles would be transported by night to the nearest church or cathedral where they would be mounted high up in the air as a demonstration of the power of the church and also as a warning to other gargoyles. You can see them of course on Notre-Dame cathedral in Paris, on Sint-Petrus-en-Pauluskerk in Ostend, in Belgium, and on Saint Catherina's on Skaleczna Street in Kraków, in Poland; and on many other abbeys and convents throughout Europe.

'Because they were attached to sacred structures, it was impossible for any alchemist or any thaumaturge to turn the gargoyles back into living creatures. And many of them were adapted as waterspouts – water-spitters, as you rightly call them – because it was believed that if their mouths were regularly flushed with water from the roof of a holy building, they would be unable to call for help from Satan.'

Theodor Zauber didn't realize that Grace had been standing in the open doorway behind him holding a glass of water and Nathan's can of beer, and listening to all of this.

'But you say that your father found a way of bringing them back to life?' she asked him.

Theodor Zauber twisted around on the couch. 'I must apologize, Mrs Underhill. I should not really be speaking of such things. It is an abuse of your welcome.'

'Not at all,' said Grace, crossing the living room and giving Nathan his beer. 'I want to hear about this. Your father created a basilisk and when that basilisk stared at me it put me into a coma that I might never have come out of – ever. If you're going to be talking about mythical creatures coming to life, I think I have a personal interest in knowing exactly what you have in mind, don't you?'

'I have already begged your forgiveness for what my father did to you, Mrs Underhill,' said Theodor Zauber. 'I hope you can accept that I am truly, deeply sorry. *Entschuldigen Sie bitte.*'

'I do. I accept your apology. But that doesn't answer my question.'

'Very well, yes. My father did discover a method by which a petrified creature could be reanimated. It may have been turned into stone, but the stone still contains all of its DNA and all of the cellular components that made it what it once was. It is like a fish that has been frozen solid. Once it is thawed, it is physically the same fish. It is not decayed, it is in a perfect state of preservation, and the same is true for petrified creatures. All they require is for them to start breathing and their hearts to start beating once more.'

'Oh. Is that all? And how exactly do you do that? I have a couple of rainbow trout in the freezer. What if I defrosted them and then gave them the kiss of life?'

'*Grace,*' said Nathan.

'No,' Grace retorted. 'Mr Zauber has come here for a reason and I want to know what it is. More than anything else, I want to know exactly *why* he wants to bring these gargoyles back to life. Especially since they're so dangerous.'

'Don't you see?' Theodor Zauber asked her. 'It would be a staggering achievement in cryptozoology! And for all we know, there are *human* statues that have been petrified in the same way. If we could bring them back to life, we might be able to speak with people who are hundreds or even thousands of years old.'

'Oh you mean those Greek statues of women with no arms and men with their dicks knocked off?'

'Grace, for Christ's sake,' said Nathan. 'At least let's hear what Mr Zauber has to say.'

'I just don't understand why he wants to revive anything so vicious, that's all. Why do you think gargoyles were exorcized and turned to stone in the first place? Because they massacred people. What else are they good for?'

'You must understand that they could save many lives,' said Theodor Zauber. 'We already know theoretically how we can turn a living creature into stone, just like we know how a human being can be cryogenically frozen. If we know that we can successfully bring them back to life, we will be able to petrify people with serious incurable illnesses and revive them many years later when a cure has been found – without the need for expensive refrigeration equipment.'

'But meanwhile you have a bloodthirsty mythical creature on your hands. Or creatures. I can't see you stopping at just one, can you?'

'All experiments can be controlled, Mrs Underhill.'

'Just like your father's experiments with the basilisk, I suppose? How many innocent people did he murder to bring *that* particular monstrosity back to life? And how many collateral killings were there? And by the way, it's *Doctor* Underhill. I'm a medical practitioner.'

Nathan said, 'I can understand how you feel, Grace. But what Mr Zauber is suggesting has a great deal of scientific and medical validity. If we can actually bring a stone statue back to life—'

'Oh, it's "we", is it? You've decided to help him already?'

'No, I haven't. I need to know a whole lot more about this, believe me. For instance, if the gargoyles are on churches and cathedrals and suchlike, how do we gain access to them? And if they're on sacred buildings, how do we use thaumaturgy to revive them? Like you say, Mr Zauber, black magic is completely ineffective on hallowed ground.'

'Aha!' Theodor Zauber smiled and tugged at his fingers one by one, so that his knuckles popped. 'Over two hundred *Wasserspeier* are no longer on hallowed ground. They are *here*, in Philadelphia, and they have been here for quite some time.'

'You're kidding me. How did they get here?'

'They were shipped over from Europe in the year eighteen twenty-nine by the British architect John Haviland, when he was commissioned to design the Eastern State Penitentiary on Fairmount Avenue – which, at the time, was the largest prison in America.'

'What the hell did he want gargoyles for?'

'Times were different then, Professor. John Haviland wanted to build a prison that looked grim and forbidding, and which would not only fill its inmates with dread but remind free citizens of what they would face if they ever broke the law. That is why it looks like a Gothic castle.

'He wanted to position gargoyles around its walls to represent the sins for which the prisoners should be asking God for forgiveness. He visited derelict churches and cathedrals all over Europe searching for them, especially to Saint Catherina's in Kraków, which was in a state of ruin at the time because of an earthquake. Then he had them transported here to Philadelphia.

'However – for one reason or another – only two gargoyles were ever erected. I think the large minority of Quakers in the Prison Society raised objections. Eventually all two hundred gargoyles were stored in the vaults underneath cell-block fourteen and forgotten. When he was studying mythology at the Jagiellonian University in Kraków, my father found out from private correspondence where they had been taken. He had ambitions to try and revive at least one of them, but of course that was never to be.'

'But now *you* want to try it?'

'I think that whatever terrible things my father may have done, we have to recognize his genius. The German rocket scientist Wernher von Braun helped to build the V-2 missiles that killed thousands of innocent people during World War Two, but without his designs America could never have sent men to the Moon. Humanity sometimes has to be sacrificed to progress.'

'Oh, you think so?' said Grace, sharply. 'What if your

grandfather had been one of the scores of elderly people that your father murdered, so that he could steal their life force? Oh, they're old, they're finished, what do they matter? Or what if you had been *me*, in a coma. I wasn't just unconscious. I was having one screaming nightmare after another.'

Theodor Zauber stood up, bowed his head and clicked his heels together, like a comic-opera German. 'It is better if I leave. I imagined perhaps that I could interest Professor Underhill in a joint experiment. I imagined that we could combine his crypto-zoological expertise with my understanding of alchemy and so-called black magic, and between us we could bring one of the *Wasserspeier* back to life.'

'Well, I think that you were being more than a little presumptuous,' said Grace. 'Quite apart from being reckless in the extreme. You wanted to bring back a *gargoyle*? What the hell were you thinking?'

'You fail to understand, Doctor Underhill. Once we establish that it is possible to revive a gargoyle, we would immediately put it to sleep to prevent it from causing any harm to anyone. It is the *procedure* that is important, you see, not the creature itself. But – I can see that you are very hostile to such an experiment, and even if I cannot agree that your hostility is rational, I do not wish to trespass on your hospitality any further.'

Nathan was about to say something, but Grace gave him a death stare and he said, 'OK. Interesting idea, Mr Zauber, but let's leave it at that, shall we?'

'I will not trouble you again, Professor. Have no fear. But if you wish to contact me for any reason at all, I am staying for the time being at the Club Quarters hotel.'

Nathan showed him to the door. Before he left, Theodor Zauber said, in the same confidential tone that he had used before, 'I hope you realize, Professor, that you are passing up the opportunity of a lifetime.'

'Well, maybe,' said Nathan. 'But I think we have a little too much history between us, don't you, the Zaubers and the Underhills? And if my wife isn't happy with what you're suggesting, then neither am I, I'm afraid. It's something you get between husbands and wives, whether you think it's rational or not. It's called loyalty.'

Theodor Zauber pressed his lips together tightly, as if he were sucking on something extremely sour. Without another word he turned away, climbed into his rented Impala and backed out of the driveway with an irritated squitter of tires. Nathan watched his brake lights disappear around the corner, and then he closed the front door and went back into the living room.

Grace was sitting on the couch looking penitent.

'I'm sorry, Nathan. I didn't mean to be so aggressive. Or so rude.'

Nathan sat down beside her and popped open his second can of pale ale. 'Don't worry about it. I'm not too interested in gargoyles right at the moment. I've got my hands full with Torchy.'

'Torchy?'

'The phoenix. We did it. We set fire to poor old Grubby and now we have Torchy. It worked.'

Grace threw her arms around him and smothered him with kisses until he gasped, '*Heyyy! Can't breathe!*'

'That is so wonderful! You actually did it! What does it look like?'

Nathan took out his cellphone and showed her the pictures he had taken of the phoenix flapping inside its cage.

'My God, I can't believe it! You actually did it!'

'He looks kind of shabby, though, doesn't he? There I was, expecting some magnificent mythical bird with rainbow-colored feathers and a golden tail. Instead, I've got myself something that looks like a beaten-up prairie hawk. But that doesn't matter. We burned the worm and it burned so hot that it shattered its case and nearly set fire to the whole goddamned laboratory. But this is what came out, sweetheart. A real genuine phoenix.'

'What did Ron Kasabian say?'

'Ron Kasabian didn't say anything because Ron Kasabian doesn't know yet. Oh, he knows we had a minor fire in the laboratory but he doesn't know what caused it. I wanted to wait for twenty-four hours at least to make sure that the phoenix was going to survive. Aarif and Kavita are taking it in turns to keep an eye on him tonight, and if he's still just as chirpy in the morning, I'll tell him then.'

'I'm so proud of you. You don't even know. And I'm so proud that you turned down Theodor Zauber this evening. I know how sorely you must have been tempted.'

She kissed him, and then knelt up on the couch and kissed him some more. Neither of them heard the front door open, and they didn't realize Denver was home until he walked into the living room. He had recently cut his hair Mohican-style and he was wearing a black AxCx T-shirt and baggy jeans that showed the waistband of his Calvin Klein shorts. His best friend Stu Wintergreen was close behind him. Stu had a mess of curly brown hair and eyeglasses with such thick lenses that he seemed to be looking at the world through two portholes.

'Hi, Professor Underhill!' said Stu, cheerfully. 'Hi, Mrs Doctor Underhill!'

'*Urrgghh*,' said Denver. 'Parents in love! Gross!'

TEN

Tuesday, 9:03 p.m.

M ary Lugano opened the door of her apartment and said, 'Yes? What is it? What do you want?'

Jenna held up her shield. 'Detective Pullet, ma'am. Ninth Division. Do you mind if I come in and ask you a few questions?'

Mary Lugano hesitated, frowning. She was a small, stooped woman in her early seventies. Her head appeared to be too big for her body, especially since she had a huge bouffant hairstyle, dyed jet-black with crimson highlights. Her cheekbones were sharp and angular, and Jenna could tell that she must have been quite a looker when she was younger, but too many years of deep suntanning had blotched her skin and given her the pursed-up mouth of a mummy. She was wearing a silk robe with a splashy pattern of red and black flowers on it.

'Can't this wait until tomorrow?' she said. 'I'm all set for bed.'

'It really won't take long, ma'am, and it's always better to talk about an incident as soon as possible after you've witnessed it, while it's still fresh in your mind.'

'Very well. Five minutes. But let me tell you that this has shaken me up something terrible. The Nectarine Tower has always been a respectable building. Safe. You don't expect anything like this. Screaming, and blood! My Lord! It was worse than one of those horror movies.'

She drew back the chain on the door. Jenna said 'thank you', and stepped into her apartment. The living room was overheated and airless and smelled of lavender potpourri and dust. It was decorated in a style that reminded Jenna of her grandmother's house, with oversized armchairs upholstered in brown brocade, and a swirly brown carpet, and table lamps with pleated brown shades. On the opposite wall hung a large oil painting of crowds of people hurrying across a city street in a rainstorm. The clouds were brown, the buildings were brown, the people's overcoats were brown, and they all carried brown umbrellas.

Mary Lugano sat down in one of the armchairs and fastidiously drew her robe around her knees. Jenna, uninvited, sat down opposite her.

'My partner said you saw something fly down from the sky. Something like a bird.'

'I *felt* it, before I saw it.'

'I'm not sure I understand what you mean by *felt* it.'

'Well, I was sitting right here, watching *Access Hollywood*. That Mel Gibson, I don't know. The language! You never heard Cary Grant using language like that.'

'OK, good. You were sitting here watching TV. Then what happened?'

Mary Lugano lifted one hand and slowly fanned it from side to side. 'I felt something flying over the top of the apartment building, very low. It wasn't an airplane. It wasn't a helicopter. It was almost completely silent except for this kind of a *swoosh*.'

'You had the TV on, but you heard a kind of a *swoosh*?'

'I don't know. Don't confuse me. It's not easy to describe it. Maybe I *felt* it more than heard it. But it was like, *swoosh*.'

'All right. Something flew over the building, whether you heard it or felt it.'

'That's right. And that was before I actually saw it. It made me shiver, like a goose walking over my grave. It was evil.'

'Can you be more specific about that?'

'What do you mean, *specific*? There's nothing specific about evil. Evil is evil. You're a detective, aren't you? Don't tell me that you can't feel evil when it passes close by.'

'OK. You felt that it was evil. Then what happened?'

Mary Lugano looked up. 'That was when I heard a thump. *Thump*! Real loud, like the time when my Jessie was run over.'

'Your Jessie?'

'My lovely golden Labrador. That was when my husband, Charlie, was alive and we lived in Bryn Mawr. Poor Jessie. The trouble was she couldn't hear too good. A truck came speeding down the street and she ran out right in front of it.'

'I see. I'm sorry. So – anyhow – you heard a thump?'

'Like I say, it was real loud. So loud that it literally *shook* the walls! Then right afterward I heard screaming. A man screaming, but just like a woman screams. Hysterical. And then this thing flew right past my window.'

'Can you describe it to me, this thing?'

'First, I only saw a shadow. It flew past the window this way, right to left, so quick that I couldn't make out what it was. But I ran to the window and I could see it circle around. It had wings, more like a bat's wings than a bird's wings; and it had two nubby horns on the top of its head; and eyes like Don Rickles.'

'You mean, like, protruding?'

Mary Lugano nodded.

'How big would you say this thing was?'

'It was big. I don't know. A whole lot bigger than any bird I ever saw. It circled around and then it flapped its wings a couple of times – like the sail on a sailboat when it catches a crosswind – and it was gone. Back upward, headed for the roof.'

'What color was it?'

'Black, I think. Or a very dark gray.'

'Did it have a beak like a bird?'

'I didn't really see. But its face was kind of pointy. More like a monkey than a bird. And it had a long thin tail like a monkey.'

Jenna jotted this down in her notebook. Then she looked across at Mary Lugano and said, 'Have a guess, Mrs Lugano – what do *you* think it was?'

Mary Lugano slowly shook her head from side to side. 'I have absolutely no idea. It reminded me of the flying monkeys in *The Wizard of Oz*, you know? It scared me. It really scared me, the way those flying monkeys did when I was a little girl.'

'OK . . .' said Jenna. 'Do you mind my asking you if you're on any kind of medication?'

'What are you trying to suggest?' Mary Lugano demanded. 'Are you trying to say that I was seeing things? The only medication I ever take is Celebrex, for my osteoarthritis, and nobody ever had hallucinations from taking Celebrex, not so far as I know. Besides – Mr Keiller, he saw it too, and so did that Japanese lady. And all of that screaming, that screaming was no hallucination. Neither was all of that blood.'

'So the flying monkey thing flew up to the roof. Then what happened?'

'I heard a man shout. Just once. Then another thump, not so loud as the first thump, but loud all the same. Then I felt the thing fly away.'

'You *felt* it fly away? You didn't actually see it?'

'No. Only felt it. I never in my life felt anything like that before. It was horrible. It was like all of the worst things you ever dreaded, all in one. So *cold*, you know? Like I said before, it made me shiver. But then it was gone.'

'That was when you went up to the roof?'

'I waited for a short while, just in case. But then I picked up my walking stick and stepped out of my door, and there was Mr Keiller from seventeen twenty-three just coming out of the elevator. He said to me, "Did you hear screaming?" and I told him I sure did. And then another gentleman appeared from downstairs, I don't know his name, but I think he used to conduct an orchestra before he retired. He said that he had heard screaming, too, although he hadn't seen anything fly past his window.

'I asked Mr Keiller if he had seen anything, and he said yes, like a darn great flying lizard, that's the way that he described it. A darn great flying lizard, with horns. Well, he didn't actually say "darn". He used another word.'

'So all three of you went up to the roof to find out what had happened?'

'That's right. Mr Keiller went first. He used to be a Marine, back in the day. Well, he's seventy-something now, but he's a big fellow and he still looks tough. We climbed the stairs and went out on the roof. At first I couldn't work out what the hell had happened up there. But then Mr Keiller took hold of my arm and said, "Don't look. Go straight back down to your apartment and call the police." Of course when he said "don't look" the first thing I did was to look, and that was when I saw a man's head, off to my left here, and a part of a leg, off to my right, and so much *blood*.'

Jenna said, 'I'm sorry you had such an upsetting experience, Mrs Lugano.'

'*Upsetting*? You have no idea! I'm going to be having nightmares about it for the rest of my life.'

'All the same, would you mind if I sent a sketch artist around tomorrow morning? It would really help if we had some kind of visual impression of what this flying monkey thing looked like.'

'I guess so, if you have to. All I want to do is forget all about it.'

Jenna stood up. 'Let me just ask you one more thing, Mrs Lugano. That feeling you had. That *cold* feeling. Did you ever have a feeling like that before?'

Mary Lugano looked up at her. She paused a long time before she answered.

'Only once,' she said, 'when my Charlie died. I'd been sitting at his bedside all afternoon, reading to him, even though he was sleeping for most of the time. Around four o'clock, though, I went into the kitchen to make myself a cup of tea. I was right in the middle of pouring it out when I went so cold that I started to shake. I knew right away that my Charlie had gone. His soul had been stolen right out of him while I was out of the room. Death had sneaked in and paid him a visit and there was nothing in the bed but a body that looked like Charlie. It took me a long, long time to feel warm again, I can tell you.'

'I'm sorry, Mrs Lugano. I didn't mean to distress you. Thank you for your time.'

Mary Lugano stood up and accompanied Jenna to the door. 'Do you have any idea what this flying thing is?' she asked her, before she opened it. 'I mean, do the police have any idea? Did something escape from the zoo? Something that they don't want us to know about?'

'I don't have a clue what it could be, Mrs Lugano. I only hope that whatever it is, it's flown off for good, and won't come back.'

'I wouldn't count on it,' said Mary Lugano. 'I get the feeling that it's circling around, looking to catch somebody else. That's what evil does, doesn't it? It circles, waiting for its moment. Just like Death did, when Death sneaked in to steal my Charlie.'

*　　*　　*

Jenna took the elevator down to Aartment 1723 where Kenneth Keiller and Christine Takenaka were waiting for her, along with Dan and two police officers. A forty-inch plasma TV was flickering silently in the background, tuned to *Everybody Loves Raymond*.

Kenneth Keiller was a huge man who almost filled the whole living room. He was at least six feet three inches tall and he must have weighed close to three hundred pounds. Once he had obviously had a bodybuilder's physique, but beer, pepperoni pizza and lack of exercise had taken their toll, and his belly hung over his belt like a small boy sleeping in a hammock. His head was shaven and his face was as podgy as the Laughing Buddha's.

Christine Takenaka was tall for a Japanese woman, flat chested and very thin. She had long black hair and the kind of features that made her look permanently vexed.

'My partner here tells me that you saw the creature pretty good, Mr Keiller,' said Jenna.

'It was only for a second,' Kenneth Keiller told her. 'It flashed right past my window and it must have been doing ninety clicks an hour, minimum.'

'But you still saw it quite clearly?'

'It was some species of lizard, in my opinion. I saw them when I was stationed in the Philippines, in the jungle. The locals call them dragon lizards, but they're only small, maybe twenty centimeters from nose to tail at most. But this one was a heck of a lot bigger than that. This one was fricking enormous. And it had horns on top of its head. And look what it did to those two poor bastards on the roof.'

'We don't conclusively know that the creature was responsible for that.'

'Oh, no? What else could have smashed them apart like that? It couldn't have been a heely-copter because we would have heard it. And to tell you the truth, they looked exactly like they'd been hit by a truck, except how do you get a truck to the top of a twenty-two story apartment block?'

'Well, we're still collecting evidence,' said Jenna. She took out her notebook again. 'Can you tell me what color it was, this creature?'

'I don't know. Brownish, I think. Brown or gray, maybe more like khaki.'

'Could you describe it to a sketch artist for me? I'm sending one round here tomorrow morning.'

'Sure thing. Any time. I'm never doing nothing much, except watching TV.'

'How about you, Ms Takenaka? Could you describe it?'

Christine Takenaka shook her head so that her silky black hair swung from side to side. 'I saw only the creature's shadow.'

'OK . . . But what size was this shadow? What sort of shape was it? Mr Keiller here thinks it looked like a flying lizard. Mrs Lugano upstairs says it looked like one of the flying monkeys from *The Wizard of Oz*. How did it appear to you?'

'It frightened me.'

'It frightened you? Why? What was so scary about it?'

Christine Takenaka raised her left hand to cover her eyes, as if she didn't want Jenna to see how upset she was.

'It reminded me of a story that my grandmother used to tell me when I was a small girl in Osaka. She told me about the *obake*, the things that change.'

'The things that change? I'm not too sure I follow you.'

'Shape-shifters, that's what they call them, isn't it? My grandmother said that they were demons that looked like statues most of the time; but now and then they would suddenly come to life and fly out across the countryside. They would search for children who had been disobedient and disrespectful to their elders, and once they had found these children they would snatch them in their claws and fly away with them. Next day their bodies would be found in a field someplace, all torn into pieces, and their hearts missing.'

'Nice bedtime story to tell your granddaughter,' said Jenna.

Kenneth Keiller said, 'You're not kidding. Jesus. My dad used to read me *Suck-a-Thumb*, and that was scary enough. The long red-legged scissorman, cutting your fricking thumbs off. Jesus.'

Christine Takenaka lowered her hand. She looked at Jenna as if she was urgently searching for reassurance. 'My grandmother said that you could always tell if one of the *obake* was after you, because of its shadow. She said they had wings like dragons and long tails. If you saw a shadow like that on the ground beside you, you should never look up – *never look back,* she told me, *never look up*! *Run as fast as you can to the nearest shelter*!

'Once, when I was walking home from school, I thought I

saw a shadow like that crossing the path in front of me. Maybe I was mistaken and it was only a bird. A black kite, maybe. Black kites are always trying to steal food. But my heart almost stopped from fright. I ran all the way home and by the time I ran into my mother's arms I was too scared even to scream.'

'So what are you trying to say to me?' Jenna asked her. She was feeling deeply tired now, but she could tell that Christine Takenaka was desperate to explain what she had seen.

'The shadow I saw tonight was the same kind of shadow. You see that apartment block opposite? I saw the shadow crossing the windows. An *obake*. Then there was all of that screaming from the roof. You cannot persuade me that an *obake* did not come here tonight. I could feel it in every bone. An *obake*, or something very much like an *obake*.'

Afterward, she and Dan went back up to the roof, where the crime scene specialists were still trying to identify which grisly lumps of flesh belonged to William Barrow and which belonged to Chet Huntley. Everything on the rooftop looked as if it had been painted red.

Ed Freiburg came over with his bloody gloves held up in front of him. 'This is going to take hours. I don't think there's any point in you guys hanging around any longer. I'll be in touch tomorrow morning.

He paused, and sniffed, and then he said, 'By the way, we found Mr Huntley's head. It was lying in the parking lot at the Carpenters' Union on Spring Garden Street.'

'My God,' said Jenna. 'That's over a block and a half away.'

'Well, that goes to show how hard that thing hit him, whatever it was. I surely don't envy your job, having to catch it.'

ELEVEN
Wednesday, 7:13 a.m.

Braydon was woken up by rain pattering against the window and at first he couldn't think where he was. He sat up, blinking his eyes into focus. He was in a small, unfamiliar bedroom, with magnolia-painted walls and a framed print of ferries on the Delaware River hanging beside his bed. It was only when he saw the sign on the back of the bedroom door saying *Cell Phones Must Be Switched Off As They Can Interfere With Vital Equipment* that he remembered that he was in one of the relatives' rooms at Temple University Hospital.

He climbed out of bed and tugged open the drapes. Outside, he could see a rainy, windswept park, and pedestrians with umbrellas hurrying across a wide intersection. The clouds were ragged and low, and they were brown, more like smoke from a burning building than clouds.

He hobbled into the bathroom, splashed his face with cold water and combed his hair. He was wearing his T-shirt, his pale blue shorts and his socks, because he hadn't brought pajamas or a change of clothes with him. He had expected to be home before midnight last night.

'Braydon,' he said to himself, 'what the hell have you done?'

He lifted his red plaid shirt and his jeans off the back of the chair and got dressed. He was sitting on the end of the bed, lacing up his Timberlands, when there was a knock at the door and a large black nurse appeared.

'Mr Harris? Good morning to you, Mr Harris. I was hoping to find you awake.'

'What is it, nurse? How's my daughter?'

'Doctor Berman would like to see you and talk to you.'

'There's nothing wrong, is there?'

'You need to talk to Doctor Berman.'

Braydon followed the nurse along the corridor and down in the elevator to the burns unit. She bustled along so quickly that

Braydon found it difficult to keep up with her, and he began to feel that he was dreaming. He passed people wearing clear plastic masks, and people with strangely-stretched faces, and other people with their heads completely wrapped in white bandages, with holes for their eyes, like *The Invisible Man.*

When he reached Sukie's room he found that Miranda was already there, talking to Doctor Berman and a tall Arabic-looking doctor with wavy gray hair. Miranda immediately turned her back to him. That narrow, spiteful back.

Braydon approached Sukie's bed. She was sleeping, her face still covered by the Jaloskin mask, and he was relieved to see that her face looked less fiery than it had yesterday. He looked across at Doctor Berman and said, 'How is she? Everything's OK, isn't it?'

Doctor Berman grimaced and rubbed the back of his neck. 'Physically, she's doing as well as anybody could expect. But she's had a very disturbed night, in spite of being sedated. In fact we had to restrain her to prevent her from causing herself any further injury. Why don't you talk to Doctor Mahmood here? He's in charge of our psychological rehabilitation program for burns victims.'

Doctor Mahmood came around the bed and laid a reassuring hand on Braydon's shoulder. When it came to his personal space, Braydon was usually highly defensive; but he wanted to appear cooperative and reasonable, especially with Miranda here, so he forced himself to tolerate Doctor Mahmood touching him. Doctor Mahmood had tangled eyebrows and a hooked nose and his eyes glittered like two black beetles. He stood so close that Braydon could smell his spearmint mouthwash and a spice that could have been fenugreek.

'Susan's mother tells me that she has always been prone to having nightmares, ever since she was very small.'

Braydon looked at Miranda's back. 'Yes,' he agreed. 'That's true. And mostly the same nightmare, every time. Scary things flying through the sky, like shadows. She calls them Spooglies.'

Doctor Mahmood nodded. 'Of course, she wasn't able to tell us what she was so frightened of, because she was wearing her oxygen mask, but we could tell from her vital signs that she was in a high state of panic.'

'I blame her grandmother,' said Braydon. 'Her grandmother

claims to be some kind of psychic, and she's always filling Sukie's head with crap about ghosts and spirits and dead people coming back as animals.'

Miranda whipped around and snapped, 'My mother has *never* claimed to be a psychic. She's a *sensitive*, which is totally different! She can sense when something bad is going to happen, and Sukie's the same. *She's* a sensitive too. The trouble with you, Braydon, is that you're totally *in*sensitive, and you always were!'

'Your goddamned mother is a goddamned witch. She even *looks* like a goddamned witch. And she's a fraud. If she can *really* sense when something bad is going to happen, why didn't she warn me on Monday that Sukie was going to get hurt? Like, Q.E.D.'

'Oh, you think she's a fraud?' Miranda retorted. 'She told me that I shouldn't marry you, and she was right, because it was just about the worst thing that ever happened to me. She told me so many times but I was stupid enough not to listen to her. If I hadn't married you, you wouldn't have kidnapped Sukie and Sukie wouldn't be lying in this bed with half of her face burned off.'

Braydon shook his head in disbelief. 'You're even dumber than I thought. If I hadn't married you, Sukie would never have been born, would she?'

'Yes, she would. I believe that some people are destined to be born, no matter what, and Sukie was one of them. She's my little girl. She's my mother's little granddaughter. The only disastrous thing in her life is that she has you for a father.'

'Who else would she have had for a father? Not that asshole of a realtor you used to go out with? What was his name? Trenton. What an asshole.'

Doctor Mahmood lifted both of his hands and said, 'Mr and Mrs Harris – please don't argue like this! I am begging you! You should be putting aside your differences and working in harmony to help your daughter to recover. If there is hostility in the air, patients are always aware of it, especially when they are very sick. Burns victims in particular need a very positive environment if they are to heal successfully. We have to nurse their minds with just as much care as their bodies.'

Miranda glared at Braydon. He could tell that she was biting her tongue to stop herself from spitting out another corrosive comment. He was almost surprised that she didn't have blood dripping down her chin like the vampire she was. She turned away again, and he could have put his hands around that stringy neck and strangled the life out of her, except that he probably would have needed to drive a stake through her heart, too.

'OK,' he told Doctor Mahmood, although he was still breathing hard. 'My apologies. I guess we're both pretty distressed right now.'

'*Distressed*?' said Miranda, with a shrill whoop of mockery. 'Distressed doesn't even *begin* to describe it! How about *shattered*? How about *totally destroyed*?'

'Of course you are both suffering equally from shock and anxiety,' said Doctor Mahmood. 'But that is why, for your Susan's sake, you both have to work very hard to reconcile your differences. It is highly likely that the antagonism between you two creates in her mind an emotional landscape in which these frightening apparitions can materialize. These *Spooglies,* as she calls them – in my clinical experience they may well represent the fear and uncertainty she feels when you two are at each other's throats.'

'My God, if anybody's a Spoogly—' Miranda began.

But Doctor Mahmood put his fingertip to his lips and said, '*Sshh*! The watchword is compromise, Mrs Harris, and your sole consideration should be your daughter's well-being.'

Miranda blew sharply out of her nostrils, like an impatient mare, but didn't say anything more.

Doctor Berman said, 'We'll be keeping a very close eye on Susan's physical progress, especially over the next five days. But we also need to keep her as calm as we can. If she has any more nightmares of the intensity that she had last night, we might have to consider a stronger sedative, which is something I really don't want to do.'

Miranda left without saying anything else, not even goodbye to Doctor Berman and Doctor Mahmood. A man whom Braydon had never seen before was waiting for her in the corridor outside. Balding, bespectacled, late thirties, in a putty-colored windbreaker. Another asshole, most likely. The man tried to put his arm around Miranda's shoulders but she twisted herself free of him.

Braydon turned back to Sukie. He wasn't surprised that she was having nightmares after being trapped in the back seat of a blazing vehicle. But he didn't agree with Doctor Mahmood that the Spooglies were anything to do with he and Miranda fighting each other. Sukie used to have nightmares about the Spooglies even when he and Miranda had been getting along well, before he had lost his job and they had lost their house and he had even lost his ability to make love to her. That was what had wrecked their marriage in the end: Miranda's feeling that he no longer loved her, no matter how much he had protested that he did, and his own feeling of impotence, both financial and sexual.

Doctor Mahmood said, 'I think it is vital for me to talk to your daughter about her nightmares, Mr Harris – only when she is well enough to speak to me, of course. If I can help her to understand what they mean, I believe that I can help her to grow out of them. I think it will also help her to deal with the obvious trauma of your break-up with your former wife.'

'All kids have nightmares, don't they?' asked Braydon. 'When I was a kid, I always imagined that as soon as my bedroom light was switched off, the bathrobe hanging on the back of my door was going to come to life, jump off its hook, and try to strangle me.'

'Eventually, though, you came to realize that this was not going to happen, and that your bathrobe was only a bathrobe?'

'Who's to say?' Braydon replied. 'The world is only what we perceive it to be, isn't it? And if Sukie thinks that Spooglies exist, maybe they do.'

Doctor Mahmood gave him an indulgent smile, and gripped his shoulder again. 'All I ask, Mr Harris, is that you try to control your feelings of animosity toward your ex-wife – at least while you are both at your daughter's bedside.'

'I'll try, doctor. But – as you saw for yourself – it ain't easy. Not by any means.'

He went to the hospital commissary and bought himself a large mug of black coffee and a lemon Danish. He sat in the corner, looking out over the courtyard in the center of the hospital complex, while rain trickled down the window. He had never felt so lonely and depressed in his life; or so guilty.

On the opposite wall a TV was playing with the sound

switched off. A reporter for WPVI news was standing outside an apartment building in the rain. Behind her, there were five or six police cars with their red lights flashing and at least twenty officers in long yellow raincoats. The caption running along the bottom of the picture said TWO KILLED BY MYSTERY FLYING CREATURE: WITNESSES TELL OF ROOFTOP 'BLOODBATH'.

Braydon could manage to eat only two bites of his Danish. He left the rest of it, and took his coffee into the relatives' waiting lounge across the hall, where there was another TV with the sound turned up. There were only three other people in it – two young men with shaven heads and tattoos who looked as if they had been involved in a fight, and an elderly woman who gave him a sweet but inane smile.

Braydon sat down in front of the TV and leaned forward so that he could hear it better. The news reporter was interviewing a woman detective in a purple rain-hat.

'. . . what those witnesses saw?' she was asking.

'Right now we're keeping an open mind,' the detective answered. 'At the time of the incident it was dark, and whatever this thing might have been, it was flying real fast.'

'But if it managed to kill two men, it must have been some-thing pretty big, surely? And highly aggressive?'

'Like I say, we're not jumping to any premature conclusions. Only one of the witnesses claims to have seen the creature clearly. The other two didn't see very much more than shadows.'

'Well, we've talked to your witnesses, too, Detective, and even if they didn't see too much, they all said that it scared them half to death.'

'If I saw a large dark shape flying past *my* apartment window, I'm sure that I'd be scared, too, especially if I was twenty stories up.'

Scary things flying through the sky, like shadows. She calls them Spooglies.

'Can you tell us the extent of the victims' injuries?'

'Not at this time. We're going to wait for the ME's report before we release any specifics.'

'One of your witnesses talked about them being literally torn to shreds. Is this true?'

'I don't have any comment at this time.'

'But their injuries *were* extensive?'

'Both victims were killed outright. I think that gives you a fair idea how extensive they were.'

'Thank you, Detective,' said the news reporter. 'Could you lastly tell me what advice you would give to the people of Philly regarding this mystery predator?'

'Stay off your rooftops, or any other high exposed area. And when you're out in the open – in a park, maybe, or up at the top of the Rocky Steps – watch the skies.'

TWELVE

Wednesday, 10:54 a.m.

Aarif was slumped in his chair, his chin on his chest, looking as if he had died during the night. On the laboratory bench next to him, inside its cage, the phoenix was sitting on its perch, much more settled now, pecking at its dull brown feathers and occasionally warbling in its throat.

Nathan approached the cage and stood looking at the phoenix with a feeling of triumph. The phoenix looked back at him, cocking its head on one side. Nathan would give it a thorough examination this morning, testing its heart rate and its blood count and its respiration, as well as its digestive functions, but on first sight it appeared to be fit and well and thriving. He looked into its feeding bowl and saw that it had eaten more than half of the strips of mouse meat they had given it, and drunk twenty-three milliliters of water from the glass tube attached to the bars.

'Torchy – I can't wait to tell the world about you,' said Nathan. 'You and me, we're going to be famous. Fame, kid! We're going to live for ever!'

He poked his fingertip through the bars and the phoenix instantly pecked at it. The sudden burst of fluttering woke up Aarif, who jerked upright and said, 'Oh! Professor! I am so sorry! I try so hard to stay awake! The bird is still OK, yes?'

'Don't worry, Aarif. The bird is still OK. In fact it looks *better* than OK. He's fantastic.'

Aarif stood up and stretched his back. 'Kavita told me that he was very restless for the first two or three hours. Screaming, flapping his wings. But then she said that he gradually calmed down. By the time I took over from her, he was sitting on his perch very peaceful, like now.

He passed Nathan a clipboard with columns of figures on it. 'You can see from the stats. When Kavita first measured his heart rate, it was more than one thousand beats per minute, as fast as a bird in flight. The last time I measured it, at a quarter after six, it was beating at three hundred forty-five, which is no more than your average crow, sitting in a tree.'

'Blood pressure?'

'High. That is the latest measurement, right there. But of course all birds have high blood pressure. I would say it is not abnormally elevated for a scavenger hawk.'

'Droppings?'

'Aha! Only one motion so far,' said Aarif. He peered into the bottom of the cage to make sure that the phoenix hadn't passed any more. 'But when I analyze it, what do you think I am finding?'

'I don't know, Aarif. What *are* you finding?'

'For the most part his motion contained all that you might expect from a carnivorous bird kept in captivity. Maybe his uric acid level was a little low. But *then* – aha! – what am I finding? A very high proportion of a blood-clotting protein that is similar to fibrin, but which appears to clot very much quicker than fibrin. You could almost call it "super fibrin".'

Nathan turned to the phoenix. 'So *that's* how you resurrect yourself, is it? Fibrous protein. You burn, you get better, because it's all in the blood.'

'I think we can cautiously assume that,' said Aarif. It was obvious that he was deeply pleased with himself. 'Once I have run some more comprehensive tests, I will contact the burns unit at Temple University Hospital, and see how many volunteers they can find for us. It will be fascinating to see how effectively this protein works on human beings.'

They were still leafing through the test results together when a tall balding man in a chocolate-brown suit walked into the laboratory. He had a long face like a horse, a likeness that was emphasized by the dark chestnut suntan of somebody who takes at least three exotic vacations every year. He stopped, and inspected the fire damage for a second or two, and then he walked over to Nathan and Aarif.

'Ron!' said Nathan, cheerfully. He nodded toward the tortured metal framework of his vivarium. 'Sorry about the mess. One of those experiments that got a little out of hand. But I'm very happy to tell you that it was highly successful.'

Ron Kasabian stared at Nathan for a long time before he said anything, and when he did his voice was a low, threatening rumble, like a stampede approaching from behind a nearby hill. 'You *do* know that this laboratory was completely remodeled only last September, at a cost of more than one and a half million dollars.' It was more of a threat than a question.

Nathan stared back at him, unblinking. 'I'm aware of that, Ron. But accidents *do* happen, particularly at the cutting edge of cryptozoology. As I say, I'm truly sorry about the mess, but I think you'll agree that the end result has made it all worthwhile.'

He nodded toward the birdcage. 'Ron Kasabian, meet Torchy the Phoenix. It worked, Ron. We set fire to the dragon-worm and this is what we got.'

Ron Kasabian approached the cage and peered at the phoenix with a distinct lack of enthusiasm. 'Scruffy little sucker, isn't he? Didn't you tell me that phoenixes have bright red beaks and shiny golden feathers?'

'His appearance is irrelevant, Ron. Aarif here has carried out some preliminary tests and we think we already have a good idea how he restores itself after being virtually incinerated. We're in business.'

'No, we're not,' said Ron Kasabian, shaking his jowls. 'Not any more, anyhow.'

'What? What are you talking about?'

'We had an emergency stockholders' meeting yesterday afternoon. By a substantial majority, the stockholders voted to pull the plug on any research that doesn't have more than a ten percent chance of commercial profitability within the next five years. And I'm afraid that your cryptozoology program doesn't cut the mustard.'

'*What*? But that's just crazy! Here it is, Ron – indisputable proof that CZ really has a future! We have ourselves a real live phoenix, Ron – a bird that we created from scratch out of a nematode! Not only that, he's a bird that can stand up to five hundred degree heat! Look at it, Ron! It's a goddamned miracle, and we made it happen, right here!'

'Yes, sure, it's a miracle,' said Ron Kasabian, 'but it's a very expensive miracle, and it's going to take millions more dollars to prove that it really has any practical application. You told me yourself that it's going to be well over two years before you can be absolutely sure that it works. And at the rate you've been burning through your funding—'

'So what are you going to do?' Nathan challenged him. 'Throw away nearly nine million dollars and three and a half years of intensive research, just because your stockholders can't see beyond their bank accounts?'

'It's called "cutting our losses",' said Nathan. 'You've overrun this year's budget by thirteen point two percent which means that you're already spending money that was earmarked for next year's R and D.'

Nathan looked at the phoenix, preening itself on its perch. When he spoke, his voice was shaking with emotion. 'Until the day before yesterday, that bird was only a myth. Like a dragon, or a wyvern, or a gryphon. But here it is, sitting in front of you. You remember *Jurassic Park*? Well, this is even more awesome than *Jurassic Park*, because this isn't fiction, this is real.

'OK – it's going to take a hell of a lot more investment to establish that Torchy's stem cells can be used by surgeons to heal third-degree human burns. But imagine the profitability for Schiller if they can. Not only that, think of your public image. Schiller, the company that gives burn victims their lives back. I can see the ads now. Burn victim *before* Schiller-cell treatment. Burn victim *after* Schiller-cell treatment. Barbecued Beast on the left, flawless Beauty on the right.'

'No,' said Ron Kasabian. 'The decision is absolutely final. The CZ program gets no more money.'

At that moment, Kavita walked into the laboratory, wearing skinny-legged jeans and a very tight red sweater, with a red silk scarf on her head.

'Hi, Mr Kasabian, what do you think of our phoenix? Isn't he just incredible?'

'Hi there, you tempting young thing,' said Ron Kasabian. 'Yes, what you've done here is amazing – truly amazing. I'm deeply impressed, and I mean it.'

'I'm sorry, Kavita,' Nathan put in. 'Impressed as he is, Ron didn't come here to congratulate us on our zoological genius. Ron came here to shut us down.'

'What? You cannot shut us down!'

'I can, and I have. Every business across America is suffering from the current financial squeeze, and Schiller is suffering just as much as everybody else – if not more, because we have to plow so much of our profits into long-term research projects. A new faster-acting medication for migraine, that's one thing. Or a week-after birth control pill, for sure. But creating phoenixes and dragons and unicorns, that's way out there, Kavita. That's a luxury that will have to wait for when times get fat again.'

'Ron, you can't do this,' said Nathan. His voice was still trembling with anger and disappointment. 'I've been dreaming ever since I first went to college of breeding mythological creatures. Now, with Schiller's finance and Schiller's facilities, I've done it. But this is only the first step. You can't ask me to stop now.'

'I'm not *asking* you to stop, Nathan. I'm *telling* you. I've already been through the figures with our accounts team, and the clinical trials you'll have to do to satisfy the FDA will cost at least a hundred million. Probably much more, with insurance. Supposing you screw up some poor bastard's face even worse than it's screwed up already – did you think of that?'

'But it's going to work, Ron. I know it's going to work.'

'Maybe it will. Maybe it won't. Unfortunately we'll never have the luxury of finding out.'

Nathan stood very still for a moment, both hands clasped together, eyes closed, almost as if he were praying. Ron looked at Aarif and Kavita and gave them a shrug, as if to say, I'm sorry, but what can I do?

'Nathan?' he said. 'Nathan, I'm leaving now. Come up to my office later and we'll talk this thing through.'

Nathan opened his eyes but he didn't answer him, or even turn his head. Instead, he walked over to the long bench on the opposite side of the laboratory, where there were two long shelves of stoppered glass bottles containing acids, alkalis and various reagents. The mid-morning sun suddenly appeared from behind a cloud and shone through the window beside him, so that the bottles were magically lit up, like lamps, and Nathan himself was given a golden halo.

'Nathan?' Ron Kasabian repeated. 'What are you doing, Nathan? I'm leaving now.'

Still Nathan didn't answer him. He ran his index finger along the line of chemical bottles until he came to a bottle of methanol. He picked it up and took out the stopper.

'*Nathan.*'

Nathan turned around. He saw Ron Kasabian and Aarif and Kavita all staring at him and frowning, because they couldn't understand what he was doing. But he knew exactly what he was doing, and he knew exactly what the consequences were going to be. He knew how much it was going to hurt, but if there was no other way to show that all of his years of study and research and disappointment had at last been vindicated, then he was prepared to bear it.

He held out his left hand and poured methanol all over it. It felt chilly, but it had almost no smell at all. He put down the empty bottle, and then he picked up the Zippo lighter which they used for lighting the laboratory's Bunsen burners.

'*Professor*—!' Aarif protested, and started to dodge toward him between the laboratory benches. Unlike Kavita and Ron Kasabian, he had suddenly realized what Nathan was about to do, but then he had been brought up in a culture where self-sacrifice by fire was not the rarity it was in America.

Nathan thought of Grace, and what she would say when she found out what he had done. But he was sure that he was right. He was sure that the phoenix could save him, and he was sure that the phoenix could save thousands of other people, too.

'*No!*' shouted Aarif. But Nathan flicked the lighter and held it under his hand. Instantly, the methanol burst into flame, and Nathan's hand became a huge fiery glove. The pain was immediate and unbearable. He had known that it would be. All of our nerve endings are close to the surface of the skin, and the first few seconds of burning are by far the most agonizing. He screamed a hoarse, desperate scream, although he couldn't hear himself screaming, and everything in his being told him to thrust his hand into the sink beside him and turn the cold water on to full.

But he could see Ron Kasabian on the other side of the

laboratory, staring at him in horror, and in spite of the excruciating pain he held up his blazing hand in a defiant salute. His fingers looked like a mockery of a menorah, with five candles instead of seven.

It was then, though, that Aarif collided with him in a shoulder tackle and seized his left wrist. Nathan's back hit the laboratory bench so hard that he heard a rib crack, and then he lost his balance and fell sideways on to the floor. Aarif dragged the dark green hand-towel from the side of the sink and wrapped it around Nathan's hand like a turban.

'Why you do this?' he shouted, hysterically. 'Why you do this? You crazy mad?'

Kavita came over and knelt beside him. Ron Kasabian took out his cellphone and punched out 911. 'Ambulance. And real quick, please. One of our researchers has just suffered a very serious burn to his hand. Yes, we can. Yes.'

Between them, Aarif and Ron Kasabian lifted Nathan to his feet and helped him up to the sink. Aarif unwound the towel. Underneath, Nathan's skin was blackened and charred, with scarlet flesh showing through the cracks. The heat had shriveled his tendons so that his fingers were curled over in a claw. Aarif turned on the faucet, making sure that it was lukewarm and not icy cold, and held his hand under the running water to cool it down. Nathan let out a whimper, and his knees buckled.

'Kavita, bring me that coat, will you?' said Ron Kasabian. 'We have to keep him warm.'

There was a red duffel coat hanging on a peg by the laboratory door. Kavita brought it over and lifted it over Nathan's shoulders. Nathan was already shivering from shock, and his teeth were chattering. He rolled his eyes toward Kavita and whispered, 'Thanks, Kavita. You're an angel.'

Ron Kasabian kept shaking his head from side to side. 'What in *hell's* name were you trying to prove, Nathan? I always thought you were nuts, but this takes the cake.'

Nathan gave him a slanted, deranged smile. 'I haven't proved anything yet, Ron. But I'm going to. And then you and your stockholders can shove your funding where you don't need Ray-Bans, because so many companies will want what I can offer them, I'll be fighting them off.'

'How does your hand feel now, Professor?' asked Aarif.

'It doesn't feel like anything,' Nathan told him. 'In fact, I can't feel it at all.'

Ron Kasabian said, 'Jesus. This is all we need. Think how this is going to play in the media. And what the hell are we going to do with this goddamn bird?'

THIRTEEN
Wednesday: 3:47 p.m.

Jenna was woken by the sound of the front door opening. She looked across at her bedside clock and thought: *Great, I've managed to get all of two and a half hours' sleep.*

She heard footsteps passing her bedroom door and she called out, 'Ellie! What are you doing home so early?'

There was a long pause and then her door opened and Ellie put her head around it. She looked just like Jenna except that she was hauntingly thin, with dark circles under her eyes. She was wearing a floppy black cowl-neck sweater, black narrow-cut jeans and a black cotton headscarf.

'Sorry, Mom. I didn't mean to wake you up. Our art teacher was sick so they let us take the rest of the afternoon off.'

Jenna was tempted to say, *have you eaten anything*? But she knew better than to nag Ellie about food. What Ellie needed from Jenna was reassurance that she looked slim and pretty, not constant criticism about her diet.

Jenna sat up in bed. 'Open the drapes for me, will you? I might as well get up. My next shift starts at six.'

Ellie went across to the window and tugged the curtain cord. It had stopped raining, but the sky was gray with low-hanging clouds.

'Everybody at school was talking about those people who got killed on top of that apartment block,' said Ellie.

'Oh, yeah?'

'Joey Krasnik thinks it was a pterodactyl that did it.'

Jenna was struggling out of her nightshirt. 'A pterodactyl? How did he work that out?'

'He said it's all down to global warming. He said there's hundreds of prehistoric creatures frozen in the polar ice-caps but now the ice is melting and they're all going to thaw out and come to life again.'

'Joey Krasnik has some imagination.'

'He said what else could it be? All of those witnesses say they saw something like a huge great bird, didn't they?'

Jenna fastened her bra at the front and then twisted it around to the back. 'Did you ever hear of herd delusion? That's when one person thinks they've seen something weird and everybody else begins to believe that *they* have, too. Let me tell you this, sweetheart: whatever killed those two poor men, I'll bet Joey Krasnik a hundred bucks that it wasn't a pterodactyl.'

'So what do you think it was?'

'Right now, I don't have the faintest idea. Right now I'm going to make myself the strongest cup of coffee ever brewed and a large baloney sandwich. I don't suppose you want anything to eat, do you?'

Ellie shook her head. 'I'm fine. I ate lunch at school.'

Jenna could tell by the way she looked down at the floor that she was lying, but she decided not to say anything more. She stood up and stepped into her waist-high elasticated briefs and then pulled on her navy-blue comfort-fit pants. *If anybody should be worrying about what they ate*, she thought, *it's me.*

She was sitting at the kitchen table eating her sandwich and watching TV when her cellphone played 'Blanket On The Ground'. It was Dan Rubik calling.

'*What*?' she snapped, with her mouth full.

'Jenna? It's Dan. You're never going to believe this.'

'Can't it wait, whatever it is? I'm trying to have some breakfast.'

'I don't think so. Another one of those statues has fallen on to Baltimore Avenue, right next to the Woodlands Cemetery.'

'You're kidding me! Was anybody hurt?'

'Not this time. Which was pretty darn lucky, considering how heavy the traffic was.'

'When did this happen?'

'Only about twenty minutes ago. I was on my way home when I heard it on the radio. I'm here on Baltimore Avenue now.'

'Any eyewitnesses?'

'There was a funeral party in the cemetery who might have seen it. I haven't had time to talk to them yet. But this trucker was driving east on Baltimore and it fell on to the road right in front of him. It's all smashed up now, like the one outside the convent, but the trucker saw it a split second before it hit the blacktop and he says it was like an angel, with wings and everything, only ugly.'

Jenna didn't answer him for such a long time that Dan said, 'Jenna? You still there?'

'Sure, I'm still here. I'll come right out now. Did you call Ed Freiburg?'

'Of course.'

Jenna put down her cellphone and looked at her sandwich and her mug of coffee. She was still hungry and tired and she badly needed a caffeine jolt. But if ugly stone angels were falling on Philadelphia out of the sky, she knew what her priorities were.

'Ellie?' she called. 'I have to go out for a while. I don't know what time I'm going to be back.'

Ellie came into the kitchen. 'OK, Mom. I'll probably go see Cathy this evening. Aren't you going to finish your sandwich?'

Jenna shook her head. She wanted so much to put her arms around Ellie and hold her tight, but she knew this wasn't the right moment. She didn't want Ellie to feel that she was grieving for the healthy, well-balanced daughter that she should have been. *Sometimes*, she thought, *you have to smile and make the best of what you've got, even if you feel like crying.*

Traffic on Baltimore Avenue was at a standstill so she had to drive along the wide sidewalk next to the cemetery fencing, with her lights flashing. By the time she arrived at the scene of the incident, it had started to rain again. Dan came over and opened the door of her car for her.

'This time we got one or two bigger chunks. Like a part of an arm, and something that definitely looks like the tip of a wing.'

'How about a head, or a face?'

'Haven't found one yet. Mind you, we got debris scattered over three hundred feet, and we're still finding pieces in the cemetery.'

Ed Freiburg walked up to them, wearing a bright yellow raincoat with the hood pulled up, so that he looked like a giant gnome. 'Hi, Jenna. Looks like more of the same to me. Good-quality limestone, with dressed and sculpted surfaces. Almost certainly a statue.'

Jenna looked up at the clouds. 'It's smashed up pretty good, though, isn't it? How far do you think it fell?'

'Hard to say until I've done all the math. But my guess is that it reached a terminal velocity of two hundred miles an hour, at least. That means it could have dropped from half a mile up, possibly higher.'

Jenna reached into her coat pocket and pulled out a pair of beige latex gloves. She snapped them on to her fingers and then she reached down and picked up one of the lumps of limestone. It was shattered on one side, smoothly carved on the other. It was a bulbous eye, staring at her out of nowhere at all.

'Where's the truck driver?' she asked.

Dan beckoned to a tall, heavily-built man with a bald head, a big nose, and a heavy gray walrus moustache. He was wearing a black T-shirt with *Speedy Trucking* printed across his chest. He came over to join them with a rolling cowboy-like walk.

'Detective Pullet, Ninth Division,' said Jenna, showing him her shield. 'I don't mean to be rude, but did you ever ride a horse?'

'Never,' the truck driver told her, in a thick, gravelly voice. 'Broke both legs ten years ago coming off my hog.' He had large gold earrings in both of his earlobes, and a tattoo of an eagle on the left side of his neck. She should have guessed he was a former Hell's Angel.

'I see,' said Jenna. 'Sorry. Do you want to describe what you saw?'

He pulled a face. 'I didn't see much because it all happened so quick. I was driving along listening to Meat Loaf and it landed directly in front of my rig, out of nowhere at all, like a goddamned bomb.'

'You told my partner here that it looked like a statue of an angel.'

The trucker nodded. 'Just like you see outside of a church, or in a boneyard. Only this angel was real ugly. I seen its face for just a second before it hit the road, and it was like *snarling*, with its teeth bare and its eyes all starey, like it was angry and scared, both at the same time.'

'Angry, but also scared?'

'That's right. I seen that exact same expression on guys when they're fighting. Angry as fuck but scared shitless, too, because they know that, win or lose, they're going to get themselves hurt real bad. But let me tell you something. It scared *me* shitless, too. I mean, more than it should have done, by rights. So it was a statue, dropping out of the sky. That's pretty goddamned scary. But it was more than a statue. It was like the Grim Reaper himself. Cold, and real evil. That's the feeling it gave me.'

Jenna looked around. It was raining harder now but at least the traffic was slowly beginning to move. 'OK, sir,' she told the trucker. 'We have your name and cellphone number, don't we, in case we need to speak to you again?'

'There ain't nothing more I can tell you,' said the trucker. 'It came down like a goddamned bomb, and God knows from where.'

It was then that Jenna's attention was caught by a man among the small crowd of spectators who were standing on the sidewalk. He was wearing a long gray plastic raincoat and a matching rain-hat, and eyeglasses. For some reason, Jenna thought he looked *furtive*. It was the way he kept glancing from side to side, as if he wanted to make sure that nobody was watching him. It reminded her of the way that shoplifters look around before they quickly lift something from a department store counter.

Her instinct was right. After a few seconds, the man crouched down as if he needed to tie up his shoelace, but at the same time he reached across the sidewalk and picked up a small lump of broken limestone, which he pushed into his raincoat pocket. Then he looked around some more, and picked up another small lump.

'Dan,' said Jenna. 'That guy in the plastic raincoat. Go collar him. He just brodied two pieces of evidence.'

'He did what?'

'He pocketed two bits of statue. Go get him. I want to ask him what the hell he thinks he's doing.'

Dan crossed the road and negotiated his way through the crowd of spectators. By the time he had reached the place where the man the plastic raincoat had been crouching down, however, the man had disappeared. Dan turned around and around, looking for him, but in the end he had to look back at Jenna and give her an exaggerated shrug.

Jenna looked left and right, too, but she couldn't see the man either. Maybe he had climbed into a car, or blindsided them by walking off behind the cover of a slow-moving bus or truck.

Dan came back. 'No sign of him. I don't know how he did it, but he's vamoosed.'

'I just want to know why he made off with two bits of statue. Put out a description . . . he couldn't have gotten far, even if he has a car.'

'OK. But my guess is that he's a souvenir hunter.'

'A souvenir hunter?'

'Sure. One of the first cases I ever worked on, there was this screwball who kept stealing mirrors from crime scenes. He thought he'd be able to look into them when he got them home and see who the perps had been, so that he could claim a reward.'

'Just put out the call, Dan.'

Jenna went over to Ed Freiburg, who was kneeling in the roadway, photographing each lump of limestone and marking its position on a chart. As Jenna approached, he stood up and said, 'Jenna! I think I may have found something interesting.'

'Oh, good. Usually, it's so ho-hum when a half-ton statue falls out of the sky.'

'No,' he said, and passed her a clear plastic evidence bag with a heavy piece of limestone inside it. 'Take a look at this.' She held it up and saw that the limestone was carved into three parallel curves, like three stone bananas.

'What is it?'

'What does it look like? Some kind of a claw. More like an animal claw than a bird's talon.'

'And?'

'Go on – look at it real close.'

Jenna examined it carefully. The tips of the claw were all stained brown.

Ed Freiburg said, 'I tested it with phenolphthalein and it's blood. Discolored, of course, from soaking into the limestone and drying out. But there's no doubt about it. Some time recently, our statue was used as a means of inflicting an injury on somebody. Impossible to say how serious an injury, but it was enough to break the skin.'

Jenna frowned at it for a while and then handed it back. 'So how do you use a statue to inflict an injury?'

'I guess you grab hold of your intended victim and ram them

up against it, hard. There's no way you could lift up the whole statue and hit them with it. Not unless you were Superman, or the Incredible Hulk.'

'God, Ed. This just gets wackier and wackier, doesn't it?' She watched him while he photographed another lump of broken stone. 'Come to that – how's the convent statue coming along?'

'Slow, very slow. But I warned you it would. We've already counted more than eighteen hundred fragments and it's not even as if we have any idea what the finished statue is supposed to look like.'

'Maybe it looked like this one. An ugly angel.'

'Well, maybe. There's definitely a strong resemblance. Same type of limestone, similar carving.'

She looked around and saw that Dan was steering an elderly woman toward her. The woman was wearing a clear plastic rainbonnet and a purple quilted waterproof coat and for some reason she strongly reminded Jenna of her own late grandmother. In fact, if she had claimed that she *was* her grandmother, resurrected eleven years after the family had interred her at Laurel Hill, Jenna would almost have believed her.

'Jenna, this is Mrs Nora Blessington. She was visiting her sister's grave when she saw the statue fall.'

'Hi, Mrs Blessington. I'm Detective Pullet. Thank you for coming to talk to me.'

Mrs Blessington looked up at Jenna with unconcealed belligerence. 'You may think that I'm suffering from senile dementia, Detective, but I can assure you that I'm as sane as you are.'

'Excuse me? What makes you think that I think that? Because I don't. At least, I don't see why I should have any reason to.'

'There you are, you see! You have your suspicions already!'

'Mrs Blessington, I can assure you that I don't have any suspicions about your sanity at all.' *Well, I didn't*, she thought, *not until we started this conversation.* 'All I want is for you to describe what you saw.'

'Hmh! I don't know if I ought to! You'll probably think that I'm making it all up, even if you *don't* think that I'm doolally.'

'Why don't you let me judge for myself?' Jenna told her. 'Believe me, I've been given some eyewitness accounts that made my jaw drop when I first heard them, but in the end they turned out to be one hundred percent accurate. And also very helpful.'

Mrs Blessington hesitated for a moment, clutching the strap of her purple pocketbook in both hands as if she were afraid that somebody was going to snatch it away from her. Then she said, very quickly and breathlessly, 'I felt a drop of rain and then I felt another drop of rain so I looked up to see how bad it was starting to cloud over because I didn't want to get myself soaked and catch my death. I didn't want to visit my sister and end up lying next to her.'

'OK,' said Jenna, as patiently as she could manage.

Mrs Blessington looked upward, and off to her right, which was a clear indication to Jenna that she was probably telling the truth. Witnesses who tell lies almost always look downward, and off to their left.

'I only saw it for a split second before it flew straight into the clouds, and at first I thought it was a bird like an eagle or a turkey vulture or something. But then it came back out of the clouds and I could see that it didn't look like any kind of bird at all, even though it did have wings. It had wings but it was more like a dog, or a monkey, maybe, or even a dwarf.'

'A *dwarf*?'

'You asked me to tell you what I saw and I'm telling you. Whatever it was, it was beating those wings but the beating got slower and slower and slower and it seemed to be having a whole lot of trouble keeping itself up in the air. It disappeared into the clouds again and I'm sure that I heard it screaming. It was a terrible scream, like when somebody knows that there's no hope for them. I only heard a scream like that once before in my life, and that was when the Keilty Department Store was burning down and there was two women and a man trapped up on a ledge and no chance of getting them down.'

'Go on,' Jenna coaxed her.

'Well, that was that. The screaming stopped and then this stone statue dropped out of the clouds and hit the road and smashed into smithereens.'

'OK. But after the statue fell into the road, did you happen to see the creature fly away?'

Mrs Blessington stared at her as if she were retarded. 'You don't understand, Detective. The statue *was* the flying thing.'

'I'm sorry, Mrs Blessington. I don't quite get it. This statue was carved out of solid limestone. It had wings, for sure, but there was no way that it could have used them to fly.'

Mrs Blessington gave Jenna a dismissive sniff. 'There! I told you that you wouldn't believe me.'

'I'm sorry, Mrs Blessington. I'm just finding it very hard to make any sense out of this. First of all you saw a dog or a monkey or a dwarf, with wings, flying through the clouds?'

'That's right. It was very high up, so I couldn't be sure exactly what it was.'

'Then you heard screaming and the statue fell out of the sky and into the road?'

Mrs Blessington nodded.

'But you didn't see the flying thing fly away, and you're trying to tell me that the statue looked exactly like it?'

'It didn't *look* like it, detective. It *was* it. It flew into the clouds and somehow it turned to stone.'

'In mid-air?'

'Yes.'

Jenna looked at Dan and raised her eyebrows. 'Thank you for your help, then, Mrs Blessington. Maybe we'll need to talk to you again, but on the whole I think not.'

'Because you think I have senile dementia? That's it, isn't it?'

'No, Mrs Blessington. I don't. But, you know, sometimes our senses can play tricks on us. We perceive things in a different way from the way they really are. You know, like mirages in the desert, seeing water where there is no water. Optical illusions.'

'It was one and the same creature, Detective, only it had turned into stone. I would swear to that on the Holy Bible, in a court of law. That was what happened. That was what I saw. But I don't have to explain it. Explaining it, I thought that was your job.'

Dan escorted Mrs Blessington back to the cemetery. Jenna looked at Ed Freiburg and Ed Freiburg was grinning.

'*What?*' Jenna demanded.

'Don't take it out on me,' said Ed Freiburg. 'I'm only the guy who puts the bits back together.'

'It's a statue, Ed. Statues cannot flap their wings and fly. Period.'

'Of course not. But I think you've got to look at this whole thing differently.'

'What are you talking about?'

'You shouldn't be asking yourself: how come these statues are falling out of the sky? You shouldn't even be asking yourself how they got up there in the first place, because the fact is they *did* get up there, and there has to be some kind of logical explanation for that. What you need to be asking yourself is, *why* are they up there?'

'How the hell should I know why they're up there? Maybe they've decided to migrate to Florida for the winter, like the birds.'

'If you could fly, just by flapping your arms, would you?'

'Of course I would.'

'Why?'

'Because I could, that's all.'

'Precisely, Jenna. Right answer.'

FOURTEEN

Wednesday, 9:17 p.m.

Nathan opened his eyes to find Grace sitting next to him. Usually, she was so placid and composed that she reminded him of one of those medieval paintings of angels. This evening, though, she looked angry and agitated. Her short brunette hair was all messed up and her green-gray eyes were as dark as a stormy sea.

'Hi,' he slurred. He was still recovering from the general anesthetic. He lifted his left hand and saw that it was covered by a large polythene glove. Inside the glove, his fingers were mottled red and tightly curled over, although he wasn't feeling any pain. A cannula had been inserted in his right wrist and connected to both a saline drip and a morphine dispenser.

'Why the *hell* did you do it?' Grace snapped at him. 'There are plenty of ways to win an argument without setting yourself on fire.'

'Not this argument.'

'I don't understand this at all. Haven't you always said that you get your own way by persuasion, not by violence? You've told Denver that often enough.'

'This wasn't violence. I didn't hurt anybody else.'

'It *was* violence. It was violence against yourself, and Ron Kasabian, and most of all it was violence against me and Denver. How are you going to make a living with only one hand?'

'I won't have to, believe me.'

'Oh, no? I talked to Doctor Berman after your operation and he said that the burns were so deep that your hand is going to be permanently scarred and contracted. It could take *months* for you to heal, and I'm still going to end up with a husband who has one hand and one monkey's paw.'

'Grace, sweetheart, I knew exactly what I was doing, believe me. Ron was going to pull the plug on us. We got as far as creating the phoenix, for sure, but the whole project is going to be meaningless unless we can show what the phoenix is *for*.'

Grace shook her head. 'You're crazy. You're crazy and you're thoughtless and I'm very, very angry with you. In fact I *hate* you for doing this.'

Nathan reached out and tried to take hold of her hand, but she snatched it out of reach.

'Don't you believe in me any longer?' he asked her. 'For all of these years, you've always believed in me. Even when I couldn't find funding. Even when every research institute between here and Seattle turned me down flat.'

Grace's eyes were crowded with tears. 'Supposing *I* set fire to myself? How would you feel about that?'

'Not very happy, it's true. But this is different. Ron Kasabian refused to pay for any clinical tests on burns patients, so what option did I have?'

'What are you telling me, Nathan? You mean you deliberately turned yourself into a guinea pig?'

'Come on, Grace. I couldn't ask anybody else to do it, could I?'

'Do you know something? You're much crazier than I thought. I thought you did this because you were angry. I thought you did it to shock Ron Kasabian. But you didn't, did you? You did it coolly and calmly and deliberately.'

'Well, I wasn't exactly cool and calm. And it hurt like hell.'

'I don't know what to say. You've left me speechless.'

'Don't say anything yet. You can give me a hard time if this doesn't work out, but I can promise you that it will.' He paused, and then he repeated, 'I *promise* you.'

Grace tugged a tissue from the box beside Nathan's bed, and wiped her eyes. He felt terrible, hurting her like this, but Ron Kasabian hadn't given him any other choice, apart from abandoning the cryptozoological program altogether, and that would have been like asking Vincent Van Gogh to give up painting.

'Do you have your cell with you?' he asked her. 'I want to call Aarif.'

'You don't have to call Aarif. Aarif is right outside – and Kavita, too.'

'I'm touched. I really am.'

Grace gave him a tight, humorless smile. 'Yes. Touched. I guess that's one way of putting it.'

Aarif and Kavita came into the room. Kavita was carrying a bouquet of purple orchids and a box of maple candies, while Aarif had brought a selection of books and magazines, including *Playboy* and *National Geographic*. They dragged chairs over to his bedside and sat looking at him with a mixture of admiration and disbelief.

'How does it feel now, Professor – your hand?' Aarif asked him. He was wearing a brown knitted skullcap and a floppy brown sweater, and he looked more like a member of the Taliban than a research zoologist.

'It's starting to throb some,' Nathan admitted, in a hoarse, whispery voice. 'But I have morphine on demand if it starts to hurt too much. How's Torchy?'

'Oh, Torchy's *fine*,' said Kavita. Her glossy black hair was parted in the center and braided, and she was wearing a black turtleneck sweater and at least a dozen Navajo bead bracelets. 'He's eating well, all of his vital signs are excellent, and he really seems to have adapted to his environment. He's even started to warble. I've made some recordings.'

Aarif said, 'We are not being closed down immediately. Mr Kasabian is giving us a month to wind up the project and finish up all of our notes.'

'Oh, very generous of him,' said Nathan. 'Hopefully, that's as much as we're going to need.'

'You should not have burned yourself, Professor,' Aarif told him, in a grave tone. 'You should have thought of what they say in Egypt, that the barking of a dog should not disturb the man on a camel.'

'I understand what you're saying. Unfortunately, this particular dog happens to finance my camel.'

'I've told Nathan myself that it was a crazy thing to do,' Grace put in. 'Crazy, and selfish.'

'But it is done now, Doctor Underhill,' said Aarif. 'We cannot extinguish a flame that is now only the memory of a flame. We have to do everything we can to restore Professor Underhill's hand. I presume, Professor, that you will be wanting me to extract stem cells from the phoenix and bring them here.'

'First thing tomorrow,' Nathan told him.

'Are you going to tell Doctor Berman what you're doing?' asked Grace.

'Of course not. He'd be too worried about a malpractice suit if anything went wrong.'

'But what would happen to *you*, if anything went wrong?'

'Grace – nothing is going to go wrong. I'm injecting myself with avian pluripotent stem cells, that's all, which potentially have the capability of rapidly healing burns. The very worst that can happen is that nothing happens, and that I'm stuck for the rest of my life with this monkey's paw, as you call it.'

'Well, terrific. But I still think you need to tell Doctor Berman, out of professional courtesy, if nothing else.'

'I'll think about it, OK?'

'No you damn well won't. I know you.'

Kavita stood up and walked around Nathan's bed and laid her hand on Grace's shoulder. 'Doctor Underhill, I know that you must be finding this very frustrating and very hard to understand. But Aarif and I have been working every day with Professor Underhill on the phoenix project and we both have such faith in what he is doing, and such respect for what he has achieved.'

'Well, so do I,' said Grace. 'But to burn his own hand, for God's sake—'

'I was as shocked as everybody else,' said Kavita. 'But many pioneering scientists take terrible risks with their health and even their lives. Think of Marie Curie. She used to carry test tubes of radium around in her apron pocket, and she died of anemia.

Think of Jeremiah Abalaka. He injected himself six times with HIV-positive blood to test his AIDS vaccine. Or Daniel Carrion, who infected himself with pus from a chronic skin lesion, to prove that it also caused Oroya fever. Which it did, and which killed him.'

Grace looked up at her and said, 'All right, Kavita. I'll give it five days. But if I see any deterioration in Nathan's condition, I'm going to tell Doctor Berman myself.'

'That's fine,' said Nathan. 'Five days will be plenty.'

Grace stood up. 'I should go now. Denver will be home at ten thirty, and I'm sure you three have a whole lot to talk about.' She leaned over and gave Nathan a kiss.

'I'm sorry I've upset you so much,' he told her. 'But trust me – please.'

'Let's wait and see,' she said. 'But this is one time when I really want you to prove me wrong.'

FIFTEEN

Thursday, 2:36 a.m.

Jimmy Hallam loved to cycle at night. Whirring along the Schuylkill River Trail in the early hours of the morning made him feel like a superhero, out on a secret mission while the rest of the city slept.

The rain had eased off about an hour ago, but the trail was still wet and shiny and reflected the street lights as much as the river that ran beside it. During the day, there was a constant stream of walkers and joggers and roller-skaters and skate-boarders, but at night it belonged almost exclusively to Jimmy.

Tonight, Jimmy was on the lookout for Biters, a gang of teenage vampires who had invaded Fairmount Park. He was Heatseeker, who could detect people hiding in total darkness because he had infrared vision. Whenever he caught sight of a Biter running between the trees, he focused his eyes on it and the vampire evaporated in a haze of blood.

Heatseeker was a character he had invented himself. He spent almost every evening in his bedroom, drawing graphic novels. His hero was the comic book artist Todd McFarlane, who had drawn *Spider Man* and *Spawn*, but Jimmy knew that he was still very far from being as good as him. He had sent some of his drawings to Marvel Comics, but they had been returned with a polite 'sorry, Jimmy, you have some potential, but a long way to go yet'.

Heatseeker was rock-jawed and muscular, and wore a dark red outfit with a staring red eye emblazoned on his chest. Jimmy on the other hand was skinny, with mouse-brown hair chopped into an undercut, a receding chin, and a prominent Adam's apple that bobbed up and down when he talked. He was twenty-one years old and he was still a virgin. In fact he had never had a serious girlfriend, although he and Elaine Draper from art college some-times went to the movies together, and picked over the quality of the animation afterward in Bootsie's burger restaurant.

Heatseeker, however, had a ravishing assistant called Melona, who had abundant black curls and enormous breasts and who always wore a skimpy red leotard and glossy red thigh-boots.

Jimmy had almost reached the Columbia railroad bridge, where the trail temporarily parted company with Kelly Drive and curved right out over the river. Heatseeker had to be especially alert here, because the vampires sometimes clustered under the brick arches of the bridge, and rushed out at unsuspecting passers-by.

He scanned the trail ahead of him, moving his head methodic-ally from side to side. After a few moments he lifted his wristwatch to his lips and said, 'I've just eyeballed three Biters hiding in the shadows. I'm going to wait till the last moment, and then zap all three of them together. Three bloodsuckers with one stare.'

'OK, Heat,' he replied. 'Affirmatory.'

As he cycled under the bridge, he focused his eyes into the darkest corner of the arch, and called out, '*Adios, suckers!*' The three Biters scrambled out of the shadows toward him, hissing with hatred, but with one penetrating stare he turned them into nothing more than a fine fog of scarlet droplets, which drifted away on the wind.

He punched the air as he emerged on the north side of the bridge. Heatseeker had triumphed again, keeping the city safe from Biters and other supernatural predators. Philadelphians

would never be aware that he was protecting them while they
slept, but Heatseeker never expected acclaim or any reward. It
was enough for him to know that the forces of evil would never
prevail.

He continued to pedal fast alongside the black, reflecting river.
In the distance he could hear police sirens, and the soft, cease-
less rumbling of a city of a million and a half people. But then
he heard another sound – a sharp, repetitive flapping, as if
somebody were shaking out a groundsheet. If they *were* shaking
out a groundsheet, however, they were doing it impossibly
high above his head. The sound seemed to be coming from
directly above him.

Freewheeling, he looked upward. At first he could see nothing
but the clouds, tinted orange by the sodium street lights. But then
he glimpsed a dark shape flying fast and high above the river,
parallel to the trail on which he was cycling. It was far too big
to be a bat, although it had wings like a bat, and its body was
all the wrong shape for a bird. With every beat of its wings he
heard *flap, flap, flap,* and there was something about that flapping
that really frightened him. It was so measured, so unhurried, as
if the creature knew exactly where it was going and what it
intended to do; and what it intended to do was serious harm.

Jimmy didn't know why he felt that way about it, but the
feeling was so strong that he almost lost his balance, and he
brought his bicycle to a juddering stop.

He watched the creature flying northward up the river, but it
had flown only about a half-mile when it turned and wheeled
around, and began to fly back again, heading his way. The *flap,
flap, flap* began to grow louder, and then he heard the creature
howling. Whatever it was, it certainly wasn't a bird. It sounded
more like a wolf, or even a man imitating a wolf.

Jimmy watched it for a few more seconds, but then he was
suddenly filled with a flood of terror. The creature was diving
directly toward him, and as it did so it was gathering speed. The
darn thing was after him, he was sure of it. He twisted his
handlebars around and began to pedal furiously back toward the
Columbia Bridge.

He turned his head only once. The creature was less than fifty
feet behind him, and the flapping of its wings was so loud that
it drowned out everything else – the police sirens, the sound of

traffic, even the noise of a helicopter that was flying over Wynnefield Heights on its way to the airport. He glimpsed the creature's face, too. It had stubby horns and huge staring eyes and a large curved beak, but unlike a bird its beak had two curved teeth protruding from it.

It howled at him again, that dreadful echoing howl. He yelped out loud in fear and pedaled even faster. He was only a few yards from the shelter of the bridge now, and he prayed that he could make it. He could hear himself sobbing as if somebody else were sobbing close behind him.

He almost made it. He was less than six feet from the brick arch where the Biters had been hiding when one of the creature's claws tore into the back of his head, right through hair and skin and striking his skull with a loud knocking noise. He screamed and pitched forward out of the saddle, while with one thunderous flap of its wings, the creature flew upward and sideways to avoid colliding with the bridge. Even so, its claw was still buried in the back of Jimmy's scalp, and it was so heavy and traveling so fast that it ripped off his hair and half of the flesh from the right-hand side of his face, pulling out his eye and tearing off his lips.

Jimmy collapsed on to his knees, too shocked to comprehend what had happened to him. He tried to stand up, but then he dropped back on to his knees again, quaking. He could feel warm blood soaking through his sweatshirt, but when he tried to look down at his chest and see where it was coming from, he realized that he was partially blinded. He tried to shout out for help but nothing came out of his mouth except a honking sound.

He crawled over to the side of the archway and made another effort to stand up, holding on to the wall to support himself. He stood there for a moment, trying to get his breath back. He felt blood coursing down the back of his throat but he couldn't spit it out because he no longer had any lips. He was gradually beginning to understand that his face had been hideously mutilated, but he didn't want to touch it to find out just how much. The pain was intense, but somehow it was beyond unbearable – so overwhelming that he felt it was being experienced by somebody else, and not by him at all.

He heard a flapping noise, and let out another honk. *Flap, flap, flap* over the river, and growing louder with every *flap*. With his one remaining eye he saw the creature flying around and around, slow and leisurely, but coming closer to the bridge every time it circled. It was going to catch him. He was sure of it. It was going to catch him and it was going to tear him apart. It was almost as if he could read its mind.

You have to get out of here, Jimmy. It's no good thinking that it won't come after you just because you're under the bridge. You have to get out of here and get yourself some help, otherwise you're going to die here, and Heatseeker is going to die here with you.

He turned around and started to hobble back along the trail. He felt as if he had no strength at all, and he could barely drag one foot in front of the other. But once he was out from under the bridge, maybe he could cross over Kelly Drive and make his way into the park, and maybe the creature would lose sight of him under the trees. Or maybe he might get lucky, and a passing motorist might see him, and take him to hospital. A Good Samaritan.

He reached Kelly Drive and stood swaying in the parking area beside the bridge. The highway was deserted, with no cars traveling in either direction, and no recreational vehicles parked anywhere in sight. The trees in the park on the opposite side of the road were shushing and whispering to each other as if they knew what was going to happen to him but didn't want him to hear.

Dear God help me. Dear God somebody help me. The pain was growing much worse and Jimmy didn't think he was going to be able to bear it. All the same, he started to shuffle across Kelly Drive toward the park, making that honking sound with every agonizing step.

He was only halfway across the highway when he heard the flapping again. This time it sounded much quicker and stronger, as if the creature were building up speed. He turned around, almost falling over as he did so, just in time to see the creature rising up from behind the bridge, its wings plunging up and down as if it were swimming the butterfly stroke through the air. Its eyes were staring and its beak was drawn back in a hideous grimace, baring its two curved fangs.

It reached over a hundred feet in the air, and then it hovered, and howled even louder than before. Its howl echoed across the river, and in every arch beneath the bridge – creating an unholy chorus that sounded like six creatures instead of only one.

Jimmy tried to run. He crossed Kelly Drive with a dot-and-carry limp, his right foot dragging behind him. He almost wished that a truck would come roaring along the highway and put him out of his pain. As he stumbled over the opposite curb, the creature's wings were flapping so close behind him that he could actually feel the draft of each *flap*.

When it hit him, it hit him as hard as a bomb going off. He was blasted apart so violently that his head went tumbling and bouncing down the highway, while his ribcage exploded and his lungs and his stomach were ripped into bloody tatters. His pelvis and his legs performed one disembodied cartwheel after another, with yards of small intestine unraveling behind them like a fire hose.

The creature let out another howl, gaining height and circling out over the river again. Almost immediately, however, it swooped back down over Jimmy's scattered remains, plucking his heart from the roadway with its beak.

Then, without another sound, it flew away, heading southwestward.

The distinctive flapping of its wings had long since died away by the time Stuart Williams came along Kelly Drive and saw what was left of Jimmy lying in the road. Stuart was a short-order chef at the South Street Diner, which was open twenty hours a day, and he had just finished an eight hour shift cooking breakfasts for other night workers and people who simply couldn't sleep.

At first he couldn't work out what all that red shiny mess was, strewn along the blacktop. He was about to put his foot down and keep on driving when he caught sight of Jimmy's head. He pulled in to the parking area, waited for a moment, and then climbed out of his car. He walked back and took a closer look, just to make sure that it *was* a human head, and not the head of some deer or some dog that had been run over, or some store window dummy that somebody had left there for a joke. But Jimmy stared back at him with one eye, his scalp torn, his mouth bloody, and there was no doubt about it. Until very recently, this red shiny mess had been a man.

'Oh shit,' said Stuart. He took his cellphone out of his shirt pocket and dialed 911.

'*What's your emergency?*' the girl on the switchboard asked him.

'I don't rightly know. It looks like some dude got himself disassembled. God alone knows how.'

'*Disassembled?*'

'That's the only way I know how to describe it, miss. There ain't one single part of him that's still connected to no other part.'

'*Please wait there. We'll be dispatching an ambulance directly.*'

'With all due respect, miss, I don't think you need to send an ambulance. All you're going to need is a bucket.'

SIXTEEN

Thursday, 7:07 a.m.

Nathan had slept only fitfully during the night and when Aarif and Kavita appeared he was dozing. Aarif stood by his bed, watching him for a while, and then he gently shook his shoulder.

'Professor? Professor, wake up.'

Nathan opened one eye and stared up at him. 'Aarif. What time is it?' He blinked, and then he said, 'I can't believe it. I was dreaming that I was out in my back yard, grilling burgers.'

'Not surprising, Professor, when you consider what you did to your hand.'

Nathan winced, and sat up. He held up his hand in its plastic glove and he could see that it was already beginning to fill with watery yellow fluid. 'If I'd known that it was going to hurt as much as this, believe me, I would have thought of some other way of making my point.'

Aarif held up the blue canvas bag that he was carrying. 'We have the phoenix stem cells in here, professor. You can have you first injection immediately.'

'That's great. How did Torchy take it?'

'He was not pleased when we anesthetized him. But he is fine.'

'What about Ron Kasabian?'

'I think he is still very angry with you. He has to make a report to the board about what happened, and explain why you burned yourself. But as I said yesterday, what is done is done, and cannot be changed. A shout can never be unshouted.'

'Too right.' Nathan looked across at the digital clock on his nightstand. 'But, hey – you'd better make it snappy. They'll be bringing me breakfast at seven thirty.'

'Everything's ready,' said Kavita. She sat down on the side of the bed and tugged on a pair of latex gloves. Then she carefully lifted Nathan's left arm and pulled up the sleeve of his pale blue pajamas, all the way to the elbow. She wiped his forearm with antiseptic wipe and Aarif passed her a hypodermic syringe.

'We decided that instead of injecting the stem cells into the burn itself, it would be better to inject them into the nearest large skeletal muscle, which is the extensor pollicis longus.'

'Oh, yes?'

She smiled at him. 'That way, we can inject you repeatedly without causing you any extra trauma or risking any additional infection. They do the same with heart patients these days, rather than inject stem cells directly into the heart muscle.'

She took the plastic cap off the syringe and held it up to make sure that there were no air bubbles in it. Then, without hesitation, she stuck the needle into Nathan's arm, and pressed the plunger. She waited for a moment, staring unblinkingly into his eyes, and then took it out.

'Didn't feel a thing,' said Nathan. 'You should have been a nurse.'

'I don't know what it's going to feel like when it starts to take effect.'

'Let's just hope that it *does* take effect. I don't think Grace is ever going to forgive me if it doesn't.'

'I talked to Grace,' said Kavita. 'She thinks that you are mad to do what you did. But all the same she admires your bravery, and your belief in yourself, and so do Aarif and I.'

'We will return this evening, Professor, and give you a further injection,' said Aarif. 'Meanwhile, all we can do is pray.'

At that moment, Doctor Berman came into the room, followed by two of his juniors – one of them a young Korean woman and the other a light-skinned black man who bore a distinct resemblance to Barack Obama.

'Professor Underhill,' he boomed. 'How's the hand coming along?'

Nathan held it up so that he could examine it. 'Making progress,' said Doctor Berman. 'It's macerating, as you'd expect, so we're getting plenty of fluid. I know it looks awful, but it's a sign that it's starting to heal. We'll change the dressing today and maybe give you a semi-permeable glove with Gore-tex in it. That should reduce the maceration.

'The main thing is to control bacterial infection. A burn wound is dynamic and infection can convert it from partial thickness to full thickness. I want you to get the use of your hand back, Professor – at least some limited use, anyhow.'

Nathan said, 'Thank you,' and smiled. He wasn't going to tell Doctor Berman that he was hoping for so much more than that. He looked across at Aarif and Aarif bowed his head as if to acknowledge that he understood the need for secrecy, at least for the time being. If Doctor Berman knew that Aarif and Kavita had just injected him with stem cells from a mangy-looking mythical bird, he never would have allowed them back into the hospital again.

'We must go, Professor,' said Aarif. 'We have a small friend to take care of.'

'OK,' Nathan told him. 'Be sure to give him a dead mouse from me. He deserves it.'

Doctor Berman and his juniors looked at each other and raised their eyebrows.

'He's a bird,' Nathan explained. 'He just did me a favor, that's all.'

'A bird did you a favor?' asked Doctor Berman.

'It's a long story,' Nathan told him.

'Well . . . you must be sure to tell me sometime.'

'Sure,' said Nathan. *Maybe sooner than you think.*

Grace came to see him after breakfast, and brought him blush pears and Florida oranges. She stayed for an hour, although she had her own practice to take care of. One of her specialties was geriatric care, and she had to visit the Burmont Rest Home out at Pilgrim Gardens, where forty-three seniors needed every kind of treatment from earwax to eczema.

She was calmer today, although she didn't hide the fact that she still felt resentful.

Nathan said, 'Kavita gave me my first injection of stem cells this morning.'

'Oh, yes? Your hand doesn't look any better. In fact it looks *revolting*. All squishy.'

'Come on, Grace, it may be a miracle cure but it's going to take time. I don't know how long. But I still believe that it's going to work.'

'I hope it does. I really do. There's a little girl along the corridor who's had all of her face seriously burned in an auto accident. I feel so sorry for her. I talked to Doctor Berman about her and he said that she can never hope to look the same again.'

'That's exactly the kind of person I'm trying to help.'

'Great. By setting fire to yourself.'

'Like Aarif says, honey, it's done now.'

'Just because Aarif has an Egyptian proverb for every possible eventuality, that doesn't mean that Aarif isn't talking out of his ass. You know me. I've never been a fatalist.'

'I'd agree with that, one hundred percent.'

She leaned over the bed and kissed him. 'Please God I hope this works,' she told him.

He managed a light breakfast of one pancake and a cup of lemon tea. After that he watched TV for a while, but gradually fell asleep again, even though his hand was still throbbing. He didn't hear the anchorwoman on Eyewitness News say, '*The body was identified as that of twenty-one-year-old James Hallam Junior, a postgraduate student from the Moore College of Art and Design. Police have given no details about how he died but say that he suffered massive trauma equivalent to being struck at high speed by a very large vehicle.*'

Nathan slept dreamlessly, but he was woken up less than hour later by a fiery sensation in his hand. He felt as if his flesh, already raw, were being dragged slowly through a blazing briar bush, so that it prickled and burned, both at the same time.

He pressed the button on his morphine dispenser to give himself another shot of painkiller, but even after five minutes had gone by, the burning was just as agonizing, if not worse. He tugged the

cord to call for the nurse, and then lay on his side in a fetal position, his eyes squeezed tight shut, grunting with pain. He could
almost *see* his pain in his mind's eye, five fingers crawling with
barbed-wire flames.

Two nurses hurried in. 'Professor Underhill? What's wrong?'

Nathan lifted his hand but his teeth were clenched so tightly
together that he couldn't speak. One of the nurses took out a
hypodermic syringe and gave him an extra shot of morphine,
while the other gently levered his left arm down and laid his
hand on a white gauze pad.

'*Dah* – that really – careful! – *ahh*!'

'It's all right, Professor. I'll be very gentle with you. I just
have to cut off this glove and change your dressing. It looks like
your hand has been weeping real bad.'

'Please, I – *hah*! *hah*! – God almighty – it's worse than when
I first burned it!'

'It might have gotten infected. Almost all burns get colonized
with bacteria in the first few days.'

'Now I'm a colony? That's terrific – *hah*! *ahh*! That really,
really hurts!'

The nurse cut away the transparent plastic with surgical scis-
sors and drew off the remains of the glove. It was filled with
watery serum, which she carefully dabbed clean with lint. Then
she sprayed his hand with antiseptic, which stung even more. He
closed his eyes tight and said, 'Jesus!'

There was a long pause. Then the nurse who was treating his
hand said to her companion, 'Edie – come over here, would you?
Take a look at this.'

Nathan heard her companion walk around the foot of the bed.
There was another pause, and then her companion said, 'How
about that? I never saw nothing like that before. I'll go call Doctor
Berman.'

Nathan opened his eyes. 'Something wrong?' he asked, trying
to lift his head up.

'No, Professor. Nothing wrong. In fact something's a whole
lot righter than it ought to be.'

Nathan looked down at his hand. The nurse had cleaned off
all of the serum, and although it was still bright scarlet, his hand
looked surprisingly unscathed. The skin on the back of his
hand had suffered full thickness burns, and Doctor Berman had

been talking about a split skin graft. The palm had been burned less severely, but it would still have needed a full thickness graft, because the inside of the hand needed to be covered with much more robust skin.

Now, however, glossy red skin had already crept back as far as his knuckles, and when he turned his hand over, he saw that his palm was healing, too. Even his life line and his fate line were reappearing, and they had been totally obliterated.

His hand wasn't simply healing; it was regenerating itself.

The phoenix, he thought. *The dragon-worm had blazed and then reappeared as a bird in only a matter of seconds*. His hand had taken a little longer, but it was still astoundingly fast by human standards. A hand that had been burned as badly as his would normally have taken months to heal, and he would have needed numerous skin grafts and months of therapy even to be able to pick up a pencil.

'It's working,' he croaked. It still hurt like hell, although the extra shot of morphine was beginning to take effect. But who cared if it hurt like hell if it was actually returning to normal, and with such rapidity? Maybe the regrowth of a few square inches of burned human skin barely even counted as a miracle when he compared it with the phoenix itself, which could reconstitute itself from nothing but a heap of ashes. But it would dramatically change the lives of millions of badly-scarred people.

Doctor Berman came in. The nurse must have interrupted his lunch, because he was still wiping his beard with a paper napkin.

'Professor Underhill?' he said. 'Nurse Johnson here tells me that something remarkable has happened.'

Nathan held up his hand, and turned it from side to side. It was still red, but it was healing almost visibly by the minute. The nurse handed Doctor Berman a pair of latex gloves and he put them on, frowning at Nathan's hand as he did so. Then he sat down on the side of the bed and examined his hand intently – first the dorsum, then the palm, then each individual finger. The renewed skin was smooth and dry. There was no bacterial infection, no further maceration, and no obvious contracture of the tendons.

Doctor Berman looked Nathan straight in the eye. 'You know that this is impossible, don't you, Professor?'

'What can I say?' Nathan told him, with a shrug.

'This is utterly and completely impossible. I have never in my entire thirty-eight-year career seen a full-thickness burn heal so quickly and so comprehensively. Never.'

'I don't know what to tell you,' said Nathan, although he would have given anything to be able to tell Doctor Berman right here and now about the phoenix project. He *would* tell him, before he left the burns unit, because if he could persuade Temple University Hospital to endorse what he had achieved, Schiller might change their minds and agree to fund the remainder of his research. First of all, however, he wanted to make sure that his hand regenerated itself until it was exactly as it had been before he had set fire to it.

'I'll come back later today,' said Doctor Berman. 'Meanwhile, you should keep your hand clean and dry, but otherwise I see no need for any further treatment. The way you're healing, it seems to be a private matter between you and God, without any need for intervention from me.'

SEVENTEEN
Thursday, 11:18 a.m.

Jenna was still sitting on the green-painted railing overlooking the river when Dan came over and said, 'Would you believe it? Another statue just dropped out of the sky.'

Jenna pushed her hair out of her eyes. There was a strong south-west wind blowing up the river this morning, ruffling the surface of the water. The blue plastic screens that surrounded the remains of Jimmy Hallam were rumbling and slapping, and even though Jenna didn't know it, they sounded almost exactly like the wings of the creature that had killed him.

'*Shit*,' said Jenna. She had been planning to go home in a minute for a shower and something to eat, and maybe even a couple of hours' sleep. 'Where?'

'Bartram's Gardens. But it seems like it came down in the wetlands, so it isn't too badly damaged.'

'Anybody hurt?'

'Not so far as I know. Nobody saw it fall. It was found by one of the volunteer gardeners, about forty-five minutes ago.'

'Right, let's go take a look. Let me tell Ed first. After he's finished up here, he can come join us. If the statue *is* reasonably intact, maybe it will give him some idea of how to piece the other two together.'

She pushed her way through a gap in the screens. Ed Freiburg was standing beside the beige, half-collapsed cannelloni of Jimmy Hallam's unraveled entrails, talking to two of his assistant CSIs. All of them had splashes of blood on the soles of their rubbers, and their hands were all blood-red, too, like three murderers conspiring together.

'Ah, Jenna, I was just coming to see you,' he said.

'Another statue came down,' Jenna told him. 'It landed in Bartram's Gardens and Dan says that it wasn't broken up too badly. Dan and me, we're on our way now.'

'OK. I'll catch up with you in – what time is it? – maybe an hour. We're still missing some parts of the jigsaw here. Or to be more specific, we're still missing some parts of our unfortunate vic.'

Jenna looked to the right, to where Jimmy's head was lying in the road, and then slowly turned her head to the left, taking in all of the scattered bones and lumps of flesh and ripped-apart organs, until she reached his bloodstained sneakers, with his feet still inside them.

'What's missing?' she asked. 'It looks like you got most of him here. Albeit kind of dismantled.'

'I'll tell you what's missing. His *heart*. And the thing of it is that we still haven't located the hearts of the other two victims, Chet Huntley and William Barrow. I thought that they might have been torn to unidentifiable shreds, maybe, or lost off the side of the apartment block, like Mr Huntley's head. If that had happened, there wouldn't have been much chance of ever finding them, hungry stray dogs being fairly undiscriminating as to what they eat for breakfast.'

'Shut up, Ed,' Jenna interrupted him. 'You're making me feel pukish.'

Ed looked around, his bloody hands spread wide. 'But now *this* poor guy is missing his heart, too, and three missing hearts out of three is too much of a pattern for me to ignore.'

'So what's your conclusion?'

'I haven't come to any conclusions yet, but I definitely have a theory. All of these three victims were killed by something of considerable mass, flying through the air at considerable velocity – far too big and far too fast to be any known bird. I was beginning to consider the notion that it might be some kind of drone – you know, an unmanned remote-controlled airplane like those Predators that the military use in Afghanistan. But then these three missing hearts place a very large question mark over that. A drone can't selectively pick a person's heart out. No drone that I've ever heard of, anyhow.'

'So what can?'

'A creature that looks exactly like these statues that have been falling out of the sky. Only alive.'

'So you're trying to tell me that Mrs Lugano and Mrs What's-her-face at the cemetery were right about what they saw? These people were killed by some species of flying monkeys, or dogs, or dwarves? Or maybe by very homely angels? But whatever these creatures were, they turned into stone in mid-air and fell to the ground?'

'Do you have another theory?' Ed asked her. His face was completely expressionless. He didn't even blink.

'I don't, as of yet,' Jenna retorted. 'But I never believed that Sherlock Holmes crap about "when you have eliminated the impossible, whatever remains, however improbable, must be the truth". So far as I'm concerned, if whatever you're left with when you've eliminated the impossible is improbable, you need to go back to square one and re-examine the evidence.'

'OK, keep your hair on. So far we haven't had time to finish examining all of the evidence *once* yet, let alone twice. I was theorizing, that's all. I was just telling you to trust your instincts, once in a while.'

'Well, don't. It gives me a migraine. I'll see you down at Bartram's Gardens in an hour.'

A large crowd of sightseers had gathered around the wetlands in Bartram's Gardens, in spite of the fact that it had started to rain again, quite heavily. The forty-five acre botanical gardens lay on the west side of the Schuylkill River, about five miles due south-west of the Columbia Bridge where Jimmy Hallam had been killed.

Jenna loved Bartram's Gardens and visited them whenever she had an afternoon to spare. They were so wild and filled with flowers that it was hard to believe that they were so close to the city center. John Bartram had built himself a handsome stone house here in the early part of the eighteenth century, and then set about planting the garden with every species of American wild flower he could find, as well as rare trees and shrubs. George III had eventually made him King's Botanist for North America.

Dan parked the car as close to the wetlands as he could, and he and Jenna climbed out. There were three police cars here already, as well as a tow truck. Their red flashing lights were reflected in the water, between the bulrushes and marsh grasses and yellow irises. On the far side of the river, there was a dramatic view of the city skyline, although the upper stories of the taller buildings were hidden in overhanging cloud.

As Jenna and Dan ducked under the police tape, they were approached by a stocky black sergeant in a leather jacket. He was fortyish, with a bristly gray moustache, but he looked as if he worked out regularly, and maybe boxed, too, judging by the way his nose was bent sideways.

'Well, well, Sergeant Dennis Williams,' said Jenna. 'Haven't seen you in a coon's age. How's that wayward son of yours? What's his name? Duane?'

Sergeant Williams nodded. 'You got a good memory, Detective. Yeah, Duane's not so wayward these days. In fact he's almost human. Surprising what a difference a couple of years can make.'

'So what do we have here? A statue, in the water?'

'That's right. But nobody can work out how the hell it got here, because it wasn't here last night, and the garden closes at five.'

He led them down to the very edge of the wetlands. About a hundred and fifty feet away, a white limestone statue lay on its side in the shallow water, half-hidden by the grass, and surrounded by orange hibiscus flowers, as if somebody had arranged them there as a tribute. Two police divers in yellow chest-high waders were trying to fasten canvas straps around it.

'Here,' said Sergeant Williams, and handed Jenna a pair of binoculars.

She focused on the statue and she could see immediately that it bore a strong resemblance to the shattered statues that had landed next to the Convent of Divine Love and Woodlands Cemetery. Half of its head was submerged, but it was facing toward her, and she could see that it had knobbly horns and protuberant eyes and a wide, curved beak. A large wing rose out of its shoulders, carved in triangular sections like a dragon's wing, rather than a bird's wing. About a third of the wing had broken off and was lying in the grass beside it.

The statue's arms and legs were disproportionately long, with claws on both of them. Its body was almost human in shape, but it was very emaciated, with a clearly-defined ribcage and a swollen belly.

Jenna passed the binoculars to Dan, so that he could take a look for himself.

'Well?' asked Sergeant Williams. 'Any ideas what it's supposed to be a statue of, or where it came from, or why anybody should want to dump it here in Bartram's Gardens?'

'Unh-hunh,' Jenna admitted. 'Not so far.' The rain started to clatter down so hard that she put up her hood. 'Who found it? Not that it makes too much difference.'

'Volunteer gardener name of Andy Fisher. He says he was starting to rake out weeds and there it was. Frightened the crap out of him. That's what he said, anyhow.'

'Think he had anything to do with it?'

'Nah. He's not exactly the sharpest tool in the box, and if this was done as some kind of a practical joke, it was done by somebody who had brains. Like, you couldn't have driven the statue out here in a truck, because the water's too deep, and you couldn't have brought it in from the river, even in a flat-bottomed boat, because there's too much goddamned grass.'

He looked around. 'Must be connected to those other statues, don't you think? They were dropped out of helicopters, weren't they? Wouldn't be surprised if this one was, too.'

'Maybe,' said Jenna. 'On the other hand, who knows? The media are all convinced that some maniac is flying round Philly in a helicopter, dropping his unwanted sculpture collection on to the heads of an unsuspecting populace. But we don't have any evidence of that yet.'

Sergeant Williams shook his head and smiled. 'I always knew

you had a reputation for being the world's greatest skeptic, Detective. But explain to me how else does a statue drop out of the clear blue yonder, except if somebody took it up there in a chopper?'

'God moves in mysterious ways, Sergeant.'

'Sure. But half-ton statues don't.'

She hung around while the divers finished strapping up the statue and hooking it up to the tow truck. The rain died away, and a watery sun appeared through the clouds, but she was feeling shivery and hungry and bone-tired.

She talked to Andy Fisher, the volunteer gardener who had discovered the statue lying in the water. He was about twenty-two, with a mop of sandy hair and a large nose and near-together eyes, like a shy woodland animal. He was wearing a blue water-proof storm coat that was much too big for him, which made him appear even more vulnerable.

'I was clearing out the weeds in the channel and then I saw the wing sticking up. I went closer to see what it was and then I saw this real scary face looking up at me out of the water.'

'But you realized it was only a statue?'

Andy stared at her as if he wanted to say something, but didn't know if she would think he was stupid.

'What is it?' she coaxed him.

He puckered up his mouth and looked miserable.

'Come on, Andy,' she said. 'I'm a police detective. I've heard everything, believe me.'

'Well, I know it's only a statue and it's only made out of stone but when I first went up to it, its eyes were closed.'

'*Closed*? You're sure about that?'

Andy nodded vigorously. 'Its eyes were closed but when I went up to it and the water splashed against its face it opened them up and it *stared* at me. One of its eyes was above the water and the other eye was under the water. But it opened both eyes and it *stared* at me.'

'Its eyes are still open now.'

'I know they are, I know they are, but when I first went up to it they were closed. I swear on the Bible.'

'OK. You saw what you saw.'

'You don't believe me. You think I'm making it up. You think I'm a retard.'

'No, I don't. Not for a moment. Like I said, you saw what you saw and that's your evidence and I respect it. This happens with every single incident that I investigate. Different witnesses see totally different things, but that doesn't necessarily mean that they're wrong, or that they're challenged in any way.'

Andy furiously scratched the back of his head as if he couldn't decide whether or not to tell Jenna any more.

'Please, Andy,' Jenna encouraged him. 'Every detail, every impression, everything helps. You may not realize it, but you could have seen something that explains everything that happened here. What this statue is, and how it got here.'

Andy looked away, off toward the wild flower meadow, but it was obvious that he was concentrating all of his attention on what he was saying to Jenna. It was as if he were trying to be somebody else, describing what Andy had told him second-hand, but making sure that he described it very precisely.

'It's alive. It *was* alive, anyhow, when I first went up to it. Maybe it's dead now. But when I first went up to it, it was alive. And I know what it is.'

'You do?'

Andy nodded, still not looking at her. 'It's a Spoogly.'

Jenna had been about to say something, but now she was left with her mouth half-open. She hesitated for a moment, and then she said, 'A *Spoogly*?'

'That's what they're called. I don't know how I know. I've had dreams about them ever since I was little – nightmares. But that's what they are. That's what they're called. *Spooglies*.'

'I see. Well . . . that sounds like a very apt description to me. I mean, that statue *is* pretty spoogly, isn't it? Not the sort of sculpture you'd want in your back yard, really. Can you imagine looking out of your kitchen window every day and seeing *that* staring back at you?'

'No. We live four floors up. All you can see out of *our* kitchen window is an air shaft.'

'Sure. Of course. I only meant that by way of illustration.'

Andy abruptly turned to face her again, but his near-together eyes still didn't seem to be focused on her. 'I've had dreams about them ever since I was little. Creatures that come flying through the night. Hundreds of them, all dark, like it's an air raid. And they're always *screaming*.'

He let out a high, eerie howl just to make his point, and several
of the police officers looked around to see where the noise was
coming from.

Jenna said, 'You've had recurrent nightmares about creatures
which look like that statue?'

'It's a Spoogly,' Andy insisted. 'It's a Spoogly. I don't know
how I know it's a Spoogly, but I do.'

Jenna walked across to the tow truck, where the statue was
gradually being dragged up the ramps at the back. Ed
was prowling around, making sure that it wasn't chipped or
damaged. He was carrying the section of broken wing in his
arms as possessively as if he had just won it in a prize draw.

'Hey, careful!' he shouted, as the statue bumped and scraped
up the metal ramp. 'Go easy, will you! That's not just evidence,
that's a work of art!'

'I guess it *is* a work of art, when you come to think of it,'
said Jenna, watching the crime scene specialists unbuckle the
canvas webbing and strap the statue securely into place on
the back of the tow truck. 'Do you think it's worth anything?'

Ed shook his head. 'Hard to say without carbon dating it and
going through some catalogs. But it looks medieval to me. Maybe
fourteenth or fifteenth century. Beautifully carved. I mean that's
craftsmanship with a capital K. You do know what it is, don't
you?'

'Some kind of demon, I guess.'

'Well, yes, but look at the mouth. It's a very specific kind of
a demon. A gargoyle. They used to put them on the sides
of churches and other buildings to act as waterspouts. I'd say it
was German or Polish. Of course all the boundaries were different
in those days, so you could be talking about Prussian or
Lithuanian.'

'Why, Ed! I didn't realize you were such a culture vulture!'

'Not really. My old man was a stonemason and he used to
carve monuments for Bertolini's discount headstones up on
Torredale Avenue. We had books and books at home, full of
pictures of sculptures, which he used for reference. When I was
a kid I was always looking through them for sculptures of naked
women.'

'At last. The truth about Ed Freiburg's degenerate boyhood.'

'Get out of here, Jenna. I'll call you later when I have some results.'

The tow truck started up and Jenna and Ed had to step back out of its way. As it drove past them, only a few feet away, Jenna saw to her shock that the gargoyle had its eyes shut, as if it were asleep.

She looked quickly across at Andy Fisher, who was standing on the opposite side of the parking lot. *It's alive*, Andy had told her. *It's a Spoogly.*

She thought about going over and telling him that she had seen the statue's eyelids closed, but he turned his back and walked off into the crowd of sightseers. She tried to see where he had gone, but he had completely melted away.

'Something wrong?' Ed asked her.

'No, nothing. But that theory of yours. Maybe it's not so improbable after all.'

EIGHTEEN

Thursday, 7:49 p.m.

Doctor Berman came into his room to find Nathan flexing the fingers of his left hand like a pianist preparing to play Beethoven's *Piano Concerto No. 5*.

He stood at the end of the bed watching him for a few moments, and then he said, 'It's almost back to how it was before you burned it, isn't it?'

Nathan clenched his fingers into a fist, and then splayed them open again. 'Yes, it is,' he admitted. 'The tendons still feel kind of tightish, but that's all.'

There was a very long pause, but then Doctor Berman cleared his throat and said, 'You want to tell me what's going on here?'

'I'm not sure I understand you. Nothing's going on, except a little light physiotherapy.'

'I'm a doctor, Professor. I deal with people every day who have agonizing and permanently disfiguring burns. To do that, I have to be a psychiatrist and a counselor as well as a surgeon.'

'OK.'

'When you were brought in here, you had full-thickness burns to your hand and you were suffering intense pain. We dealt with the pain by giving you morphine. But you also faced the prospect of losing the use of your hand, maybe for good. That should have been very daunting and distressing, especially for a man in your profession.'

He paused again, and took off his spectacles.

'The thing of it is, Professor, you were *not* daunted and you were *not* distressed. Not especially, anyhow. Maybe I sensed a little apprehension, yes – but only that kind of "fingers crossed" apprehension when a person is hoping that everything goes according to plan. Now that I've seen how rapidly your hand has restored itself, I think I know why.'

'All right then, doctor,' said Nathan, guardedly. 'You tell me.'

'I think you were ninety percent sure that your hand was going to heal as quickly as that, because you treated yourself somehow to make sure that it would. I've been Googling your research this morning, Professor. As far as I can tell you've been trying to recreate extinct species in the hope of discovering cures for diseases and medical conditions that are currently incurable. Such as MS, Lou Gehrig's disease, and Alzheimer's, and reconstruction after third-degree burns and other serious traumas.'

'You're right,' said Nathan. 'Well, you're ninety-nine percent right. My objective is certainly to find ways to cure all of those conditions, and more. But the creatures that I've been trying to bring back to life aren't so much extinct as mythical.'

'*Mythical?*'

Nathan nodded. 'I'm talking gryphons and wyverns and chimera. They all flew and swam and walked on this planet once, for real, and their DNA is still traceable. My idea was to recreate them in the laboratory, and then extract their stem cells to give human beings some of their attributes. The trauco, for instance, which was a mythical humanoid from Chile, was supposed to have been capable of making even the most infertile woman pregnant. Stem cells from a trauco could make IV redundant.'

'So what about your hand? What creature's stem cells did you use to heal that – if that's what you did?'

'A phoenix. We successfully recreated it in the laboratory on Monday, using a dragon-worm whose DNA we had combined with that of an Egyptian scavenger hawk. We burned it alive, and out of the flames came the phoenix.'

'So I assume that when your colleagues came to visit you, they injected you with stem cells from this phoenix?'

'Twice only. Once this morning and once at four p.m. this afternoon.'

Doctor Berman carefully put his glasses back on. 'You do realize what could have happened to me if this little experiment had gone wrong, don't you? That would have been the end of my career.'

'I *do* realize, and I'm truly sorry. But I couldn't think of any other way. Schiller was cutting off my funding so I couldn't afford to test the phoenix stem cells on any other burns victims. You can imagine the medical insurance premiums. They would have been staggering.'

Doctor Berman stared at him. 'You burned yourself *deliberately*? You did it on purpose?'

'How else was I going to find a willing burns victim?'

'*Gott in Himmel*. You must have been damn confident that it was going to work.'

Nathan said, 'Confident? Not totally. I have to admit that when my hand was actually on fire I wished to hell that I hadn't done it, and that's an understatement. I never knew burns could hurt so much.'

Doctor Berman came around to the side of the bed. 'May I?' he said, and took hold of Nathan's hand. He examined it closely, and then he shook his head and said, 'It's remarkable. It really is. Do you think it will have the same effect on any type of burn?'

'I don't see any reason why not. And my research has indicated that it doesn't matter how old the scar tissue is. Somebody might have been burned by napalm in Vietnam, thirty years ago, but even after all this time their skin could be regenerated.'

'Remarkable.' Doctor Berman bent Nathan's fingers back. 'You have almost total flexibility, and your skin is barely even discolored, let alone scarred.'

He thought for a moment, stroking at the prickly silver stubble on his double chin. Then he said, 'One of the patients we're treating here at the moment is a five-year-old girl. She was trapped in a blazing auto wreck, and she suffered very serious burns to her face and hands. We're giving her the very best treatment we know how, but she's still going to end up badly disfigured.'

'You want to try the phoenix treatment on her?'

'I'm not sure. If it had any unwanted side-effects, I could wind up in very deep trouble.'

'Well, Doctor, I can't give you any guarantees. But it's worked on me, hasn't it, and so far I feel fine. All I can say is, if you *do* decide to try it, my team and I will give you all the help you need. *And* we'll keep it totally confidential. Except if that little girl gets healed, of course. Then we'll want all the publicity we can get.'

Doctor Berman said, 'Why don't you come take a look at her?'

Nathan climbed out of bed. He put on his slippers and Doctor Berman handed him the dark blue robe that was hanging behind the door. Together they walked along the corridor until they reached the room where Susan Harris was being treated, her face still protected by the shiny Jaloskin covering. Braydon was dozing in an armchair beside her bed, but when they walked in he opened his eyes with a jolt and said, '*Jesus!*'

'Sorry,' said Doctor Berman, laying a hand on his shoulder. 'Didn't mean to startle you.'

'No, no,' said Braydon. 'Don't worry about it. I was having this really scary dream, that's all. More of a nightmare.'

'Well, you've been under considerable stress, Mr Harris. It's not surprising that you're having nightmares. I'll prescribe something to calm you down, and you should sleep better. Meantime, I want you to meet Professor Nathan Underhill.'

'Sure. Great,' said Braydon, standing up and holding out his hand. 'Are you a patient, too?'

'Professor Underhill has been undergoing some minor procedure, that's all. We'll be discharging him tomorrow morning, most likely. But he was very interested to see what treatment we've been giving your Susan.'

Nathan approached the bed. Sukie was fast asleep, breathing deep and slow, with a slight catch in her throat. Even beneath the Jaloskin, Nathan could see how severely her face had been seared. No matter how expert it might be, conventional treatment would still leave it looking like a taut, expressionless mask. The twisted face of the doll lying beside her on the bed was a horrible parody of what she would eventually become.

'What – are you some kind of burns specialist?' asked Braydon.

Nathan nodded, and then turned around. 'You could say that, sir. I'm so sorry for what's happened to your little girl. But I know that she's being given the best possible care here at Temple. Doctor Berman here is something of a genius when it comes to burns.'

'Thanks, Professor,' said Braydon. 'Thanks, Doctor Berman.'

'By the way, Mr Harris,' said Nathan. 'What was your nightmare about? You practically jumped out of your skin when we came in here.'

Braydon gave a dismissive flap of his hand. 'Ah, nothing. It was just like a nightmare that Sukie always has. I must have been thinking about it, that's all, and when I fell asleep I started to have the same nightmare myself.'

'OK.'

'It was all about these huge shadowy creatures flying through the sky. Like dragons, you know? And they were making this terrible screaming noise. Sukie calls them Spooglies. For some reason they scared the living crap out of me, excuse my language.'

'I think they would have scared the living crap out of me, too,' said Nathan. 'Make sure that Doctor Berman gives you that Rx. Nightmares like that you can do without.'

They said goodbye to Braydon and went back out into the corridor.

'Well?' asked Doctor Berman. 'What do you think?'

Nathan said, 'I can't give you any guarantees, but I think there's every chance that the phoenix treatment will give young Sukie her face back, just as it was.'

'So – if I agreed to go ahead with it – how soon could you call in your associates?'

'I can arrange for them to give her the first injection tomorrow morning, early. Do you want to say seven a.m.?'

'Very well. Seven a.m. I just hope I know what I'm letting myself in for.'

'Fame and fortune, Doctor, with any luck.' He lifted his left hand and said, 'See? You have my hand on it.'

NINETEEN
Thursday, 11:37 p.m.

Nathan was nearly asleep himself when he heard the door of his room open, and somebody step quietly inside. It didn't disturb him. The nurses came in to check up on him at least twice during the night. But after more than a minute, he realized that whoever it was, they still hadn't left.

He lifted his head from the pillow. At first he couldn't see anyone, but then he gradually began to make out the dark shape of somebody sitting in the armchair on the opposite side of the room. He could smell a grassy aftershave, too.

He reached across and switched on his bedside lamp.

'*Shit*,' he said, and he jumped almost as violently as Braydon Harris had when they had startled him awake from his nightmare.

Sitting with his legs crossed and a sloping smile on his face was Theodor Zauber, dressed entirely in black – black three-piece suit, black silk shirt, black necktie, black polished shoes. His hands were steepled as if he were about to deliver a lecture, or say a prayer. The bedside lamp was reflected in both lenses of his spectacles.

'What the hell are *you* doing here?' Nathan demanded.

'Please do not overexcite yourself, Professor Underhill,' said Theodor Zauber. 'I am sure that you have suffered quite enough trauma in the past twenty-four hours.'

'How did you get past security?'

'Ah, that. You know that my late father taught me the arts of thaumaturgy. I can pass through any security and nobody sees me. You remember Obi-Wan Kenobi in *Star Wars*?'

'What do you want? I thought I made it pretty damn crystal clear when you came around to my house that I didn't want anything to do with you and your gargoyles.'

'I know what you did, Professor. I know that you deliberately burned yourself. I also know that you have achieved a miraculous recovery.'

'Who told you that?'

Theodor Zauber tapped the side of his nose with his fingertip. 'Like I said, I am a thaumaturge. People will willingly talk to me without realizing who they are talking to and what they are saying.'

Nathan said, 'Great.' The last thing he needed right now was Theodor Zauber trying to cajole him into helping him. His encounters with Theodor's father had taught him a healthy respect for alchemy and the so-called magical spells that were devised by medieval sorcerers. Without the instructions contained in *Kitab Al-Ajahr, The Book of Stones,* he could never have recreated a phoenix. Although he rarely said so at zoological conventions, he believed that modern scientists could learn a great deal from the dark arts practiced in the Middle Ages.

But it was almost midnight, and he had enough on his plate with his own experiments. More than that, he didn't like Theodor Zauber. He had too much self-esteem, just like his father. And, just like his father, he seemed to have no regard whatsoever for other people's lives. If a few people die in the course of this experiment, so what? The outcome will be worth it for mankind as a whole.

'I think you need to leave now,' Nathan told him. 'I don't want to discuss this any further. Not now, not ever.'

'Ah, but you must,' Theodor Zauber retorted. 'I have reached a critical stage now with my gargoyles and I urgently need your expertise.'

'What gargoyles?'

'The many gargoyles that I have in my possession.'

'What? I thought you said that they were all stored under the Eastern State Penitentiary, in the vaults.'

'Until February of this year, they were, yes. But then the board of directors wanted to clear most of them out so that they could open a new exhibition area. They sought tenders to remove them, and my bid was successful. I now have more than a hundred of them in premises of my own.'

'You're kidding me.'

'Not at all, Professor. It is the most extraordinary collection of gargoyles that you have ever seen. From France, from Germany, from Poland. They are all gathered together, frozen in time, waiting for the moment when they can be brought back to life.'

'So what exactly do you want *me* to do?'

Theodor Zauber stood up and walked across to the window. 'I have been attempting, perhaps rashly, to bring them back to life myself, using a formula devised by Artephius for reversing the process of petrification. To turn the gargoyles into stone, he used his "secret fire". To change them back, he mixed a liquid he called "quenching water".'

'So you've been trying to mix your own "quenching water"? But no luck, huh? That's too bad, Mr Zauber. I'm sorry you got nowhere with it. Maybe you should take up something else for a living, like stage hypnotism. You seem to be pretty good at that.'

'No,' said Theodor Zauber. 'The whole point is that I *have* had success. I have already brought several gargoyles back to life. They can walk, they can feed, they can articulate their feelings in cries and screams. They can *fly*.'

Nathan sat up straight. 'Is this some kind of hoax, Mr Zauber? If it is, I don't find it very rib-tickling, I'm afraid.'

'Why would I tell you anything but the truth, Professor? Besides, don't they always say that we Germans have no sense of humor?'

'You're trying to convince me that you have actually succeeded in breathing life back into a creature made of stone?'

'You don't have to take my word for it, Professor. You can see for yourself.'

With that, Theodor Zauber tugged the cord that drew back the blinds. Nathan's room was on the top floor, and out of the window he could see the ten-story building opposite, which was the physiotherapy wing. Most of the building was in darkness, although a pattern of windows was still lit.

'What am I supposed to be looking at?' he asked.

Theodor Zauber pointed upward. 'The roof. Come closer, Professor. You won't be able to see anything from over there.'

Nathan hesitated, but then he swung his legs off the bed and walked across to the window. To his discomfort, Theodor Zauber laid his hand on his shoulder, as if they were old friends.

'There, Professor. Do you see it, sitting right on the very edge of the roof, next to that satellite dish?'

Nathan could see it quite clearly – a silhouette that looked like one of the gargoyles perched on the steeples of Notre-Dame cathedral in Paris. It had a hunched back, with dragon-like wings folded over it, and stubby horns, and a curved beak.

'So how did you manage to get *that* baby up there?' he asked Theodor Zauber. 'If that's a real gargoyle, and not a Styrofoam replica, it must weigh all of half a ton.'

'I told you. I brought it back to life. It *flew* up there.'

Nathan peered at the silhouette more intently. 'It's not moving. If it flew up there, I'm a Dutchman. This *is* a hoax, isn't it?'

'It is not moving, Professor, because it is waiting for me to give it permission to go looking for what it needs. I brought it back to life. I am its master.'

Nathan turned away from the window, shaking his head. 'What kind of a sucker do you take me for, Mr Zauber? Now – please. I'd very much appreciate it if you went, and let me get some badly-needed sleep.'

'No, please! Come back here. You *must* see this. I promise you that you will never forget it.'

Nathan took a deep breath. 'Very well,' he said. 'But make it quick, whatever it is, and then I want you to go.'

He rejoined Theodor Zauber at the window. The gargoyle was still crouching exactly where it had been before, motionless.

'Look down there,' said Theodor Zauber, and pointed to the hospital parking lot ten stories below. There were only twenty or thirty cars parked in it tonight, and the only people that Nathan could see were two hospital orderlies standing in a dark corner between the buildings having a surreptitious smoke. The tips of their cigarettes glowed red in the shadows.

'OK, what is it you wanted to show me?' asked Nathan.

Theodor Zauber turned the handle and opened the window as far as the safety catch would allow, which was only about two inches. Nathan could feel the cool night breeze blowing in.

'As I told you, I have reached a critical stage with my gargoyles. I can use the "quenching water" to turn them back into living flesh, and a static electrical charge to start their hearts beating again, just as Artephius would have done. So far I have succeeded with four of them, including this one you see sitting on the rooftop opposite. And – as I explained, they can walk and they can feed and they can scream and they can fly.

'The problem is that after quite a short time, they rapidly start to transmute back into stone. At my first attempt, only an hour passed before this started to happen. The next two took a little longer, but they still suffered the same fate. The "quenching water" reanimates them very quickly, but the effect is only temporary, and I cannot find a way to overcome this problem. Not with alchemy, anyhow.'

'I see,' said Nathan. 'So this puts paid to your idea of turning terminally ill people into stone and bringing them back to life again when a cure's been discovered. Pity. In its way, it was a very cool idea. Now, is that it? Because I'm dying to get back into bed.'

Theodor Zauber turned to stare at him. Behind his spectacles his eyes were as cold as two pebbles found on a Baltic beach in winter.

'There *is* a way that a gargoyle can stop itself from transmuting back into stone – or at least postpone the process. Artephius himself wrote about it. He called it "the baptism of blood". If the gargoyle can devour a human heart every three or four hours – a living heart, which is still beating – then it can carry on living indefinitely.'

'Erm . . . slight problem there,' said Nathan. 'Where are you going to find an almost endless supply of beating human hearts?'

'The whole world is crowded with beating human hearts, Professor. But I am not seriously talking about feeding my gargoyles on them. I am simply saying that – knowing this – it might help us to find a way to stabilize their physiology, once I have turned them back into living flesh.

'The problem for me is that I do not have the expertise to do this. Of all the scientists in all the world, the only one who could do such a thing – the only one who understands how mythical creatures can be brought back to sustainable life – the only one who believes it is possible, is you.'

Nathan said, 'There's a much simpler solution, Mr Zauber.'

'And that is . . .?'

'That is for you to abandon this screwball research altogether, before somebody gets seriously hurt, or even killed. At some point you'll have to petrify a living person, but if you can't *un*-petrify them, they'll wind up being a statue for ever.'

'How can I abandon it? It is the future of medicine! It is the future of mankind! You persisted with your gryphon and your phoenix experiments even when it seemed as if there was no hope for them! Now you have reached your moment of triumph, and so will I, if you help me! I can *never* give this up!'

'Read my lips,' said Nathan. 'I-am-not-going-to-help-you. Period.'

. 'I can pay you handsomely, Professor. When my father died, he left me a great deal of money. And now that Schiller have cut off your funds—'

'*No*,' Nathan repeated. 'I think your concept is extraordinary, as a concept, but I can't see any way of taking it forward without the risk of multiple fatalities. This isn't Nazi Germany, Mr Zauber. You can't conduct life-threatening experiments on living people. This is twenty-first-century America, where every life is held to be equally valuable, no matter how poor you are or how sick you are or how old you are.'

Theodor Zauber continued to stare at him for a few seconds with those Baltic pebble eyes. Then, without warning, he turned back toward the window and let out a harsh, high-pitched scream, more like an angry animal than a man.

Immediately, the gargoyle crouched on the roof of the physio-therapy building swiveled its head and shook out its wings. Nathan had been so sure that it was a statue that he felt a thrill of shock.

'*Fliegen*!' screamed Theodor Zauber. '*Finden Sie Ihre Fest*! *Das ist ihr Meister sprechen*! *Finden Sie Ihre Fest*!'

'What the hell are you doing?' Nathan shouted at him, snatching at his sleeve.

Theodor Zauber twisted himself away. '*Fliegen*!' he screamed, one more time. Then he turned to Nathan with his voice shaking and spit flying from his lips, 'I am going to bring back these gargoyles to life, Professor, whatever it takes, and if you refuse to help me to do it safely then damn the consequences.'

'Jesus! And I thought your old man was crazy!'

'I am not crazy, Professor! I am determined. We can learn from the past but we cannot live in the past. If we do not take risks, if we do not make sacrifices, we will all die, eventually, even if we look as if we are still living and breathing.'

Nathan looked out of the window. The gargoyle had now raised itself up on its legs and stretched its wings to their widest extent.

It lifted its head and let out a high, eerie howl. Then it launched itself into the air, its wings beating in long, steady strokes. Even though the window was open only two inches, Nathan could hear the repetitive *flap, flap, flap* as it gradually gained height.

It flew up almost vertically until it was hovering at least two hundred feet above the parking lot. It kept itself aloft with languid beats of its wings, and every now and then it let out another howl.

'So you've managed to bring a stone gargoyle to life,' said Nathan. 'I'm impressed. In fact I'm *very* impressed. But I'm still not going to help you.'

'What if you had no choice?'

'But I do have a choice, and my choice is no.'

He couldn't keep his eyes off the gargoyle, with its horns and its bulging eyes and its curved beak. It was like something out of a nightmare. In fact it was like something out of Braydon Harris' nightmare. '*It was all about these huge dark creatures flying through the sky. Like dragons, you know? And they were making this terrible screaming noise. Sukie calls them Spooglies.*'

Theodor Zauber said, 'Very well. I did not want to do this, Professor, but regrettably you leave me no option.'

Again, he screamed out, '*Finden Sie Ihre Fest!*' and as soon as he did so, the gargoyle half folded its wings and peeled off head first to the left as if it were diving off a high diving board. It swooped and looped, heading downward toward the parking lot. It looked as if it was taking its time, but it seemed to know exactly where it was heading. Nathan saw it briefly flicker against some of the lighted windows in the physiotherapy building, but then it disappeared into the shadows.

He heard a faint, echoing thump. He looked at Theodor Zauber but Theodor Zauber shrugged and said nothing. He pressed his forehead against the window to try and see what was happening below them in the parking lot, but it was too dark. After a few seconds, he saw the gargoyle climbing up into the air again, its wings plunging up and down. It tilted off to the right, over West Ontario Street, and for a split second he saw it silhouetted against the street lights. Then it was gone.

'What just happened?' demanded.

Still Theodor Zauber said nothing.

'*What just happened?*' Nathan yelled at him.

'The consequences of your decision, that is what happened,' said Theodor Zauber. 'The gargoyle is now a living creature, *ja*? And like all living creatures, it will do anything to survive. Just as you will. Just as your wife and your son will.'

'Are you threatening me? You'd better damn well not threaten me.'

'I am repeating my polite invitation to you to join me in my research, Professor. At the same time I am warning you of what will happen if you continue to refuse.'

Nathan went over to his bedside table and picked up his phone. He punched zero for the operator and waited while it rang. Theodor Zauber remained where he was, watching him, still smiling that slanted, creepy smile.

'Switchboard? This is Professor Nathan Underhill in ten-twenty-two. Could you send up security, please? I have an unwanted visitor.'

'*Right away, sir.*'

Nathan folded his arms and stood facing Theodor Zauber. Neither of them spoke. Outside, Nathan could hear shouting and an ambulance siren give a single whoop. Then – after less than a minute, he could hear rubber-soled shoes squelching along the corridor.

'If you are adamant that you will not help me, Professor, I will leave you,' said Theodor Zauber. 'But I fear that you will be sorry. We have a saying in German – *ein Unglück kommt selten allein*.'

The door burst open and two security guards came in – a huge black man and a broad-shouldered white man with a shaved head.

'You got trouble, sir?' asked the black security guard.

'Yes,' said Nathan. 'This gentleman is disturbing me. I want him out of here. Now.'

Theodor Zauber gave Nathan a mocking salute and then carefully edged his way past the two security guards and out of the door. He was close enough for them to touch him and yet they didn't seem to be aware that he was there.

The black security guard looked around and said, 'What gentleman, sir? I don't see no gentleman.'

Nathan gave an exaggerated shake of his head, as if he had just woken up. 'I'm sorry. I apologize. I must have been having a nightmare.'

The black security guard was about to say something when his radio beeped, and a panicky voice crackled, '*Newton? You and Bradley'd better get your asses down to the parking lot, ASAP.*'

'What's happened?' he asked.

'It's a nightmare, that's what's happened.'

The two security guards looked at Nathan in complete bewilderment. Then, without saying anything else, they hurried off.

TWENTY

Friday, 6:17 a.m.

B y the time a wan gray dawn began to smear itself across the sky, Jenna had been at the crime scene for over two hours. She was wearing her thick brown quilted parka and her Ugg boots, but she was still feeling the cold, and she shuffled her feet as she waited for Dan to bring her a cup of hot coffee.

As it grew lighter, the halogen lamps around the parking lot were switched off, one by one, and the crime scene looked less like a movie set and more like the back yard of a South Street slaughterhouse. The remains of the hospital orderly were still strewn across the asphalt, but the forensic team had finished photographing them and marking the location of whatever entrails they could identify.

Dan came out of the rear entrance of the hospital carrying three cups of coffee. He was wearing a droopy khaki anorak and baggy black sweat pants, and his eyes were puffy from lack of sleep.

'Ed!' called Jenna. 'Coffee's up!'

Ed Freiburg came over, tugging off his latex gloves. 'What?' he said. 'No donuts?'

Dan handed him and Jenna a cup of coffee each and then rummaged in the pocket of his anorak and produced a paper bag. 'You think I'd forget donuts? That's the first thing they teach you at detective school. Buy coffee. Then buy donuts. When you've finished drinking the coffee and eating the donuts, then – and *only* then – examine the evidence and interview witnesses.'

Jenna popped the lid off her cappuccino and sucked at the froth. 'This is the exact same scenario as the last three fatalities, yes?'

Ed sniffed, and nodded. 'Pretty much. He was struck at a steeper angle than the others, but I don't think there's any doubt. I'd say that the back of his shoulders took all of the initial impact. His head flew forward, into the angle between the two buildings, where it was fielded by one of the bicycle racks. The rest of his body was compressed into the ground with such force that he literally exploded.'

'What about his heart? Did you find that yet?'

'Not yet. But it's still too early to say for sure. The other vics were hit at such a shallow angle that their internal organs were all strung out in a long line. This guy was *squished*. You know, like hitting a tomato with your fist.

He looked up at the surrounding buildings. 'I'd say that what-ever did this, it came down almost vertical from a considerable height. It would have had to, to build up so much momentum.'

'So – any preliminary opinions?' asked Jenna. 'Another one of your homely angels, maybe?'

'Not saying it was, not saying it wasn't. But it weighed a heck of a lot, and it must have been traveling at close to terminal velocity. Two things for sure, though. A, it was alive, and b, it could fly. If it had been an inanimate object, like a grand piano, or a statue, it would still be here. And if it couldn't fly, it would have been killed or seriously injured on impact, and it would also still be here.' He bit into his donut. '*Yecch*, cinnamon. I really hate cinnamon.'

'It's been proven that cinnamon is good for the memory,' said Jenna. 'It also relieves arthritis.'

'I still hate it. I'd rather forget everything I ever knew and have agonizing pains in my knees. Did you interview the witness yet?'

Jenna checked her wristwatch. 'I'm going to try in a couple of minutes. He was in too much shock when I first tried to talk to him.'

'Yeah, well, not surprised,' said Ed, looking across at the bloody torso that was lying on top of its folded legs as if it were praying to get its head back. 'How are you going to brief the media?'

'Don't know yet. That's up to Captain Wilson. So far we've told them that the two guys who were killed on top of the Nectarine Tower were probably hit by a helicopter, and that James Hallam Junior was more than likely struck by a speeding semi. This guy – I have no idea. But "grand piano falling from the sky" – that isn't a bad suggestion. Squished by a Steinway.'

Once they had finished their coffees, Jenna and Dan pushed their way through the revolving doors into the hospital reception area. One of the hospital administrators was waiting for them – a large, flustered woman in a tight powder-blue suit. She had a wildly fraying bun of dyed red hair and bright crimson lipstick that looked as if she had applied it in the dark.

'This is so *awful*,' she said. 'Do you know how it happened yet? It wasn't negligence by the hospital, was it?'

'No, you don't have to worry about that,' said Jenna. 'Nobody's going to be suing you for reckless endangerment. How's our witness? Is he ready to answer a few questions yet?'

'I think so. I'll take you along to the recovery room. If you'll just come with me, please.'

She bustled over to the elevators. Jenna looked at Dan and raised her eyebrows and then they both followed her. As they went up to the fifth floor, the woman lowered her voice and said, '*So* . . . do you know how poor Eduardo was killed?'

'We're working on it,' said Jenna. 'We have to wait for the ME's report before we can say anything officially.'

'You can't even give me a *hint*?'

'I'm afraid not. And we'd rather you left the media to us. There are some details that we don't want to be made public just yet awhile.'

'Really? Such as?'

Jenna puckered her mouth and said nothing.

'Oh, of course!' said the woman, pretending to pull a zipper across her lips. 'Mum's the word!'

She led them into a private room where the surviving hospital orderly was resting on a bed – shoeless, but fully dressed in bright blue scrubs. He was Hispanic, about forty years old, but already balding, even though he had a heavy black moustache and stubble.

'Hi there,' said Jenna, producing her shield. 'Detective Pullet,

Ninth Division. This is Detective Rubik. Do you mind if we ask you some questions about your friend Eduardo?'

The orderly looked back at her listlessly. 'I don't see what happen,' he said, hoarsely. 'It is too dark. It is too quick.'

'What were you and Eduardo doing, out in the parking lot?'

'Nothing. Just for fresh air.'

'We found fresh cigarette butts on the ground. Were they yours?'

'We are not permitted to smoke in hospital vicinity.'

'I won't tell anybody if you don't. Were they yours, those cigarette butts?'

'*Sí*,' he admitted. 'We go only for one cigarette. We finish them, and we are ready to go back inside. Eduardo is telling me he have fight that morning with his wife. She hit him with a skillet, on his head. And just as he say this, I hear screaming sound, *ow-ow-ow-ow-ow*, and then *bang*!'

'Bang?'

'Something is drop on top of Eduardo, and he blow up like bomb. Just blow up, *bang,* and blood is spray everywhere, and his head fly away.'

'Did you see what this something was, that dropped on top of him?'

The orderly shook his head. 'I don't know. It is very big. *Enorme. Como una tienda negra grande.*'

'Like a big black tent,' Dan translated.

'*Sí*,' said the orderly. 'Like when a big tent fall down and you are bury inside. I hear screaming sound, *ow-ow-ow-ow-ow*, and also sound like thunder. I feel wind, too. *Woof*, and then *woof*, and then *woof*, and then it is gone, and Eduardo—'

He tried to carry on, but his eyes filled with tears and his lips quivered with grief.

Jenna took hold of his hand and squeezed it. 'Tell me, that screaming sound, that wasn't Eduardo screaming?'

The orderly shook his head.

'So a big black tent came screaming down and hit Eduardo so hard that he blew up like a bomb?'

The orderly nodded.

Jenna stood up. 'Thank you for your help,' she said. 'You don't mind if I maybe talk to you again when you're feeling a little better?'

'Of course,' said the orderly. He wiped the tears from his eyes with his hairy forearm.

Jenna and Dan went down to reception, where the hospital administrator was still waiting for them. As soon as they stepped out of the elevator, she came hurrying up to them, her little fists clenched.

'I thought you ought to know that there was a security alert just before this tragic incident,' she told them. 'I can't tell you if it was relevant or not, but you never know, do you? Jessica always says that the devil's in the details.'

'Jessica?'

'You know. Jessica Fletcher, in *Murder, She Wrote.*'

'Oh, OK,' said Jenna. 'Good old Jessica. So – anyhow, what exactly was the nature of this security alert?'

'One of the patients in the burns unit complained that there was an unwelcome visitor in his room. This was at eleven forty yesterday evening. We sent two of our security guards to check, but when they got there, there was no sign of anybody except the patient himself. He tried to persuade the security guards that he must have been having a nightmare, but they were very dubious about that, because he's a very intelligent man, very rational. They think that there might have been an unwelcome visitor in his room, but for some unknown reason the patient changed his mind and decided not to report it.'

'And what do *you* think? You watch a lot of *Murder, She Wrote.*'

The woman blinked rapidly. 'I really don't know. But if there *was* an unwelcome visitor in this patient's room, why was he unwelcome? And how did he get in – because there is no record of any visitors for this particular patient in the visitors' log. More to the point, how did he get *out,* because nobody saw him.'

'You should have been a PI,' Jenna told her. 'Can you tell me the patient's name, please? I think it might be a good idea if we go talk to him.'

'Professor Nathan Underhill. He's in ten-twenty-two.'

'Underhill? Why do I have the feeling that I've heard of him?'

'He's a zoologist. Quite famous, as a matter of fact.'

'All right, then. Let's see what this quite famous zoologist has to say for himself.'

*   *   *

Nathan was already dressed and sitting in his armchair drinking black tea when Jenna and Dan knocked on his door.

'Professor Underhill?' said Jenna. 'We're police detectives. Do you think we could have a moment of your time?'

'Police detectives?' Nathan asked her. He put down his cup and stood up. 'Does this have anything to do with what happened last night? I heard that somebody got themselves killed, down in the parking lot.'

'That's right. Somebody got themselves killed. To tell you the truth, somebody got themselves *very* killed.'

'I'm sorry to hear it. What happened?'

'Well, that's what my partner and I are looking into. One of the hospital administrators tells us that you called for security, round about the same time this fatality took place.'

'I – *ah* – yes. I did. But I don't see the relevance.'

'We're just trying to build up a picture of everything that occurred last night. It helps us to place where everybody was, and if anybody was likely to have witnessed anything meaningful.'

Nathan would have done anything to be able to tell this detective that he had seen a living gargoyle diving off the roof of the building opposite, and that its creator had been here, right here in this room, making threats against him. But she would simply think that he was delusional, and worse than that, it could put his family in danger. Theodor Zauber had staged this grisly performance to show Nathan that he was completely ruthless, and that he would allow nobody to deter him from getting what he wanted.

Apart from that, even if he explained to her what had happened, how was she going to *find* Theodor Zauber – a man who was capable of walking past the noses of two security guards without them seeing him?

Nathan said, 'I was asleep. I thought that there was an intruder in my room, but I guess I must have been dreaming. My doctor has had me on morphine for the past twenty-four hours, and the dream was so totally vivid that I believed it was real. That's why I called security.'

'Did you call security before you woke up, or after?'

'Well – after, of course.'

'But when you woke up you must have realized that there was nobody there.'

'No – it was dark and I was still convinced that there was somebody here. They could have been hiding behind the drapes, or under the bed.'

'Under the bed?'

Nathan shrugged. 'Isn't that where boogeymen always hide – under the bed?'

Jenna wasn't amused. 'Was it anybody in particular, or just some unknown intruder?'

'It was dark.'

'But you felt threatened?'

'Wouldn't *you* feel threatened, if you thought that there was somebody in your bedroom in the middle of the night?'

'I don't know. I think it would depend entirely on who it was. If it was George Clooney, maybe not.'

Jenna went to the window and peered down into the parking lot, ten stories below.

'You didn't see or hear anything unusual?'

Nathan said nothing. Withholding information from the police was difficult enough, but he found it almost impossible to tell an outright lie.

'No screams?' asked Jenna. 'No thumping noises? Nobody shouting out for help? After all, the window's open.'

Still Nathan said nothing. Jenna came up close to him and stared at him intently.

'What is it?' she said. 'What are you not telling me?'

He turned his face away. 'I'm sorry,' he told her. 'I can't help you.'

'I have a feeling that you can, but for some very obscure reason you just don't want to.'

Dan's cell warbled. He flipped it open and said, 'Rubik.' Then, 'OK. Sure. OK. We'll be down there directly.' He closed his cell and said, 'Captain Wilson's arrived. He's going to make some kind of statement to the media, and he wants us to brief him first.'

Jenna pulled a face. 'OK,' she said. 'We'll leave it like that for now, Professor Underhill. But a man was brutally killed here last night, and it wasn't an accident, and I intend to find out how it happened, and who was responsible. Or *what*.'

TWENTY-ONE
Friday, 8:47 a.m.

When Aarif and Kavita stepped out of the elevator on the tenth floor, they found Nathan and Doctor Berman and three young interns already waiting for them.

Aarif was sporting a red and white sweater with a reindeer pattern all around it, while Kavita was wearing a very short black wool dress and black rock-chick boots.

'It's not Christmas yet, Aarif,' Nathan told him.

'I am a Muslim, Professor. To me, a reindeer is only an animal, *rangifer tarandus*, so I can wear a reindeer sweater all the year round. But for this little girl with the burned face, maybe today *will* be Christmas.'

He held up his black medical case, and smiled.

Kavita said, 'Torchy was much calmer this morning when we took the stem cell sample. He seems to have gotten used to it. There's something else about him, too. His feathers are beginning to change color. He's looking much brighter. And his beak is turning pink.'

'Maybe he's going to look like Voltaire's description of a phoenix after all,' said Nathan. 'I can't wait to see him again.'

'Show me your hand,' said Kavita. 'Is it all healed?'

Nathan held out his left hand, and then held out his right hand for comparison. It was now impossible to tell which hand had been so badly burned. Kavita took hold of both hands and looked up into Nathan's eyes.

'I admire you so much, Professor. You know that I have nothing but respect for what you did. It was in such a great scientific tradition. But please don't hurt yourself again. Not for *any* reason. Every time you hurt yourself, you hurt me, too – more than you know.'

Nathan nodded, and said, 'OK. I promise.' He wasn't quite sure what Kavita was trying to say to him, but he could sense that her feelings for him went beyond the formality of professor and research assistant. He was flattered, but also slightly disturbed. Kavita was extremely pretty, but he was extremely married.

Doctor Berman led them into Susan Harris' room. Sukie was sleeping, although her lips were moving as if she were talking to somebody in her dreams.

Nathan said, 'We'll inject the phoenix's stem cells into her *pterygoideus externus*, her external jaw-muscles, which is the nearest we can get to the burns on her face. One injection into each jaw muscle now, and then another in twelve hours' time. She'll probably need a third injection tomorrow morning, but at the moment it's too soon to be sure of that.'

Doctor Berman nodded. 'OK. But I want everybody here to be aware that I am personally taking full responsibility for this procedure. If anything goes wrong – if the patient's condition deteriorates because of what we are doing here today, then the buck stops with me.'

'You trust me that much?' asked Nathan.

'I examined your hand when they brought you in here, Professor, and I was convinced that you were going to suffer the most serious scarring and contracture, and that the burns to your first web would limit thumb abduction to the point where your left hand was virtually useless. But look at it now. No scars, ninety percent flexibility.' Doctor Berman looked away and said, 'Don't quote me. Any of you – you ever *dare* to quote me. But you've convinced me, Professor Underhill. Stem cells from mythical creatures? I'm a believer.'

Suddenly, her voice muffled by her oxygen mask, Sukie blurted out, '*No! Don't look up! Don't look up!*' She flapped her hands as if she were trying to swat wasps away.

Kavita took hold of her hand and said, 'It's all right, sweet thing. Everything's going to be fine. You just hold on a little longer.'

'*But they're up there! They're up in the sky!*'

Nathan looked at Doctor Berman, but Doctor Berman simply shrugged and said, 'Delirium. It's the shock, and the physical trauma, and the painkillers.'

But now Sukie was reaching up with her bandaged hands and trying to pull off her oxygen mask. '*They're up there! Hundreds and hundreds of them! They're up in the sky and they have tails and claws and they're coming to kill us! And they're so greedy!*'

'Who are you talking about, honey?' Nathan asked her, trying to calm her down. 'Who is it exactly, up in the sky?'

Sukie lay silent for a moment, shivering and sniffing, like a crack addict brought in from the street. Nathan looked across at Doctor Berman and said, 'What? How much did you give her? She's out there on Planet X.'

Doctor Berman checked Sukie's vital signs and then bent over her bed with his stethoscope, and listened to her heartbeat.

'*Well*?' said Nathan. He knew that he might sound aggressive, but he didn't want to inject Sukie with Torchy's stem cells if there was any risk of heart failure or other complications.

Something else disturbed him: the way she had screamed *they're up in the sky and they have tails and claws and they're coming to kill us*! It reminded him of an engraving by the eighteenth-century artist Gustav Doré that he had come across during his research of mythical creatures. It showed twelve flying demons called Malebranche from Dante's *Divine Comedy*. Malebranche meant 'Evil Claws' and the demons were led by Malacoda, which meant 'Evil Tail'.

Dante was said to have invented the Malebranche, but Nathan had suspected from the first time he had seen Doré's illustration that he had based them on gargoyles, from the days when gargoyles had flown in flocks across the skies of Europe, swooping on sheep and cattle, and – according to Theodor Zauber, anyway – on tens of thousands of unsuspecting men, women and children.

A living gargoyle had been perched here at Temple University Hospital only a few hours ago. Had Sukie somehow sensed its presence? Had her father, too? If they had, then *how*?

Doctor Berman stood up and shook his head. 'She's fine. Heart rate's just over one hundred, which is a little high, but her respiration is twenty-two, which is acceptable, and her blood pressure is in the fifty-fifth percentile, which is also acceptable.'

Nathan looked down at Sukie, with her shiny Jaloskin face. 'You're happy to go ahead, then?'

'She might be a little upset, emotionally, but physically she's fine.'

'All right then, doctor. So long as you think we're doing the right thing.'

Aarif took out a hypodermic syringe and injected Sukie in the left side of her jaw. She had quietened down now, and she didn't even flinch. He took out a second hypodermic and injected stem cells into her right jaw muscle.

'Well, then, that's it,' said Nathan. 'All we can do now is wait. I'm going to go home and change and have something to eat. Then I'm going to the lab to take a look at Torchy. But I'll be back in a couple of hours to see how she's progressing.'

Kavita said, 'Would you like me to drive you home, Professor? I have my car here.'

'That's OK, Kavita. It's way out of your way. I'll take a cab.'

'It's no trouble, really. Besides, I would like a chance to talk to you about the phoenix.'

'OK,' said Nathan. 'That's very kind of you. Appreciate it.'

As they drove northward on Wissahickon Avenue in Kavita's bright red VW Beetle, Nathan said, 'You've really been great, Kavita. You and Aarif – the work that you've been doing. There's only one word for it and that's "inspired".'

Kavita glanced across at him and smiled. 'No, Professor. You're the one who's inspired. I can't believe that Schiller tried to cut off your funding.'

'Well . . . if young Sukie gets her face back, maybe they'll change their minds.'

There was a long pause, and then Kavita said, 'It could be . . . maybe they've changed their minds already.' She was trying to sound offhand, but Nathan could detect an odd flatness in her voice.

'What are you saying? You're kidding me. Where do you get that from?'

She stopped at a red traffic signal at West Rittenhouse Street. 'Mr Kasabian promised me that he's going to talk the board again tomorrow, and see if he can persuade them to allocate us another three years' finance.'

'Ron said that? *Really*? But Ron was dead set against it.'

Kavita didn't look at him. The sun was shining through the trees beside the intersection and playing patterns across her face as if she were wearing a black lace veil.

'Ever since I came to work with you, Professor, Mr Kasabian has shown an interest in me.'

'What kind of an interest? You mean a personal interest?'

Kavita nodded. The traffic signal changed to green and she shifted into drive.

Nathan stared at her. 'I never really noticed. You mean like a *lecherous* interest?'

'Yes.'

'I don't believe it. He's the CEO, for Christ's sake. He's married, with three kids in high school.'

'I know. But that did nothing to stop him. From the very first day, he asked me almost every day to go out for a drink with him. And he kept on making suggestive remarks. "Are you wearing anything under that lab coat?" That kind of thing. He invited me to go to Seattle with him when he went to that pharmaceutical convention. He even asked me if I would come with him to Paris.'

Nathan said, 'And now all of a sudden he's changed his mind about our funding? I hope you're not going to tell me what I think you're going to tell me.'

Kavita's eyelashes were sparkling with tears. 'Professor – he was going to close down the phoenix project, for ever! If that happened, it would be a tragedy! It would mean the end of the most wonderful time I have ever had in my entire life.'

She wiped her eyes with the back of her hand, and then she said, 'I *love* the phoenix project. It's like the three of us being magicians. Every day we make something impossible become real. And we're going to bring so much good to so many suffering people. Look at that poor little girl today, with her face all burned up.

'I *love* it,' she repeated; and then she turned to Nathan and said, 'I love you, too, Professor. I love you with all of my heart. How could I lose both the project and you? I couldn't bear it.'

'Listen,' said Nathan, 'why don't you pull over here? You don't want to drive when you're upset.'

Kavita turned into West Johnson Street, a quiet suburban side street lined with trees, and parked halfway up the curb. 'I'm sorry,' she said. 'I'm so stupid.'

'You're not stupid at all,' Nathan told her. 'You're one of the brightest, cleverest research assistants I've ever had working for me. Every reading you give me, every analysis, they're always one hundred percent accurate.' He paused, and then he said, 'I know that doesn't sound very romantic, but it means that I rely on you, Kavita. I couldn't have created Torchy without you.'

Kavita pulled a crumpled Kleenex out of her sleeve. 'Look at my mascara. It's a mess now. God, I'm stupid.'

Nathan waited while she dabbed her eyes and blew her nose. Then he said, 'You still haven't told me what made Ron Kasabian change his mind about my funding.'

Kavita took a deep breath. 'Late yesterday evening, maybe ten p.m., when I was settling Torchy down for the night, Ron came into the laboratory. He told me how sorry he was that I was going to be leaving, and asked me if I would go out with him for one last drink. This time I said yes.'

'Go on,' said Nathan.

Kavita wouldn't look at him, but stared straight ahead along West Johnson Street as if she thought she recognized somebody in the distance.

'He took me to the Swann Lounge at the Four Seasons for cocktails. Well – he had a couple of Martinis but I only had one glass of white wine. We talked about the phoenix project and I told him how much it meant to me, and how upset I was that Schiller had cut off our funding.'

'And what did Ron say?'

'He said that I was a fantastic-looking girl and what a great future I had ahead of me. Maybe as a personal favor to me he could find a way to keep the phoenix project going, at least for a few months longer. Maybe he could divert some of the money that Schiller have been investing in that new denture cleanser.'

'Jesus. What a Casanova.'

Kavita gave a bitter little smile, but still didn't look at him. 'I have to say that he was completely honest about what he wanted in return. If he was going to do *me* a personal favor, then he expected me to do *him* a personal favor. Or *favors*, rather, for as long as our funding continues.'

Nathan said nothing, but waited for Kavita to finish.

'He booked a room,' she said. 'We went upstairs.' She hesitated, and turned her face away, and then she added, 'He wasn't very good.'

Nathan whacked his forehead with the heel of his hand. 'Christ almighty, Kavita! How could he have done that? How could *you* have done that?'

'Because I thought it would save the phoenix project! Because I couldn't think of any other way! Because I love you!'

'Do you know what I'm going to do? I'm going to cut off Ron Kasabian's pecker and feed it to Torchy for breakfast. What a bastard! Do you seriously think that I'm going to take any more of Schiller's money if you have to prostitute yourself for it?'

'I'm sorry,' Kavita sobbed. 'I'm so, so sorry. I thought it would make everything right. I told you I was stupid.'

Nathan took hold of her hand. 'You're not stupid, Kavita. You're super-intelligent. But sometimes super-intelligent people can't imagine the depths of moral shittitude to which people like Ron Kasabian are capable of sinking. Listen, if we can prove beyond doubt that the phoenix project works – if this little girl's face regenerates itself – then we should be able to find funding from almost anyone. Maybe even the federal government.'

She looked at him with a tear-stained face, and her mascara had run so badly she looked like Alice Cooper. 'Do you hate me? Do you think I'm worthless?'

He took her crumpled tissue and wiped her eyes. 'You made a mistake, that's all. You should never sell yourself for any reason. Not your beliefs, not your principles, not your body.'

'I'm sorry,' she repeated, dismally.

'Don't be. Here – let me drive the rest of the way home. We can both freshen up and then we can go see Torchy. And Ron Kasabian, if he's there, and tell him what we think of him. When you said he wasn't very good . . .?'

'I don't want to talk about it. I'm too ashamed of myself. But, yes. He had hardly started when he was finished.'

'OK. I'm sorry. I won't bring it up, ever again. And if I have anything to do with it, neither will he.'

TWENTY-TWO
Friday, 11:37 a.m.

G race was off-duty that morning, so while Nathan went upstairs to shower and change, she perked a pot of coffee and whipped up some of her famous egg and pepper omelets. Kavita sat on one of the kitchen stools and talked to her while she cooked. As he went upstairs, Nathan could hear her telling Grace how Torchy's plumage was beginning to shine, and how docile he had become since his fiery and bad-tempered debut.

Passing Denver's bedroom, Nathan was sure that he could hear a faint, persistent *tish-tish-tish* that sounded like music. He stopped and listened. Denver was supposed to be at school, so he must have left his iPod playing. But when Nathan opened the door, he found Denver sprawled on his bed with his earphones on, his eyes closed, punching the air in time to the AxCx song he was listening to, and mouthing the words in a high, catarrhal whine – what his friends would have called singing *a crapella*.

'*Hear the pounding, army of the night*! *The call of metal summons us tonight*! *We rule the night!*'

Nathan walked up to the side of his bed and grabbed hold of his ankle. Denver shouted out, '*Aaahh*! *Fuck!*' and sat up so quickly that his earphones were pulled out of his ears. He blinked at Nathan as if he couldn't think who he was.

'Why aren't you at school?' Nathan demanded.

'Why aren't you in hospital?' Denver retorted.

Nathan held up his hand, right in front of Denver's nose, so that Denver went cross-eyed trying to focus on it. 'I'm not in hospital because my hand is all healed already. What's your excuse?'

Denver clamped his hand to the left side of his head. 'I have a really bad earache.'

'You have a really bad earache and you're listening to that racket? Get real. You have a really bad earache because you wanted to cut your math class, and earache is one of the few ailments that nobody can tell for sure if you're faking it or not.'

'Dad – I swear to you. I have an earache. It's like this unbearable throbbing, you know? I think I got an infection in my ear when I went swimming on Monday.'

'And what does Mom say?'

'Mom said it was OK to take a day off, seeing as how it's Friday anyhow.'

'Mom is much too soft.'

'Dad, really, I'm not faking it. I promise. I feel terrible.'

'OK,' said Nathan, reluctantly. 'But it's a pity you're feeling so bad, because Kavita's downstairs.'

Denver swung his feet off the bed. 'Hey, I'm not feeling *that* bad that I can't be polite.'

Nathan smiled and shook his head. 'Go on, then. Go talk to her. Ask her about the phoenix. I won't be long. I'm just going to take a shower.'

'Dad,' said Denver, as Nathan turned to leave the room.

'What is it?'

'Do you think Kavita would go out with me? Like, on a date? I know I'm a couple of years younger than her, but you know, I think I'm quite mature for my age.'

'One day, maybe. But not today. She's been through some personal stuff recently, and I don't think she's really in the mood for dating.'

'Oh. OK. Is she OK?'

'Oh, sure. But she's only just found out that the world can be a much crappier place than she imagined. Happens to us all, eventually. It's called "disillusionment". Or "growing up".'

They ate breakfast together in the kitchen, with the sun shining across the table and lighting up the jar of marmalade like an orange lamp.

Grace said, 'I was so angry about Nathan burning himself. Spontaneity I don't mind at all. But spontaneous stupidity – that does make me mad. I get so many patients who do stupid things on the spur of the moment and end up hurting themselves really badly. My waiting room is almost like an open audition for *Jackass Four.*'

'But Professor Underhill has proved something so amazing,' said

Kavita. 'If that little girl's face regenerates . . . it's like a miracle, almost.'

'There's a kid at school,' Denver put in. 'He has these twisty purple scars all over his legs because his brother pushed a lighted firework down his pants. He's real self-conscious when he has to wear shorts. But if you could fix somebody like him, that would be great.'

'I think we can fix anybody,' said Nathan. 'In a few years' time, the phoenix treatment is going to be the standard cure for burns, worldwide, and we're all going to be very, very famous and very, very rich.'

'I thought you said you didn't get into this cryptozoology stuff for the money,' said Denver. 'I thought you said you were doing it for the good of mankind.'

'Do you want a new Mustang or not?' Nathan asked him.

When they had finished brunch, Kavita left to drive herself downtown, while Nathan stayed behind to go through his mail and talk to Grace.

'I can't believe you let Denver play hooky,' he told her. 'You know there's not a damn thing wrong with him. Earache, my ass.'

'I know there's nothing wrong with him. But didn't you ever skip school for a day, when you were his age? I know you think it's important to be strict if you're a parent. But I think you need to be indulgent, now and again. It makes your kids realize that you're human, after all. And it also makes them feel ever so slightly guilty, and where there's guilt there's chores, like taking out the trash or raking the lawn.'

'You're more devious than I thought, Doctor Underhill,' grinned Nathan, and gave her a kiss.

As he drove to the Schiller building, he listened to the local news. The lead item was the killing of Eduardo Sanchez Delgado in the parking lot of Temple University Hospital.

'Police are still declining to commit themselves as to the exact cause of Mr Delgado's death. His fellow orderly was the only eyewitness, and according to police he is still in shock and unable to give a coherent description of what happened. However, several hospital patients and employees who saw Mr Delgado's body after the incident say that it appeared that he had been crushed, as if by a very heavy object.

'Detective Jenna Pullet, who is leading the investigation, appealed for anybody who was in the vicinity of the incident to contact her.

'"*Any detail, no matter how trivial or unimportant you may think it is, can assist us in determining how Mr Delgado met his death. If you saw anything out of the ordinary, or heard anything unusual, please contact me on two-one-five six-eight-six thirty-ninety. Your call will be kept strictly confidential.*"

'Detective Pullet was asked by our correspondent if the death of Mr Delgado could be connected in any way with the stone statues that have apparently been falling from the sky on to various locations around Philly over the past week. As we reported earlier, a third statue, almost intact, appeared to have been dropped into the wetlands at Bartram's Gardens sometime during Wednesday night or early Thursday morning.

'"*Our forensic teams are still examining the statue that was recovered from Bartram's Gardens and reassembling the fragments of the statues from the Convent of Divine Love and Woodlands Cemetery. I'm afraid that it's far too early for us to make a positive identification of any of them.*"

'"*And still no clue where they might have come from?*"

'"*Not so far. But as soon as we find out for sure – don't worry, you'll be the first to know.*"'

Henry, the Super, gave Nathan a salute as he walked into the lobby of the Schiller building.

'Top of the mornin', Professor! Real glad to see you got your hand fixed up so quick! That was some kind of amazin'.'

'Hi there, Henry. How's it going?'

'Just fine, so long as I stay well clear of that crazy pigeon of yours. I swear that bird would peck out my eyes and have them for breakfast, given half a chance.'

'Really? Still? Kavita told me that Torchy had really chilled out.'

'With *her*, maybe. But no way with nobody else. A couple of building contractors come in yesterday afternoon to give us an estimate for redecoratin' your laboratory, but that bird of yours made such an all-fired fuss, a-screamin' and a-flappin', they came hot-footin' out of there like their asses was alight. The sooner you can find a new roost for him, the happier I'm goin' to be.'

'Well, between you and me, Henry, that shouldn't be too long now.'

'Praise the Lord, Professor. But welcome back, all the same.'

Nathan crossed over to the elevator and went up to his laboratory. Most of the debris from the holocaust of Torchy's birthing had been cleared away now, including the twisted steel bars of his cage. Aarif was hunched over one of the benches, peering at stem cell samples with his microscope. He was wearing a red knitted hat and an ankle-length *djellaba*, in maroon wool. Kavita meanwhile was standing in front of Torchy's cage. The door was open and she was taking readings of Torchy's heart rate and respiration and other vital signs, and scraping up faeces for chemical analysis.

Torchy himself had grown by at least a third since Nathan had last seen him – and Kavita had been right about the transformation of his beak and his plumage. In fact, she hadn't done him justice. His beak had now flushed a deep rosebud pink, and the feathers around his neck were gleaming in crimsons and yellows and iridescent greens, while the feathers on his body were gradually turning into burnished gold. His tail looked like a fine spray of yellow broom.

Nathan approached the cage and as he did so Torchy cocked his head on one side, and shuffled his claws uneasily on his perch.

'Take it real easy, Professor,' said Kavita. 'He doesn't remember who you are, and he's very suspicious of strangers.'

'OK,' said Nathan, lifting up both hands to show Torchy that he meant him no harm. 'No need to get edgy, son. I'm your father, after all.'

Without looking up from his microscope, Aarif said, 'That is no guarantee. Whenever *my* father comes into the room, he always makes *me* feel edgy. I know he loves me, but he is such a demanding man. In Egypt we say that a father curses his son, but is just as angry with anybody who says amen.'

'Amen to that,' said Nathan.

Kavita held up a test tube. 'I've already extracted the stem cell sample for this evening's injections. So – just as soon as I've finished all of these readings, we'll be ready to go.'

'That's great,' Nathan told her, and laid his hand on her shoulder. Instantly, the phoenix let out a shrill, furious screech and beat his wings, so that his cage was filled with a storm of golden feathers. Still screeching, he threw himself toward the open door, but Kavita managed to slam it shut and latch it before he could burst out of it.

'Please, Professor – please back off!' Kavita begged him. 'Torchy is so-o-o protective.'

'You're not kidding, are you? It looks like you've got yourself a guard-phoenix there. He hasn't hurt himself, has he, crashing against his cage like that?'

'Scavenger hawks are known for the fierceness with which they defend their young,' said Aarif. 'I have heard of men who have been blinded by scavenger hawks when they accidentally came too close to their nests.'

Nathan approached the cage again, and the phoenix ruffled its feathers and warbled in its throat as if it were warning him off. 'The question is,' he said, 'what are we going to do with Torchy if we have to close this project down?'

'That's a question for later,' said a deep, harsh voice. 'For the time being, it looks like the project is staying active.'

TWENTY-THREE
Friday, 1:26 p.m.

Nathan turned around. Ron Kasabian had walked into the laboratory. He was wearing a tan suit that was almost the same color as his face, and tan Gucci loafers.

'Well, well! How are you feeling today Nathan?' he said, with that lopsided grin that he put on to convey sincerity. 'Kavita told me that your hand is almost completely healed up.'

Nathan lifted it up to show him, turning it this way and that and wiggling his fingers. 'See – I told you that this phoenix project would work.'

'So you did. But then again, you can hardly blame me for being skeptical. You were eating up so much budget, with nothing to show for it but this chicken here.'

'Oh, I don't think you were being skeptical, Ron. I think you were being short-sighted and unimaginative rather than skeptical.'

Ron Kasabian tried to look amused. 'Maybe you're right, Nate. Maybe I was too hasty in cutting off your funding. It looks like there could be some profit in this phoenix project after all.'

'Not for *you,* Ron, unfortunately,' said Nathan.

There was a dead silence, except for the phoenix warbling. Ron Kasabian said, 'Excuse me?'

'You heard me. I said that you won't be getting anything out of it. I'm through here. I quit. I'm closing the project down. At Schiller's, anyhow.'

Ron Kasabian's grin disappeared, and his voice grew harsher. His words were conciliatory, but his tone was distinctly threatening. 'You burned your own hand just to prove me wrong, Nate, which was a very brave thing to do. OK, I admit it, I might have made a misjudgment, but now I'm willing to recommend a temporary resumption of funding. So why would you quit now?'

'Because nobody exploits the loyalty of my research assistants. You understand what I'm saying?'

'I'm not so sure that I do.'

'Well, let me spell it out for you,' said Nathan, walking across to him and poking his chest with his finger. 'You took advantage of Kavita because you knew how devoted she is to this project, and you knew how devoted she is to me.'

Ron Kasabian turned to Kavita, his jaw working as if he were masticating a particularly gristly mouthful of steak.

'You told him? You *told* him? What kind of a stupid slut are you?'

'She's not any kind of slut,' Nathan snapped at him. 'What you did to her, that practically amounts to rape. And if you think I'm going to continue working on a project that's been financed by sexual harassment, then you have another think coming. It's over, Ron, and you'll be lucky if I don't report you to the cops, and Schiller's board of directors, both.'

Ron's nostrils flared. For a moment, Nathan thought that he was going to be able to control his fury, and simply stalk back out of the laboratory. But then he lost it. His face reddened and his eyes bulged like Theodor Zauber's gargoyle. The veins in his neck stood out as thick as ropes.

'You fucking stupid slut!' he bellowed. He pushed Nathan

roughly to one side and went for Kavita, seizing her by the shoulders and shaking her so hard that her face became a blur.

'Didn't I tell you not to say anything to anybody? That was the *deal*, you slut! What did I tell you?' His voice rose to a barely-comprehensible scream. '*What did I fucking tell you?*'

Nathan hooked his arm around Ron Kasabian's neck, trying to pull him away. Aarif came around the laboratory bench and grabbed his right arm. But Ron Kasabian was a big man, and he was incandescent with rage. He swung his right arm sideways, with his fist clenched, and he punched Aarif so hard in the face that Nathan heard his nose crack. Blood sprayed out Aarif's nostrils and he staggered backward, stumbling over a stool.

'Get off her, Ron!' Nathan shouted. 'Let go of her! Are you crazy?'

Ron Kasabian didn't hear him. He was deafened by his rage. Nobody disobeyed Ron Kasabian, ever – especially women. He slapped Kavita's face one way and then the other. Kavita started to scream – an urgent, piping scream that sounded like a kettle boiling over.

Nathan jumped on Ron Kasabian again, and managed to force his head back. Ron Kasabian released his grip on Kavita, and twisted himself around, so that he could punch Nathan hard in the ribs. Nathan gasped, but punched him back. Without hesitation, Ron Kasabian head-butted him, so hard that their skulls knocked together – *klokk*! – and Nathan toppled backward on to the floor, hitting his shoulder. Dark stars swam in front of his eyes.

Half concussed, he saw Ron Kasabian going after Kavita again, and forcing her back over one of the benches. Kavita tried to bring her knee up between his legs, but Ron Kasabian slapped her again, even harder this time. He was shouting something at her, but by now he was so angry that he was incoherent. 'You – fucking – swore to me – never – do that – *ever* – betray me – nobody – fucking – *ever*! Do you hear me? *Evaaaaaaaaaaahhhhhh!*'

Nathan grabbed the stool nearest to him and heaved himself back on to his feet. He took two steps toward Ron Kasabian, but as he prepared to jump on him again, he saw a bright flare of light from Torchy's cage – like a white flower opening up, a flower with petals made of incandescent magnesium. It was almost too dazzling to look at directly, and Nathan had to shield his eyes with his hand.

Inside his cage, the phoenix had raised his head and spread his wings wide, and he was on fire. Not in the sense that his feathers were alight. He *was* fire, he had *become* fire. First of all, he had been a dragon-worm, then a bird. Now he had transformed himself into pure white flame, a flame that was hissing like a pressure lamp.

Ron Kasabian lifted his head to stare at it, although he kept his grip on Kavita's throat. Kavita herself tried to wriggle herself free, but Ron Kasabian clutched her throat even more tightly and banged her head against the bench. 'Stay there, you fucking slut!' Nathan guessed that however angry he was, he must have realized by now that his outburst had lost him his job, and possibly his marriage, too, if his wife got to hear what he had done, and there was nobody more dangerous than a man who has nothing else to lose.

'Ron!' he shouted. 'Let her go, Ron! It's over!'

'Go screw yourself, Nathan!' Ron Kasabian shouted back, without even turning to look at him. He was transfixed by the white feathery fire in the phoenix's cage, which was blazing brighter and hotter with every passing second.

Suddenly, the fire-bird flapped his wings – once, twice, three times – and then flew right through the bars of his cage as if he were made of nothing more substantial than flames. He flew at Ron Kasabian with a soft roaring sound, and then he let out a screech that made Nathan's scalp prickle.

Ron Kasabian tried to dodge to one side, ducking his head down, but the phoenix caught his shoulder pad in its claws, clinging so ferociously that there was nothing he could do to beat it off.

'*Get it off me!*' he screamed. '*For Christ's sake, get it off me!*'

But the phoenix flapped its fiery wings on either side of his head, again and again, so that his hair caught alight, and his cheeks were seared scarlet. He lurched toward the door, knocking over stools and colliding with workbenches, but the phoenix flapped its wings harder and harder, until his entire head was enveloped in fire, and then the sleeves and lapels of his suit began to burn.

'*Get it off me! Oh God, get it off me! It hurts! It fucking hurts! I can't take it! God, I can't take it! It hurts!*'

The smoke alarms began to sing *meep-meep-meep-meep-meep*. Nathan hurried across to the door, and hoisted the bright yellow fire extinguisher out of its rack. Ron Kasabian was flailing around and around with the phoenix perched on his shoulder, blazing from the waist upward. It looked as if the phoenix was flapping its wings in order to create a downdraft, so that the flames were licking at Ron Kasabian's thighs and down toward his knees, greedy for more and more oxygen.

Nathan punched the button that started the extinguisher and white foam spurted out of the nozzle. But this fire was just like the fire in which the phoenix had first been created: it was so hot that it seemed to swallow the foam and evaporate it. Within a few seconds, Ron Kasabian was burning from head to foot, a sacrificial figure made out of nothing but flames. He collapsed to his knees, his arms by his sides, and then he keeled over sideways and lay burning on the floor.

The phoenix let out another screech, but this time he sounded more triumphant than vengeful. He lifted itself up into the air and hovered for a moment over Ron Kasabian's body, a bird made out of nothing but brilliant white fire. Nathan could just make out his eyes, as pale as glass. Then the phoenix tilted toward his cage, and flew back in through the bars. He settled on his perch, and as soon as he settled his incandescence began to dim, and his flames died down, and within a few moments he was back to his substantial self, with his rose-pink beak and his gilded feathers and his yellow tail. He let out a self-satisfied *skrarrrkkk*.

'Call nine-one-one,' said Nathan, in a croak as dry as Torchy's. Smoke was still rising from Ron Kasabian's body and the laboratory reeked of his half-cremated flesh.

'I did already,' said Aarif. He was dabbing his bloody nose with a white hand-towel. 'Fire, police and ambulance.' The smoke alarms were still *meep-meeping* as if they were peeved at being ignored.

Nathan went over to Kavita. She was rubbing her neck where Ron Kasabian had tried to throttle her. Both of her cheeks were crimson and bruised, and Nathan could tell that she would probably have a black eye tomorrow. She was trembling with shock.

'How did that happen?' she coughed. 'I mean, that was *impossible*. How did Torchy change like that? He flew right through the bars of his cage as if they weren't even there.'

'Are you OK?' Nathan asked her. He was shaking, too. 'Jesus – if I'd thought for a moment that Ron would go apeshit like that—'

Kavita glanced toward Ron Kasabian's blackened body and then looked away.

'He's dead, I'm afraid,' said Nathan.

Kavita gave a complicated shrug. 'He was a bully and a pig. He didn't deserve to die like that, but he brought it on himself.'

She paused, still trembling, and then she said, 'In bed, he was just the same. Trying to make me do things that I didn't want to do. Shouting at me when I refused.'

She paused again. 'He even expected me to—'

She started to say something more, but then she thought better of it and closed her lips. Ron Kasabian was dead now, after all.

Nathan walked across to Torchy's cage and peered in through the bars. Torchy clawed his way along his perch to the far side of the cage, as far away from Nathan as possible.

'He definitely doesn't like me,' said Nathan.

Kavita said, 'Don't worry. He will grow to like you, when he sees how well you take care of me.'

'We need to run some more tests, but I think you'd better do the honors until I'm sure that he's not going to burn me to a cinder, like Ron here.'

'Of course,' said Kavita. 'But I think I need to go now. I can't bear the smell.'

Nathan said, 'I want another DNA sample, and we should also check if his fundamental cell structure has altered in any way. How the hell does a living bird turn itself into pure fire, without any apparent scorching or loss of substance? And how does it turn itself back into flesh and feathers? And what triggers a change like that? Is it fear, do you think, or protectiveness, or is it natural avian aggression?'

'Professor, I feel sick.'

'OK,' said Nathan. 'I'm sorry. Why don't you and Aarif both go down to the lobby? But I think I'd better stay here. The police will be here at any minute, and besides, I want to keep an eye on Torchy.'

Aarif and Kavita left the laboratory, circling around the benches so that they kept as far away from Ron Kasabian's smoldering body as they could. Nathan stayed close to Torchy's cage, but not too close. He didn't want to set off another exhibition of avian pyrotechnics.

He was deeply shaken by the way in which Ron Kasabian had been burned to death, right in front of them, but as a zoologist he had so many questions about how and why it had happened. He had read every myth and every legend about the phoenix that he could find, including *O Pássaro Ardente De Egipto – The Burning Bird of Egypt*, by the fifteenth-century Portuguese alchemist and ornithologist Aldo Sombrio. There were only two known copies – one of which had been water-damaged during the Second World War in a flood at the Biblioteca Nacional in Lisbon – but it contained more details about the origins of the phoenix than anything else he had read. All the same, it hadn't mentioned that the phoenix could transform itself into pure fire, and then back again into a solid, screeching, bad-tempered bird.

He went across and hunkered down next to Ron Kasabian's body. Ron Kasabian was lying on his right side, with his arms and legs drawn up into the monkey-like position adopted by the victims of so many fires. His eyes were open but his eyeballs were opaque, and the skin on his face was charred in curled-up layers, like the pages of a burned book.

'Jesus, Ron. Why did you have to lose it like that?' Nathan asked him, but he already knew the answer to that. As long as he had known him, Ron Kasabian had been arrogant and insecure. He had been afraid to take risks in a business that was inherently risky, and Nathan had quickly come to the conclusion that he had been promoted far beyond his capabilities. That was why he had always acted so aggressively. He obviously hadn't expected that Kavita would stand up to him, or that she would be defended with such ferocity by a mythical creature that could incinerate him where he stood.

Nathan was still hunkered down next to him when three firefighters came in, followed by Henry and then by two paramedics.

'Holy Moses, Professor!' said Henry, taking off his cap. 'Not *another* fire?' Then he realized what was lying next to Nathan on the floor.

'That ain't – that ain't Mr Kasabian, is it? That's – *shee-it*! – that *is* Mr Kasabian! How'd he get all burned up like that?'

Nathan stood up. The leading firefighter looked around to make sure that there were no spot fires still burning, and then he said, 'Want to tell us what happened here, sir?'

'I couldn't honestly tell you,' said Nathan. 'Spontaneous combustion, I guess you could call it. Mr Kasabian was standing here talking to us, and suddenly *whoof*! Up he went like a Roman candle.'

'*Whoof*?' repeated the firefighter. His eyes were very pale hazel, and he had a bristly ginger moustache. He looked like the stubborn type.

'Whoof,' said Nathan, nodding in agreement.

The firefighter knelt down next to Ron Kasabian's body. He lifted off his helmet, bent his head down and sniffed. He sniffed again, all the way down to Ron Kasabian's tan Gucci loafers, with their fringes crisp and curled-up from the fire. Then he looked up at his companions and said, 'I can't smell nothing in the way of accelerants, but Jimmy – why don't you go bring Muttley up here? Maybe *he* can.'

'Muttley?' asked Nathan.

'He's our fire dog. He can detect one thousandth of a drop of part-evaporated gasoline in a room twice this volume.'

'Mr Kasabian wasn't set alight by any accelerants, officer. Not that we saw. Not unless his clothes were already saturated when he came in here, but we didn't smell anything.'

'So, what are you telling me? Your friend walked in here and caught fire without no warning at all? He looks like he was given a going-over by a goddamned flame-thrower.'

'I can't believe it,' said Henry. 'Only a half-hour ago, Mr Kasabian was axin' me about my hernia operation. Now look at him.'

One of the paramedics said, 'We'll leave you guys to get on with it, OK? There's nothing we can do for this poor bastard. We'll contact the ME.'

The paramedics left; but as they did so, they stepped aside to let Detective Pullet and Detective Rubik in through the door.

Jenna came in and looked around. Then she stalked right up to Ron Kasabian's body, bent down and peered at it closely.

'Do we know who this is?' she asked, looking directly at Nathan.

Nathan said, 'Mr Ron Kasabian, CEO of Schiller Medical Research Inc.'

'And do we know what happened to him?'

'He caught fire,' Nathan told her. He nodded toward the empty fire extinguisher lying on the floor. 'I tried to put him out, but I couldn't. He was burning far too fiercely.'

'He caught *fire*?' asked Jenna. 'How, exactly?'

'We don't know yet,' the firefighter put in. 'Until we do, we're reserving judgment.'

Jenna walked across to Nathan and stood facing him. 'Professor Underhill,' she said.

'Yes?'

'Professor Underhill, this is the second time in less than eight hours that you've figured as a witness in an inexplicable fatality.'

'Yes.'

'Why don't you make my life a little easier, Professor Underhill? Why don't you tell me what the hell is going on?'

TWENTY-FOUR

Friday, 3:07 p.m.

Henry showed them through to the boardroom and brought them coffee and bottles of spring water. Jenna and Dan sat down at the shiny mahogany table with Aarif and Kavita. Aarif's nose had not been fractured out of alignment but the paramedics had given him a cold compress to hold over it. Both of his eyes were already swollen like dark red plums, and Nathan had told him to go home, but he had insisted on staying. He was determined not to miss any of the stages of Sukie Harris' stem cell treatment.

Nathan remained standing, looking out of the window at the downtown skyline. The sun had come out, and was glittering on the river, and the pale blue sky was streaked with thin horses' tail clouds. The scene reminded Nathan of some of the illustrations he had seen in books of mythology, with strange creatures flying around the spires of medieval cathedrals.

Jenna said, 'This is where you do your research, Professor? Here at the Schiller building?'

'That's right. Schiller have been funding me for nearly a year now.'

'And what exactly is it that you're working on?'

'Is that relevant?'

'I don't know. Is it?'

Nathan turned around. 'It's no secret. I've been trying to recreate mythical creatures. I believe that their stem cells could help us to treat some incurable illnesses.'

'When you say mythical creatures . . .?'

'Creatures out of mythology. Basilisks, wyverns, gryphons. Right up until the Middle Ages there were dozens of them – from the adlet, which was like an Inuit werewolf, to the ziz, which in Jewish mythology was a giant bird whose wings could block out the sun. Some of them were purely imaginary, but many of them really existed. You saw that bird in my laboratory. My researchers and I created that bird only a few days ago. Or shall we say *re*-created it. It's a phoenix.'

'A phoenix? Are you serious? Isn't that the bird that sets fire to itself, to get reborn?'

'That's the one.'

'So is there any kind of connection between your re-creating a phoenix and Mr Kasabian catching on fire?'

Nathan pulled out a chair and sat down. The surface of the table was so shiny that everybody sitting at it was reflected like the figures on playing cards.

'Unlike the phoenix, Detective, I don't think there's any chance that Ron Kasabian will be coming back to life.'

Jenna looked at Nathan narrowly. He hadn't really answered her question, and she felt the same way about him that she had felt back at Temple University Hospital – that he wasn't giving her the whole picture. Maybe not *lying*, exactly, but failing to give her some critical facts. She was convinced that there was a link between the death of Eduardo Delgado at the hospital and Ron Kasabian's immolation here at Schiller Medical Research, and she suspected that Nathan knew what it was. The question was: why was he being so guarded?

Dan opened his notebook. 'The way that the victim was burned – could we run over it again? He came into the laboratory, right? How long was it before he combusted?'

'I don't know,' said Nathan. 'Only a couple of minutes.'

'Did he *say* anything before he caught fire?'

'We exchanged a few words, yes.'

'Just a few words? You didn't argue? It looks like your two assistants here both suffered some injuries.'

'They sustained those when Mr Kasabian caught fire. They fell.'

Jenna turned to Aarif. 'You fell flat on your nose? You didn't put out your hands to save yourself?'

Aarif shrugged. 'I tripped over a stool. I hit my nose on the edge of the bench.'

'And how about you?' Jenna asked Kavita. 'I've attended more domestic disputes than you've had hot dinners, young lady, and I know a slap when I see it.'

'That was Professor Underhill,' said Kavita. 'I hit my head and he thought I was unconscious so he slapped me to bring me round.'

Jenna stared at her disbelievingly for a moment, but then she turned back to Nathan. 'Prior to catching light, did Mr Kasabian complain of feeling strange, in any way?'

Nathan shook his head.

'Was there any chemical in your laboratory that could have accidentally set him alight?'

'Only methanol, and he would have had to empty a whole bottle over himself and set himself alight with a match.'

'Or somebody would.'

'What are you trying to suggest? That one of *us* killed him?'

'I don't know. Did you? The circumstances are highly suspicious, to say the least. And to be quite frank with you, I don't buy this falling over on your nose and this slapping story. Did you and Mr Kasabian have any kind of dispute?'

Nathan said, 'Yes. We'd had a serious disagreement over money. Mr Kasabian had recommended to the Schiller board that they discontinue funding my research.'

'Oh, yes?'

'This morning, though, he came in to tell us that he had changed his mind, and that our funding would continue – at least for the time being.'

Jenna sat back, tapping her ballpen on the tabletop. 'So there was no longer any bone of contention between you? No reason for you to argue, or to get physical?'

Nathan shook his head.

Jenna's cellphone played 'Blanket On The Ground'. She said, 'Excuse me,' and flipped it open.

'Mom? It's Ellie. OK if I stay over at Hermione's tonight?'

'What about your homework?'

'It's *Friday*, Mom. I can do it tomorrow.'

'Did you eat lunch?'

'I had vegetarian pizza.'

'How much? Come on, tell me the truth.'

'I had one slice. But I ate all of it, I swear.'

'OK, then. But make sure that you eat something at Hermione's. I'll call you later, when I finish work.'

She snapped her cellphone shut. She looked across the table to see Nathan smiling at her.

'*Kids*,' he said.

Jenna refused to smile back. 'I might need to talk to you again, Professor, once the medical examiner has taken a look at Mr Kasabian's remains, and I get a full report from the fire department.'

'OK,' said Nathan. He checked his watch, and then turned to Aarif and Kavita. 'Right now we have a pressing appointment with a certain young lady, don't we, compadres?'

TWENTY-FIVE

Friday, 5:35 p.m.

When they arrived back at Temple University Hospital, they found that Doctor Berman was still in theater, finishing up his treatment of an auto mechanic who had been splashed in the face with car-battery acid. They waited in the beige-painted visitors' lounge at the end of the corridor, under framed prints of lakes and forests. Kavita closed her eyes and tilted her head back and attempted to rest, while Aarif lay back on one of the couches, keeping the folded white compress pressed to his nose. Nathan sat next to the tropical fish tank, trying to read *National Geographic*, but he couldn't stop picturing the way that Torchy had blazed through the bars of his cage, flown at Ron Kasabian and set him on fire. After a while he tossed the magazine back on to the table.

Twenty minutes passed and then Braydon Harris came into the lounge, carrying a cup of coffee. His eyes were swollen and his hair was sticking up at the back like a bedraggled cockatoo. He was wearing a light green zip-up windbreaker with a pattern of brown stains down the front, and grubby gray Nike sneakers.

He sat down opposite Nathan and nodded, 'Hi, Professor.'

Nathan said, 'Hi there. How's it going?'

Braydon sipped his coffee. It was still scalding hot, and he said, 'Ouch. Shit. No wonder they call it the burns unit.' He put down his cup and then he said, 'Taking a break?'

'I'm waiting for Doctor Berman,' said Nathan. 'How's your daughter doing?'

'I haven't seen her yet. They're changing the dressings or something like that.'

'I don't think you should worry about her too much. The surgeons here can practically work miracles.'

'I hope to God. As if she hasn't been through enough already, what with her mom and me separating. Kids always have to bear the brunt of it, don't they?'

'Sure. But they're pretty resilient. Tougher than adults, sometimes.'

'I'm not so sure about my Sukie. She's kind of sensitive, you know. One of those real shy kids who wouldn't say boo to a goose. And she's always having those nightmares.'

'Come on . . . nightmares are not necessarily bad. Having nightmares is how kids deal with things that frighten them, and things they don't understand. Don't tell me *you* never had nightmares, when you were young? I always thought that the robe that was hanging on the back of my bedroom door was going to jump down and strangle me. Then I used to have nightmares about getting lost in the woods, and there were wolves coming after me.'

'Yeah, but my daughter has that *same* nightmare about the Spooglies, over and over, and always has.'

'Have you ever taken her for counseling?'

Braydon shook his head. 'Her mom – my gorgeous ex-wife – she doesn't believe in shrinks. She thinks that Sukie has some kind of psychic gift, like my ex-mom-in-law. They've always been into that stuff, the two of them. Seances, Ouija boards, all that crap. She thinks that Sukie's nightmares are some kind of message from beyond, you know, like *w-o-ooo-ooo-ooh*!'

He paused, and tried sipping his coffee again, but it was still too hot. 'I talked to the psychiatrist here, Doctor Mahmood, and he said pretty much the same as you, that her nightmares were caused by stress. You know, her mother and me always yelling at each other. But I still don't understand why she should always have nightmares about these goddamned Spooglies. She even drew me a picture of one.'

Nathan took out his iPhone and Googled Doré's engraving of Malacoda, the leader of the Malebranche. When he had located it, he passed his iPhone over to Braydon, and said, 'Sukie's drawing . . . did it look anything at all like this?'

Braydon peered at it. 'Jesus. That's exactly what it looked like. *Exactly*. What the hell is this?'

'It's a gargoyle – a flying creature that was supposed to have plagued the whole of Europe in the Middle Ages. According to the myths about them, they came out at night in their hundreds, whole flocks of them, and swooped down on cattle and sheep, and carried them off. People, too, apparently. Men, women and kids.'

Braydon blinked and passed Nathan's iPhone back. 'I thought gargoyles were those ugly statues you see on the tops of churches.'

'They are. But the myths suggest that they were alive, once, and it was only because they were hunted down by exorcists and turned to stone that they became extinct.'

'Yeah, but like you say, they're only a myth, right? Why should Sukie have nightmares about a myth?'

'I don't have any idea, to be frank with you. But I would be very interested to find out.'

At that moment, Doctor Berman came in, still wearing his green theater scrubs.

'Ah . . . Professor Underhill. We're ready for you now.'

'How's Sukie?' asked Braydon. 'Can I see her now?'

Doctor Berman smiled and held up his right hand with his fingers spread. 'If you could just give us five minutes, Mr Harris?'

'Sure. But she's OK, isn't she?'

'In five minutes, I promise you, you can see for yourself.'

Doctor Berman led Nathan and Aarif and Kavita along the corridor to Susan Harris' room.

'Is she making any progress?' asked Nathan.

Doctor Berman looked back over his shoulder. 'You could say that,' he replied, evasively.

They went into Susan Harris' room, where a nurse was plumping up Sukie's pillows and making her comfortable.

Nathan slowly approached her bed and said, 'My God.'

Sukie was no longer wearing the shiny Jaloskin covering that had been protecting her burns while they healed. She was no longer wearing an oxygen mask, either. She was still connected to a saline drip, and her vital signs were still being monitored, but she was sitting up in bed with a crooked smile on her face.

Her mousy-colored hair was still burned on one side like stubble in a cornfield, and she still had no eyebrows, but the only signs that her face had been seared so severely were a pinkish patch on her forehead and a pattern of pinkish spots on her cheeks. Her lips were redder than they should have been, with two or three black crusty scabs, but Nathan could see that they were healing fast.

She wasn't a particularly pretty little girl. In fact she was rather plain, with an overbite and a weak chin. But she had huge brown eyes that were immediately appealing, and what Nathan warmed to, most of all, was the way in which her face had regenerated so quickly, in less than a day.

'I never saw anything like it,' said Doctor Berman. 'If she continues to improve at this rate, she should be ready for discharge in a day or two. Best of all, I don't think she'll have any visible scars on her face at all.'

He took a deep breath, and then he said, 'When they took the Jaloskin off, and I saw Sukie's face, I have to admit that I had tears in my eyes – and, believe me, I've been treating burns victims for twenty-six years, and I'm not the sentimental type.'

Nathan took hold of Sukie's hand. 'How are you feeling, Sukie?'

'Much better, thank you.'

'Does your face hurt at all?'

'No, but it feels *stretchy*.'

'Stretchy, that's OK. Stretchy is good. Stretchy means that it's getting better.'

'I *am* hungry, though.'

'You're hungry? Haven't they been feeding you in here? What would you like to eat?'

'A Twinkie,' said Sukie.

Nathan turned to Doctor Berman. 'Is that OK? A Twinkie?'

'It's not on the usual dietary sheet for burns patients, but I guess it wouldn't hurt. So long as it's not deep-fried.'

Aarif opened his medical bag one-handed and Kavita took out a hypodermic with the stem cell sample. Nathan said, 'I just have to give you two injections, Sukie. One in each side of your face. You'll feel a little scratch, but that's all. Once I've done that, you can have as many Twinkies as you like.'

He injected Sukie, once in each jaw-muscle. She said, '*Ouch!*' with each injection, and gave him an exaggerated frown, but then she smiled again, and Nathan could tell that she was already feeling better. As for himself, he felt almost like God.

TWENTY-SIX
Friday, 9:23 p.m.

That evening, Grace was too tired after her day's rounds to think about cooking, so Nathan called Cosimo's and ordered pepperoni pizzas. When the pizzas arrived, Denver and his friend Stu took theirs up to his bedroom so that they could listen to death/grind CDs, while Nathan and Grace ate theirs sprawled on the living room couch, in front of the television.

'What's going to happen to your phoenix project now that Ron's dead?' asked Grace.

Nathan chewed and swallowed. 'I'm not sure. For the moment, I'm going to try to carry on as normal. I'll probably have to produce a new budget presentation for the board, but once they see evidence of what the phoenix stem cells can do, I don't think I'll have any trouble at all in getting them to approve more funding. Doctor Berman says that he'll give me his unqualified endorsement.'

'But what about the phoenix attacking Ron like that? I mean, that could happen again, and somebody else could get burned.'

'Torchy was being protective, that's all. He saw Ron going for Kavita, and he wanted to stop him from hurting her. I don't think that kind of situation is ever likely to arise again.'

Grace finished her pizza and wiped her mouth on a paper napkin. 'All the same, darling, you don't know *how* Torchy turned himself into pure flame like that, and until you do—'

Nathan said, 'Don't worry. I'm determined to find out how he does it, and what it is that triggers him off. It's crucial that we know. After all, it could be the key to how he can recreate himself, and how his stem cells can regenerate people's burns. Kavita went back to the lab tonight to take more readings, and I'll be running some more comprehensive tests tomorrow.'

He had told Grace that he had been interviewed by the police after Ron Kasabian's death, but he had not yet told her that he had been also been interviewed by the same detectives after the death of Eduardo Delgado at Temple University Hospital, and why. He didn't want to frighten her by telling her what had happened when Theodor Zauber had visited him at the hospital, and the threats that Zauber had made against him and his family.

'The gargoyle is now a living creature, ja? And like all living creatures, it will do anything to survive. Just as you will. Just as your wife and your son will.'

He hoped that Theodor Zauber had been bluffing, but if he was anything like his father, Nathan knew that his threat was serious. He had urged one of his gargoyles to smash an innocent man to pieces, after all, just to prove what they were capable of, and to prove that he had no conscience about ordering them to do it.

'How about a nightcap?' he suggested, picking up their pizza plates.

'A glass of that Merlot would be good,' said Grace.

Nathan went through to the kitchen and took two glasses out of the hutch. He was just about to pour them two glasses of red wine when he heard a thunderous crash from upstairs, and the explosive sound of a window breaking. The impact was so violent that the entire house shook, and a row of side plates rolled off the shelf on top of the hutch, one after the other, and shattered on the floor.

The crash was immediately followed by a hideous screeching sound, like a train jamming its emergency brakes on, only shriller and louder.

Nathan hurtled out of the kitchen and collided with Grace, who was coming into the kitchen to find him.

'What was that?' she gasped. 'Something's hit the house!'

'*Dad*!' screamed Denver, from his bedroom. '*Dad, come quick!*'

'Stay here!' Nathan told Grace, and bounded up the staircase. He was only halfway up when there was another crash, even louder than the first, and the house jolted so much that he had to grip the banister rail to stop himself from losing his footing.

'*Dad*!' Denver called out, and this time his voice was shrill with panic. '*Dad! There's something trying to get in here! Stu's been hurt real bad!*'

Nathan ran across the landing and along the corridor to Denver's bedroom. When he threw open the door he could hardly believe his eyes. The entire window had been smashed in, including the frame, and the carpet and bed were strewn with sparkling fragments of glass and broken pieces of glazing bars. Part of the wall on the left-hand side of the window had been ripped away, too, and the torn wallpaper was flapping in the wind.

Outside, the trees were thrashing as if they were trying to uproot themselves in terror. The street lights were flickering through the leaves so that everything in Denver's bedroom seemed to jump and jerk like a scene from an old Charlie Chaplin movie.

Denver was crouched down behind his bed, while Stu was lying on his back with a large triangle of glass sticking out of his right thigh. His jeans were flooded in bright red blood, and he was shivering with shock.

'What the hell happened?' asked Nathan, kneeling down beside him.

'Something crashed in through the window!' Denver told him, so frightened that he was almost screaming. 'It was like a monster or something! It crashed in through the window and there was glass flying everywhere! Then it came crashing in again, and I thought it was going to bite me!'

Nathan said, 'Go downstairs, call nine-one-one for an ambulance, right now.'

Stu groaned, and tried to sit up, but Nathan pushed him gently back down again and took off his thick-lensed eyeglasses. 'Just lie still, Stu. I'm going to take out this piece of glass and see how bad you're bleeding. I won't hurt you, I promise.'

Denver hesitated at the door, but Nathan told him, '*Go*! Call nine-one-one!' and he went.

Nathan took hold of the thick brown woolen throw from Denver's bed and used it as an impromptu glove. He gripped the triangular piece of glass in Stu's thigh and carefully drew it out. Then he unfastened Stu's belt and tugged his jeans down to his knees. There was a diagonal slit high up in the inside of Stu's skinny white thigh, about seven inches long, which was pumping out blood like the mouth of a harpooned fish. Nathan guessed that the glass had cut his femoral artery, and that he was in imminent danger of bleeding out.

Grace appeared in the doorway. 'Denver just told me that Stu's been hurt. He's called for an ambulance.'

'A damn great piece of glass went into his leg,' said Nathan. 'Quick – hand me that towel.'

Grace took the white hand-towel from the ring beside Denver's washbasin, and folded it up. 'Here,' she said, 'I'll do this. Press the heel of your hand into the crease of his groin – that's it, just there – as hard as you can.'

She wrestled Stu's jeans right off, and then she held the towel firmly against his wound. Meanwhile, Nathan knelt down next to him, positioned the heel of his hand over the pressure point at the top of his leg, and leaned forward with all of his weight, so that he would restrict the pumping of blood through his femoral artery. Stu said, '*Ow*!' and tried to struggle out from under him, but he was already growing weaker, and Nathan held him firmly against the floor.

'God, I hope those paramedics get here soon,' said Grace. The hand towel she was using as a pressure bandage was already soaked bright red, and she tugged the bottom sheet from Denver's bed and bundled it up so that she could press it down on top of the towel.

'What the hell happened here?' she asked Nathan, looking

across at the shattered bedroom window. 'It looks like a bomb went off.'

'I have a pretty good idea,' Nathan told her. 'But first let's make sure this kid doesn't die on us.'

Denver came to the bedroom door and stood watching them for a while. 'He's going to be OK, isn't he?'

'Sure,' said Nathan, even though Stu's face was white now and his lips were pale blue. The blood from his femoral artery was creeping inexorably into the sheet and by the look on Grace's face Nathan could tell that she was beginning to think that they had lost him.

'He can't *die*,' said Denver.

Nathan heard the scribbling of an ambulance siren. 'Go down and let the paramedics in, OK? Tell them what's happened. Tell them that Stu has a severed artery in his right leg and that he's bleeding bad.'

'Should I tell them about the monster?'

Grace looked up sharply and said, 'What monster?'

'The monster that bust in through the window,' said Denver. 'It was like some kind of dragon or something.'

'Don't say anything about the monster,' Nathan told him. 'It'll only confuse them. Just tell them about Stu, OK?'

'OK,' said Denver, doubtfully, and disappeared downstairs again.

'What *monster*?' Grace demanded. 'What is he talking about, for Christ's sake?'

Nathan said, 'I'll tell you later, I promise. All I care about right now is saving Stu.'

A few seconds later, two paramedics came running up the stairs, a thin blonde woman and a young Korean. The woman took over from Grace, applying a fresh dressing to Stu's thigh, while the young man fitted an oxygen mask over Stu's face and then ran down again to fetch a stretcher. Nathan stayed where he was, keeping up the pressure on Stu's artery. The pale blue carpet all around was soggy with blood.

It took another ten minutes before the bleeding appeared to slow down. The woman paramedic wrapped Stu's thigh in another dressing, and then she and her companion lifted Stu on to the stretcher and carried him downstairs.

'Which ER are you taking him to?' asked Nathan, as the young man closed the ambulance doors.

'Albert Einstein Medical Center. You know how to get there?'
'Sure. Yes. We'll see you there. Please – take care of him.'

TWENTY-SEVEN
Friday, 10:33 p.m.

A small crowd of neighbors had gathered in his front yard. His next-door neighbor Jim Lightly came up to him with his wife Jean. Jim was a lawyer for Philadelphia City Council, serious and bespectacled with a shiny bald head even though he was only thirty-nine.

'What the Sam Hill happened here, Nathan? Jean and I were on our way up to bed and then *ker-ash*! And then *ker-ash* again. We thought a plane had come down, didn't we, Jean? We were expecting to see bodies and bits of plane all over.'

'Who's been hurt, Nathan?' asked Jean. She looked toward the open front door of the house, where Grace and Denver were putting on their coats and their shoes. 'Thank God it wasn't Grace.'

'It was a friend of Denver's, Stu Wintergreen. He and Denver, they were trying some kind of science experiment.'

'Science experiment? Looks more like they were trying to build a home-made bomb! Was this Stu hurt bad?'

'We don't know yet. We're just off to the hospital. Listen, Jim, maybe you can do me a favor and keep an eye on the house for me while we're gone.'

'Of course. What are neighbors for?'

Several more neighbors came up to him to express their shock and offer their sympathies. Grace came to the door and called out, 'Nathan? Come on! We're ready to go! I've called Stu's mom and dad and they're going to meet us at the hospital!'

The neighbors dispersed with a chorus of, 'If there's anything we can do for you, Nathan, you just holler.' 'We're always here if you need us.' 'You take good care, you hear?' 'Hope that young boy gets better.'

Nathan turned back toward the house. He looked up at Denver's bedroom and the jagged widescreen hole where his window had been. He could see Denver's AxCx and Misery Index posters on the wall, and also a high spray of Stu's blood in the shape of a shepherd's crook. For the first time that evening he felt afraid.

'Nathan!' Grace repeated.

'OK, I'm coming!'

As he started to climb up the steps to the front porch, however, he heard a faint, echoing howl, high in the sky above him. He stopped and twisted around and looked up. At first he saw nothing but the moonlit clouds, but he was about to continue up the steps when he heard another howl, louder this time, and much harsher. It sounded triumphant, challenging, heartless. A dark shape was circling high above – a shape with widespread wings and a long, lizard-like tail. It circled once, twice, three times, directly over the top of the Underhills' house, as if it were warning him that it knew where he lived and it might come back to cause even more damage and destruction.

'*Nathan!*' called Grace. She didn't sound at all happy. 'Nathan – what are you doing?'

The dark shape flapped away in a south-westerly direction, toward Manayunk and the Schuylkill River, like a ragged black sheet blown by the wind. Nathan stared at it until it was out of sight, and then he went back into the house. 'Sorry,' he said. 'I was just inspecting the damage. Jim's going to take care of things until we get back.'

They climbed into Nathan's car, backed out of the driveway and headed east toward the Albert Einstein Medical Center.

Grace turned around in her seat. 'All right, Denver. So what's all this about a monster? Were you and Stu smoking something you shouldn't?'

'It *was* a monster, Mom,' Denver insisted. 'We were sitting there minding our own business, eating pizza and listening to music, and then this *thing* came busting right through the window. I mean like a goddamned *bomb*.'

'This *thing*? And don't blaspheme.'

'I don't know what it was. It had a kind of a curvy beak like a buzzard and great big starey eyes and claws like goddamned *swords*, you know? Like there was glass flying everywhere and this thing kept screaming at us like it was trying to force itself right into the room and tear us to pieces.'

Grace turned to Nathan. 'Do you believe him?' She paused, and then she said, 'Oh. Of course you believe him. You told him not to mention anything about it to the paramedics. And you didn't do that in case they buckled him up in a straitjacket and carted him off to the psych ward, did you?'

'No,' Nathan admitted.

'So what are you not telling me? Or shall I put two and two together? This monster exists, doesn't it? It really exists?'

'Yes, Grace, it does. It's a gargoyle. It's one of Theodor Zauber's gargoyles. He came to visit me in the hospital and he asked me again if I would help him. I said no, I wouldn't. He said that I would regret it, and he gave me a very graphic demonstration of *why* I would regret it. There was a gargoyle sitting on the hospital roof. A real, living medieval gargoyle. Zauber called out to it, and it dived down and killed that hospital orderly.'

'A *gargoyle* killed him?'

'That's right. I was talking to one of the interns who saw what was left of him. He'd been out in Afghanistan with the Army medical corps, and he said that the poor guy looked as if he'd stepped on a roadside bomb, only much worse.'

'And you didn't tell the police about Zauber? Why on earth not?'

'Do you really think they would have believed me? And even if they managed to track him down, him and his gargoyles, what could they do then? These are mythical creatures that have been turned to stone. Do you think the police are seriously going to believe that he can bring them back to life again, so that they can fly, and attack people? All he has to do is deny it. Besides, he was threatening to set his gargoyles on *you*, and Denver, and that's why I didn't tell you what happened at the hospital, and that's why I didn't tell the police, either.'

'But he *did* set a gargoyle on us, didn't he? Regardless of the fact that you didn't tell the cops. It's lucky that Stu wasn't killed. It's lucky that *all* of us weren't killed.'

'Don't worry,' said Nathan, as he turned into the parking garage of Albert Einstein Medical Center. 'I'm not going to let Zauber get away with this. I'm going to find him, and I'm going to put a stop to this gargoyle insanity for ever.'

'What *is* a gargoyle, anyhow?' Denver asked him.

'You should know what it is already, the number of times I've talked to you about it.'

'Sorry. Maybe I wasn't exactly listening.'

'It's another mythical creature, just like that gryphon I was trying to recreate, and like that basilisk that put your mom into a coma. Just like the phoenix we've managed to bring to life.'

'Oh, great. Another mythical creature. Why can't you just breed rabbits or something?'

They went into the hospital's main entrance and the receptionist directed them through to the emergency room. It was Friday night, so the waiting room was crowded with people with minor injuries – young men and women who had already drunk too much and fallen down flights of stairs, elderly people who had fractured their hips or their wrists or their ankles, a nightclub doorman who had been hit in the face with a beer glass.

Nathan went up to the nurses' station and asked if they could see Stu Wintergreen. 'They brought him in about fifteen minutes ago. He had a deep laceration in his right leg.'

'Please wait here, sir,' said the nurse, and disappeared for almost five minutes. A small boy who had fallen out of his top bunk bed and broken his finger went on crying and crying and wouldn't stop. After a while, Nathan was sorely tempted to put him out of his misery by strangling him.

'So how do you propose to find Theodor Zauber?' Grace demanded.

'I expect he'll find me. He'll want to know if tonight's attack has persuaded me to change my mind. Believe me, Grace, Zauber needs me if he's going to make his gargoyle project work. He can turn his gargoyles into living flesh but he doesn't know how to make them stay that way.'

The nurse reappeared, followed by a short, tired-looking young doctor who strongly reminded Nathan of Michael J. Fox.

'Hi,' he said. 'I'm Doctor Brainerd. Are you Stuart's parents?'

'No . . . but they should be here any minute. Stu's a friend of my son here. They were together in my son's bedroom when Stu got injured.'

'How did it happen?'

Nathan was trying to think of a convincing explanation when Denver said, 'The wind caught the window and it slammed real hard, and the glass broke.'

Doctor Brainerd looked as if he were too exhausted to worry about the plausibility of this scenario. 'OK . . .' he said. 'Stuart sustained a very deep cut which severed the main artery in his right leg. The problem with severed arteries in the lower part of the body is that the blood is always under more pressure than the upper part of the body, which means that a patient is likely to bleed out very quickly.'

Grace said, 'I'm a doctor myself, Doctor. Doctor Grace Underhill, from the Chestnut Hill medical practice.'

'Oh, good. In that case you'll know that a patient only has to lose five or six pints of blood before they expire.'

'What are you saying?' asked Nathan. 'Didn't you give Stu more blood?'

Doctor Brainerd shook his head. 'There was no point, sir. Stuart was dead on arrival.'

Denver opened and closed his mouth. His eyes were suddenly filled with tears. 'He's *dead*? I don't believe it! He can't be dead! We were eating pizza and listening to music! He can't be dead!'

'I'm very sorry,' said Doctor Brainerd.

Nathan looked at Grace and Grace looked back at him with an expression of such anger that he couldn't think of anything to say. He had believed that if he kept quiet about Theodor Zauber's threats that he could protect his family from the gargoyles, but instead his silence had led to the death of his son's best friend. He might just as well have stabbed Stu himself.

They were all still standing in shock when Nathan heard a voice calling, 'Nathan! Grace! We just got here! How's Stu?'

He turned around and saw Kenneth and Frances Wintergreen pushing their way toward them through the crowds of emergency patients.

Grace said, 'What are you going to tell them, Nathan? Are you going to tell them truth?'

TWENTY-EIGHT
Saturday, 7:55 a.m.

Jenna came into the office carrying a plastic cup of cappuccino and a box of jelly donuts. She hung her parka over the back of her chair and sat down at her desk. 'That is the very last time I have breakfast at Joe's,' she said, snapping the lid off her coffee.

'You say that every single morning, without fail,' said Detective Brubaker. 'What was wrong with it this time?'

'I ordered corned beef hash, not fatty pink slurry. And what that man can do to eggs . . . it ought to be a misdemeanor, at the very least.'

'Murder most fowl,' said Detective Brubaker, and when Jenna didn't respond he said, 'F-o-w-l, get it?'

'I get it, for Christ's sake.'

Detective Brubaker eased himself up from his desk and came across with a torn-off sheet from his notepad. 'Jokes apart, we had a real strange call passed across from the Fourteenth District about a half-hour ago. They know that you've been working on these unexplained objects dropping out of the sky and they thought it might interest you.'

'Oh, yes?'

'A taxi driver said he was passing through West Mount Airy around nine thirty yesterday evening when he saw something fly into the second story of a private house. He says he only caught a glimpse of it and at first he thought it was a guy on a hang-glider who had gotten out of control.'

Jenna put down her coffee cup. 'A guy on a hang-glider? Are you serious? Where the hell could anybody have hang-glid from, in West Mount Airy? Is that the word? Or is it "hang-glided"?'

'I don't think it matters, because our taxi driver soon realized that he couldn't have been a guy on a hang-glider because he circled around and collided with the house a second time. I mean like really smashed into it. Then he flew off.'

Jenna took the note and studied it with a frown. 'Did they send out any officers to check this out?'

'Yes, they did, because they'd had several calls from neighbors, too. They all reported two loud crashes, and severe damage to one of the windows at the front of the property. It seems like somebody in the property got badly hurt, too, because the residents called for an ambulance. Officer Dolan at the Fourteenth promised to call me back when he had further information on that, but so far he hasn't.'

'Did any of the neighbors see this mystery out-of-control hang-glider who couldn't have been an out-of-control hang-glider?'

'Nope. The only eyewitness was our taxi driver. His name and his number's at the bottom of the page, works for Victory Taxis.'

'Do we know whose property this was?'

'No. But I can call Dolan and ask him.'

'It's OK,' said Jenna. 'I'll do it. Thanks for taking the message.'

'You're welcome,' said Detective Brubaker. 'That'll cost you a donut. In fact, that'll cost you two donuts.'

Jenna opened the box and he helped himself. She picked one out, too, and took a large bite. She punched out the number of the Fourteenth District and they answered so promptly that she still had her mouth full and a drip of raspberry jelly on her chin.

Officer Dolan was just about to end his shift, but she caught him at the front desk.

'Thanks for calling about that flying thing,' she told him. 'I appreciate anybody who does real joined-up police work.'

'To be honest, it was my partner, more than me. He said it reminded him of all that wacky stuff about statues falling out of the sky, and I remembered seeing that interview you did on the TV.'

'Have you found out yet if anybody was hurt?'

'Yeah. I had a call from the ER at Albert Einstein Medical Center about ten minutes ago. Hold on, let me check my notes. Yes, here. The casualty was a seventeen-year-old male name of Stuart Wintergreen. He was hit by flying glass when the window of the property was smashed in, and he suffered a severed femoral artery.'

'What's his condition now?'

'He bled out before they could get him to hospital. He died.'

'Jesus,' said Jenna. 'Do you have any idea what it was that hit that house?'

'None at all.'

'Do you have an address?'

'Sure. Six-oh-five, West Mount Airy Avenue. Home of Professor Nathan Underhill and Doctor Grace Underhill.'

'You're kidding me.'

'Excuse me?'

'No, no – I'm sorry. You just took me by surprise, that's all. Professor Underhill seems to be involved in every single case I've been investigating lately.'

'Yeah. I get people like that. They turn up at every crime scene and every fire and every traffic accident. You look through the photographs and there they are, in every single picture, standing in the background. My partner reckons they're aliens.'

'I think your partner may be right.'

Jenna gulped down the rest of her coffee and left her desk with a donut gripped in her mouth like a giant teething ring. Dan was waiting for her in the parking lot outside, with his engine running. It was starting to rain.

'Suits you,' he said, nodding at the donut.

Jenna took it out of her mouth. 'You want some?'

Dan bit into it and then handed it back. 'This Professor Underhill . . . maybe it's just a series of coincidences, you know – him being around when that guy from Schiller got burned, and that hospital orderly got torn to pieces, and this kid got killed.'

'Oh, you think? I don't believe it for a moment. There's a connection between all of these fatalities, and it's my hunch that Professor Underhill knows what it is.'

'If he knows what it is, why hasn't he told you? There's no circumstantial evidence so far that he was responsible. I don't know about this kid.'

'Stuart Wintergreen,' said Jenna, checking her notebook. 'Seventeen years old, attended West Airy High School. Model student, apparently. Loved dogs. Wanted to go to Penn Vet when he graduated to study veterinary medicine.'

They had only just reached Pennsylvania Avenue when Jenna's cellphone played. It was raining harder now, and the rubbery squeaking of the windshield wipers made it difficult for her to hear.

'Jenna? It's Ed Freiburg. I've identified that statue that we found in the wetlands at Bartram's Gardens. You want to come over to Arch Street and take a look?'

'Maybe later, Ed,' said Jenna, but then she thought, *if there is a connection between Professor Underhill and these falling statues, the more I know about them before I go to question him, the better.* 'No – change of plan. I'll come on over right now.'

'What's up?' asked Dan.

'Turn around. Ed Freiburg has something to show us.'

'Nothing disgusting, I hope. I just ate breakfast.'

They met Ed in the large chilly garage at the rear of the CSI building on Arch Street. It was mostly used for the forensic examination of vehicles that had been involved in crimes or suicides or suspicious accidents, and there were two SUVs parked side by side, one burned out and the other with its driver's door riddled with bullet holes. The garage was high-ceilinged and neon-lit, and it echoed with the banging of hammers and the persistent nagging of circular saws.

The statue that had been retrieved from the wetlands at Bartram's Gardens was standing at the far end. Ed came over to greet them, wearing a noisy blue Tyvek suit and a baseball cap. He was carrying a large Manila folder in one hand and a hotdog in the other.

'Breakfast,' he remarked, holding up the hotdog. Then he nodded at the statue and said, 'He's a real beauty, ain't he? America's Next Top Gargoyle.'

The statue scowled back down at them – over ten feet tall, carved out of grayish-white limestone, with horns and bulbous eyes and a distinctive beak with sharp teeth protruding from either side. It had curved claws like scimitars and it looked no less threatening for having been damaged. Its broken wing lay on the floor close beside it.

'Its eyes are open,' said Jenna.

Ed stared at her. 'It's made out of limestone, Jenna. It couldn't close its eyes if it wanted to. Not that it could ever want to do anything, because it's an inanimate object.'

'OK . . . so you've found out what it is.'

'Yes, I think I have.' He opened his folder and leafed through the first two or three pages. 'It took me some time, because it's a really *rare* inanimate object. But I was able to track it down because it has a very distinctive chemical composition. It's made out of limestone from a quarry south of Kraków, in Poland. The quarry's flooded now, and they call it Zakrówek Lake, but back in the fourteenth century, it was the source of building materials for several of the early churches in Kraków, including Saint Catherine's, in the old Kazimierz quarter, which is where *this* baby came from.'

Dan approached the statue and looked up at it, wrinkling up his nose. 'Ugly looking dude, isn't he?'

'He's a gargoyle, Dan. Gargoyles are ugly by nature. I believe that this particular one is called a *draghignazzo*, which means "nasty dragon". It's mentioned in Dante's Inferno as one of the demons who guarded the Fifth Pit of Hell.'

'How did it get here, to Philly?' asked Jenna. She couldn't take her eyes away from it. It seemed to be staring at *her* directly, and she had the irrational feeling that if she broke eye contact, it would instantly come to life and attack her. She had interviewed dozens of sociopathic criminals who had the same unblinking look in their eyes, and she knew from experience that you never turned your back on them, ever, not even for a moment.

'I checked it out on the Internet. Saint Catherine's was plagued with bad luck right from the moment it was built. In the fifteenth century, even before it was finished, there was an earthquake in Kraków and half of it collapsed. There was another earthquake in seventeen eighty-six, when Saint Catherine's was the only building in the entire city that was damaged.

'This particular gargoyle toppled off the south porch and killed a young priest who had something of a reputation as an exorcist. Because of that, it was never put back up again when the church was restored. The priests kept it in the vaults, and they actually chained it up with heavy iron chains to prevent it from escaping. Superstitious, or what?'

Jenna blinked, and for a split second she thought that the gargoyle blinked, too. *I dare you*, she thought. *I dare you to close your eyes and show me that you're really alive.*

Ed said, 'When the architect John Haviland was building the Eastern State Penitentiary in the 1920s, he wanted to have

gargoyles placed all along the parapets, each one of them
representing a different sin, to frighten the inmates into mending
their wicked ways. He got to hear about our pal the *draghignazzo*
here – after all, it was quite a legend in gargoyle circles – and
had it shipped over to the USA. I think the priests at Saint
Catherine's were pleased to get rid of it, especially since Haviland
paid them five hundred dollars for it.'

'I never saw any gargoyles on top of the Eastern State
Penitentiary,' said Jenna.

'That's because they never put any up. Haviland gathered
together dozens of them, all from different parts of Europe, but
they ended up being stored in the cellars underneath cell-block
fourteen.'

'And that's where they are now?'

Ed took a last bite of hotdog and shook his head. 'Not any
more they're not. Earlier this year, the penitentiary's directors
sold them all off.'

'Do we know who bought them?'

'A company called A-One Chemicals, with a registered office
in Delaware. I tried to track them down, but they don't have a
website and they don't appear in any business directories. There's
an A-One Chemicals in Deer Park, Texas, but they make cleaning
solvents and they wouldn't have any use for more than a hundred
gargoyles.'

Jenna said, 'Dan – you want to follow that up? Go talk to the
accountants at the penitentiary. They must have a record of who
paid them for the gargoyles, and how. And somebody must have
hoisted them out of that vault, and trucked them someplace.'

'Sure. I'll get right on it.'

'So how about it, Ed?' Jenna asked him, although she didn't
take her eyes away from the *draghignazzo*. 'How did it end up
in Bartram's Gardens? Was it floated there, or dragged there? Or
was it dropped there?'

'All the indications are that it fell, and from pretty high up.
That's how its wing got broke. You can see for yourself that it
has no abrasions or chips or vegetation stains on it, which you
would have expected if it had been dragged.'

'So we're back to your theory about flying creatures who turn
to stone in mid-air?'

'That's about the size of it.'

'I can't go back to the captain and tell him that. He'll send me off on psych leave.'

'In that case, Jenna, you'll have to do what you said before. Go back to square one and find some new evidence.'

Jenna said, 'Yes. And I know where to start. When something wacky happens, you need to go looking for the wackjobs.'

TWENTY-NINE
Saturday, 10:43 a.m.

Sukie was sitting up in bed eating a bowl of Cheerios when Nathan and Aarif and Kavita came in to see her. Her face was still flushed but all of the blisters and the scarlet searing had melted away. She looked as if she were suffering from nothing worse than a bad case of sunburn.

Braydon was sitting beside her. He had shaved and showered and changed into a clean blue button-down shirt and he was so delighted that he couldn't keep still.

'How are you feeling, Sukie?' asked Nathan, sitting down on the opposite side of the bed.

Sukie smiled and said, 'Great, thanks.'

Braydon said, 'Doctor Berman told me what you did, Professor Underhill.'

'Well, maybe he shouldn't have. We used your daughter as a guinea pig and we didn't ask your permission.'

'I might have said no,' Braydon told him. 'In fact, I probably *would* have said no. But look at her now. I don't know how to thank you. I mean, bless you – all of you, from the bottom of my heart.'

Kavita said, 'You should know that Professor Underhill tested the procedure on himself, before he tried it on your daughter. He deliberately burned his own hand, very badly, but when we injected him with the stem cells from the phoenix, his hand was healed in only twenty-four hours. In fact, in less than that. That was what persuaded us that it was probably safe to go ahead.'

'So far as I'm concerned, it's a miracle,' said Braydon. 'But

I've learned something else, too. Every kid needs two parents, their father and their mother, and no matter how much their parents might have grown to hate each other, they need to talk, even if they talk with clenched teeth. A child's happiness is worth infinitely more than any of that adult-bickering shit.'

He turned around and took hold of Sukie's hand. 'Do you know something, sweetheart? You're more to me than all of the treasure in the world. And look at you now. These people have saved your life. You'll never have to hide your face or put up with people staring at you like you're some kind of freak.'

Nathan said, 'Braydon – is it OK if I ask Sukie a couple of questions about her nightmares?'

Braydon frowned at him. 'Her *nightmares*? Why would you want to do that? I mean, why is that relevant, in any way at all?'

'You want me to be frank with you? You've told us that Sukie has been having nightmares for years about these Spooglies, right?'

'Yes,' said Braydon, suspiciously. 'But I don't understand why you're asking me this.'

'I'm asking you, Braydon, because Sukie has been repeatedly having very vivid nightmares ever since she arrived here in the ICU, and because yesterday a young man was killed in my house by something which bore a distinct resemblance to one of her Spooglies.'

'*What*? What are you talking about? The Spooglies . . . they're just something out of her imagination.'

'I'm not so sure,' said Nathan. 'I think that they could be real, and that they're coming to life, and your Sukie can sense them. She can *feel* them, Braydon, these Spooglies of hers. For some reason, her mind is tuned in to the Spooglies' wavelength, just like some dogs can hear whistles that are totally inaudible to the rest of us.'

'Say, what? I don't understand what you're talking about.'

'I know it's difficult to get your head round it. But I have strong reasons to believe that Sukie's Spooglies are very much like the phoenix I created. Mythical creatures that have been extinct for hundreds of years, but which have now been revived.'

'Revived? Revived by who? And what the hell for?'

'That's what I'm trying to find out,' said Nathan. He wasn't going to tell Braydon about Theodor Zauber and his efforts to turn his gargoyles back into flesh and blood. Not yet, anyhow. It was difficult enough for him to grasp the concept that his daughter's burns had been healed by a firebird that Nathan and his assistants had recreated from a classical legend.

'OK . . .' said Braydon, with obvious reluctance. 'But don't do nothing to upset her. Otherwise, that's it, I'm pulling the plug.'

Nathan shuffled his chair a little closer to the side of Sukie's bed. 'Sukie,' he said, 'is it OK if I ask you some questions about the Spooglies? You won't be upset, will you?'

'I guess not,' said Sukie, shyly.

'When you dream about them, are they always flying in the sky?'

'Most of the time.'

'Do you ever see them anyplace else, like in a building, or a house?'

Sukie nodded. 'I never used to. But I do now. Sometimes, not always.'

'I see. What kind of a building is it, do you know?'

Sukie shook her head. 'They're all down in the cellar. It's dark down there but I can see their eyes shining. Their eyes are green, like green lights. And I can hear them making a noise like katydids, like *chirp-chirp-chirp* and *shuffle-shuffle-shuffle* and sometimes they scream.'

'Wow. Do you know how many Spooglies there are, down in that cellar? Like twenty, maybe, or thirty?'

'I can't see them very well because it's so dark but more than a hundred I think.'

'More than a hundred? That's an awful lot of Spooglies, isn't it? Do you have any idea where this cellar might be?'

Without hesitation, Sukie pointed to the right-hand corner of her room, next to the door. 'They're over there.'

'What do you mean, sweetheart?' Braydon asked her. 'Do you mean they're *here*, someplace in the hospital?'

'Uhnh-hunh. They're over there, but a long way away.'

'How do you know that, Sukie?' Nathan asked her.

'Because that's where they are. I can feel them. I can *hear* them. They're over there and they're waiting to fly. They want to fly now but they're not allowed to, not yet, and that's why they're going *chirp-chirp-chirp* and *shuffle-shuffle-shuffle* and screaming.'

'Do you know why they're not allowed to? Is somebody telling them that they can't?'

'I don't know. It's too scary. When they fly it's going to be horrible and people are going to get torn to bits and pieces.'

Sukie was gradually growing more and more distressed. She was twisting her blanket in both hands and Braydon took her cereal bowl away in case she jolted her bed-table and spilled it.

'When they fly there's going to be hundreds of them and nobody will be able to get away and they'll be everywhere! And they'll be screaming, and so will we! And there's going to be bits and pieces of people all over, like arms and legs and bodies and heads!'

Sukie was panting now, and her voice rose higher and higher. Braydon said sharply, 'That's enough, sweetheart! That's it! No more talking about Spooglies, OK? They're only a bad dream, that's all.'

'But, Daddy, they're *not*!' Sukie protested, and her eyes filled up with tears. 'They're real! The Spooglies are real, and they're over there! I know they are! I can *feel* them! I can *hear* them!'

Nathan laid his hand on Sukie's arm and said, 'It's OK, Sukie. I'm sorry if I upset you. You've been very, very helpful. If the Spooglies *are* real, I can tell you this: my friends and I will find out where they are and make sure that they never ever get to fly, and never hurt anybody. And we're also going to make sure that you never have nightmares about them, ever again.'

Sukie sniffed, and nodded. Braydon held her close to him and said to Nathan, 'Maybe you and your people had better leave now. Don't think that I'm not grateful for what you've done, because I am. But all this stuff about Spooglies . . .'

'I understand,' Nathan told him. 'But I'd like you to know that Sukie may have saved some lives here today. Not just two or three lives, but maybe hundreds.'

'Please,' said Braydon. 'Just go.'

Outside the hospital, Aarif said, 'You believed her, that little girl? You believe that the gargoyles are really there, in some cellar, in the direction in which she was pointing?'

'Yes,' said Nathan, 'I do.'

'But what is the use of knowing the direction if we do not know how *far* it is, this cellar? She was pointing – what – to the south-west. She could have been pointing to the next street, or she could have been pointing toward Maryland, or West Virginia, or even further. How can we tell?'

'That's a problem I'll have to work on,' said Nathan. 'Meanwhile, why don't you two go back to the lab and check up on Torchy? I need to get home and sort out my house.'

Kavita said, 'I am so sorry about what happened to Denver's friend. Do you really think it was a gargoyle that killed him?'

'I'm sure of it. Theodor Zauber is trying to frighten me into working with him, and I have to admit that he's not far away from succeeding. That's why I want to try and find where he's stored all of the gargoyles he bought from the Eastern State Penitentiary.'

'What will you do, if you can find them?'

'What do you think? Smash them to pieces, before they smash *us* to pieces.'

THIRTY

Saturday, 11:47 a.m.

The doorbell chimed. Nathan thought it was the builders, who were supposed to come and give him an estimate for replacing Denver's bedroom window, but when he answered it he found Detective Pullet and Detective Rubik standing in the porch.

The wind was getting up, and dry leaves were chasing each other around the driveway.

Jenna said, 'You don't need to see my shield, do you, Professor?'

'What do you want?' Nathan asked her. 'I already spoke with an officer from the Fourteenth District.'

'I know you did. But he called me. The thing of it is, I've been assigned to investigate these mysterious limestone statues that keep dropping out of the sky, and these mysterious flying creatures that have been tearing people apart, and I'm beginning to come to the insane conclusion that – somehow – they are one and the same.

'What's more, Professor, it sounds to me as if the thing that damaged your house and caused the death of your son's friend bore a very close resemblance to one of these statues and/or flying creatures.'

Nathan didn't answer, so Jenna stuck her two index fingers up on the top of her head and said, 'Horns?' Then she flapped her arms and said, 'Wings?'

Still Nathan said nothing, so she bugged out her eyes and pressed her nose flat with her finger. 'Maybe it had bulging eyes and a beak?'

'I didn't see it myself.'

'But your son saw it, didn't he? How did he describe it?'

Nathan said, 'You'd better come in. I think we need to talk about this.'

'Well, hallelujah,' said Jenna. 'He done seen the light. And about time, too.'

Nathan led them into the living room. Grace was sitting at the coffee table, filling in reports for her practice at Chestnut Hill medical center.

'Grace, honey. These are detectives.'

'Detective Pullet and Detective Rubik,' said Jenna. 'We've come to ask you some questions about what happened to Stuart Wintergreen, among other things.'

'Sit down, please,' Nathan told them.

Jenna said, 'I've just been to see the statue we hauled out of the wetlands at Bartram's Gardens. You heard about that?'

'Of course.'

'Our chief crime scene investigator has identified it as a gargoyle – from Poland, originally, but shipped over here when they were building the Eastern State Penitentiary. Apparently it was supposed to be positioned on the roof to frighten the crap out of the inmates, as well as about a hundred more gargoyles, but for some reason they never got around to putting them up.'

'I know all about them,' said Nathan. 'I also know who they belong to.'

'And you didn't tell me the last time I talked to you? Haven't you heard about something called "obstructing a police investigation"?'

'I was being mortally threatened, Detective. My family was

being mortally threatened. After that hospital orderly was killed, I knew that the threat was deadly serious. But I thought there was a good chance that I could track the guy down and destroy his gargoyles before he could use them to kill anybody else.'

'Let me get this absolutely straight,' said Jenna. 'The stone statues and the flying gargoyles, they really *are* one and the same?'

Nathan said, 'Yes. They are. I know it's really difficult to believe, but in the Middle Ages, in Europe, there was a plague of gargoyles – thousands of them. They killed cattle, sheep, and countless numbers of people. But in the end an alchemist called Artephius found a way to turn them to stone, and a whole bunch of exorcists was sent out by the Vatican to hunt them down. The Brotherhood of Purity, they called them.'

'So once upon a time, these gargoyles used to be actual living creatures?'

'That's right, before they were petrified. But now this German thaumaturge called Theodor Zauber has discovered a way to turn them back into living creatures.'

'*Thaumaturge*? What's a thaumaturge when he's at home?'

'A magician. A sorcerer. A worker of miracles. Theodor Zauber's late father Christian Zauber was one of the greatest sorcerers of the twenty-first century, and his son has followed in his footsteps. He can do things that would make you doubt your sanity, and bringing gargoyles back to life is one of them.

'His idea was to turn terminally ill people into human statues – just like cryogenics except that you wouldn't need the freezers. Sometime in the future – when doctors eventually find a treatment for whatever disease was about to kill them – they would be *un*-petrified, if that's the right word, and then, hopefully, cured.'

'But?'

'Why do you say, "but"?'

'Because there's always a "but". Because this Zauber character threatened to set his gargoyles on you. Why did he do that?'

Nathan explained how Theodor Zauber had found that his newly-revived gargoyles were unable to stay living and breathing for more than a few hours before they started to turn back into stone, and how they needed an almost endless supply of fresh human hearts to keep them alive. He explained how Theodor

Zauber had asked him to join him in his enterprise, and give him the benefit of his cryptozoological expertise. The sorcerer desperately needed a scientist, but the scientist had said no.

'Do you have any idea of Zauber's current location, or where he stores these gargoyles?' Jenna asked him.

'No,' said Nathan. 'None whatsoever.'

He did tell her, however, about Sukie Harris, and how Sukie Harris had pointed south-westward from her hospital bed.

'She's convinced that the gargoyles are stored somewhere in that direction. But as my assistant said, that could mean that they're three blocks away, or three hundred miles.'

'Do you think that Zauber will try to contact you again?' asked Jenna. She was frustrated and annoyed with Nathan, but at the same time she could understand that he had been trying to protect himself and his family, as well as his reputation. She had dealt with a similar case only last year, when the Black Mafia had threatened the family of a very reputable lawyer unless he repre- sented one of their members in a drugs prosecution. Before he had given in, the lawyer's two German shepherds had been decapi- tated and their heads impaled on each side of his cast-iron gates.

Nathan said, 'Yes. I'm sure he'll be in touch. He seriously believes that this petrification scheme is the future of medicine. He's convinced that it's going to make him rich and famous, and it doesn't even occur to him that killing innocent people is wrong, so long as he achieves his dream.'

'OK, then,' said Jenna. 'When he does get in touch, I want you to arrange to meet him. We'll be there, too.'

'He's pretty elusive, I warn you. He can walk in and out of places and nobody even sees him.'

'There's nobody born who can get past me, Professor, I promise you. Thauma-thingummy or not.'

'Like I say, I'm just warning you.'

Jenna and Dan stayed for another hour and a half, asking questions and taking notes. As simply as he could, Nathan explained his cryptozoological research to them, and how he had developed the phoenix, and this time he confessed what had really happened when Ron Kasabian had been burned to death.

Jenna said, 'You realize there could be a case here for crimin- ally negligent homicide? Not that any jury would believe anything that you just told me, not for a moment.'

'Right now, it's only important that you believe it,' Nathan told her.

He described how Theodor Zauber had visited his room at Temple University Hospital, and how Theodor Zauber had urged the gargoyle to plunge from the top of the physiotherapy building and kill Eduardo Sanchez Delgado.

When she had finished, Jenna closed her notebook and said, 'You won't tell anybody else about any of this, will you, Professor? Especially not the media. You know it's true and now I know it's true, but if it gets out before we can properly substantiate it, we're going to look like we're barking mad.'

Nathan and Grace stood together at the front door watching Jenna and Dan climb into their car and drive away.

'I'm so angry with you,' said Grace. 'I'm so angry I don't know what to say to you. Stu's dead because of you.'

'Stu's dead because Theodor Zauber is a psychopath. Like I said before, if I had told the police about the gargoyles, they never would have believed me. And even if they had, what then? You think they could have protected us? How do you stop a gargoyle from crashing into your house?'

'Those detectives believe you now.'

'You think so? I don't know. I don't really believe it myself.'

'But if only you had told them sooner, they could have done something. They could have found Zauber and arrested him.'

'On what charge, Grace? Owning a large collection of grotesque medieval statues?'

'I don't know. Making threats against you.'

'My word against his. No, Grace, when it comes down to it, there's only one person who can stop Theodor Zauber and his gargoyles, and you're looking at him.'

THIRTY-ONE
Sunday, 9:42 a.m.

He came out of the shower, toweling his hair, and went into his dressing room. He was standing naked in front of his mirror, wondering if he had put on any weight around his midriff, when an amused voice said, 'Very well endowed, Professor. I'm impressed.'

He shouted out, '*Ah!*' and turned around, bundling the towel between his legs. Sitting in the pale blue basketwork chair in the corner, his legs crossed, was Theodor Zauber, dressed in his usual black suit and glossy black shoes.

'How in God's name did you get in here?' Nathan demanded.

'God's name had nothing at all to do with it,' Theodor Zauber replied. 'It was the name of another, equally powerful. You should know me by now. I am able to go wherever I please. *Ich bin wie Glas transparent.* I am no more visible than a window. By the way, I am sorry about *your* window. What damage those gargoyles can do!'

'Do you think I care about the goddamned window? It's young Stu Wintergreen that I care about. You killed him, you bastard. He was only seventeen years old and now he's dead.'

Theodor Zauber gave a one-shouldered shrug. 'It's very regretful, Professor. But you know what they say about omelets and eggs. I did warn you what might happen if you persisted in being so uncooperative.'

'Stu Wintergreen was nothing to do with you and me. He was an innocent kid who had the whole of his life in front of him.'

'Well, now the whole of his life is behind him. What can I say? There is nothing that can bring him back to us now, not even the greatest spells devised by the greatest sorcerers of all time. Dead is dead, Professor. But you can make sure that he did not die in vain, your Wintergreen boy.'

'What do you mean?'

'If you agree to join with me now, and work to perfect the

petrification process, his death will have had some lasting value. If you like, we can name the process after him, in his memory. The Wintergreen Process. I like the sound of that. It sounds like fresh growth emerging at a time when everything is chilly and barren. Life, emerging out of cold stone.'

'Do you seriously think that I would consider working with you after what you've done?'

'Have I not managed to persuade you yet? You saw what happened to that poor fellow at the hospital; and now you have seen for yourself that you and your family are not safe anywhere, even inside your own home. If you do not agree to assist me, Professor, I will have no option but to continue trying to find a thaumaturgic method to prevent my gargoyles from reverting back to stone. That will mean bringing more and more of them to life, and sacrificing the lives of many more innocent people.'

Nathan took a deep breath, making the most reluctant decision of his life. 'OK,' he said. 'Let me do some background research today, and see if there's anything practical I can do to help you. Then maybe you can show me the gargoyles and I can try out some preliminary chemical tests on them. Where do you have them stored?'

Theodor Zauber smiled. 'All in good time, Professor.' He checked his wristwatch. 'Why don't you meet me at ten o'clock tomorrow morning at the Eastern State Penitentiary? That would be an appropriate rendezvous, don't you think? Then you can tell me what you have discovered about reanimating gargoyles, if anything, and we can discuss how we can go forward together with our research.'

'I see. You don't entirely trust me, even though you're threatening to kill my wife and my son, and who knows how many other people?'

'I have learned to trust *nobody*, Professor, regardless of the duress they may be under. Many people will not hesitate to sacrifice others for the greater good, even the ones they love. Like my father, for instance, and like myself.'

Nathan said, 'My God. You're a piece of work, aren't you, Herr Zauber?'

'All living things are "pieces of work", Professor. You and I devote ourselves to finding out what these "pieces of work" are made of, and how they are put together. Also, how one may take them apart.'

He paused, and then he said, 'I will see you tomorrow, then, at the penitentiary. I must ask that you tell nobody, however – especially the police. Otherwise, the consequences may be doubly terrible. *Ein Blutbad*, as we Germans so graphically describe it. A massacre.'

Nathan went across to his closet and took out his navy blue toweling bathrobe, and put it on. When he turned around again, tying up the belt, Theodor Zauber had gone.

Immediately, he went out on to the landing. Grace was coming up the stairs, and she said, 'What's the matter, darling? You look like you've seen a ghost.'

'Theodor Zauber was here.'

'*What*?'

'He was right here, in my dressing room, talking to me. Then he just vanished. You didn't see him come downstairs, did you?'

'No. Nobody. But it was very strange . . . halfway up the stairs I felt like somebody brushed past me.'

'That was Zauber. He can do that. It's some kind of hypnotic thing.'

'What did he want?'

Nathan went into the master bedroom and crossed quickly to the window. He was just in time to see Theodor Zauber climbing into his rented Impala. Theodor Zauber looked back at the house as he was fastening his seat belt, and Nathan was sure that he smiled up at him.

'He wanted the same as he wanted before, the bastard. He needs help to reanimate these gargoyles of his. He can bring them back to life, but after an hour or two they start to turn back into stone again.'

'*Could* you help him?'

'I think so. It's all a question of modifying the coding in their chromosomes. At the moment, being petrified is their default state, because of the way in which they turned to stone. What I would have to do is alter their chromosomes so that their default state is flesh and blood. It's a bit like reprogramming a computer.'

'More to the point,' said Grace, '*would* you help him?'

'I think you know the answer to that. It's time to disinfect the world of Zaubers. This particular line of Zaubers, anyhow. He's asked me to meet him tomorrow morning at the Eastern State Penitentiary.'

'And you're going?'

'Of course. If I can find out where Theodor Zauber keeps his gargoyles, I can make sure that none of them ever comes to life again. I know enough about recreating mythical creatures to know how to exterminate them, too.'

'You're not telling Detective Pullet?'

'What's the point? Like I said before, she couldn't arrest him for possession of legally-purchased statues. And how could she ever prove that Theodor Zauber had brought them to life, so that they could fly, and attack people? He would simply have to say that the whole idea was absurd, and it *is*, when you think about it – like the phoenix, and the gryphon, and the basilisk.'

'I guess so, when you put it like that. But you will be careful, won't you?'

Nathan heard a soft rumbling noise. It sounded like distant thunder, but actually it was the tarpaulin that the builders had rigged up as a temporary cover for Denver's bedroom window, rumbling in the wind.

He held Grace close, and kissed her forehead, and she smelled of roses and citrus, like she always did.

'I'll be careful. I promise.'

THIRTY-TWO

Monday, 9:07 a.m.

Monday morning was one of those gray, grainy days when Philadelphia looked like a tinted black-and-white photograph of itself. A cold wind was blowing from the north-west and there was a feeling that winter was beginning to wake up, somewhere on the Canadian prairies, and shake his coat of icicles.

Nathan visited the Schiller building first, to see how Torchy was developing. Kavita was there, in the laboratory, but Aarif had taken the morning off to have his nose X-rayed. It was still swollen and he was having difficulty breathing.

The phoenix was larger and grander and more dazzling than ever, with plumage that shone like gold leaf. On the floor of his cage, Kavita had made him a comfortable nest of dried grass and feathers and dried flowers and laced-together twigs, and instead of sitting on his perch he now preferred to sit here with his head regally raised, looking from side to side as if he had nothing but contempt for everybody who approached him.

Kavita nodded toward the laptop at her workstation. On the screen was a picture of Sukie Harris, happily smiling. Her skin was almost completely healed, and even the redness had faded.

'Doctor Berman sent that across at seven thirty this morning,' said Kavita. 'He's expecting to be able to discharge her by Wednesday. He also says that he'd like to arrange a meeting with us as soon as possible, so that we can discuss the phoenix procedure for more of his patients.'

Nathan examined the picture on the laptop closely. 'She looks terrific, doesn't she, when you consider how seriously she was burned? I can't wait to test it on some more patients. Third-degree burns, especially.'

He went across to Torchy's cage and peered inside. Torchy ruffled his golden feathers and made that threatening warble in the back of his throat.

'He still doesn't like me, does he?'

'I think he's a woman's bird,' said Kavita. 'In fact, I don't think he realizes that he's a bird at all. He thinks he's my mate.'

'Well, I don't mind that, so long as he keeps on supplying us with stem cells. Unfortunately, we have to get approval from the FDA and the Department of Health and Human Services before we can do any more tests. I know Doctor Berman is itching to get started – so am I. But the last thing we need is for somebody to hit us with a major lawsuit. Which they inevitably will, even if the phoenix procedure has cured them completely. And we don't yet know if there are any long-term side-effects.'

'*You* still feel well, don't you, Professor?' Kavita asked him.

'So far. But I'll feel a whole lot better once we've gotten rid of Theodor Zauber and his goddamned gargoyles. I'm supposed to be meeting him at ten o'clock this morning. I think I've managed to convince him that I'm prepared to help him. Well, *half*-convince him, anyhow. He still won't tell me where his gargoyles are stashed.'

Kavita said, 'I did a whole lot of research last night on gargoyles. Do you know of Zosimos of Panopolis?'

'Sure. Good old Zosimos of Panopolis, where would modern science be without him? He was practically the first known alchemist, wasn't he, back in three hundred AD, in Greece? Wasn't he the guy who thought that fallen angels fell in love with human women, and married them, and taught them chemistry and metalworking and how to paint their eyelids? And as far as I remember there followed much licentiousness and fornication.'

'That's right. But he also wrote about gargoyles, and how to petrify them, centuries before Artephius, even though he never actually managed to do it, like Artephius did.'

'No, I didn't know that.'

'Well, neither did I until I looked it up. But I thought one thing was really interesting. Zosimos warned that once a gargoyle was petrified, you can break it up, but you can never destroy it simply by smashing it to pieces. That is why gargoyles were always mounted on the tops of churches and cathedrals, rather than shattered. If they were shattered, the fragments would always come back together again, somehow, but if they were attached to a sacred building, they could never escape, for as long as the building remained standing, and they could never call on Satan to rescue them, because their mouths were purified by rainwater from the sacred building.'

'Now that *is* interesting,' said Nathan. 'In fact it's more than interesting. If I can manage to locate Theodor Zauber's gargoyles, I'll have to know how to destroy them, and if smashing them to pieces isn't going to do it—'

'That's right,' said Kavita. 'But Zosimos believed that he had worked out the answer to that little problem. He theorized that you can exterminate gargoyles by changing their chemistry. All you have to do is expose them to intense heat and then drench them with water. Zosimos said that this will "purify" them with holy fire.'

Nathan thought about that, and then nodded. 'He was right, chemically speaking. If you heat limestone it changes from calcium carbonate into basic calcium oxide. All you have to do then is drench it in water, and you get a fierce exothermic reaction. Up to one hundred fifty degrees Celsius, which changes it into quicklime.'

The clock on the laboratory wall now read 9:26. Nathan said, 'Listen, Kavita, I'd better get going. I'm meeting Zauber at the Eastern State Penitentiary.'

'Why does he want to meet you there, of all places?'

'I don't know. I think he's trying to frighten me, that's all.'

'I think you *should* be frightened.'

Nathan kissed her on the cheek. 'Who says I'm not?'

THIRTY-THREE

Monday, 10:04 a.m.

Theodor Zauber was waiting for him outside the prison's main entrance on Fairmount Avenue, wearing a long black overcoat and mirror sunglasses.

The Eastern State Penitentiary occupied an entire city block between Corinthian Avenue and North 22nd Street. Its facade was built of gray stone, like a medieval castle, with forbidding square towers and battlements. Two gargoyles were perched above either side of the entrance, holding chains in their claws to remind inmates that this was a place of punishment and retribution. There was already a shuffling line of visitors outside the door, and a party of Japanese tourists listening to their tour guide.

'When the prison was opened in eighteen twenty-nine, each prisoner was kept in solitary confinement, with only one small skylight in the ceiling of his cell, the Eye of God, to make prisoners feel that the Lord was always watching them.'

Nathan crossed the street. Theodor Zauber took off his black leather glove and held out his hand but Nathan didn't shake it. 'Please yourself, Professor,' said Theodor Zauber, tugging his glove back on again. 'I merely thought that if you and I were going to be colleagues in our research, we might as well behave in a cordial manner.'

'You want me to be *cordial*? After wrecking my house and killing my son's best friend? Like you said, I'm only agreeing to help you under extreme duress.'

Theodor Zauber said, 'I regret very much that I have had to apply so much pressure, Professor. But you left me no alternative, did you?'

'Forget the crocodile tears. Just tell me what you want me to do, OK?'

Theodor Zauber produced two tickets from his coat pocket. 'Here – let us go inside. Have you ever visited this penitentiary before? It is most educational, and most entertaining. I came here last week, and lay down on the very bed that Al Capone used to sleep in.'

'You and he deserve each other. Spiritual bedfellows.'

They went inside the penitentiary. It was chilly, and echoing, and even though the last prisoner had left over thirty years ago, it was still gloomy and smelled of despair. It was a preserved ruin, and no attempt had been made to restore it, so the cream-colored paint on the walls was peeling and the cells were cluttered with broken chairs and old newspapers and other detritus, and most of the toilets had been smashed.

Theodor Zauber led the way up the narrow spiral staircase to the central guard tower, his polished shoes clanging on the iron treads. When they reached the top and stepped outside, Nathan could see the way that the fifteen cell-blocks had been built, like the radiating spokes of a wheel. He could see for miles in every direction, although the sky was as gray as the penitentiary walls.

Theodor Zauber took a deep breath and pummeled his chest with his fists. 'Refreshing up here, yes? *Auffrischung*, as we say in Germany.'

'You think so?' Nathan retorted. 'I think it's cold enough to freeze your nuts off, as we say in America. Do you want to make this quick?'

'Very well. You know that I can restore life to the gargoyles by using the formula that Artephius devised for "quenching water". But for reasons that I cannot fathom, their revivification has only a limited duration. I have tried a hundred different variations of the same formula but it makes no difference. After only a few hours, at the very most, they always begin spontaneously to transmute back into stone. If they are flying, they drop out of the sky.

'As you know, they can prolong their animation if they can find a living human heart and devour it. But I do not want to see dozens of innocent people slaughtered any more than you do, Professor, especially since – at the moment, anyway – they are dying in vain. That is why I am appealing to you to lend me your cryptozoological expertise. You can save so many lives, believe me.'

Nathan went across to the rusted guard-rail and looked down over the rooftops. Who could imagine what it must have been like, locked up in here for year after year with no other human contact except for the prison governor and the prison guards? Each cell had its own small exercise yard, with walls so high that prisoners had no contact with each other. The idea had been that intense isolation would lead to spiritual and social reform, but in practice it had driven many inmates insane.

Without turning around, Nathan said, 'I did some preliminary research yesterday and I've come up with one or two ideas that may help to prevent your gargoyles from reverting so rapidly into limestone. But if I'm going to test them out, I'll have to have at least two or three gargoyles to work on, and I'll have to know what this "quenching water" is made of.'

'Of course. Yes. But first I really need to know that I can trust you.'

Nathan raised both hands, although he still didn't turn around. 'What can I say, Herr Zauber? You have me over a barrel, don't you? Of course you can trust me.'

'You *do* believe that it can work, don't you, petrifying people? You believe that it can be a success?'

'Theoretically, yes. I'm not so sure that you'll find many takers, even if they're terminally ill. But who knows? The worst that can happen to them is that they leave their loved ones a statue of themselves.'

'*Zynisch, aber wahr,*' said Theodor Zauber. 'Cynical, but true. Meet me tomorrow at six o'clock in the evening in the parking lot outside the Bala Cynwyd Shopping Center on West City Drive. Bring with you any equipment that you think you may need.'

At that moment, however, they heard footsteps clattering up the stairs. It sounded like five or six people, and they were coming up fast. Theodor Zauber threw Nathan a look of perplexity and backed away from the staircase. Nathan was about to tell him that *he* didn't know what was going on, either, when Detective

Pullet appeared, with her gun drawn, closely followed by Detective Rubik and three uniformed police officers.

'Theodor Zauber?' snapped Detective Pullet. 'Put your hands on top of your head and get down on your knees.'

'Why?' asked Theodor Zauber. 'What do you imagine that I have done wrong?'

Jenna crossed the guard tower, her boots crunching on broken glass. 'I don't *imagine* that you've done something wrong, sir. I *know* that you've done something wrong. Theodor Zauber, I'm arresting you for the murders of Chet Huntley, William Barrow, James Hallam Junior and Stuart Wintergreen. Hook him up, Dan.'

'Wait,' Theodor Zauber protested. 'This is absurd. You have absolutely no evidence of this. I have never heard of any of these people. I have never met them, and I have certainly never done them any harm.'

'Well, you can explain that back at the district,' said Jenna. 'But let's put it this way: if a man is the owner of a dangerous dog, and he lets that dangerous dog loose to go out and attack other people, whether he knows these people or not, then who do you think is responsible in law? Not the dog, sir, and you'd better believe it.'

Jenna came over to Nathan. She holstered her gun and stood in front of him with her hands resting on her hips. 'It was my distinct impression, Professor, that when you arranged to meet Theodor Zauber, you were going to inform me in advance. Or was I mistaken?'

'I'm sorry, but I didn't see how you could realistically charge him with any offense. I thought that if I could find out where his gargoyles were stored—'

'You could do *what*, exactly?'

'I thought that I could destroy them, and that would be an end to it.'

'So now we have the truth, Professor!' Theodor Zauber barked at him. 'You had no intention of helping me with my research! You did the same to my father! You lied to him and cheated him and destroyed his entire life's work, and then you took his life, too! And now you want to do the same to me! Well, I can assure you that you won't get the better of me!'

Jenna turned back to Nathan. 'Did you really not think that I would put a tail on you? Every time I questioned you, I knew that you weren't giving me the whole picture. It's a funny thing, but after you've questioned thousands and thousands of liars and bluffers and double-talkers, you get to recognize who's telling you the truth and who isn't.'

'You really think you can charge Zauber with all of those murders and make it stick? I mean, where's your proof?'

'We should have more than enough forensic evidence. Zauber's prints all over the gargoyles, for beginners. And your expert testimony, too, that it's scientifically possible to turn a stone statue into a living, flying creature.'

Nathan gave her a disbelieving shake of his head, 'How can I possibly stand up in court and testify to that, when I don't have any idea how he does it? That's why I wanted to meet him alone. He says he has some stuff called "quenching water" which he uses to bring the gargoyles back to life, but I don't have a clue what's in it or how it works. Right now, all we have is speculation. He only has to say that he *can't* bring a gargoyle back to life, and never has done, and who do you think a jury's going to believe?'

'Well, we'll see about that,' Jenna told him. 'Right now he's coming to the district for some gentle interrogation, and we'll take it from there. Dan – can you escort our prisoner downstairs, please? And make sure he doesn't trip. I don't want to be accused of police brutality.'

Dan said, 'What prisoner?'

'Herr Theodor Zauber, of course.'

'Herr who?'

'Theodor Zauber. Do you want me to spell it for you?'

'Not really. There's nobody here.'

Jenna turned her head. Dan was right. The only people standing in the derelict shell of the guard tower were her, and Dan, and the three police officers who had accompanied them up the stairs, and Nathan. Theodor Zauber had vanished.

'Where the *hell* did he go?' said Jenna.

'Who?' asked Dan. He seemed to be genuinely baffled.

'The prisoner! Theodor Zauber! The man you were just about to hook up! Look – you're even holding your goddamned cuffs in your hand, ready!'

Dan frowned, and pressed his fingertips to his forehead, as if he were trying to remember something important that had completely slipped his mind.

Jenna turned to the uniformed officers. 'He must have walked right past you! Why didn't you stop him? What are you, *blind*?'

One of the officers said, 'Excuse me, Detective, I have to say that I resent that remark.'

'Then why didn't you stop him, for Christ's sake?'

'I'm sorry, Detective, I don't know who you're talking about.'

'*Aaahhhh!*' screamed Jenna, in frustration. 'Why do you think we came up here? To feed the pigeons? To admire the lovely view, maybe?'

Another officer said, 'We came up here – we came up here to—' he stopped, and then he said, 'I don't know *why* we came up here.'

Nathan said, 'Detective—'

'What?'

'It's no use, Detective. They honestly don't know. Theodor Zauber has the gift of hypnotizing people. He's done it to me. One second he's there, the next second he's gone, and you don't remember seeing him go, or if he was ever there at all. There's nothing magical about it. It's nothing more than standard clinical hypnosis, but he happens to be very, very good at it.'

'So we've lost him.'

'For now, yes. But I think there's a chance that he'll get in touch with me again. He may be angry with me, but he still needs my help.'

'I don't believe this,' said Jenna. 'I've only just managed to persuade myself that stone statues can come to life, and now the man who can do it has disappeared in front of my eyes. I was worried that my captain was going to send me off on psych leave. Now I think I'll volunteer for it.'

THIRTY-FOUR

Monday, 3:13 p.m.

Nathan returned to his laboratory in the Schiller building. In the absence of any vetoes from the Schiller board of directors, he was continuing his work on the phoenix project as if nothing had happened. He had heard no more about future funding, or whether Schiller would support the project to its logical conclusion – which would be to breed phoenixes on a large scale so that their stem cells could be used to heal burns sufferers all over the world.

Kavita was running tests on Torchy's glands. She was wearing a white lab coat but a red silk scarf tied around her head, pirate style, and large gold earrings.

'How's it going?' Nathan asked her.

'There's at least twenty percent more prolactin in his pituitary gland than there was the last time I tested him, and almost twice as much corticosterone in his adrenal gland. Normally, birds only produce hormones in this quantity when they're getting ready to migrate, and need a huge amount of stored energy for very long flights. I think it's possible that Torchy releases all of this tremendous energy in one burst to become incandescent.'

Nathan went over and looked at the results that she had printed out from the QX diagnostic computer. 'That looks highly likely, Kavita. Good work.'

He was about to suggest some further blood tests when his cellphone bleeped. He checked the number but he didn't recognize it.

'Nathan Underhill.'

'Ah, Professor Underhill. Here is Theodor Zauber.'

'Herr Zauber – I was wondering if you'd call me. What happened at the penitentiary this morning, that was nothing to do with me. I had no idea that the police had a tail on me.'

'And you expect me to believe that? You think I am some kind of *dummkopf*?'

'No, I don't. But I wouldn't do anything that puts my family at risk.'

'You can protest as much as you like, Professor. It is plain to me that I cannot trust you.'

'So what are you going to do now? If you want your gargoyles to come back to life and stay alive, you'll *have* to trust me, won't you?'

'You told that police detective that your intention in meeting me was to find out where they are and destroy them. Was that a lie?'

'Of course it was a lie. I couldn't let them think I was really going to help you, could I?'

Theodor Zauber was breathing very hard, as if he were trying to control his temper. 'No,' he said, 'I cannot risk you discovering where my gargoyles are. I will just have to carry on my experiments without you. If I bring enough gargoyles back to life, I am bound to find out eventually how to prevent them from transmuting back into stone.'

'You said yourself that if you do that, a whole lot of innocent people are going to get killed.'

'Well, so be it. My father took many lives in order to further his research. I will have to do the same. You have only yourself to blame, Professor. You could have prevented this, but you chose instead to double-cross me. When the people of this city start to be torn to pieces, look in the mirror and ask yourself who is responsible.'

'Listen, I *will* help you!' said Nathan. 'Just give me the chance to prove that you can trust me! We could start with only a couple of gargoyles, in any location you choose.'

'Too late, I'm afraid. You admit that you lied to the police. How do I know that you are not lying to me? You have poisoned the well, Professor. Now you and many others will have to pay the price for that.'

'*Zauber*—' Nathan began, but Theodor Zauber had gone. He tried to call the number back, but the cellphone had been switched off.

'*Shit*,' he said, under his breath.

Kavita looked up from her readings. 'What's wrong, Professor?'

Nathan was already punching out Grace's number at Chestnut Hill Medical Center, so that he could warn her not to go home this evening.

'What's wrong?' he replied. 'I think I just set the end of the world in motion.'

He called Grace, and then he called Denver, and told them not to go home when Grace had finished her surgery for the day and Denver had finished football practice, but to meet him at the Doubletree Hotel downtown.

After what had happened to Stu, Nathan had asked Denver if he wanted to take some time off school, but Denver had preferred to go back to his studies and his sports. 'I don't want to think about Stu, Dad, even for a second. Every time I close my eyes I see him lying on the floor, all covered in blood. And that screaming monster trying to bust in through the window.'

Next, Nathan called Detective Pullet. She was on a coffee break and she had her mouth full of lemon Danish.

'I just had a call from Theodor Zauber. He's extremely pissed, to say the least.'

'Did you get his number? I doubt if we'll be able to trace it, but we can try.'

'I have it on my cell. I'll send it to you. But trying to arrest him like that – you blew any chance I had of finding out where he's keeping those gargoyles.'

'Look, I'm sorry. I had no idea that he would be able to give us the slip. I mean, how was I to know that he was a hypnotist?'

'There's no point in beating yourself up about it, Detective. But I have to warn you that he's going to bring a whole lot more of those things to life, and everybody who's out on the street is going to be in danger of being attacked.'

'We can't put out a warning like that,' said Jenna. 'Either people won't believe us, or else there'll be total panic, like that *War of the Worlds* broadcast. The whole city could come to a standstill.'

'I don't know,' Nathan told her. 'Maybe you could find some way of wording it so that people will just keep their eyes on the skies. Maybe you could tell them that the city is being plagued by a flock of unusually aggressive crows.'

'Unusually aggressive crows? You can't be serious.'

'People remember *The Birds*, don't they? Tell them it's a similar problem to that.'

'I don't know. I think I need to talk to my captain.'

Nathan said, 'Our number one priority is locating Theodor Zauber. Maybe you could put out a description.'

'Again, I'll have to talk to my captain. It took *me* long enough to believe that these gargoyles are really real, but he's the most skeptical man I ever met. He doesn't even believe in global warming.'

'Please keep me up to date, Detective. I'm taking my wife and son to stay at the Doubletree Hotel until this is all over.'

'OK, Professor. And if you hear from Zauber again, let me know *immediately*, you got it?'

'I hate to say this, but I think we'll be hearing from one of his gargoyles before we hear from him.'

THIRTY-FIVE

Tuesday, 1:47 a.m.

Jay and Tory and Kenny and Pat were sitting in one of the brightly-painted children's playhouses in the Palumbo Playground on Fitzwater Street, passing a joint around.

The night was chilly, and their breath fumed almost as much as the skunk they were smoking, but they were all wearing thick coats and scarves and Jay was wearing a huge black woolly hat.

The city had quietened down, but there was still a restless swooshing of traffic all around them, punctuated by horns blowing, and sirens whooping.

'You know what my old man said to me yesterday?' said Jay. 'He said, what are you staying at school for? He said when he was my age he was working in the spoon factory, making spoons. I said, that's the reason I want to stay at school. I don't want to make no spoons.'

'I know,' said Kenny, 'you want to be an unclear physicist.'

'It's "nuclear", you dimwit. Besides, that's not what I want to be anyhow. I want to be like a New Age Diddy. I want to have my own record label and my own line of men's clothing and my own chain of restaurants. But I don't want to be such an arrogant asshole as Diddy. I believe in swagger, like he does, but I believe in, like, *restrained* swagger.'

'I want to be a model,' said Tory. She had long blonde hair and big gray eyes and a pert little nose. She was wearing an oversized pink padded windbreaker and gray woolen leggings. 'In fact I want to be America's next top model.'

'You won't have no-o-o trouble at all,' Jay assured her. 'Models don't need no brains, do they, so you have all the necessary qualifications already.'

Tory slapped him and Jay laughed and lifted his arm up to protect himself. 'Temperamental, too! That's good! All the top models got to be temperamental!'

Pat was coppery-haired and pale and wore a dark brown duffel coat. 'I always dreamed of being a nurse,' she said.

'A *nurse*?' said Jay. 'That is one genuinely shitty job. Long hours for crappy pay, and all that wiping old people's asses.'

'I *did* dream of being a nurse but I changed my mind. Now I want to be a manicurist. Or maybe a dog-groomer or a pole-dancer.'

'Hey, I like a girl with ambition.'

Kenny said, 'Me, I want to be ride-pimper. Just give me a workshop and a set of tools and a fifty-nine Chevy Impala and I'll be h-a-p-p-y for the rest of my life.'

Pat passed him the joint and he took a deep drag at it, and then went into a coughing fit. 'That is seriously strong shit, man. Where'd you score it? Jesus!'

Jay was about to answer when they heard a harsh screeching sound, directly above their heads. Then another screech, off to their right. And another, and another.

'What the hell was *that*, man?' said Kenny. He turned around and peered across the playground, shielding his eyes against the nearby street light.

There was more screeching, and Jay stood up and leaned out of the side of the playhouse. 'Sounds like buzzards,' he said.

'*Buzzards*? In the middle of the city? And how do you happen to know what buzzards sound like?'

'I seen enough cowboy movies. Those are definitely buzzards.'

'Oh, the great bird expert, all of a sudden.'

They heard three or four more screeches, and then a loud flapping of wings. Tory stood up, too, and took hold of Jay's arm. 'They sound *big*,' she said. 'And *look*! There they are! They're flying all around us!'

She pointed upward. Although the playhouse was under the trees, they could make out at least three shadowy shapes. They were circling around and around, about fifty or sixty feet above them, their wings making a steady, dull thumping sound, like somebody beating carpets.

At first, they couldn't see anything at all. But then, without warning, a huge gray creature swooped around the side of the playhouse, so close that its horny wing-tip clanged against one of the yellow-painted metal uprights. It turned its head as it flew past, and they saw bulging green eyes and a curved beak and fangs. It screeched, and then it flapped its wings and disappeared upward.

The four of them stared at each other in shock. Tory was stunned into silence but Pat was panting in terror as if she had just run the hundred meters. 'What the *fuck* was that?' said Kenny, in the thinnest of screams. 'That wasn't no buzzard, that was a fucking *dragon*!'

'Let's just get the hell out of here,' said Jay. 'Like – let's go, man! These things look like they want to fucking eat us!'

They jostled their way toward the playhouse steps, but before they could clamber down them, they heard a high-pitched whistling sound. One of the creatures collided with the side of the playhouse with such a devastating impact that it felt as if they had been hit head-on by a speeding truck. They were all thrown backward on to the floor, tumbling over each other, and Kenny hit his head on one of the railings with an audible *klonk*.

The steps were ripped up sideways, so that now they led nowhere at all. Three of the playhouse uprights were so badly bent inward that one side of the roof almost touched the handrail.

'Jump out!' Jay shouted. 'Jump out and run for it!'

Both Tory and Pat were screaming, but Kenny was still lying on his back looking stunned. Jay snatched hold of his sleeve and tried to heave him upright. 'Get up, man! They're trying to kill us!'

Tory managed to lift one leg over the handrail, but she was just about to drop down to the ground when one of the creatures landed right next to her, noisily folding its wings and making a hoarse rattling noise in its throat.

Tory started screaming again, and Jay let go of Kenny's sleeve and tried to make a grab for her hand. But the creature was much too quick for him. It dug its claws into the back of Tory's pink windbreaker and lifted her off the handrail like a hawk picking up a field mouse. With a few drafty flaps of its wings it rose up into the air and carried her high over the playground, screaming and thrashing her arms and legs.

'*Tory!*' shouted Jay. He vaulted over the handrail but he was still in mid-air when a second creature plummeted down and hit him. It struck him so hard and so fast that he exploded, his head flying over the railings and rolling across Fitzwater Street, underneath a passing car. His detached arms flew up in the air, turning over and over as if they were being juggled like Indian clubs. His whole body burst open, and was strewn across the play area in a chaotic tangle of lungs and intestines.

The creature that had hit him turned in mid-air and then came swooping back down. It landed among his remains, its wings still outstretched, scratching through them with its claws until it found his heart. It let out a screech of triumph, and then it shredded his heart with its beak and teeth, greedily devouring it.

Pat was still crouching on the playhouse floor on her hands and knees. Every now and then she let out a low, quavering moan. Kenny was lying beside her, half-concussed and not at all sure what was happening.

'Pat?' he said, trying to lift up his head and look around. 'Pat – where's Jay?'

'Mmmpphhh,' said Pat.

'What? I don't understand you. Where's Jay? Where did Tory go?'

Pat stared at him. 'Those flying things . . . they took Tory away. Right up in the air. She's gone. Then one of them came down and smashed Jay to bits.'

'What? What do you mean, smashed him to bits?'

'I mean smashed him to bits! Smashed him into pieces! There isn't any Jay any more!'

Kenny managed to roll himself on to his side and sit up. He reached around and touched the back of his head and said, 'Jesus. That hurts.'

'One of the flying things took Tory and then the other one came down and smashed Jay to bits.'

'OK, OK, take it easy,' Kenny told her. He looked around, and then he said, 'Seems like they've gone now, anyhow.'

He used one of the bent uprights to help himself stand up. Now he could see what was left of Jay, glistening in the street light. He clamped his hand over his mouth and retched.

'Jesus,' he said, with his eyes watering, and he crossed himself. 'You weren't fucking joking, were you?'

'We need to call somebody,' said Pat, her voice quaking. 'We need to call nine-one-one.'

Kenny looked up. 'What were those things? Like, what the fuck were they?'

'I don't know. Just call nine-one-one.'

Kenny took his cellphone out of his coat pocket. He punched out 911, but he had lifted his phone only halfway up to his ear when there was a shuddering bang on the metal roof, right above his head. This was followed by a furious flurry of scratching. He looked up and saw eight curved claws hooked around the edge of the guttering.

'*Pat,*' he said, and pointed upward. '*It's landed on the roof.*'

There was a rattling noise, and some more scratching, and then another harsh screech. A creature's head appeared, upside down, staring at him with yellowish-green eyes. Kenny took one step backward, and then another. The creature didn't move, but continued to stare at him. It was hideous, this thing, whatever it was, but it was expressionless, and it was impossible to tell what it might be thinking. Maybe it wanted to smash him to bits, too. Or maybe it was just curious.

He slowly raised his cellphone to his ear. A voice was repeating, 'Nine-one-one. What is your emergency, please?'

Kenny had never felt so frightened in his life. 'We're at the Palumbo Playground. We've been attacked by these things.'

'What things, sir?'

'These flying things, like demons.'

'Excuse me, sir. Did you say "demons"?'

'They've taken one of us. Tory. And they've killed another one, Jay.'

'When you say "demons", sir, are you talking about a gang called The Demons?'

The creature blinked at him, its eyelids closing upward, like a frog's, and he saw a gray forked tongue flicker out of its beak.

'No, I mean real demons! They have horns and tails and they can fly, and they killed my best friend Jay and took a girl called Tory. For Christ's sake, you have to send somebody before they kill us, too!'

'A patrol car is already on the way, sir. Just try to stay calm.'

'How can I stay calm when there's one of them sitting on the roof and it's staring at me like it wants to bite my fucking head off?'

'Please, sir, stay calm. You don't have to use that kind of language.'

'My best friend has been smashed to pieces! What other kind of language do you suggest I use? Fucking Arabic?'

'Sir—'

Before the emergency operator could say any more, however, the creature came scuttling into the playhouse in a sudden rush, dragging its wings in behind it. It came across the ceiling, upside down, and gripped Kenny by the neck with its claws. Kenny tried to cry out, but the creature's claws were so sharp that they pierced his carotid artery and penetrated his windpipe with a hiss of air. He dropped his cellphone and desperately seized the creature's forearm, trying to pull its claws out, but the creature was far too strong for him, and he was already spurting bright red blood out of his neck and all down his coat.

Pat whimpered, climbed on to her feet, and started to climb awkwardly over the handrail. She managed to swing both legs over and drop down on to the rubbery play surface. Then, still whimpering, she ran toward the yellow gate that led out into the main playground area. She was so terrified that she found it difficult to make her legs move one in front of the other, and to keep her balance. She almost felt like falling to her knees and letting the creatures catch up with her.

She was two-thirds of the way toward the gate when she heard screeching, directly above her. She didn't look up. She didn't dare, she just kept stumbling on, past two other playhouses and a swing set.

She heard another screech, and the *flap-flap-flapping* of wings. Oh God, she thought, it's going to get me. It's going to fly down and smash me into bits, the same as it did to Jay. But still she kept on running, and still she didn't look up. Maybe she was going to die but she didn't want to see her own death coming.

She was only ten feet away from the gate when something fell on to the play surface next to her, and bounced. It had a long mane of bloody blonde hair and she realized that it was Tory's head. She stopped, totally shocked, as the head rocked to a rest beside the fence. Then, suddenly, she was struck on the shoulder by something heavy and wet, a severed leg, and then by a deluge of warm blood and slippery human remains.

She looked up. Her face looked as if she were wearing a scarlet mask and her hair was drenched. The creature was slowly wheeling around in the air and gliding off to the west. She could see the street light shining through the thin grayish skin that covered its wings. It let out a screech, and then started to flap away. Pat didn't know it, but it had taken what it had come for, which was Tory's living heart. The rest of Tory, it had simply dropped to the ground, unwanted.

THIRTY-SIX

Tuesday, 3:12 a.m.

Stephen let Kayley out of the front door of the Utopia Diner, set the alarm, and locked the door behind him.

'What a great night,' he said, buttoning up his brown tweed overcoat. 'And did Lenny tell you who was sitting at table twelve? Don Williams from *Playboy* magazine, who writes all of their Best Bar reviews. Not only that, he smiled a lot. *And* he told Lenny that the lobster mash was to die for.'

Kayley stood on tiptoe and gave him a kiss on the cheek. 'I can't believe it's all working out so well. It's better than we ever dreamed of, isn't it?'

They walked south along Second Street together, arm-in-arm. At this time of the morning, it was almost deserted. This was a part of Old Town Philly that until five years ago had been tatty and neglected. Stephen Mars had been one of the first bar owners and restaurateurs to start bringing it back to life, and now the Utopia Diner was rapidly making its name as one of the city's classiest nightspots, where moneyed thirty-somethings came to eat sophisticated tapas and crab cakes and drink Martinis and admire themselves in its mirrored walls. In the past year, more than fifteen new bars and restaurants had opened up all around them.

Stephen had risked everything he owned. He had mortgaged his house and invested all of his savings, but now his self-belief was beginning to pay dividends.

Kayley said, 'How about we take a couple of days of down time? We don't have to do anything special. Stay in bed all day and watch TV.'

'Maybe. I don't know. I have the year-end accounts to go through, and all the new winter menus.'

'You *never* take any time off. It's bad for you. Look what it did for your marriage.'

'Yeah, I know. But I'm always worried that if I take any time off, something disastrous is going to happen when I'm not there. Like everybody in the diner is going to go down with E. coli poisoning, or the building's going to burn to the ground.'

'Stephen, you have the most brilliant staff ever. You have to trust them now and again. Lenny is absolutely the best manager I've ever worked for.'

'I'll think about it, OK?'

'I wish you would. You know, we could even have sex.'

'Sex, huh?' Stephen nodded in exaggerated approval. 'That would be a novelty.'

Stephen and Kayley hadn't been attracted to each other at first sight. For starters, Stephen had been married to Margie when they met, whom he had dated since high school, and he and Margie had a boy aged seven and a girl aged three. And he was a workaholic. He had joined a realty company in Glenside when he left college, but he had quickly struck out and started his own business selling multimillion-dollar properties in and around Jenkintown.

He was tall, dark and serious, and he always looked as if he had something on his mind. This was because he always did, and it was always business.

Kayley on the other hand was businesslike without being driven. She was small, with a raven-haired bob and a pale, heart-shaped face. She had always wanted to be a dancer but she was much too full-breasted and apart from that she had absolutely no sense of musical timing. Instead, she had found work behind the bars of several downtown hotels, and then at a trendy cocktail bar on Market Street called Lucca's. That was where Stephen had first seen her, and from where he had eventually bribed her away to run his bar at Utopia. To begin with, he had been impressed by her efficiency and her people skills, more than her breasts.

When Utopia had first opened, Stephen and Kayley had worked together from morning till night with hardly a word spoken between them. Then one night last September, they had worked until it was too late for Stephen to go home. He had booked a hotel room at the Sheraton on Society Hill, and when he locked up the diner, he had simply said, 'Why don't you stay with me tonight?'

He had never been quite sure why he had asked her, and Kayley had never been quite sure why she had said yes, but she had. They had been lovers ever since.

They had reached the concrete parking structure on Second Street where Stephen always left his Toyota, and they were just about to walk into the low main entrance when they became aware of a howling noise, somewhere in the distance. They both stopped, and looked at each other.

'What is *that*?' asked Kayley. 'Is that a train whistle?'

'I don't think so,' said Stephen, looking around. 'Where's it coming from? It's more like – I don't know – *singing*.'

But the noise quickly grew louder and louder, and more and more discordant. Soon it sounded like hundreds of mourners at a funeral, all keening at once – a dismal, penetrating, high-pitched chorus that set their teeth on edge and made windows rattle all the way down the street. Dogs began to bark and car alarms were set off, even as far as Lombard Street. The noise became so overwhelming that Stephen and Kayley had to clamp their hands over their ears.

'*What is it?*' Kayley shouted. But Stephen didn't have time to answer her before she could see for herself what was causing it. In the sky above them, which was already dark, scores of darker shapes appeared, howling as they flew. They were slowly circling over Old City Philly in a swirling black cloud, their wings flapping and their long tails twisting like snakes. They flew in unison, like a flock of migrating birds, dipping and turning as the cross-wind caught them.

The stocky black night attendant came out of the parking garage with his baseball cap on backward and stood beside them, staring up at the sky.

'Now *that's* what I call scarifying,' he shouted, over the howling. 'What the hell *are* those things? They sure enough ain't bats, and they sure enough ain't birds. No birds that *I* ever saw before, anyhow.'

'I don't have any idea what they are,' Stephen shouted back at him. 'They look like some kind of flying reptile to me. I expect they're harmless.'

As soon as he said that, though, they heard a woman screaming, somewhere in the next street. Chillingly, it reminded Stephen of a middle-aged woman he had seen two weeks ago on 52nd Street, whose pelvis had been crushed by a bus. It was the same cry of agony and utter hopelessness. Then they heard more screams, both women and men, from the direction of Market Street, which is where they had just come from. A few seconds later, they heard shots, six or seven of them, and a man shouting.

'Maybe we'd better get out of here,' Stephen suggested. 'I don't know what's happening but I don't like the sound of it. Otis? You got my keys?'

'Sure thing, Mr Mars. Coming right up.'

They heard more screams, and more shouting, and then an ambulance siren whooping, and then another. The flying creatures kept up their keening, which rose and fell as the wind caught it, and made it sound even more unearthly, but now they were *screeching*, too – sharp, harsh, exultant screeches. Stephen grabbed Kayley's arm and said, 'Come on. Maybe those things aren't so goddamned harmless after all.'

They had just entered the fluorescent-lit interior of the parking structure when they heard a man shouting, '*Help me! Help me!*' and the sound of running feet.

Stephen said, 'Stay here, OK?' and stepped back out on to the sidewalk.

He looked northward up Second Street, and saw a young man in a light gray suit running toward him, grimacing with effort, his orange necktie flapping over his shoulder like a flame. He wasn't just running, he was *sprinting*, as fast as he humanly could.

'*Help!*' he choked. '*For God's sake, help me!*'

At first glance, it appeared to Stephen as if the young man was being followed by his own giant shadow, which jerked and jumped as he ran past storefronts and alleys and parked cars and street lights. But then he realized that it wasn't a shadow at all. It was one of the dark creatures that they had seen swarming in the sky. Its wings were flapping steadily and evenly, its wing tips scuffing the road surface with every downbeat. It didn't look as if it was in any kind of hurry, but it was gaining on the young man with every second.

As they came closer, the creature let out a screech, and then a howl that made Stephen feel as if his scalp were shrinking.

The young man turned his head to see how close the creature was. He stumbled and almost fell over, but he managed to keep running. He didn't shout for help any more. Instead he clenched his teeth and lowered his head and ran even faster.

'*In here!*' Stephen shouted, as the young man approached him, and jabbed his finger toward the entrance to the parking structure. Then he turned back to Kayley and said, 'Get back! Keep out of the way! It's one of those creatures!'

'What?' said Kayley, but then she took two steps back, and then two more, and then clambered over the steel barrier that lined the side of the entrance, and crouched down behind it.

The young man had almost reached the parking structure. Stephen could see his face quite clearly, as if he were running in slow motion. He had fair hair and fair eyebrows and his cheeks were flushed crimson. He reminded Stephen of a friend of his from school, but of course it couldn't have been – ten years too young.

'Come on!' Stephen shouted at him. 'You can make it!'

But the young man couldn't have been more than thirty feet away from him when the creature slammed into him from behind, sending him sprawling across the road. He rolled over and over, all arms and legs, still trying desperately to get away. He reached the opposite curb, and almost managed to climb on to his feet. But the creature jumped on him with one hideous hop, and caught his shoulders in its claws. Stephen heard them crunching into his muscles.

'*Daaaaaaaaaaah*!' the young man screamed, and the creature mocked him by throwing back its head and echoing his scream with a screech.

Stephen crossed the street toward them and shouted out, '*Let go of him, you bastard*!'

Even as he did it, he realized how futile it was. Whatever it was, this creature, it wasn't going to understand him, and what was more, it wasn't going to be afraid of him. It swiveled its head toward him, still clutching the young man by his shoulders, and let out another screech, as if to warn him to stay away.

Stephen stopped where he was, in the middle of the street. He had never seen anything so fierce and so terrifying and so ugly in his life. The creature looked like a hunchbacked man, only it was probably seven feet tall, or even taller. It had two curved horns, and a curved beak, and staring green eyes. Its body was emaciated, so thin that its ribcage was visible, but it had a pot belly with a navel that protruded like the tied-up neck of a party balloon. Its wings were folded now, and their pale gray skin was wrinkled, but Stephen had seen for himself how wide they could stretch when they were open.

Kayley called out, '*Stephen*! *Stephen, come back here*!'

Otis said, in a panicky voice, 'I tried to call nine-one-one, Mr Mars, but all of their lines is jammed!'

Stephen stayed where he was, breathing deeply. The young man had his face in the gutter and he was sobbing with pain. The creature was making a rough sandpapery noise in its throat, punctuated by clicks of phlegm. Its eyes blinked once, and then twice, as if it were waiting for him to come nearer.

'Let him go,' Stephen told it. 'Do you understand what I'm telling you? Let him go! What did he ever do to you?'

With a sound like a huge umbrella opening, the creature spread its wings. For a moment it stayed where it was, crouched in the street, but then it climbed to its feet, holding up the young man so that his feet swung clear of the ground. The young man gasped out, '*Tell my wife*! *Tell her I love her*! *My name's Gerry – Gerry McManus*!'

He didn't have the chance to say any more, because the creature gave three or four thunderous flaps of its wings and rose up into the air, carrying him away. He started screaming again as it lifted him high over rooftop level, and Stephen could see him kicking his legs.

Kayley came out from the parking structure, followed by Otis. She clung on to Stephen's arm and said, 'My God, that poor man! What *was* that thing?'

'Looked like one of them ugly statchers you see on the tops of churches,' said Otis.

'That's right,' said Stephen. 'It looked like a gargoyle.'

'That's the word I was looking for,' Otis told him. 'But them there grah-groyles, they're only statchers, ain't they? They don't go flying around and grabbing people.'

Stephen looked up into the night sky and shaded his eyes. 'Whatever it was, I doubt if we'll ever see *that* poor guy again.'

They were still standing there when they heard more howling, and then the unmistakable *flap-flap-flap* of leathery wings.

'Stephen?' said Kayley.

Stephen looked back up Second Street. Under the street lights, no more than five blocks away, he saw another creature flying toward them, its green eyes gleaming. Then he realized that there was another one close behind it, and slightly above it, and another, and another. It was almost as if they were flying in close formation.

'I think it's time we got the hell out of here,' he said. He took hold of Kayley's hand and turned back toward the entrance to the parking structure. As they did so, however, they heard more howling, from the opposite direction. At least five more creatures were flying toward them from Lombard Street.

'Holy shee-it!' said Otis. 'They're coming from every-damn-place.'

'Come on – *quick*!' urged Stephen, and the three of them ran into the parking structure and up the first ramp. They stopped at the top of the ramp, where they could still see the entrance.

'Maybe they won't follow us,' said Stephen. 'They won't be able to spread their wings in here, will they? The ceiling's too low.'

'I hope you're right,' said Kayley. 'The way that poor guy was screaming . . .'

They heard the howling and the flapping of wings grow louder, and then the clattering of claws on the sidewalk outside, and a

chaotic chorus of infuriated screeches. Stephen crossed his fingers
and said, '*Please, God,*' under his breath.

But God wasn't listening, not that night. Howling and
screeching, the creatures came crowding into the parking structure, their wings folded, more than a dozen of them as far as
Stephen could see, although he didn't stop to count them. He
seized Kayley's hand and they ran across the next level of the
parking structure and up the second ramp. Otis followed close
behind, panting for breath and saying '*shee-it, shee-it, shee-it,*'
with every step.

They heard the creatures rushing up the first ramp, their folded
wings rustling and their claws clicking on the shiny concrete
floor like castanets.

'What are we going to do?' gasped Kayley.

'Keep on going up to the roof,' said Otis. 'There's a fire escape
in the space between this building and the next one and it's real
narrow. I don't think these suckers will be able to follow us down
it, not with those wings and all.'

'OK, then,' said Stephen. 'Let's go.' The creatures could obviously sense that they were gaining on them, because their howling
had risen higher and higher, and it was echoing all around the
entire parking structure, all five stories of it, like some opera
composed with the malicious intention of driving its audience
mad.

They ran up the next ramp, and the next. The howling and the
screeching had become one endless cacophony, and Kayley was
sobbing with fright and exhaustion. As they came to the last
ramp, which led up to the roof, Stephen looked back and saw
the leading creatures pushing and jostling each other as they
reached the crest of the previous ramp. Their claws were raised
as if they were ready to tear their quarry to pieces and their green
eyes glowed like lamps.

'Come on, Kayley!' Stephen urged her. 'You can do it!'

They ran to the top of the last ramp and now they were out
in the cold night air, with the lights of Old Philly glittering all
around them. They could hear yelling and screaming from every
direction, and smoke was rising from Washington Square, thick
with orange sparks. The howling of the creatures was louder than
ever, mingled with the howling of police and ambulance sirens
and the blaring of fire trucks.

The sky was beginning to grow pale, and they could see creatures swooping and diving in every direction. Only two blocks away, a creature lifted a young woman high up over the rooftops and ripped her open in mid-air. She tumbled into the street below, her arms and legs wildly waving like a rag doll.

'Fire escape's this way!' Otis shouted, and started to run over to the opposite corner of the roof.

They were less than halfway there, however, when a creature came flapping down from the sky and perched on the retaining wall next to the fire escape. It looked different from the creature that Stephen had encountered in the street, with longer horns and a face that was more human. He could have sworn that it was grinning at them, as if it were daring them to push past it and try to make their way down the fire escape.

Another creature landed close beside it, and then another, and another. Soon they were surrounded by creatures, some with bird-like beaks and others with faces like scowling men. Their claws shuffled and scratched on top of the retaining wall, and occasionally one of them let out a screech, or an echoing howl.

Then, behind them, they heard more scratching and more screeching. The creatures that had been pursuing them up inside the parking structure had reached the roof, and were making their way toward them.

'What in the name of God are we going to do now?' asked Otis.

Stephen squeezed Kayley's hand. 'I don't think we have a whole lot of choice, do you?'

'There ain't no way I'm letting those things tear me to pieces. No, sir.'

Stephen turned to Kayley. She looked strangely calm.

'I'm sorry,' he said. 'I wanted us to spend so much more time together.'

'I know,' she told him. 'But at least we'll be together for the rest of our lives.'

Stephen reached out and took hold of Otis' hand, too. Otis looked up at him and nodded.

'Are we ready?' shouted Stephen, over the screeching and the howling. Two or three of the creatures had already hopped down from their perch on the retaining wall and were coming toward them. One of them had a face like a wild boar, with tusks that protruded from its lower jaw, while another had a face like a medieval picture of Satan, with slanted eyes and a demonic smile.

Holding hands tightly, Stephen and Kayley and Otis dodged between the creatures toward the space that they had vacated on the retaining wall. The creatures screeched and snatched at their clothes with their claws, but they couldn't stop them. Without a word, the three of them leaped together over the wall and into eternity.

THIRTY-SEVEN
Tuesday, 5:01 a.m.

As the smeary sky grew lighter still, the creatures flapped up into the air again, and gathered in a huge flock over Penn's Landing, by the river. They circled around two or three times, like a flock of birds, not howling now but still giving voice to an occasional triumphant screech.

After a few minutes, they turned toward the south-west and began to fly away. Soon they had disappeared from sight altogether, leaving behind them an Old Philly where the streets were spattered with blood and littered with human body parts. Cars and taxis had been torn open and their drivers dragged out. The side of a bus had been ripped off so that a creature could attack its passengers, and now its windows were blinded with blood.

A creature had flown into the front of a fire truck as it sped along Market Street. The driver had been wrenched out of his seat, right through the shattered windshield, and now the fire truck was embedded in the facade of Sonny's Famous Steaks. Its fire crew lay scattered all around it, so comprehensively dismembered that the only way to tell how many men had been killed was to count their helmets.

THIRTY-EIGHT
Tuesday, 11:24 a.m.

Nathan's cellphone warbled. He flipped it open and said, 'Nathan Underhill.'

'Professor? It's Detective Pullet.'

'Hey – at last! I've been trying to call you all night but I couldn't get through.'

'It's been total madness. I imagine you've been watching the news?'

Nathan glanced across at the TV screen on the opposite side of their hotel room. Grace had turned down the sound but it was still showing images of bloodstained sidewalks and bodies covered with blankets and coats. Denver was lying on the bed next to him, but after staying awake for most of the night he had now fallen asleep.

'Professor, we *have* to find where Theodor Zauber has got these gargoyles hidden. Don't you have any more ideas?'

'No, I don't, apart from drawing a line on the map from Sukie Harris' hospital bed in the direction she was pointing and checking every single building that it passes through. But, like I say, Zauber could be six blocks away or six hundred miles.'

'We're talking more than three hundred fatalities, Professor. We can't have another night like this. The governor has already put the National Guard on standby in case the gargoyles come back tonight.'

'I saw that artist's impression of Zauber on the news. Did anybody recognize him?'

Jenna said, 'Forty-seven people thought they did, and we sent police officers to investigate all forty-seven of the men they named. No luck though. Two of the supposed Zaubers were even Korean, for Christ's sake, and another of them was black.'

'I don't know what else to suggest,' Nathan admitted. On the TV screen, a streamer headline underneath the anchorwoman read CREATURES FROM HELL KILL 334 IN PHILLY: MASSACRE ON MARKET STREET.

'Maybe it's going to be the only way, drawing a line on the map. I'll take one of our crime scene specialists to the hospital and have young Sukie point to where the gargoyles are again, so that we can get the direction exactly right.'

'Spooglies, she calls them. Ask her to show you where the Spooglies are.'

'She calls them *what*?'

'Spooglies. Because she thinks they're spoogly, I guess.'

'*That* is one hell of a coincidence, Professor. Or maybe it's not a coincidence. I interviewed one of the gardeners when that gargoyle was found at Bartram's Gardens. A young kid called Andy Something. He told me that he'd had nightmares about gargoyles ever since he was little, just like Sukie Harris, and *he* called them Spooglies, too.'

Nathan sat down on the edge of the bed. Denver snuffled in his sleep and turned over and said, quite loudly, '*No*! Not hot dogs!'

Nathan said, 'It sounds to me like Sukie Harris and this gardener could both be sensitive to gargoyle activity.'

'What do you mean?'

'It's the same sensitivity that many animals have, especially dogs. They can sense things like impending earth tremors, and they can tell if somebody is harboring aggressive thoughts about their owner, even if that person is outwardly trying to give the impression of being friendly.'

'You mean they're, like, psychic?'

'You could call it that. But so-called "psychics" are simply people who have a highly-developed sensitivity to other people's auras.'

'Auras? I thought that was all hippie new-age stuff.'

'Not at all. All of us continuously give off a strong electro-photonic vibration, especially when we're angry or upset or belligerent. It's called the Kirlian Effect, and it's even been photographed. Zauber's gargoyles are extremely vicious and their physiognomy is in tremendous turmoil, so they probably give off a very intense vibration indeed. Sukie and this gardener could well have the ability to pick up on it.'

Jenna thought for a moment, and then she said, 'There was somebody else who picked up on it, too. A Pink Sister from the Convent of Divine Love on Twenty-Second Street. I interviewed her when the first gargoyle dropped out of the sky. She said that she felt the gargoyle fly overhead, even though she never actually saw it, and she said that it felt "dark and cold and evil-hearted". Those were her exact words.'

Nathan said, 'This could be what we're looking for. Three people who are all sensitive to the aura given off by gargoyles.'

'I don't think I follow you.'

'Triangulation, detective. We ask all three of them to point to where they can feel the strongest gargoyle activity. Then we ask your crime scene specialist to draw all three lines on a map, and where they converge . . . that's where we'll find Theodor Zauber.'

Jenna said, 'It's worth a try, isn't it? But – ah – I don't think I'll tell my captain what I'm doing, not just yet. A five-year-old kid and a mentally-challenged gardener and a nun who's been shut up in a convent for the past seventeen years . . . they're not your classic reliable witnesses, are they?'

'How about meeting at Temple University Hospital? We can take the first bearing from Sukie Harris, and go on from there.'

'OK, Professor. I guess I've tried nuttier ways of solving a crime, but I can't remember what they were.'

Nathan and Jenna met in the hospital reception area. Jenna had brought Ed Freiburg with her. He had been working all night and he looked bug-eyed and exhausted.

Up in the burns unit, Sukie was dressed in a bright red cable-knit sweater and jeans and was all ready to go home. Both Braydon and Melinda Harris were there, as well as Doctor Berman and Doctor Mahmood.

Sukie was coloring a picture of a pony with a pink Cosmic crayon. Jenna hunkered down beside her and said, 'How are you feeling, Sukie?'

'I'm *fine*, thank you.'

'She had no nightmares last night,' said Doctor Mahmood. 'I don't know if there is any significance to this, in the light of what has happened.'

Nathan said, 'She doesn't know about it, does she?'

Melinda shook her head.

'Maybe there is a connection,' said Nathan. 'I believe that those creatures that attacked the city last night were the same creatures that Sukie has been having nightmares about. The Spooglies. In reality, they're gargoyles.'

'I do not understand you,' said Doctor Mahmood. 'Gargoyles are made of stone, are they not?'

'Well, yes, they are normally. It's a little too complicated to explain right now, but take it from me that they *are* gargoyles, and that we need very urgently to find out where they've been hidden. What happened last night, we don't want that to happen again, at any price.'

Jenna said, 'We need to ask Sukie to point out exactly where she thinks they are.'

'No,' said Melinda. 'Absolutely not. Don't you think she's been through enough?'

'Ma'am,' Jenna retorted, 'three hundred thirty-four innocent people were killed last night. Torn to pieces, all of them. What do you think *they* went through?'

Braydon laid his hand on Melinda's shoulder. 'Come on, Melinda. These people are asking for our help. It was my fault that Sukie got burned, but Professor Underhill here, didn't he fix her up? I've learned a hard lesson out of this, and that's to swallow my pride and listen to other people's advice and allow other people to help me. The least we can do is help them in return.'

Melinda looked across at Sukie, sitting at the table by the window, the tip of her tongue clenched between her teeth, trying not to crayon over the lines.

Braydon said, 'I don't know how it all got so hostile between us, Melinda. Maybe you don't want us to get back together, but at least let's be friends, for Sukie's sake. Or at least let's *pretend* to be friends.'

Doctor Berman stepped forward and laid a hand on each of their shoulders. 'In my entire career, I have never seen a patient with third-degree burns to the face heal as quickly and as perfectly as Sukie. Maybe it's not my place to say so, but I do think you both owe Professor Underhill a serious debt of gratitude.'

Melinda remained tight-lipped for a moment, but then she said, 'Very well. You can ask her, so long as you don't upset her.'

'Thank you,' said Jenna. 'This could save a whole lot of lives.'

Next, Melinda turned to Braydon. 'Yes,' she said, as if she had just swallowed a mouthful of white wine vinegar. 'I *can* pretend to be friends.'

Jenna said, 'Sukie, will you do something for me? Will you show me again where the Spooglies live?'

Sukie nodded, without looking up from her coloring. Ed Freiburg opened his satchel and took out a Coherent laser compass, a yellow box about nine inches long and six inches wide.

'This man is called Ed. Ed has this really cool light. He's going to shine a light along your arm so that we can find out exactly where the Spooglies are.'

Sukie put down her crayon. 'Are you going to put them in prison?' she asked.

Ed said, 'No, we're not. We're going to send them off to Disney World, that's all, so that they never come back and give you nightmares, ever again, because they'll be having too much fun with Winnie the Pooh.'

Without hesitation, Sukie pointed to the south-west. 'They're *there*,' she said, emphatically. Ed switched on his laser, and a narrow beam of green light shone along her arm toward the opposite side of the room.

Jenna looked at Nathan. She said nothing, but they were both praying that this triangulation was going to work.

They drove to Bartram's Gardens and managed to catch Andy Fisher as he was leaving to go home. The wind was rising and the sky had turned charcoal-gray and they could hear thunder in the distance, like the cannons of an approaching army.

'Andy,' said Jenna. 'Can you feel where the Spooglies are hiding?'

Andy blinked at her, and then looked at Nathan and Ed. 'The Spooglies – they killed all of those people last night.'

'We know they did,' Jenna told him. 'That's why we need to find out where they are. We want to stop them from killing any more people.'

'I don't know *where* they are,' Andy told her. 'And if I knew where they were, I wouldn't go there, ever.'

'But do you know which direction they're in?' asked Nathan. He pointed to the north, and then to the east, and then to the south. 'Are they over *that* way, or *that* way, or *that* way?'

'I don't know,' said Andy, wringing his hands together.

'You don't know?' Nathan retorted, with mock impatience. 'What are you, stupid or something?'

'I'm not stupid! You can't call me stupid! You're not allowed!'

'What do you mean, I'm not allowed? If you're stupid I can *call* you stupid! All I'm doing is telling the truth.'

'It's discrinimation.'

'Oh! It's discrinimation, is it? Thank God I'm not guilty of discrimination!'

Andy clenched his fists in distress. 'If I tell you – if I tell you – they'll come find me! They'll come find me, and they'll tear me to pieces, the same way they did all of those other people!'

Nathan went up to Andy and put his arm around his shoulders. 'Andy,' he said, 'they won't find you. You know where *they* are but they don't know where *you* are. They don't even know you exist.'

'That Spoogly opened its eyes and it saw me.'

'Maybe it did and maybe you were just imagining it. Whichever it was, that particular Spoogly is all locked up in the CSI laboratory now and its wing is broken off and it's not going to come and find you, I promise.'

Andy's eyes darted from side to side. 'I'm scared of them,' he said. 'If they don't come find me for real, they'll come find me in my nightmares.'

Nathan hugged him even tighter. 'Andy, they won't. I promise you.'

'You said I was stupid.'

'Yes. That's because you won't tell me where they are. So I want you to prove that you're not stupid.'

Andy sniffed, and nodded. 'OK.'

Nathan waited for almost half a minute, but Andy said nothing. All he did was repeatedly sniff.

'Andy,' said Nathan.

'Yes, sir?'

'*The Spooglies, Andy!*' Nathan roared at him. '*Where the fuck are they?*'

Andy made a whinnying noise like a nervous foal and pointed in a westerly direction, toward Elmwood and the Holy Cross Cemetery.

'That's terrific,' Nathan told him. 'Now keep your arm as still as you possibly can while Ed lines up his laser.'

Ed Freiburg shone his green laser beam along Andy Fisher's arm and took a note of the compass bearing. 'OK then,' he said, 'that's two readings. That's enough for a rough triangulation, but

I think we ought to go for the third, just to make sure. These two kids only had to waver their fingers a couple of inches and our final reading could be miles out.'

'You're sure they won't come find me?' asked Andy.

'Cross my heart and hope to die,' said Nathan.

'But I don't want to die!'

Sister Mary Emmanuelle came along the long echoing corridor to greet them. She looked even paler than she had when Jenna had first talked to her, and there were plum-colored circles under her eyes.

'You wanted to see me again?' she asked.

'Yes, Sister. This is Professor Nathan Underhill and this is Ed Freiburg, one of our criminologists.'

'How can I help?' asked Sister Mary Emmanuelle. 'I'm afraid I have nothing more to add to what I told you before.'

Jenna said, 'You look like you haven't been sleeping very well, if you don't mind my saying so.'

Sister Mary Emmanuelle crossed herself. 'I've been having nightmares. It's like a moral struggle inside my mind. I believe that God is testing me.'

'Nightmares about what?' Nathan asked her. 'Nightmares about creatures like gargoyles?'

Sister Mary Emmanuelle nodded. 'I know that they are nothing more than a metaphor for evil, but the nightmares have seemed very real.'

Jenna said, 'Do you know what happened last night?'

'No. I was praying from midnight until four in the morning.'

'What happened last night was that hundreds of gargoyles attacked the old part of the city and killed over three hundred innocent people.'

Sister Mary Emmanuelle stared at her. 'You're serious, aren't you? It really happened?'

'Somebody has found a way to make stone gargoyles come to life,' Nathan told her. 'We need to find that somebody urgently, before any more people get killed. Those nightmares, Sister – you weren't just going through a personal moral struggle. You were seeing what really happened. You sensed it. You know that feeling you had when the gargoyle first flew over the convent? That feeling of coldness? Do you have any of that feeling right now?'

'I don't understand what you mean.'

'Let me put it this way. When you think about those creatures in your nightmares, those demons or gargoyles or whatever they are, can you sense where they're hiding?'

Sister Mary Emmanuelle opened and closed her mouth, and then she said, '*Yes*. I thought I was being neurotic. I thought it was lack of sleep, or because I've been fasting. I've been fasting, you see, to purify my body, and thus to purify my mind.'

'It's not you who's evil, Sister, it's those gargoyles, and the man who's been reviving them. The evil isn't inside your head. It's out there someplace, and we have to find it. Do you think you can point to where you can feel it?'

Without another word, Sister Mary Emmanuelle turned around and pointed westward. Ed Freiburg took out his laser compass and said, 'You don't mind, do you, Sister?'

'Of course not. If you can find those creatures, and exorcize them, I will do anything to help you.'

Ed leveled his laser along Sister Mary Emmanuelle's arm, and it shone directly on to a painting of Jesus on the opposite wall, a brilliant green dot of light directly between the Saviour's eyes. Ed jotted down the compass bearing and then said, 'God bless you, Sister.'

'And God bless you, too. All of you.'

Back in his van, Ed Freiburg opened his laptop and brought up a map of Philadelphia and its western suburbs. He tapped in the compass bearings that he had taken, and three red lines converged on Clifton Heights, less than eight miles to the west.

'Got him,' he said. He magnified the map and brought up the street view. It showed a single-story concrete building with a double garage door at one side. 'Thirty-three East Baltimore Avenue. It's an abandoned factory where they used to repair fire extinguishers.'

Jenna said, 'Right. This is where I have to explain everything to my captain and ask for some serious backup. I just hope that he believes me.'

'After what happened last night, Detective, I don't think he has much alternative, do you?'

'Well, we'll see. Wish me luck, won't you?'

'Before you do that,' said Nathan, 'I think I know a way in

which we can destroy those gargoyles once and for all. But I'm going to need you to trust me and give me some support. Believe me, if you go in there with all guns blazing, Theodor Zauber will have every chance of reviving at least some of his gargoyles and it could be a massacre.'

'So what are you suggesting?' asked Jenna. 'You go in alone and appeal to his better nature?'

'No . . . I want to take my colleagues in with me. But that's all. No SWAT team. No tear gas. No guns.'

'I don't think I can allow that, Professor. If anything goes wrong—'

'If anything goes wrong, it will be my own fault, Detective. But my colleagues and I are the only people who have the knowledge and the means to destroy these gargoyles so that they never come back to plague us again.'

'I really don't know,' said Jenna. She puffed out her cheeks in indecision. 'If you or your colleagues get yourselves killed, I'm going to lose my shield for sure.'

Ed said, 'What's your gut feeling, Jenna? Remember what I said to you before, when you didn't believe that statues could fly?'

'You said that I should trust my instinct, once in a while.'

'And your instinct in this particular case is what?'

Jenna checked her wristwatch. 'I'll give you two hours, Professor. If you haven't managed to find Zauber and finish off his gargoyles by then, I'll have to call for backup. But let me tell you this: if you die, I'll kill you.'

THIRTY-NINE

Tuesday, 2:07 p.m.

By the time Aarif and Kavita arrived at 33 East Baltimore Avenue, ragged black clouds were sailing in from the west like a fleet of pirate ships with torn sails, and lightning was flickering on the horizon. The wind was getting up, so that dust devils whirled up all around them and sheets of newspaper came tumbling down the street.

Nathan and Jenna and Ed Freiburg had parked their car and their van two blocks away, outside a tired-looking convenience store called Skippy-Save. The former fire-extinguisher factory looked deserted. There were no vehicles outside it, and all of the windows were covered with corrugated iron, except for two grimy wired-glass windows in the front door.

Aarif and Kavita pulled their red Explorer into the parking lot and climbed out. Aarif was still wearing a blue Band-Aid across the bridge of his nose, and both of his eyes were still rainbow-colored. Kavita was wearing a brown headscarf that made her look even more Mohawk than usual, a tight black sweater and black jeans, with black thigh-boots.

'So this is where our villain is hiding out?' asked Aarif.

'We don't know for sure,' Nathan told him. 'But it looks to me like a pretty likely location to hide a couple of hundred gargoyles.'

Jenna checked her wristwatch again. 'Can we move this along?' she said, impatiently. 'I'm *this* close to changing my mind and calling my captain.'

'Go on,' Nathan told Aarif, with a nod, and Aarif went around to the rear of the Explorer and lifted the tailgate. Between them, he and Kavita lifted out a large bell-shaped object covered with a black cloth. As they slammed the tailgate shut, there was a screaming sound from inside the cloth, like a frustrated child.

'What the hell have you got in there?' asked Jenna.

'That, Detective, is our secret weapon. Show her, Kavita.'

Kavita lifted up the cloth to reveal Torchy, his feathers gleaming so brightly he looked as if he had been fashioned out of twenty-four karat gold. He was warbling indignantly and jerking his head from side to side as if he refused to look at any of these humans who were treating him with such disrespect.

'That's the bird from your laboratory,' said Jenna.

'That's right. The mythical phoenix. And if there's one thing I've learned, it takes one myth to fight another myth.'

'Are you going to explain to me exactly how you think you can stop Zauber with a *bird*?'

'No,' said Nathan. 'For beginners, I don't have any idea if this is going to work or not. But we won't know for sure until we try. Are we ready to go over and pay Theodor Zauber a visit?'

Ed had armed himself with a crowbar and a pair of bolt cutters. 'Let's just hope he's really in there, and that this isn't a wild phoenix chase.'

They skirted around the side of the factory in case Theodor Zauber was keeping a watch on the street outside through one of the two small windows in the front door.

Jenna went first, with her gun drawn, followed by Ed and Nathan and then Aarif carrying the phoenix cage, and Kavita bringing up the rear. Torchy, under his black cloth, was unusually silent, as if he could sense that there was something evil and dangerous very close by.

Jenna went up the concrete steps to the front door and jiggled the handle.

'Locked,' she said. 'Ed – do you want to do the honors?'

'You know that we don't have a warrant,' Ed reminded her.

'Of course I know that we don't have a warrant. But we heard screaming from inside the building and so we had cause to break in and investigate, didn't we?'

Ed gave his bolt cutters to Nathan to hold, and then wedged his crowbar into the side of the front door. It took only three hefty tugs before the wood splintered and the lock gave way. They stepped into what had once been the factory's reception area. There was a plywood desk, a tipped-over chair, and a very dead yucca, its leaves trailing black and dry over the sides of its pot like a giant tarantula.

Their shoes crunched on grit and broken glass. Jenna checked the back of the door and said, 'There's a key in it. That means that somebody locked it from the inside.'

They paused, and listened. Torchy shuffled on his perch but still didn't warble or screech. On the walls around them there were half a dozen yellowed posters for different kinds of fire extinguisher, as well as a group photograph of the staff of Flame-Ban, Inc, all grinning inanely.

'Maybe Theodor Zauber is not here after all,' said Aarif. He sounded almost hopeful.

Jenna went across to the door beside the reception desk labeled PRIVATE: STAFF ONLY. The door was slightly ajar, and so she leaned close to it and listened. At first there was nothing, but then she thought she heard humming. It sounded

like classical music, the *Blue Danube* or something else
Strauss-like.

'There's somebody here,' she said.

Nathan joined her by the door and listened, too. After a few
seconds, he said, 'Zauber. I'm sure of it.'

'So what do we do now?'

'We go in,' he said. 'Or at least, *I* go in, with Aarif and Kavita.
You cover me.'

Jenna said, 'If Zauber's armed, or if he attempts any kind of
violent retaliation, I do warn you that I'll shoot him.'

'Of course you will. You're a police officer. That's what police
officers do for a living, isn't it?'

Nathan turned around and beckoned to Aarif and Kavita. 'Come
on, you two. Keep close behind me.'

He opened the door. He found himself in a short corridor, with
offices on either side, both empty except for a bent filing cabinet
and a bicycle wheel. The corridor gave out on to a metal platform
with a handrail, which overlooked the main factory building.

Nathan walked along the corridor as quickly and as quietly as
he could, with Aarif and Kavita following him. When he reached
the platform, he stopped and said, '*Holy shit.*' He could hardly
believe what he was looking at.

The factory floor was over a hundred feet square, and it was
filled with at least three hundred gargoyles – a grotesque crowd
scene of hideous creatures with wings and claws and hunched
backs, and faces that represented every kind of depravity that
nature could devise. Nathan recognized gargoyles from churches
and cathedrals in every European country, from France and
Belgium and Germany and Poland, but there were many that he
couldn't identify, which looked as if they might be Japanese or
Indian.

Their faces were contorted into snarls, leers, and maniacal
stares. Some of them had the beaks of vultures or carrion crows,
while others had the faces of pigs or wolves.

Although all of them had been turned into stone, and none
one of them was moving, there was an overwhelming aura of
malevolence in the factory, as if all of the oxygen had been taken
out of the air and replaced with a cold, odorless gas that made
anybody who breathed it in feel weak and hopeless and afraid.

This was a host of evil; a legion of sheer terror. This, petrified, was a representation of the depths to which men and animals were capable of sinking. This was the massed army of hell itself.

On the far right of the factory floor stood a long trestle table, cluttered with glass jars and copper bowls and test tubes, as well as bunches of different grasses and twigs. Two gas burners were flickering at one end of it, and behind them, his face distorted by the reflection from the flames, was Theodor Zauber, wearing a long dark brown lab coat. He was loudly humming the melody from the *Voices of Spring* waltz.

With a long glass rod he was stirring a pale blueish liquid in a large glass globe, and spooning into it some carefully-measured powder. He looked up and saw Nathan standing on the metal platform. Immediately, he stopped humming, but he continued to stir the liquid and drop more powder into it.

Nathan looked up. There were fire-sprinkler pipes all the way across the ceiling, and he just hoped that the system hadn't been shut off. He walked down the steps and across the factory floor, weaving in between the gargoyles.

'Well, well, you have discovered my lair!' said Theodor Zauber. 'You are even more astute than I imagined, Professor. You like Strauss? *Frühlingstimmen*, my favorite.'

'Do you know how many people you murdered last night?' Nathan demanded. Unexpectedly, he found that he was so angry that his voice was shaking.

'I listened to the news at noon,' said Theodor Zauber. 'At last count, three hundred and forty-one. But I did warn you, did I not? You are responsible for those deaths, just as much as I am. So – tell me – why have you come here today? To join me and to help me, or to tell me how much you regret the consequences of your own stubbornness?'

'I've come here to finish this,' Nathan told him. 'It's over – you and your gargoyle project.'

Theodor Zauber stirred the pale blue liquid a little more, and then smiled. 'I think not, Professor. You know what this is? This is the quenching water that brings these poor petrified creatures back to life. A combination of calcium, sodium and potassium to create a strong electrolyte which will induce muscle activity, as well as the secret ingredients which Artephius mixed in, including the finely-ground bark of the fortune tree.'

'You're not hearing me, Zauber. It's over. You need to stop

stirring and give yourself up. The police are outside. They agreed to give me the chance to persuade you to surrender yourself without any violence.'

Theodor Zauber flared his nostrils. 'You think this is over? This is only the beginning! Look at all of these gargoyles! Look at them! They are magnificent in all of their ugliness, and they will make me great one day! You think you can stop me? *You*? You and your petty dabbling with birds and worms? This is where evil can be used for the greater good! This is where God and Satan join together to conquer death!'

Nathan said, 'You're crazy, do you know that? You're worse than your father, and he was hanging off by his hinges. Use some intelligence, Zauber. The police are outside and it's over!'

Theodor Zauber stopped stirring. He looked down at the quenching water that he had prepared, as if he were thinking. Then he picked up the glass globe, held it high over his head in both hands, and tossed it over the nearest gargoyles. It smashed, and splashed over at least three of them.

'*Es ist Zeit, damit Sie zum Leben kommen!*' he screamed. '*Es its Zeit, damit Sie kämpfen!*'

With that, he took hold of the trestle table and heaved it over, along with everything on it – jars, test tubes, gas burners and bunches of grass. It fell on top of Nathan and knocked him backward on to the floor, with smashed glass and ceramic scattered all around him. Theodor Zauber pushed his way between the gargoyles and headed for the steps that led up to the metal platform.

'*Aarif, stop him!*' Nathan shouted, levering himself out from underneath the table. Aarif whipped the black cloth from Torchy's cage, and held it up high. The phoenix screamed and spread his wings, as aggressive as he had been when he was first recreated.

'You think I am afraid of some bird in a cage?' shouted Theodor Zauber. He started to clamber up toward the platform, but Kavita went to the top of the steps, gripped the handrails for support, and kicked him hard in the chest with her black high-heeled boot.

Theodor Zauber staggered backward, his shoes clanging, but he managed to snatch at the handrail and stop himself from losing his balance. Grunting with effort, he hoisted himself back up the steps and when Kavita kicked out at him a second time, he seized her boot and pulled her down with him. The two of them rolled over and over in a tangle of arms and legs until they hit the bottom step.

Nathan climbed to his feet and body-swerved between the gargoyles toward the steps, but he was seconds too late. Theodor Zauber had dragged Kavita to her feet and had his left forearm hooked around her throat. Kavita was wide-eyed and choking for breath.

'You want me to break her neck?' Theodor Zauber shouted, with spit flying from his lips. 'You want your lovely assistant to die in front of your eyes? I can do it, you know!'

At that moment, Jenna appeared behind Aarif, closely followed by Ed. She pointed her gun at Theodor Zauber and snapped, 'Zauber! Let her go!'

'Oh, no,' said Theodor Zauber. 'This time, it is a Zauber who is the winner!

He turned toward his gargoyles and shouted at them again. *'Hören Sie mich, meine Freunde*! *Es ist Zeit, damit Sie zum Leben kommen*! It is time for you to come to life, my friends!'

Nathan heard an extraordinary crunching noise, like concrete churning in a concrete mixer. He turned around, too, and saw that the three gargoyles that Theodor Zauber had splashed with his 'quenching water' were actually moving. Blotchy gray limestone was subtly changing into pale gray reptilian skin. Eyes were lighting up with an eerie greenish glow. Wings were unfolding and claws were spreading wide.

The nearest gargoyle took one step toward Nathan and then threw back its head and screeched. It had long knobbly horns like a mountain goat, and a predatory beak with curved fangs protruding from it. It shook its wings open with a leathery bang, and then took another step forward, and then another, with the other two gargoyles following it.

Nathan could hear its breath rasping in its throat, as if its insides had still not completely changed from stone into flesh.

Jenna shouted, 'Call them off, Zauber! You hear me? Call them off!'

'Too late!' Theodor Zauber shouted back at her. 'They want human hearts, these beauties! Living, pumping hearts! Nothing I can do or say will stop them from ripping them out of you!'

Jenna grasped her automatic in both hands and fired at the

leading gargoyle. The noise of the shot was deafening, and echoed all round the factory. The gargoyle screeched at her but didn't stop shuffling forward. She fired at it again, and then again, and then fired a shot at each of the other two gargoyles. They screeched in unison, like some kind of hellish duet, but her bullets didn't even make them flinch. Only the densely-packed crowd of stone gargoyles was holding them back, and now they were pushing them out of their way, toppling some of them over.

Nathan knew that the moment had come. He had brought Kavita for a reason, and he prayed that he hadn't taken too much of a risk. If she got hurt, or was killed, he would never be able to forgive himself.

He zigzagged between the stone gargoyles until he was only three feet away from Kavita and Theodor Zauber. Kavita was struggling and gasping, but Theodor Zauber had her in a headlock and he wasn't going to let go.

'Stay back, Professor!' he shouted. 'If you come any nearer, I swear to you that I will kill her!'

Nathan lunged forward and seized Theodor Zauber's sleeve, but Theodor Zauber swung Kavita between them and jerked her head back so hard that she let out a cry of pain.

'I warn you, Professor!'

Just then, though, a rippling golden light began to shine from the top of the steps. It quickly grew brighter and brighter until it was so dazzling that it was impossible to look at. It lit up the whole factory with all of its gargoyles as intensely as a bleached-out photograph. Nathan had to cup his hand over his eyes, and he could see that Aarif was doing the same, while Jenna and Ed had turned their faces away, toward the corridor.

Kavita had closed her eyes tight, while Theodor Zauber was doing everything he could to stay in her shadow.

The three living gargoyles all howled and screeched, and when Nathan looked around at them, he could see that the light was making them thrash their heads from side to side and collide blindly with the stone gargoyles that were assembled all around them.

The light was so bright now that it was like the core of the sun. It was the phoenix, transforming himself into pure incandescent energy. He spread his wings wide, and rose through the bars of his cage as if he were no more substantial than flames.

For a few seconds he hovered in the air, his wings beating so that flags of fire flew in every direction. Then he screamed, and swooped down toward Kavita and Theodor Zauber with a loud flaring sound like an acetylene cutting-torch.

Theodor Zauber stumbled backward, and as he lost his footing, Kavita twisted herself free of his headlock and pushed him hard in the chest with both hands. He fell sideways on to the concrete floor, hitting his head.

The phoenix was on him instantly. It caught his black coat in its claws and pecked viciously at his face, so that his head was engulfed in a mass of fire. He screamed and tried to stagger on to his feet, but the phoenix beat his wings against him, again and again, fanning the flames. Within a few seconds he was blazing from head to foot, as if he had been doused in gasoline and set alight.

He dropped heavily back on to the floor, jerking and twitching. As he did so, one of the gargoyles let out a long, hair-raising howl, and the three creatures began to push aside the rest of the stone gargoyles that stood in their way, and advance toward Nathan and Kavita with their claws raised. The half-ton gargoyles rumbled like falling boulders.

'Time to get out of here, fast!' said Nathan, and took hold of Kavita's arm. He pushed her up the steps ahead of him, and Aarif was ready at the top to grab her hand.

The gargoyles howled again, and came lurching toward the platform. Before they could reach it, however, the phoenix blazed up from Theodor Zauber's still-burning body, screeching and beating his wings, and attacked them. The gargoyles snarled and screeched and lashed at him with their claws, but he was burning at such a high temperature that they couldn't even get close to him. He was no longer a bird, he was a nuclear reaction, a continuous explosion of air and gases and mythical cells. He was consuming himself, burning up his own existence at a ferocious rate, but the gargoyles were his natural enemies, both physically and morally, and he was determined to destroy them, even at the cost of his own recreated life. The phoenix was fire and light and purity, while the gargoyles were unmitigated evil, turned into stone.

Nathan pushed Aarif and Kavita along the platform until they reached the corridor.

Jenna said, 'What's happening? What do we do now?'

'Nothing!' said Nathan. 'We get the hell out of here as fast as we can! This place is going to go sky high!'

'I'll call the fire department!'

'Don't! They won't be able to stop it and they won't be able to contain it! They'll only get themselves killed!'

He looked back at the factory floor. The phoenix was now a huge ball of fire, and he could feel the waves of heat that were rippling out of it. The three living gargoyles were retreating from it, still howling, but the temperature inside the building was rising every second.

It was then that the sprinklers were set off. Water suddenly began to spray from the pipes across the ceiling, drenching the gargoyles from one side of the factory floor to the other.

The exothermic reaction was instant. The limestone gargoyles detonated like an atom bomb, and the whole factory floor was blotted out by a blinding flash, followed by a blast of heat and a shock wave that almost knocked Nathan over.

As he pushed Aarif ahead of him along the corridor, he looked back and saw lumps of limestone tumbling through the white-hot inferno – heads and wings and torsos and legs.

They hurried through the reception area, out of the front door and into the parking lot outside. It was raining now, and thunder was mumbling over Darby Creek.

They stopped, and waited. Shafts of light were shining from behind the sheets of corrugated iron that covered the factory's windows, like the shafts of light from a movie projector, and they could hear a soft but threatening roar.

Then the factory blew up, sending a geyser of fire high into the air. Chunks of concrete were thrown in all directions, bouncing into the roadway beside them. A loud bang echoed and re-echoed, and more debris fell from the sky, pieces of wooden window-frame and plasterboard and shredded paper.

After that, though, there was nothing but the rain and the wind and the distant thunder. Several cars stopped close by, and their bewildered drivers climbed out to see what had happened.

Jenna went across to Nathan and said, 'I guess you were right, then. I owe you one.'

'It was all a question of science,' said Nathan. 'Science, and mythology. And those are my two specialties.'

Jenna looked around. 'No pieces of gargoyle anywhere. Not that I can see.'

'All converted to quicklime. That was the science bit.'

'And what was the mythological bit?'

'Believing that the gargoyles were real. Believing that creatures like that used to exist, once upon a time, and that they've left enough of their DNA behind for us to bring them back to life.'

'Well,' said Jenna, 'good luck with that.'

FORTY

Wednesday, 4:46 p.m.

Nathan was sitting in the kitchen, working on his laptop, when the doorbell chimed.

'Denver,' he called out, 'do you want to answer that?'

Denver heaved himself off the living-room couch and went to open the door. Nathan heard voices, and then Denver called back, 'Dad, it's for you!'

He saved his work and went through to the hallway. Standing at the front door was Detective Pullet, accompanied by a thin young girl in a black cowl sweater and skintight jeans. Detective Pullet was carrying a large red cardboard box, tied with a red satin ribbon.

'Detective Pullet,' said Nathan. 'Why don't you come on in?'

'I hope we're not intruding,' said Jenna. 'This is my daughter Ellie, by the way. I wanted to come by and say thanks for everything you did yesterday, that's all.'

'You didn't have to do that,' Nathan told her. 'But come in, anyhow.'

Jenna and Ellie stepped into the hallway and Nathan showed them into the living room. Nathan thought Ellie was strikingly pale, with dark, haunted-looking eyes, but all the same she was very pretty.

'I brought a cake,' said Jenna. 'I hope you like lemon drizzle frosting.'

'My favorite. Here, Denver, why don't you take it into the

kitchen? How about a cup of coffee to wash it down with, Detective, or maybe a soda? Or maybe a serious drink, even?'

'Please, call me Jenna,' said Jenna. 'Ellie, give Denver a hand cutting the cake, would you?'

'OK,' said Ellie, without much enthusiasm.

When Denver and Ellie had taken the cake into the kitchen, Jenna said, 'Actually, Professor, the reason I'm here is to ask for your help. I have to write a report about what happened yesterday, and I'm darned if I know what I'm going to say. Like I told you before, my captain is the most skeptical man I ever met.'

'Call me Nathan,' said Nathan. 'And I'm sure I can help you. What you need to do is explain all the scientific bits and forget about the mythology. I've learned from bitter experience that most people simply don't believe in mythological creatures. Or can't believe in them. Or *won't*.'

They sat down on the couch and Nathan wrote some notes for her about calcium carbonate and calcium oxide and exothermic reactions. After twenty minutes or so, they heard laughter coming from the kitchen.

Jenna said, '*Ssh*,' got up from the couch and went quietly across to the kitchen door. When she looked in, she saw Denver and Ellie sitting side by side at the kitchen counter, grinning at each other. Denver had taken the lemon drizzle cake out of the box and cut it into slices. Ellie had her mouth stuffed full of cake and was licking the frosting from her fingers.

Jenna returned to the couch.

'Everything OK?' Nathan asked her.

'Let's just say that since I met you, Nathan, my life seems to have become so much simpler.'

FORTY-ONE
Wednesday, 7:38 p.m.

Ed Freiburg didn't bother to switch on the lights when he walked into the CSI workshop on Arch Street. The street lights outside were enough for him to see where he was going, which was only to pick up the forensic toolbox he had left next to the gargoyle they had recovered from Bartram's Gardens.

He hunkered down and opened up the box to make sure that all of his tools and his luminal spray bottles were in place. Then he closed it and locked it and stood up. He took one last look up at the gargoyle, with its horns and its curved beak and its one broken wing.

The gargoyle's eyes were closed, as if it were hibernating.